I0823284

Fire Sword and Sea

ALSO BY VANESSA RILEY

Historical Fiction

Island Queen

Sister Mother Warrior

Queen of Exiles

The Lady Worthing Mysteries

Murder in Westminster

Murder in Drury Lane

Murder in Berkeley Square

The Rogues and Remarkable Women Romances

A Duke, the Lady, and a Baby

An Earl, the Girl, and a Toddler

A Duke, the Spy, an Artist and a Lie

Betting Against the Duke

A Gamble at Sunset

A Wager at Midnight

Fire Sword and Sea

A NOVEL

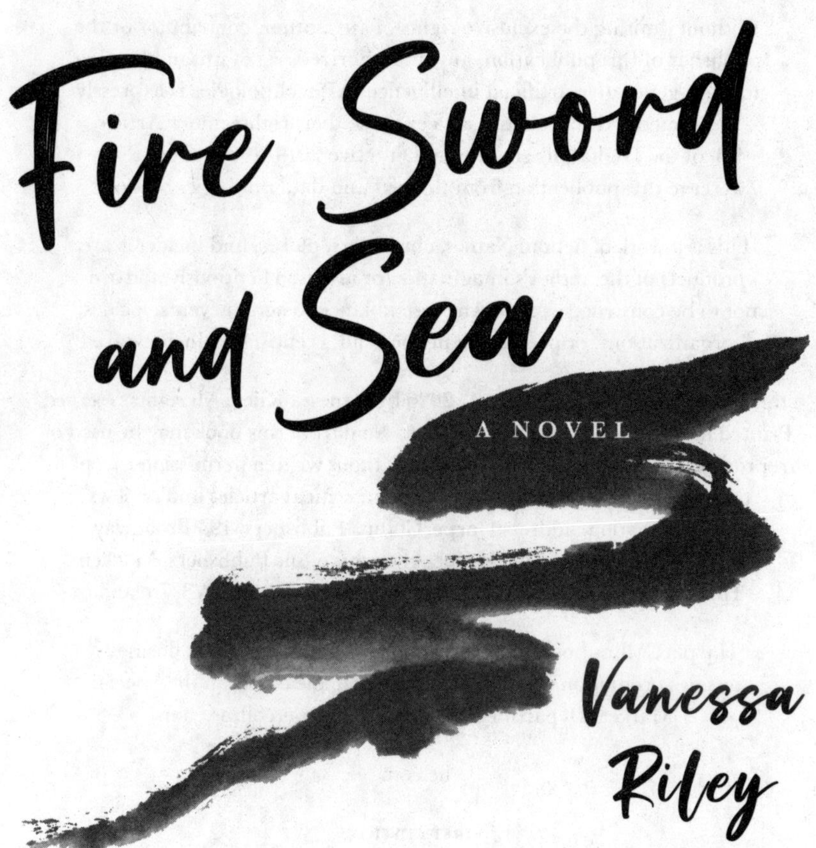

Vanessa Riley

wm

WILLIAM MORROW

An Imprint of HarperCollins*Publishers*

This is a work of fiction. Names, characters, places, and incidents are products of the author's imagination or are used fictitiously and are not to be construed as real. Any resemblance to actual events, locales, organizations, or persons, living or dead, is entirely coincidental.

For information, address HarperCollins Publishers, 195 Broadway, New York, NY 10007. In Europe, HarperCollins Publishers, Macken House, 39/40 Mayor Street Upper, Dublin 1, D01 C9W8, Ireland.

HarperCollins books may be purchased for educational, business, or sales promotional use. For information, please email the Special Markets Department at SPsales@harpercollins.com.

hc.com

FIRST EDITION

Library of Congress Cataloging-in-Publication Data

Names: Riley, Vanessa, author.
Title: Fire sword and sea : a novel / Vanessa Riley.
Description: First edition. | New York, NY : William Morrow, 2026. |
Identifiers: LCCN 2024060911 | ISBN 9780063271043 (hardcover) | ISBN 9780063271067 (ebook)
Subjects: LCSH: Women pirates—Fiction. | LCGFT: Action and adventure fiction. | Historical fiction. | Novels.
Classification: LCC PS3618.I533 F57 2026 | DDC 813/.6—dc23/eng/20250108
LC record available at https://lccn.loc.gov/2024060911

ISBN 978-0-06-327104-3

26 27 28 29 30 LBC 6 5 4 3 2

For the women who do right.

For the women who do wrong for the right reasons.

For the women who burn it all down, find beauty in ashes.

For the dreamers left behind—keep sailing.

Cast of Characters

Denizens of Tortuga	Alternate Names and Titles
Jacquotte Delahaye	Madame Le Basque Jacques Delahaye Delahaye Helmsman Captain Delahaye Captain of the *Canopus*
Uzoamaka Delahaye	Mother of Jacquotte and Josiah Uzoamaka of Kissi
Pierre Delahaye	Father of Jacquotte and Josiah
Old Jean	Mentor of Jacquotte Friend of Uzoamaka Jean of Kissi
Sarah	Madame Sayon
Mille	Madame Mille, brothel owner
Hasneau	Monsieur Hasneau, second in command
Neveu	Jacques Neveu de Pouancey Governor Neveu
Governor d'Ogeron	Bertrand d'Ogeron
Governor de Franquesnay	Jacques de Pardieu de Franquesnay, de Franquesnay
Governor Du Casse	Jean-Baptiste Du Casse

Denizens of Petit-Goâve	Alternate Names and Titles
Bahati	Dockworker Quartermaster
Wulf	Dirk De Wulf Dirkje De Wulf
Quincy	Dockworker
Margaret	Wulf's wench Warehouse owner
Lizzôa Erville	Madame Erville Lizzôa
Celia	Celia Chilango Chilango Bosun
Monsignor Robilere	Monsignor François Robilere Monsignor of L'Église de L'Assomption of Petit-Goâve, the monastery of Petit-Goâve
Anne	Anne Dieu-Le-Veut Madame Chérel
Joseph Chérel	Chérel

Denizens of Port Royal & Jamaica	Alternate Names and Titles
Michel Le Basque	Michel d'Artigue Captain Le Basque Le Basque Captain of the *Marauder*
Samuel Axe	Retired filibuster
Lieutenant Governor Henry Morgan	Filibuster, Pirate King
Gramma Nettles	Housekeeper
Tomás	Michel's ward "His Eyes"

Other Characters	Alternate Names and Titles
Governor of Curaçao	Governor Johannes van der Bosch of Curaçao
Captain Nicholas Trott	Governor of Nassau
Captain Nickels	Captain of the HMS *Florence*
Hackney	Boatswain Hackney
Dender Smith	Captain Dender Smith Captain of the HMS *Florence* Captain of the *Canopus*
Aurangzeb	Mughal emperor Grand Mughal Aurangzeb
King Louis XIV	Le Roi Soleil
Danseker	Zuth Danseker Zuthimalin Danseker
Mel	Calico Mel
Laurens de Graaf	de Graaf Captain of the *Neptune*
Thomas Tew	Tew

Author's Note

This novel begins in 1674, along the shores of a remote West Indies island, a few years before what is considered the start of the Golden Age of Piracy. Tortuga, a haven for outcasts and land grabbers, changes leadership as Spain, France, and England wrestle for control. The result is continued instability and an influx of multilingual seekers of asylum.

I want you to feel fully immersed in this novel. While the real individuals portrayed—Jacquotte Delahaye, Anne Dieu-Le-Veut, Michel Le Basque, and Laurens de Graaf—would have spoken in English, French, Spanish, or various African dialects, I have chosen to tell their story in modern language. This approach ensures that you, the reader, can vividly experience the turbulent and often violent lives they led. As the infamous pirate captains and their comrades seek their fortunes, they battle diametrically opposed forces:

Two world powers—Spain and the Mughal Empire.
Two emerging nations—England and France.
Two opportunities—naval careers versus legal piracy.
Two systems—diverse frigate crews above, transporting the enslaved below.
Two feminine norms—wenches or wives.

Content Guidance

If you are a reader who appreciates learning about sensitive content, this is for you. *Fire Sword and Sea* contains graphic and historically accurate depictions of rape, murder, prejudice and enslavement of men, women, transgender, queer, and pregnant characters. The seventeeth century was a violent time, yet it also allowed for transformation and radical agency. I hope you'll join these daring pirates on their heroic journeys.

Fire Sword and Sea

Twilight

The first lady pirate of my acquaintance was Uzoamaka Delahaye. Escaping her master's whip, the enterprising laundress stole a silken dress from the mistress of the habitation, boots from the oldest son's closet, and a reed Moses basket from the pantry. Hiding her four-year-old daughter within the woven straw, Uzoamaka lugged the basket through the jungle and over a mountain to the shore. Awaiting the right time, the twilight before the dawn, she took command of a sloop and escaped Hispaniola. An Icarus floating in the sky, not from boyhood to manhood but enslaved to true freedom, she crossed her beloved sea.

For a moment of time, Uzoamaka—my mother, ma maman—flew high, living an exciting adventure. Then she sailed into the sun and married, losing her wings and her life.

One

1674. Basse-Terre. Tortuga

When my mother left this world, she bore a curse on her lips, sweat on a pained brow, and a dead-arse stare pinned on me. "You, Jacquotte Delahaye," she whispered, "you're my legacy. Make somethin' of your life."

Me hiding outside the tavern she built, with ale-soaked hands, refusing to go inside . . . isn't what she meant.

The growing darkness hides me. White cobbles near my feet grab bits of the fleeting daylight, holding onto it, illuminating a path around the tavern. I should follow it and flee.

But I'm too angry to move. Accidentally—not so accidentally—spilling ale on a patron shows a weak temperament. Weakness is a disgrace.

If I'd been smarter, I'd have held in my fury, left the tavern and all those silly men, and chased the twilight to the shores. But I wasn't. I dumped a tankard of ale on a lousy patron's lap. On the habitation where I was born, back in Hispaniola, my actions would've gotten me whipped.

"Mademoiselle Delahaye, come back!" That's the upstairs fille hired to watch my baby brother while I cook.

My gut tightens. Something could be wrong with Josiah. Part of me wants to check. The angry part of me remembers that this woman is paid monthly in silver, a whole piece of eight, to protect him. Is she trying to shirk her responsibilities on to me?

"Mademoiselle Delahaye. You're needed back in the kitchen," she says. "The pottage does look good."

I should tell her to get a bowl. Everyone loves my pottage, the bouillon I cook. In a big copper pot, I make a broth stewing vegetables—carrots or potatoes or whatever I can grow or purchase cheaply—and chopped fish, scooped over a *sop.* That is what a British filibuster calls the little scrap of bread that sticks to the bottom of the bowl.

I'm privileged to run my father's kitchen. Since I was old enough to walk, I helped my mother in these tasks, working beside her slaughtering goats, ripping the hides from boars, gutting fish. Not many women could brag of their knife skills like Delahaye women.

"Mademoiselle. Come in. No one is mad."

Ignoring this call, I press my back flatter against the wall and draw deeper into the shadows. No footfalls near. Like Père, let this person relent and let me be.

I love my father, but he doesn't understand me. I'm fourteen, and he thinks he can shape my will. He won the fight to have me wear womanly gowns instead of the breeches I wore as a child. My temper is such that I don't lose many other battles.

Blowing out hot breaths, I watch dusk hover over my garden. It's peaceful and reminds me to count my blessings. I should be more grateful that Père cares about me and my little brother. Yet, knowing how my mother suffered from shackles, why can't he condemn the announcement that slave women will again return to Tortuga?

"Jacquotte?" A different female voice calls for me. "Jacquotte, I know you're out here. You left fire in the hearth!"

Madame Mille? Silly woman. You always leave coals warming if you aren't done cooking. I'd be in there now, starting a second batch of pottage, if Père had silenced the patrons and stood up for what's right. Instead, he apologized for my behavior like I am in the wrong.

No, I'm not. I took a stand.

My rebuke of the governor's lieutenant stopped his chortles. It was rash, but he should know the French side of the island ended enslavement over forty years ago. Basse-Terre became a beacon of freedom. That's why Maman chose to live here.

"Jacquotte Delahaye," Mille says. "You stubborn fille, come now."

Why is she searching for me? Mille hates me and my dead maman.

"Did you find her, Madame Mille? She didn't go to her room." Père sounds concerned. He left the fancy politicians to hunt for his wayward daughter. Is he coming to force me to apologize?

"Monsieur Delahaye." The brothel owner's tone becomes sickeningly sweet, like an overripe banana. "You mustn't be guiding Jacquotte with a strict-enough hand."

"We are managing, Madame Mille," he says.

"Of course, monsieur. It's not every day ale is spilled or emptied . . . by accident."

"Oui, madame. Jacquotte is excitable." Père's tone tightens.

"Your daughter is easily angered, monsieur. But it's to be expected. She's part Guinea. Their blood is warm."

I wait for a response.

Nothing. No defense. My father's soft heart refuses to hear her insults. I'm not as generous. Madame Mille should have her painted face scrubbed, her white wig knocked off, and maybe her corset loosened so she can breathe instead advertising her breasts. Unencumbered lungs and a voice are gifts.

"This my fault," Père says. "She heard the men joking"—he clears his throat—"about the *shipment.* D'Ogeron has brought more prisoners. They are in pens in Cayonne. Pens."

"Oh." Mille sounds surprised. "The shipment?" she asks, her pitch rising. "That's what you call the whores from Paris?"

"Madame Mille, please. Jacquotte may overhear. She'll misunderstand—"

"Misunderstand what, Monsieur Delahaye? The criminal women collected from the rues of France are going to be imprisoned in

Fort de Rocher then sold to the highest bidder. What is there for Jacquotte not to comprehend?"

My father sighs hard. I hear his boots pound back into the dining room.

And I match the rhythm, running toward the beaches of Cayonne to see for myself.

* * *

My feet sink into cool, powdery sand. The path feels like walking on fine ash. Above my head, coconut palms snap their leaves. Like loud clapping hands, the noise keeps me looking up as I follow the jungle path to Cayonne.

It's hard for stars to send their light through the canopy of branches. It's a shame. They are so pretty. My favorite is the Crux. The Southern Crux, or Cross, as the Brits say, twinkles, the stars leading men to Tortuga.

Something scampers behind me. A nighthawk? A monkey? I live and die a thousand times, jumping at every thud and creak. Then I hear the crash of waves. The salty air, strong and inviting, reaches my nostrils. My heart flips out of my bodice and back. I've made it to the beaches of Cayonne.

Dropping to my knees, I kiss the sand. Maman did the same when we first landed here. I remember how happy we were, dancing along the shore, the waves lapping against our toes. She'd stolen a boat. We'd arrived to freedom.

It's been four years since she died. At ten, I thought the world ended. At fourteen, must I again relearn cruelty? Yet, as I search the beach from the jungle to the dock and warehouses, I see pens. But no captive women. I breathe easier. Maybe Mille and Père were teasing because they knew I was listening.

My father, the person Maman sacrificed so much for, couldn't be complicit with making women captives. I realize how low my faith in him has fallen. This must change.

Rushing to the water, I dip my hands into a foamy wave and

wash sticky ale and sand from my fingers. Perhaps all the wild talk is about what they want for the future. Those men in the tavern weren't confused. They want Tortuga to become like Hispaniola, a place dependent upon chattel slaves.

* * *

High tide, low tide, I sit on the beach watching the sea. The black curtain of night rises, erasing where sky and water intersect. I've been here most of the night, alone. It's too early for the washer-women or laundresses to start their boils, too soon for fishermen to begin, too late for wenches to fill empty beds.

The second twilight arrives and makes the dark sky turn a little gray. In less than an hour, the sun will bring new warmth and begin the day. The receding tide exposes treasures—shells, shiny rocks, bits of rope.

A nighthawk swoops low. His screech buzzes my ear. He's flown close, as if my braids are a suitable nest. The bird, the hunter, might find a meal by the warehouses. The open-air buildings on the far side of the docks sell spices and cloth and allow men to trade their humanity for silver. I'm sure a fat rat would be at home there.

I pick up a shell and try to catch a piece of the fleeing sea. Foam sweeps over my thumb. Good and warm, light and honest, the comfort of the water reminds me of my mother, her purification rituals, her scent.

"Maman, help me find a way to apologize to Père," I say aloud. "There are no pens here. No prisoners will be sold."

"This isn't the only beach in Cayonne." The voice, dark and scratchy, isn't my mother's. Startled, I peer over my shoulder and see my friend Old Jean. A man of the same tribe as Maman, he won his freedom long, long ago.

"What do you mean, monsieur?"

He comes alongside me. The outline of his pointy cap drapes the left side of his face. Made of ebony velvet, the hat probably cost a lot when he bought it. He's the most prosperous Guinea man I know.

His dry lips part. "Cayonne stretches far. If the rumors are true, this wouldn't be where I'd hunt. There are more convenient places to hold captives meant for Fort de Rocher."

"Does my father condone this practice?"

"Jacquotte, I'm the last to know these things. Asking about a Blanc man's business isn't wise."

His eyes, frowning and dark, express the sorrows he's seen. Yet, deep in them are stars and hope. "Come sailing with me," he says. "If you want to catch the wind, you need to chase it."

Rearranging my gown of rough silk and muslin, I stand and brush away the sand that clings near my knees. "You were at the tavern, Old Jean. Tell me you heard them brag about enslaving women."

"Not sure what I heard, but I saw you do the stupidest thing."

"Dumping the ale was wasteful."

"Worse, child. You let them know you're mad. That gives away your power." With his silvery hair pushed back, he adjusts his hat. "Never do that."

Shamed again and I've not even seen daybreak. I lower my chin. "So you are saying it's true."

He takes my arm and pulls me forward. "I think Uzoamaka Delahaye is here. Let's ask her. She's in the waves, telling me the best spots to cast my nets. She'll know the truth."

"Isn't it too early to fish?"

He chuckles. The sound is rich and filled with a sense of calm. "Then we wait on the water until it's time. Your maman asked me to guide Jacquotte. Come. Let's sail and find her."

For a moment, I think of being no trouble and returning to hide in my garden. Then Père will scold me and make me promise to be good and quiet and cook. The men of Basse-Terre want a woman to be a pottage pot, constantly feeding and filling others until she runs dry.

"Come on, Jacquotte," Old Jean says. "I don't have all night."

Indecisive, I take a few steps. "You sure you want me to come? I haven't been so smart."

"You're smart." He looks up at the fading stars. "You come from Kissi women. Let's go pray that Uzoamaka meets us in the sea."

The Kissi are the lifeblood of the Guinea. They believe in communing with the ancestors that have passed on to the next journey. For a moment, I feel the pride of these people and the joy of stolen tribal members who are freed, no matter the cost—even death.

"Jacquotte. Don't dawdle. Let's be on the water at dawn." Old Jean tips his pointy hat and heads to the docks, leaving me to decide.

A breeze rattles the close palms that hang their trunks, like long extended necks, over the beach. The steady rhythm, the shaking leaves soothe me. The jungle wishes to accompany Père's organistrum, the musical instrument with strings that he and Maman played. My mother used to say it sounded similar to her father's kora, a gourd with leather strings pulled tight across its belly. Her memories of these melodies surely brought the master's son and the enslaved laundress together.

The clapping palms are a sign.

"Old Jean, wait!" Jogging, kicking up sand, I catch him and help untie his boat from a pillion. The glorious ketch with its two masts wiggles free into Maman's waters. I brace against the side, waiting on the wind to help me catch a fantôme.

Two

1674. The Sea About Tortuga

Maintaining his balance, Old Jean stands in the ketch and yanks at the halyard, the rope raising the white sail up the mainmast. The boat moves gently in the waves. The dock and the horrid warehouses grow smaller the farther we drift. I imagine pinching them betwixt my index and thumb and plucking them into the sea. Wouldn't it be great to cause such destruction?

Twilight transitions to daybreak. I lift my hands and see my shortening shadow on the deck. "It's magical out here."

"See. You've calmed. Being out here always does that." He cups his palm to his brow. "No red in the sky today, Jacquotte. We'll have no worries, for it is written in Pope Alexander's book that foul weather comes from a sky that's red and lowering."

His voice switches from his Creole French to formal French when he quotes anything written. He's learned such formalities from his days enslaved at a monastery. Through the years, he's told me everything of his life while filling in missing pieces about the Kissi people.

"Did I ever tell you about how I gained my freedom? The monks sold me to explorers?"

Explorers? It's hard enough to imagine men of God having slaves, but for the monks to sell them to explorers, that seems very odd.

"Is this going to be another d'Artigue story? It seems most of your stories involve that filibuster."

"I guess I've mentioned that name before."

"Oui, you have." I mimic his voice and say, "D'Artigue was one of the few Blanc men I trust."

"Laugh if you must, Jacquotte. But d'Artigue was special. He and his son have too many airs to be ordinary pirates. D'Artigue signed on to the explorer's crew."

"To hunt Spanish treasure? All the buccaneers and filibusters in the tavern lust for such?"

"Until the world finds more gold, only the Spanish and the Mughals have it. Men search the Caribbean hunting for lost treasure in the wrecks of the armadas. The explorers made me put on a helmet and walk along the sea bottom for ingots."

My mouth drops open. "Walk beneath the sea! You're not a fish."

"Chattel don't have much choice," he says. "But I was promised my freedom if I trusted the hose on the helmet to deliver air. I took the risk. D'Artigue manned the tube, and when I recovered gold, he made sure I was freed. Kept his word. That's why he and his son are the only Blanc men I trust."

As if he realizes he's said too much, he turns and checks the bow sail. Even if he keeps some things to himself, he's told me more about life than Père.

Old Jean claps his hands. "It shall be a good day for fish."

Spear hooks shift on the deck, as he sorts them and picks the right one. "Did I tell you about the time Uzoamaka caught a butterfish in the Ọya River? She took a hook like this. Got him on the first try."

"You use nets here."

"It's the way in the Caribbean. Uzoamaka mastered this way as well."

Every time I sail with Old Jean, his stories make me feel as if my mother is with us. Since her death, fishing with him, sailing his ketch have become the only things I look forward to. Though I once loved cooking, it's a prison, a symbol of the confined life women are bred to have. How does one break free? How can I dream of freedom beyond this?

Old Jean folds his arms, his happy expression fading into a full frown.

"Say it, monsieur. I see you're burdened."

"Jacquotte, you know a maiden alone out in the dark is not safe. The men here can be desperate. The governor's soldiers—"

"You mean the filibusters he hired, *those* soldiers?"

"They are all soldiers for France. Piracy is legal when you have le Roi Soleil's permission. A mulattress, no matter how light her skin is or how fair her red hair, will never gain justice. Hell, their own women gain none."

My skin is tan. My hair takes after my father's coloring, but with a fine, curly texture. Unlike pale, three-year-old Josiah, I'll never be confused for fully French or Blanc. Old Jean is convinced that our skin is light not only from French blood but the light KhoeSan ancestors that came to Kissi.

Nonetheless, skin coloring offers no protection for women. "Old Jean, why are men immune to troubles?"

"We have our own, Jacquotte." His laughter sounds rich. "It's not all bad. Your father's well off, and he'll make a good match for you, someone respectable to marry. It's best your soul is tied to someone that's good."

Tying of souls? I look at the gown that I'm forced to wear. It's an indication of things to come. Père has a soft spot for politicians. He could be angling and positioning for an agreement to wed me to one once I reach a suitable age. But what is a suitable age in Tortuga, where women are scarce?

"Tell me of your père's plans. What or who has he said?"

"Plans? I've only heard about helping my brother and running the tavern."

"That's all he's said?" Old Jean sucks his teeth. "Waste of a man. Doesn't he understand it's a father's duty to plan his daughter's life?"

"Monsieur. I have plenty of time for plans."

"You think so? Little girl, life has a way of changing that."

At fourteen, I wouldn't exactly call myself a little girl. I'd rather call myself enterprising, an adventurer.

"You need to be ready." Old Jean stretches, making his jacket billow about his chest. "Monsieur Delahaye should be thinking good and hard. You deserve a good bride's wealth. He should set a high lowola. That's what Uzoamaka would want."

"Lowola?"

"The bride's wealth." He huffs like my question is ignorant. "It's what the groom must give your father to prove he can provide for you and to compensate for your loss to Delahaye when you marry."

"If that doesn't sound like being sold to the highest bidder, I must be confused."

Old Jean sucks on his teeth again. "Your father is feckless. But he's in good with the leaders of Tortuga—"

"The bragging men you mean? Maman told me that Kissi women were listened to. Their words were revered. They led."

"Elder females led. Now, stop interrupting," he says with a half smile, then starts pointing. "Grab the rudder. On the big ships, it's a whipstaff. Steer it so we'll fly through the ship lanes."

I dream of those big ships as much as I do this ketch. Palming the rudder, I guide the boat. We pick up speed and soon come to the tip of Tortuga. Old Jean turns the sail to keep us to the French part of the island and away from the Spanish side. I wouldn't mind drifting beyond the imagined border and spying a galleon or even a frigate belonging to King Carlos II.

He heads us back, putting the ketch closer to the land but at a safe distance from the wild mangroves. These tangled roots thrive along the edges of the island and can ensnare unsuspecting boats. They're beautiful and grow green and yellow flowers. During the warm season, some bear jade-colored fruits, which can quench a thirst. With salty, undrinkable water everywhere, these gems save lives. Runaways from Hispaniola's habitations live off them. Maman and I did until we were caught on her first try at escaping.

Old Jean grabs the rudder from me. He makes the ketch turn to the left. "Don't be gentle with a boat. She needs to know you believe in what you're doing. Take her where you want."

Fingers tightening and relaxing about the handle, I try again and become more confident. My heart beats a little faster. He's never let me set the course. I stare at him and catch his proud deep-set eyes. "You're going to let me be captain?"

Laughing, he puts his back flat against mainmast. "Oui. We go until I tell you to head back. I know how angry you are. Sailing will calm you. It will help you think more deeply about the risks you take."

A legacy has to take risks. "I can defend myself. I practice fencing with my father's rapier. I dream about battles."

"Dreams aren't true, Jacquotte. And fighting an invisible person is different than attacking the governor's lieutenant, who can arrest you and use an army to seize your family and property. Everything can be lost. Do you know how much bitterness I must swallow to keep a jealous Blanc from taking my ketch?"

He closes his eyes. "I do not wrestle with what I cannot control. Out here, I look at the mountains. They sing to my spirit. Look at them, Jacquotte. The Montagnes du Nord are bigger than our problems."

Père loves them too. They overlook the place of his birth at his Parisian parents' habitation. Partially shrouded in fog, the mountains only lets us see so much.

With Old Jean snoring, I command the rudder. I intend to sail the length of Cayonne, hunting for the truth about enslavement returning to Tortuga.

* * *

With a favorable wind and a steady hand, I have the ketch easing through the blue-green waters. Porpoises play in the distance. A shift in the breeze makes me glance at Tortuga's hills full of forests and caverns. The batteries of Fort de Rocher are exposed. A cannon looms.

I direct the boat to where I can more easily view the fort. If there are pens on that section of Cayonne, I'll know instantly.

My heart pounds. I angle the rudder and slip so close to the mangroves their petals fall onto the deck. The smell of the sulfur from flowers dropping seeds into the water overwhelms, but Old Jean doesn't wake.

I spy an opening in the trees. It's wide enough for a frigate to pass. Aiming the rudder, I drift the ketch inside to a bay. A huge, sleek hull looms, with three-masts, with square sails and one triangular one. A flag bearing a blue cross on white cloth waves from the stern. It's a French second-rate frigate, here with le Roi Soleil's blessing.

Without adjusting the ketch's sails and awaking Old Jean, I ease closer. All seems quiet on the frigate, but their handiwork offloading women into iron cages set up along the beach can't be unseen. I count at least twenty women.

My stomach caves inward. "Enslavement has returned to Tortuga."

"Jacquotte, what's happening? What are you looking at?" Old Jean sits up. "Oh."

He cannot miss this. The sin is right there in the shadow of Fort de Rocher.

"Blanc women? Damnation!" Old Jean covers his mouth. He takes command of the rudder. "We must get out of here before we're spotted."

"But—"

He puts a finger to his lips, hushing my complaint. Soon, the ketch whips around and with the next gust of wind sails out of the mouth of the bay. When we are far away, he says, "They'll confiscate my boat if they think I'm interfering! Hell, they could sell us both into slavery again. Non. It's not worth the risk."

He puts his hands to the rudder again and skirts the mangroves with such ease. Old Jean drives his boat even closer than I did. The seeds, the petals—the stench is bad.

"You know this is wrong," I say. "We must help these women."

"We? Oh, non. Don't get no ideas, Jacquotte Delahaye. Just because I teach you about boats doesn't mean you can take mine to war."

Folding my arms, I lean against the mizzenmast. Its shadow splits me in two, the part that burns because I want to fight and the sensible side that knows we'll fail and suffer. "How does evil end if good people do nothing?"

"You listen. Let the Blancs save the Blancs. It's their women. Let them have at it. Your Guinea blood will decide whose you are and where you belong. It's not to be made an example to keep others in line."

Making a neat bundle, he curls rope around his palm and then to his elbow and back. "Whether they get husbands or become wenches for Madame Mille or even toil in fields, it's not our business."

I put my head down. "I want to do something."

"You and I are the currency exchanged all over the world for food or water or medicine, anything they value. Those Blanc women will be fine. Their children will not be enslaved. They're not us."

Old Jean hasn't lived this long as a free Guinea man with means and his own boat by chance. He is a success—safe, minder of his destiny, keeper of his treasures . . . and secrets.

"Now, Uzoamaka Delahaye didn't raise a foolish child. So don't sulk, Jacquotte."

He speaks her name to chastise me, but Maman is the fire that stirs my soul.

"We're almost at the docks, and look who's come looking for you."

Père and Josiah stand along the beach. My father sees Old Jean's boat and waves.

"The family Uzoamaka fought and died for are waiting for you. What say you, Jacquotte? Ready to go back home?"

A big wave crests and slaps the boat. A spray of water kisses my cheeks. It doesn't sting but leaves salt like tears on my skin. It is a sign. Maman cries for me and those women, but she needs me safe at home. "Take me to the docks."

If there's a next time, I'll have a plan worthy of my mother that will keep me safe while I set the captives free.

Three

1674. Basse-Terre. Tortuga

A week of being confined to our home and tavern isn't the punishment Père expects it to be. I spend time gardening and cleaning my kitchen. I keep a tidy ship, so to speak, that somewhat mirrors my father's efforts in the dining room. He swabs it daily as if it is a ship's deck.

I examine every surface—my oak table for food preparation, my wall hooks for pots and spoons, my tripod kettle for cooking outdoors, and my pink-and-gray brick hearth. From the reredos at the back of my hearth, I scoop ash, which I'll save to make lye soap. My pottage cauldron holds a shine. The copper pot sparkles but has a green patina along the rim that I can't make disappear no matter how much I rub.

My busy brother plays in the corner stacking old plates. Three-year-old Josiah looks at me with big greenish-brown eyes. He has Père's cleft in his chin. But at age three my brother still hasn't learned to speak.

At least he is safe, not getting into or causing trouble. I bend and congratulate him on his perfect stacks. "Excellent," I say and kiss his forehead and pray he finds his words.

He stands, hugs my legs, then goes back to restack the plates.

One more check about the room. I move to the shelves to

straighten demijohn neck jars of olive oil and a pewter tankard filled with my special mix of spices for my pottage, a blend of herbs, salt, and dried peppers.

Père purchases spices from the warehouse at the docks. It always bothers me having to get things from there, but my father pays in silver, no other exchange.

A large iron pot cools on the floor. Earlier, I boiled ashes with goat fat to make lye-water soap. Once it becomes solid, I'll have enough to scrub every inch of the kitchen every day for a week. "Josiah, I think we can go get the water for the pottage."

He dances around the large table where I prepare vegetables and season meat. Père's tavern is the only place in the little ville to purchase a hearty meal and a drink of ale or sweet rum.

The slatted door separating the dining room and kitchen opens. I hold my breath and await my father's inspection.

Père's boot heels clack on the tile floor. He moves to the stacks of clean bowls and plates, then touches the surface of the worktable like his fingers will find grime, but his skin touches nothing but smooth ridges from the grain of the freshly cleaned surface. He sorts through my kitchen knives hunting for that one dull one, but I've shined and sharpened each to the best of my ability.

He moves to the empty pails. "Jacquotte, you're to go to the well and back."

"Oui, Père. Josiah and I are both going. He can chaperone and see that I finish quickly."

My father starts to leave but turns back, his reddish whiskers drooping. "I'm not wrong to chastise you in this matter. You must understand this."

I keep silent and hope my stare reminds him of Maman's.

He puts his hands together as if to pray. "Except to go to the well, you aren't to leave the tavern. You will cook, serve, then go to your room. We'll have another rowdy crowd. Men are noticing you. What if the Spanish raiders from the other side of Tortuga had struck? You could've been taken in the dark. Then what, Jacquotte?"

"Obviously you'll complain to one of your loyal customers, to see if I can be bought back." I point to the pewter tankard. "They say that's worth fifteen to twenty Guineas. I'm just one, so you can negotiate a better trade."

"That's not funny, Jacquotte."

I pick up the pails. "I will return—"

"Those women aren't slaves. They committed crimes. This is their punishment."

I give Josiah a pail and make ready to walk out the door. "Père, you have no worries. Your governor has completed the auction. Mille has new women to entertain your patrons, and I hear several men have bought slaves. Pardon. Wrong word. I meant, bought wives, but that means the same thing."

His countenance dims. The striped pourpoint that wraps his thin shoulders begins to sag. He opens the door. "You may think me a coward, and in some respects, I am. We are all servants to Governor d'Ogeron. His way provides protection for Basse-Terre. We could grow as big as the cities of Hispaniola. Tortuga and the Delahayes being a success is the best revenge."

Revenge? Is this about besting his own father? "This bending of principles is to win a competition against the slaver Delahayes of Hispaniola?"

His lips snap closed like he didn't mean to speak this truth. He huffs and says, "We compromise to survive."

* * *

I take several deep breaths of the crisp morning air then start to the well. The cobbled path leads there. The ancient watering hole is in front of the tavern. We take our time. Once I'm sure Josiah won't wander away, I draw fresh water from the well.

In lieu of a church, this is the center of Basse-Terre. The ville sits on a flat plateau. Nine of the original houses of the settlement and the tavern form a ring. Two-story homes with sandstone and coral bricks and thatched roofs stand between the jungle and larger habitations.

My father wants our tiny city to grow to be big like Santo Domingo. If tobacco takes hold here like it does in Hispaniola, enslaved Guineas will again toil upon the island.

Josiah tugs on my apron and points to a fallen palm frond. Then he makes a sweeping motion with his hands. Does he want to sweep the dirt? I wish he would say what he wants—to get the leaf, to twirl it, to clean?

Then I resign myself. "If we both spoke up, I'm sure you'd agree with me, and we'd drive Père mad."

Crash.

A pail is tossed from the house farthest to the right.

A loud argument follows, and I hear horrid shouts. "Wench! Pute! Get the water!"

That angry voice belongs to our neighbor Monsieur Sayon. The former filibuster is a little older than Père but thick with muscles from his years at sea.

Pulling a threadbare shawl over her head, a woman I've never seen before stumbles from the Sayon cottage. She looks tired. Perhaps ten or fifteen years older than me with raven hair that looks purple in the sunlight, she bends and picks up the pail. The way she seems to cower protectively makes my stomach queasy.

When Monsieur Sayon sees me gawking, he calls out, "Hurry back, wife."

Then he struts back into his cottage. I groan. He bought a woman at the auction.

When she comes closer, I see the stony look on her face as she gazes toward her husband's house. This woman's angry but, like Old Jean, swallowing her bitterness. Yet, the way she swings the pail in her hands, I think she's tempted to throw it back at Monsieur Sayon.

I like her instantly. "Bonjour, Madame Sayon. It would be my pleasure to fill your pail."

I crank the handle the final turns, and the bucket in the well rises. I take it and fill her vessel. "There. If you ever want pottage, come to the back of the tavern. The door to my kitchen is there."

The woman is thin, like she hasn't eaten much in a long time. She nods and starts back to Monsieur Sayon's house. Then she stops. "My name is Sarah. Thank you for the water and for being nice."

"I mean it. I'm Jacquotte Delahaye."

"Hope to call you friend, Mademoiselle Delahaye." Sarah seizes a big breath. "Also hope you have a shovel and soft ground. Don't know if this fool will make it a whole week."

That reply makes me love her. My soul leaps at the thought of another fighter in Basse-Terre.

Père comes out of the front door. "Jacquotte, do you need any . . . help?"

His eyes grow big at the sight of Sarah. He bows.

Sarah nods and keeps going. She has no time for pleasantries. Maybe she suspects Père is one of the men who allowed this to occur.

Josiah and I start back down the cobbles.

Père intercepts us and takes the pails from me. "You've done enough. Go rest until it's time to start the pottage. Jacquotte, I do love you."

I can't argue. I know he does. "The pails are heavy. Thank you."

Père takes the lead, and we follow. Maybe he watched from the grand front window of the tavern and saw Sayon's shoddy treatment of his newly purchased bride. Perhaps this is Père's way of showing contrition.

Doesn't truly matter.

I've just met my future. Unless I figure out a new destiny for myself, I will become enslaved as someone's miserable wife.

Four

1675. The Cayonne Hills. Tortuga

Early in the morning after a hearty breakfast of cassava bread, roasted plantains, and cuts of boar belly, Père takes Josiah and me on a walk. We stay in the jungle.

Up, up, up into the hills, there's no scent of seawater. The fragrance is pines and earthy ferns. I can't pout. During the day, the trees and vines are magical. The flowers and fruits are a feast for the eyes, with colors varying from pale green mangoes to bright-orange cashew apples.

"Keep up," Père says to me as he jostles Josiah on his shoulders.

Traveling the trails, he points to caverns and fruited bayahonde trees. His love of raw, hilly Tortuga beams from his countenance.

I'm cheered to see him so happy.

His lively steps guide us up a hill, then he takes a sharp turn.

Jumping over the fallen trunk of a bamboo tree, I trail behind.

"Something special," Père says and swipes off his pointy tan hat. "You'll be rewarded with the sweetest smells and best views."

Nodding and gawking at everything around us, I have to agree. The air is cooler up here. In another month, the wet season will bring more damp heat and make even the breeze feel sticky. Then these dry paths can become treacherous, turning into raging rivers overnight.

Père has retrieved the rapier I always borrow. He whacks at the brush that has overgrown the dirt path. I study the way he holds the sword, the way his fingers curl about the hilt. I'm proud and envious.

The beautiful weapon would normally go to a son. But I suspect Josiah may never be ready for the responsibility.

"Watch your brother," Père says as he lowers him to me. "There are buccan traps everywhere in this part."

"Traps? I have the eyes of a nighthawk, sir."

Père begins to laugh and takes Josiah's hand. "Then you take the lead."

I don't have a sword, so I take up a thick branch and swing it about, poking the brush like my father does with the rapier.

Making the first bend in the trail, I know I'm doing a good job.

Then Papa reaches out and catches me by my corset strings, tugging me backward. "Nighthawk's eyes, is that so?"

When I try to move forward, he holds out his arm. "Non."

He takes my branch and tosses it onto our path.

What I think are fallen leaves drop away. It takes a moment to hear the branch strike the bottom. I edge closer and see a deep pit. The abyss is bad enough, but the sharp pointy sticks standing straight up will rip through the flesh of anyone unlucky enough to fall.

"Nighthawk, you walk onto that and you're dead," Père says. "The buccans are trapped by these all the time. I found that one yesterday."

Ah, the fatback. That's where that treat came from.

He smiles as we watch Josiah pick up leaves along the trail.

Père takes a whack at hibiscus stringers and a shrub that blocks his next turn. "I worry about Josiah. He's starting to wander when unattended."

It's terrifying. Josiah doesn't understand the harm that can come to him.

Père picks up a pink flower and puts it into my loosely braided hair. "You know he'll never survive without help."

I touch the petals, which feel delicate and soft beneath my fingertips. Then I grasp Josiah's hand more tightly.

It's now more evident he'll never speak. Maman's birth pains, the cord wrapping his neck have stolen my brother's voice and maybe some of his hearing. Living in Tortuga isn't easy. Being mute and possibly deaf will make surviving ten times worse.

Clutching a pine branch, Père gazes out toward the mountains of Hispaniola. As always, only the silhouettes appear behind a foggy curtain.

"They call that the Chaîne de la Selle," he says. "The tallest mountain is Morne La Selle. Those are the highest one can see from Santo Domingo. It's my guide as much as the fort. It's how I know my way and all the traps." He points to the left. "There's a small lake that fills in the rainy season. Right now, it's a dry hole leading to caves. Above us are the masonry walls of Fort de Rocher, with batteries of bronze cannons."

"I don't see soldiers marching today. Is that because the governor has sailed?"

Père trims a wider path through the brush. "Governor Bertrand d'Ogeron has died in Paris. We await his replacement."

Did my ears lie? I school my face. It would be wrong to celebrate openly the evil man's demise.

Sheathing his rapier into the sling at his side, Père leads us off the trail into a grove of tall trees. "Your mother and I used to walk here all the time. In the morning, she glistened. I'm glad we found our happiness, even if it wasn't meant to last."

"Why was it on her to save us?" My voice is low, trying to keep my pitch respectful. "Maman said it was a crazy time. But I've hungered to hear your reasoning. I'll accept that it wasn't what you planned, or that circumstances beyond your control kept you from doing what was right. I just want your words, not Maman's excuses."

He puts a hand to his graying reddish beard. "I was a fool and a coward. When my père discovered our love, he banished me. He said I had to buy Uzoamaka as I would any other slave. Off earning my own way, I wasn't even able to witness your first breath or steps."

This sad tone sounds true. Père turns. His gaze is again toward the Chaîne de la Selle. "D'Ogeron allowed me to start a tavern. When I earned enough money, the family wouldn't sell her to me. My father condemned me, told me I'd never be anything important. I was coming up with a new plan, but Uzoamaka took matters into her sweet hands."

I was young, but I remember how cruel that family was to my mother and other chattel. "Being a man who believes in rules, it must be terrible when things don't work as they should. And Maman suffered. It cost her everything to believe in your love."

"Those Delahayes have no honor. Be a woman of honor, Jacquotte."

Whatever I thought to say dies on my tongue. I accept this challenge as a blessing.

* * *

In silence we walk a little farther. Twenty minutes of twists and turns, and we reach a plateau that smells of honey. Almond trees form a room of white blossoms all around us.

Père uses the rapier and cuts blooms, handing one to me, another to Josiah. "Eat. It's all edible now."

I set my brother down, and we mimic what Père does, popping the petals into our mouths. It's good—jasmine and sweet.

"You're smiling, Jacquotte. You like it. The tropical almonds are young and tender. It'll take months before they mature and form a protective bitter shell around the delicious nut. Then the hardness must be thrown away. Having served its purpose, it takes pride in standing aside."

This sounds like a political speech. Is Père preparing to lose influence under a new governor? How will this change the tavern? Us?

"Eat, children." Père takes another bite and licks his lips as it explodes with juice.

I take a bite of mine. My teeth slice the gooey almonds.

Josiah, finishing his, begins to grin.

The three of us on top of the world enjoying a treat. "The Delahayes of Tortuga have survived so much. Père will survive a change in governor."

He hugs us. "You two are my treasures. I have to protect what matters." He hands me his rapier then scoops up Josiah.

Something happens when I hold the rapier high. My arm tingles, and I marvel at how good the weight feels in my palm. "This is better than my kitchen knives."

Père steps back like I've drawn it against him. "You look like you know how to hold a weapon."

I fail to mention that I practice every evening, jabbing the waybreads and stabbing gourds. Instead, I spin. The steel tip whizzes as I aim at an almond bloom. My strike is clean and precise—just the flower, no leaves, no stem. "Teach me to be better. This feels right."

He shakes his head. "Non. That's not for you. A woman—"

"It would be Josiah's, but we both know he'll never wield it. It should be mine. Then when you're no longer able to protect us, you'll know I can."

My words force to him think, and I step into his path. He nods. "I'll teach you a little, but the rapier will be for your son." His face sobers. "I'm being asked by men of Basse-Terre about marriage contracts. Even Old Jean has mentioned a name. Wealthy men are ready to settle their lives with a wife."

"You said I'm not ready."

Again he nods, but his gaze stays low. "You're not ready, but soon. The way you keep the kitchen shows me you are ready to run your own house."

"So my punishment for speaking my thoughts is for you to give me a husband?"

"Daughter, I'm trying to prepare you." He steps closer, and I see the goodness in his eyes. "You'll need a good man by your side, someone who'll protect you and Josiah and your freedom."

Heat fills my belly. "My freedom? When will Josiah and I be free of becoming chattel?"

The sadness in his eyes is plain. His failure to formally free us means *never.* I ache with new rage.

"We've had enough this midday, Jacquotte. Let's head back."

"Let me see the sea." Keeping the rapier, I cut my way to the edge of the plateau. Instead of blond beach and blue water, I see the masts and sails of a French frigate. Stretching, I find the missing soldiers. They're erecting iron pens in the sand. "I guess there's a monument to the late governor after all."

My father holds Josiah tighter.

"I do not control other men. They'll rot in hell for what they do. I will rot for my failures. But I do control you, and I'll find a good man for you to wed. He'll swear to care for Josiah. Then I will know I've done my best."

He picks another blossom and gives it to his son. "Come along, Jacquotte. We know our duty. It's time to act in one accord."

Père's plan liberates me. What consequences can I suffer that are worse than becoming another man's property by marriage or auction?

None. So it won't matter if I do the worst and free d'Ogeron's last boat of captives.

Five

1675. Basse-Terre. Tortuga

Men sing in the dining room below. I sit on the floor of the balcony, my toes tracing the knots in the oak planks very close to my bedchamber door. Père had me go up as soon as the pottage was ready to serve. Tonight he's paying some of Mille's filles to help out. They're making a time of it, flirting, pulling their bodices so low a nipple could pop out.

The jokes start again about the new shipment.

"The tavern looks its best from here." Madame Mille has come up the stairs that lead to the dining area below. She stops beside me on the balcony.

"Does it look like Paris, Madame Mille, or Sodom and Gomorrah?"

"It looks like Basse-Terre. It's an opportunity." She peers down at me, folding her arms over her lacy stomacher. "But it could be a harbinger of ill. With d'Ogeron gone, there will be a battle for power."

Don't men always battle for something? I glance at the dark ceiling beams of the dining room from which still hangs Maman's empty birdcage. Why is it still there?

A roar of laughter echoes. "Yes, she's a spitfire. Only thirteen, but what a mouth on her."

For a moment, I think he's speaking of me, but at fifteen, I'm past that age.

Nose upturned, Mille shakes her head. "The soldiers are perverted. They'll auction off a child as a wench."

It takes some seconds for my shock to evaporate; Mille has a conscience. "Then you agree this should stop."

She looks down at me. "I know what I don't like, but I'm also wise enough to know it's none of my affair."

I leap up and face the woman who operates a brothel a few feet away from where I rest my head. "Maybe that should change."

"Listen, princess," she says, "I'm only trying to look out for you. Uzoamaka was nice to me. She never looked down on me. Don't be a fool. Your father's talking to very well-off men for you. Consider yourself lucky, unless you wish to work for me."

"No thank you, madame."

Mille is a crafty woman. Cunning in a man is respected; in a woman, it's a threat. While I don't fault her for what she does or how she makes her pieces of silver, I wonder why she's shared her opinions openly with me.

She brushes her hand through her high wig. Bits of her natural brown show at the edges. I try to move away, but she calls me back. Her voice is loud, getting louder. She'll draw attention.

"Yes, Madame Mille? Is there something else you wish?"

"My rooms could use dusting."

They need more than dusting. The sheets need to be burned. "You have plenty of filles. I'm sure they could do your cleaning."

"They are busy earning. Since you have time to go meet with your secretive young man, you have time to clean for me."

She's full of assumptions of my behavior. That is better than the truth, so I allow her slander. I won't threaten her with the kitchen knife strapped to my thigh. I'll save my fury for Cayonne. "Madame Mille, I'll clean the two bedchambers closest to the one I share with my brother. But you must watch him while I'm away. Keep him comforted if he awakens and finds me missing."

"Two rooms?" She rolls the pearl bracelet about her wrists.

"That's a good bargain. And I like Josiah. He's quiet and humble. You might try that."

It takes everything in me to curtsy and not tell Madame Mille what I think of her and her advice. With a nod, I pass Mille and descend the back stairs. I breathe easier in the cool twilight. I've passed my first obstacle to liberating the captives.

* * *

The fading twilight passes into dusk, but the tavern's glow makes Maman's cobbles bright. I sneak through my garden and round the corner, walking past the window where Old Jean sits.

If he has seen me, he says nothing, and I think to myself that I'll roast a plantain special for him.

The last challenge is the big window at the front of the tavern. Maybe I should've gone the other way around the tavern, but that side is darker. I have no time to fight off a drunk or criminal.

I take a couple of steps and hide beside the well. Scanning the big window, I see Père serving up my pottage. The crowd is singing and drinking.

Before I can slip away, I see a woman coming toward me. Head down, I become a statue.

She's on the other side of the well. She surely sees me.

"Mademoiselle Delahaye?" It's Madame Sayon.

"I didn't mean to startle you." I try to keep my voice low. "How are you tonight?"

She stops pulling at her shawl. She can't hide the bruises on her neck any more than I can hide my body from her notice. "Work has to get done, even after dusk."

"Monsieur Sayon is a brute." I blurt this. "He needs to be dropped into a buccan pit."

Releasing a small laugh, Madame Sayon begins to crank the well's handle.

"Do you need help from whoever you're avoiding?" she replies. "I can't ask for the same. A wife can't fight back."

My eyes flick from Madame Sayon to the path to Cayonne. She'll be able to attest that Jacquotte Delahaye left the tavern. A Blanc woman as a witness is as good as a man's testimony if soldiers suspect me.

As if she senses my indecision, she looks me in the eye. "Go do what you have to do. I won't tell. A woman alone outside at this time of night must have something important to do."

"I do have something to do, Madame Sayon. I should get to it."

"Call me Sarah. I hate that name. I hate him. But I've nowhere to go. My family has cast me away. At least I have a roof over my head. There's food. I cook it. I've started my own garden. It's enough."

"Doesn't sound like enough. It sounds like barely existing."

"When you have nothing, this is good. Your père has a fine business. Your gown is very nice. Though you have no shoes on, I've seen you wear them. You are better off than I was."

She works the crank. The bucket comes to the top gushing water, more fulfilled than either of us.

"Sarah, I need to know if you think it would've been better to stay in the pens. Or to be in prison at Fort de Rocher? I need to know."

Basically confessing to my plan, I await her words. I already feel my mission to free the imprisoned women of Cayonne is doomed.

After filling one pail, Sarah lowers the bucket into the well again. "The soldiers abuse you in Fort de Rocher. They take turns and laugh."

When she has the bucket high again, Sarah releases the handle. It spins as the full bucket drops at speed to the bottom. The time before impact is like falling into a buccan pit. I feel as empty and as hollow.

She glances away, toward the tavern. "If someone is going to try to free them, it's better to do it before they go to the fort."

"My mother freed women. She smuggled the captives into the jungle. Some journeyed to the mountains and became Maroons. I think they are happy with that choice."

"And the others, Jacquotte?"

I swallow harshly. The memories of the floggings return like my own flesh is being whipped. "They were caught and punished. Some killed. Maman, she was hurt bad, but she tried again."

"Sounds like a brave woman. Most people don't help when they can." She starts turning the handle again. "I was trapped in the belly of a boat for three months. Two Guinea women were sold for provisions in Nassau. The soldiers made jokes that we were next, unless . . ."

Sarah's face wets with tears. "I don't know if I'd have the strength to flee if some brave soul came to try. I don't know."

I turn to the tavern, readying to crawl back inside.

"But I would've liked to try." Her whisper reaches my ear. I still.

"If anyone asks, Jacquotte, you came to stay with me. We had mint tea from leaves in my garden. You stayed the night."

She reaches down and puts a palm on my shoulder.

I hold her hand tightly. "Merci, Sarah."

"Leave me your fine outer dress. I will keep it clean. No one will know that you were rooting around in the dark."

That makes sense. I strip to my stays and shift, and hand Sarah the dress.

"Go now. If you decide you can't, you've done more than any. You're not a coward for trying." Stars highlight her honest face, her gentle dark eyes. "Come to my house when you're done. The door in the back will be open."

One quick glance at the tavern shows men drinking and singing and ogling Mille's filles. No one looks to the well. No one sees me so undressed. It's now or never.

I offer Sarah a gallant bow, then I head to Cayonne. No one follows. I am again alone under a canopy of leaves and darkness.

Six

1675. The Bay of Cayonne

Boats anchored along the shore bob in the sea. The water looks shiny and black and able to swallow them whole. I don't see Old Jean's ketch, but I know it's there. With something that powerful, I could sail from here to the secret bay in a matter of minutes and gather up at least ten or fifteen of the prisoners and take them to Hispaniola before dawn. But I will never put Old Jean at risk.

Though concerns about how to get these women away start to bubble, I commit to figuring this out once I have them freed. Trudging past the salt pool where sails are seasoned to ready them for ships, I keep looking over my shoulder. The jungle devours Basse-Terre. I keep going, looking up at the stars and the shadowy mountains. When I think I might've lost my way, everything opens. Stars and Morne La Selle never lie.

Light from logs on a fire exposes two iron pens staked into the ground near the water's edge. There are least ten women in one, and a sole captive in another. The lone one looks like a child. The scrawny little thing could never count as a woman. The dead governor's madness sent a child to Tortuga to become a wench or an abused wife.

* * *

Barely holding in my emotions, I step from the shadows and head to the pens. No one screams. No one gives away my position, but one woman says, "Fille fantôme."

I freeze. I'm no fantôme.

She says it again and then bows and prays at me, "Mère Marie! Sauve-moi! Mère Marie! Mère Marie, sauve-moi de la bête."

Another woman starts to laugh. Her giggles sound like she's drunk. The closer I get to the pen, the stronger the stench of ale becomes. The smell is stronger than the tavern before it's cleaned. That must be why the soldiers can leave these captives unguarded. They get them sotted.

The chant starts again. "Fille fantôme!" I'm their ghost girl coming from the jungle. Unsure of how much time I have, I go first to the pen of the lone girl. She doesn't seem drunk. This one can surely run and hide.

Sinking into the sand, I hoist my knife and pick at the lock. The blond girl inside stares at me. I put a finger to my lips. "Shhh!" Before I can do the same to the others, the girl says in immaculate French, "You've come to put me through more hell. I will yell."

"Sispann. Arrête. Alors vous nous ferez tuer toutes les deux." My French isn't as good, but I try to tell her to stop, that she'll get us both killed. I try again, "Morte, de touye," and point to us.

Her eyes are wide. I persevere, twirling my blade, prying up one bolt of the lock and then the other. When it all falls away, I ease open the door.

The girl doesn't move. I try to get her attention, and she turns her face to me. Her hair falls in matted braids. Her round cheeks look puffy, as if she's been struck.

I try again. "Ou lib! Tu es libre! Leave."

Her flat voice responds, "But where do I go?"

"Hispaniola," I say, "but hide in the jungle tonight. Go anywhere but Basse-Terre."

"You are trying to trick me. The Devil has come to trick me."

Sweat rolls down my brow. I've risked great trouble for this one girl. I should've worked on the more crowded pen first. The firelight makes my skin look darker than it is. Surely that couldn't be why she refuses? Yet, I can think of no other reason.

If the difference between her white skin and mine dictates that I can't be her rescuer, so be it. My gaze goes to the route I came. No one has followed me. I have time to go to the other pen.

This lock is trickier. "When I free you, hide tonight. Boats go to Hispaniola all the time. They won't find you there."

Finally, I loosen one of the bolts. My poor kitchen knife has dulled. If I live past this night, I'll have to take it to a whetstone to fix what I've ruined. The cries from the other women start again. "Bon fantôme!"

"Patience." My whisper is unheeded. The ale that wets their tongues keeps them chanting.

I should be cheered that they have such faith, but I begin to realize they won't all escape. The soldiers will hear the ruckus. The women are so drunk, I'm not sure they'll know how to hide.

Nonetheless, I keep trying. I can't give them hope then creep away.

Bang. Bang. I hit my knife at the last unmoving bolt. It's stuck.

A shadow covers me. My pulse pounds. I've been caught. I throw up my hands. "Maman, forgive me."

"I'm not your mère." A harsh voice tells me to move aside. *Smash.* The blond lump has come out of her pen. She's picked up a rock and strikes at the lock.

Together, we lift the heavy thing and beat against the iron lock. *Boom. Boom.* We strike until everything falls away. We've done it.

I jerk the pen's door open. They chant, "Perle noire!" The women wander the beach calling me a black pearl. That's something my mother would be proud to call me. This is a sign I've done good.

"Stop!" A voice rings out over our heads. The command is in English. "Halt or die!"

Soldiers round the bend. The lead man speaks French. "Arrêtez! Arrêtez, les femmes!"

They raise swords and begin to run toward us. We scatter. Every woman moves in a different direction.

My blond shadow and I head to the hills. Some of the women pick up rocks and shells and pelt the soldiers. I trip over one fleeing soul. My knife tumbles from my fingers. There's no time to retrieve it. I have to flee.

One woman picks up a burning log and tosses it. It strikes a filibuster, and his clothes catch fire. He becomes a screaming flame.

I move faster. This new light exposes paths into the jungle. As my feet hit the dirt, I hear a flintlock belch. A woman cries out, but my shadow and I keep running for our lives.

Seven

1675. The Hills of Cayonne

Terror and confusion, I've created them on the beach. I fly up the trail deeper into the jungle. It's dark. It's hard to see, but stopping will be worse. I veer off the well-worn path. Keeping to it will make me too easy to track.

The thick leaves hang overhead. They hide me but block the moonlight. A breeze whips the palm leaves. The snapping no longer encourages me. I must now hide like a wild animal.

Bending closer to the ground, I keep climbing, ducking tree limbs, looking for buccan traps. Moss gathers under my fingernails.

Needing to catch my breath, I slow, and the girl who didn't want to flee runs into me. We stumble and roll together. Flat on my back, I lie there until the world stops spinning. Whether I like it or not, the blonde and I are together. If one is caught, both will be.

A spark flashes in the distance. *Boom.* A signal has been sent to the frigate. More soldiers will flood the beach.

"How many guns does it have?" I whisper.

"What? Why?"

"If it's second- or third-rate—heaven help us if it's first-rate, that's a lot of cannons. That means a good many soldiers could be coming to search for us."

"It has fifty guns," she says.

"That's fourth-rate. The frigate can blow away this hill." My throat feels tight. It constricts more with each sound of a gun firing. "If I could save any one of them, I'd turn back."

"You're no fool. You can't reason with brutes or bullets." The girl's voice sounds strong and calm. "The cannons won't fire at us unless they see us. It's too dark. So, keep moving."

Can't fault her logic. I obey. Head down, I crawl forward. Putting my hand out, I almost tip over when my palm meets nothing. "Stop. A trap."

Moving around the edge, I guide my blond shadow farther up the hill. Under all the branches and leaves, the stars can't find us, but traps don't discriminate. They'll swallow pigs, goats, men, and stubborn souls.

"Keep going," my shadow says.

"I've done badly." I confess, "I have no plan. You're free. Go to it."

"I thought it was a trick." The blonde moves to my side. "When you said Hispaniola, the place I want to go, I thought you'd been sent by that evil filibuster. That my dreams were being used to punish me."

Her words humble me and remind me why I've done this. "Then keep up." I push at branches and begin crawling again. "You may be the only survivor tonight. If we make it to morning, I'll try to help you get to Hispaniola."

Soon the trees seem to thin. We've worked our way higher. With less dense trees, starlight finds us. They are a map for me to make out where we are. "Fort de Rocher is ahead. Caverns should be near. We might need to hide in them."

"You stopped again. I'm too close to my dreams to fail." The fool girl charges forward like she's lived in Tortuga all her life.

But I know where we are. I speed up, grab her elbow, and spin her back. "This is dangerous. You almost fell into that hole."

"Hole?"

"It's a buccan trap." I reach down, grab a rock and toss it. A few seconds pass before the sound of it hitting the bottom echoes.

Before either of us responds, a twig snaps.

The glow of flames appears out of nowhere. Someone tracks us and yells, "Come out!"

A man with a torch has followed us into the jungle. If he catches us, this soldier will kill us.

* * *

We don't move. When the man with the torch goes the other way, we creep lower, hiding behind a patch of growing ferns. A branch of bayahonde hangs over our heads.

The blonde grasps my shaking hand with her trembling one.

Smoke from the torch comes closer. The flames show the man. The girl's eyes grow giant. She must recognize him.

Dirty, stained shirt. Long, brown hair tied with a reddish scarf. Big pantaloons and boots. He is dressed like any filibuster I've seen in the tavern.

And that's our doom. A soldier might have mercy, but not a pirate.

He comes within three feet of us. "Anne. Je sais . . . sais que tu es là . . ."

She covers her mouth and squeezes my fingers so tight I'm sure the blood stops flowing.

The torch swings to our left.

Thwack. The filibuster's sword smacks bushes and branches near us.

"You caused this. I know you did. Anyone dead is your fault, Anne. We'll catch the ones loose in Basse-Terre too."

Women made it to the ville? Not all of them have died! I have to cover my mouth to keep from screaming with joy. It wasn't all for naught.

The man retraces his steps and heads again toward us. His torch illuminates everything—branches, leaves, bayahonde pods, the hungry buccan trap.

"Come out now, and I'll see you are spared."

He's lying.

The girl shaking beside me scoops up fallen pods, big ones with thick, prickly skins, and flings them. They smack a tree a distance away from us. The noise is loud.

The filibuster turns to where the pods hit. He sneers and heads that direction.

Then he's gone, into the buccan trap. The spikes impaling his flesh sound like my knife gutting fish. He dies fast, before uttering another word.

The torch that dropped with him extinguishes.

Darkness falls around us again.

One should feel bad for a life ending without the chance for repentance, but I feel nothing but satisfaction. I congratulate the buccan trap for killing a horrid boar.

"I'm Anne, Anne Dieu-Le-Veut," she says in the perfect French of missionaries. "We should know each other's names before we are found and killed."

"J-Je m'appelle Jacquotte. Jacquotte Delahaye. We just might live."

We remain quiet, waiting for more soldiers. Then I risk stating my truth. "I am a fool. I did not have a plan beyond opening the pens. I know women died tonight. I'm lucky you have good aim."

"Jacquotte, we all wanted out of the pen. They didn't want this life or anything waiting in Fort de Rocher. But I wish to go to Hispaniola. I'll get there, because you came for me."

I feel her trying to rise. "We need to stay here. It's not safe to move yet."

She ducks back down. "As long as you stay, Jacquotte, I stay."

We crouch next to each other, hoping to remain alert and alive.

Eight

1675. The Hills of Cayonne

A nighthawk thrashes overhead. Easing my sleepy eyes open to darkness, I hear a group of the majestic birds diving onto prey. Something soft scratches my forehead. I panic, swing my arms, and strike a fern. Then I exhale. My soul hunts for rhythm. I want Maman to tell me in drums, in the tempo of the Kissi, she's happy with me. I reach for her, but she's not there. Her presence, silent and full, slips away.

I must settle for the call of the birds. It's not Maman, but they announce I have lived through the night. With my eyes fully open, I embrace twilight, that moment when it's not so dark, but it's not daylight. The purple sky possesses enough light for me to see the girl asleep at my feet.

"Hello," I say. "Anne. Awaken. We must go."

She whimpers and curls up more tightly.

"Anne, you have to hide. I have to go back to my family. No one can know what we've done."

She doesn't move.

Panicking, I place my hand to her nose. The breath hitting my fingertips makes me happy. I clutch her shoulder. "Come on, Anne. We're not safe."

"I have to get to Hispaniola," she mumbles.

"You mentioned going there before. You know about the big island?"

She nods. "When I found out they were taking women to the Caribbean, I had to go. I must get to Petit-Goâve."

I blink at her, realizing that she isn't an unfortunate soul who'd been rounded up for some crime. "You planned to be enslaved?"

"I saw a moment to join the women who'd be taken to the new world. I took it. The East India Company is very lax at the port of Lorient, especially for transport."

"Didn't you know what they'd do to you? That they auction women off to wive strangers or force them to wench? Some, the guards abuse."

"I didn't know all the risks, but I knew my future would be better here. My cousin lives in Petit-Goâve. He has made a fortune in these waters." She sounds so confident, as if none of the dangers would harm her.

That's crazy, but what can I say after risking everything to be a fantôme? "You can't even be fifteen. Your parents—"

"They are dead." She looks away, taking away her shiny eyes. "I'm thirteen. But I'm braver than many. I've had to be."

My heart aches for her. "This cousin will take you in if you get to Petit-Goâve?"

"Oui. You must help me get there."

She's crazy, but so am I. "Let's head to the docks. I'll see if I can get a friend of mine to sail you to Santo Domingo, that's the closest city on Hispaniola. From there, you'll disappear. No one must suspect you've escaped from Tortuga."

"Santo Domingo is not Petit-Goâve." Her bruised face becomes so serious. "You must help me get there. That's where the opportunities are."

I'm not going to argue. With at least two men missing or assumed dead, the filibusters for hire, the sailors on the frigate, and the soldiers at Fort de Rocher will become relentless in their search. "We have to go now. I'm not going to be executed because you are stubborn."

She grabs my arm. "The beach is that way."

"Can't be spotted anywhere near the pens. Haven't you been listening to me?"

"Oh, oui," she says. "If we are seen, we are guilty."

Being seen equals guilt—her words feel truer than anything. That's a woman's plight here in Tortuga, and everywhere.

"They haven't discovered us yet." I help her stand. We dust off the rich island dirt that grows the sacred ferns.

"Jacquotte, a soldier may already be at the docks looking for prisoners."

"I'm the leader now." Though not a good one. This will be the last time I'll have that distinction. "I'll learn to plan better. I have a good plan now."

Taking the path I followed with Père yesterday, I lead Anne toward Basse-Terre. The trogons sing for us as we walk through the jungle. The canopy of leaves shrouds us from above. It's cool, and the ground is moist. The smell of sweet rose mallows greets us.

Peering ahead, looking for trouble, I ask, "Was getting here worth it?"

She lifts her chin high. "I am here. I'm alive. I still have my dreams. Oui. Much better." Catching me staring at her thin body and bruised face, she grabs the bodice of her gray gown. "Been struck a few times," she says. "You get used to it. Then you get even."

A smile shows through. She's probably thinking of the buccan trap. A vulture flies over us. His call sounds greedy.

"Hungry birds will get rid of the evidence." There's not an ounce of regret in her ruddy countenance. I like that.

"Anne, I'm about to involve one of my dearest friends to save you. You seem smart. Becoming a burden on this cousin is worth risking the punishments to get here?"

"My cousin is special. He's a buccaneer. If I'm wily enough, I'll join his crew. I can become a buccaneer too."

If this were a jest, I'd laugh, but the look on her face is so serious. She's risked everything for a foolish dream.

"You should come too, Jacquotte. We—"

"Buccaneers are men. This I know. They sup and drink at my father's tavern."

She shakes her head. "Women have been buccaneers. They've done it in disguise."

I didn't do all this for this girl to lie to me. "Women have not done that. They cook and clean. They become wives and mothers. Or they work in brothels. Those are the only things we get to do."

"Jacquotte, if you keep asking for permission, you'll never get what you want."

Her rebuke shuts my mouth hard. I hear Maman's laughter in the bleating of the coco palms. A wind comes up from the sea so strong that I almost lose my footing.

Maman didn't ask permission to flee.

She didn't wait for my father to win her release. She stole a vessel and won her freedom. If my mother hadn't had me and the obligations she felt toward my father, would she have kept sailing? Would she still be alive? Oui, she'd be enjoying the sea she loved, claiming treasures, opening her arms and grasping as much of the world as she could.

Anne takes my arm. "Women have been pirates in secret. A buccaneer's crew only cares about the work getting done. Come with me, Jacquotte. I already see you have adventure in your soul."

I pry out of her grip. "I have responsibilities here. I have a little brother who's probably awake and looking for me." I ache, listening to my excuses. My stomach feels like I've taken my kitchen knife and gutted my insides. When will I learn to stop asking for permission for the future I want?

More light shows in the sky. Sunrise will expose us. "Neither of us can be anything if we don't get to the docks," I warn.

Anne matches my speed and runs beside me. "Jacquotte, I think fleeing to Petit-Goâve is *our* next adventure."

Ignoring her, I search until I see the masts of Old Jean's boat. "Come. My friend is a fisherman. He won't turn us in, but we'll have to convince him to help."

As quickly as we can, we move down the wooden docks. A dozen boats are anchored beyond the reefs, while others are close, tied to pillions. The makeshift warehouse remains dark, but workers and fishermen will be here soon. In another hour or two, women in Basse-Terre will rise and go to the well or come here to buy fish or goods. Sarah must be awake. I hope she isn't fretting about me not returning.

"Come on, Anne. We need to hurry."

In front of Old Jean's boat, we stop. My stomach is full of knots as I hear men singing, coming down the trail from Basse-Terre. Soldiers in French blue justaucorps with big, folded-back cuffs on the sleeves have joined with filibusters-for-hire.

Nine

1675. The Docks of Basse-Terre, Tortuga

The minute the armed men step on the sand, I know we're caught. I brace. I hold hands with Anne. I pray.

And the god of good, the favored god of Maman, the one watching over the Kissi in the fields, makes us invisible. These men don't look at us or even toward the docks.

Anne squeezes my fingers. "I owe you. Someday, I'll repay this debt."

We aren't safe yet, so she owes me nothing. I knock on the boat hull as if it's a door. "Old Jean, are you awake? I need a favor."

"Your friend will be back soon." A silky baritone answers me. An unknown man sits up from where he was lying on the deck of the ketch. "Mademoiselle Delahaye, what brings you out today?"

How does he know me when I don't know him? "Monsieur, where's Old Jean? This is his boat."

"It is." The fellow stands and stretches. He stares at me, barely acknowledging Anne.

"Monsieur?" I repeat. I sound agitated and protective. This is my friend's boat. "Will he be back soon?"

"Oui, and I am Captain Le Basque. I assume that's your next

question." He leaps off the boat and lands, his boots drumming the rickety planks.

He stands before me. I drink him in like a good bouillon—dark hair, pleasant smile, sea-blue eyes. Le Basque bows, sweeping his light-brown hat into his hand. Showy white ostrich feathers rise from its band.

"It's a pleasure to greet other early risers," the captain says. He stands there waiting, staring. Then I remember I'm only wearing a shift and a corset.

My stomach tightens. "I'm sorry, monsieur, but I have a problem that only Old Jean can solve. Where is he?"

The man folds his arms. "He'll be back soon. You sure you do not know me, Jacquotte Delahaye, the daughter of Pierre Delahaye?"

I don't wish to look back toward the beach, so I focus on him and try to remember where we've met. He does look familiar, and it's obvious he knows me and Old Jean.

I give up. "This is my friend, Anne—"

"Anne Dieu-Le-Veut," she says with a nod.

"Mademoiselle, it's a pleasure to meet you. Your friend doesn't seem confident that she recognizes me. Mademoiselle Delahaye probably is familiar with my old name. I was Captain Michel d'Artigue, but I now am Captain Le Basque."

That name I know.

I've heard it quite a bit from Old Jean. But d'Artigue was a ship's captain from Old Jean's pirate days. This man doesn't look old enough to be that captain. My brow rises. "Le Basque? You can just change a name?"

"Oui. My crew prefers a bold title. I must consider them, and does it not roll off the tongue with flair? Le Basque! I am from Navarre, which is the Basque country of northern France."

He grins at me, the man's vanity looming over us. Unlike most filibusters, this one is clean—clean-shaven, combed hair tied back with a silver ribbon, and a new-looking coat the color of oxblood.

I blink a couple of times and try not to seem panicked. "My friend needs to get to Hispaniola right away. Can you help me find Old Jean?"

He steps closer to me. "What will you give Jean for the trip? Perhaps I can make a better arrangement."

Up close, Captain Le Basque smells as clean as he looks, like he's washed his face with good soap that holds a scent of rosemary. Nothing like the stark lye soap I make in the kitchen.

"Mademoiselle?"

"I usually trade Old Jean a meal at the tavern for favors. I'd do the same for you."

The captain offers a pouty frown. He looks boyish. "You have served me before. I do enjoy your pottage, but that's not enough."

My gut hurts again. It twists like it's about to burst when he takes off the luxurious coat. I'm dead when this handsome man drapes it about my shoulders.

"You're not dressed for an early morning excursion to Cayonne."

"We were in Basse-Terre," I say quickly. "Nowhere near any beach."

His hands move toward my heated cheeks. He doesn't touch my skin, but he pulls twigs from my braids. "Nowhere near Cayonne, eh?"

"What happened was . . . oh, it's not important. Captain, you must have a ship. Can you take my friend to Hispaniola? Now?"

"Every captain has a ship at least once." His tone is light, but I'm desperate.

As much as I want to sound sweet, my teeth grit. My voice lowers. "Where's yours?"

Le Basque lifts his hands as if to surrender. "I'd do anything the fair Mademoiselle Delahaye asks, but my men will be working on repairs today." He points to a beautiful ship anchored by the reefs. "The *Marauder* is out of commission."

"A frigate?" Anne says. "It's been in a battle. Who did you battle?"

The grin on Michel's face becomes bigger. "Just a little skirmish."

"A little skirmish? The foremast has a section missing." I point to the ship with its burnt sails. "I've repaired headsails for the ketch, it's a serious task. A section out of a mast is from a siege."

"Astute, mademoiselle. We were lucky." His eyes remain full of humor, and fastened on me.

I glare at him too, making my eyes as intense as his. It's easy. I like the look of him. And I love his frigate, even if it was fifth-rate.

Before I can get more information on Old Jean, Le Basque says, "If I'd known you'd be up early with your friend, who is also underdressed, I'd have been delighted to ask for your assistance to mend my sails. Ladies sewing for the *Marauder* sounds fitting for my ship, as she herself is quite the lady. And she'll be ready again to defeat any English or Spanish fleet that comes my way."

Cursing, dark and deep. Footfalls follow, pounding the dock.

My pulse slows as I spy Old Jean storming our way. He steps around us and slugs the captain in the shoulder. "What are you doing, Michel? I leave your arse—"

"Mon ami, we must control our language. You . . . well, we have visitors this morning. But tell us what has you so upset on this glorious day."

The old man grinds his teeth. "Damned filibusters-for-hire. They're at it again, but worse. They've slaughtered some of the women they brought from Paris."

Michel's grin disappears. "Why would they do that?"

One of Old Jean's thick, bushy eyebrows rises as he looks at Anne. "The captive women they were going to auction this afternoon escaped last night. Soldiers are saying they were attacked by the prisoners. A women set a guard on fire. If you kill one of theirs, they kill double in retaliation."

I try to appear shocked. "Did any escape?"

"Don't know. But they're scouring the beach. The few women they did recapture are babbling about a fantôme breaking open their cage."

"That's unfortunate," Captain Le Basque says. "But we have

guests, mon ami. The good daughter of Monsieur Delahaye and her Anne."

Old Jean stares and tugs at his pointy hat. I see his eyes narrowing. "Mighty early, Jacquotte and Anne. It's good you two weren't involved with last night's escape." He tugs at the sleeve of Anne's prison garb, the tell-tale gray gown given all the captive women. "You two wouldn't know anything about what happened in Cayonne, would you?"

Captain Le Basque folds his arms. His mustache twitches. "Women causing havoc? When do they not?"

"Old Jean, I need to get Anne away. Can you take her to her family in Hispaniola?"

More shouting comes from the beach. A dozen soldiers in wide blue hats and the powdery-blue justaucorps arrive. Their jackets are open, showing white shirts and lacy neckties. They look dignified and very warm. They split up and begin talking to each fisherman who's come to the docks.

"Time is wasting. For the spirit of Uzoamaka, Old Jean, please take Anne to Hispaniola."

"Uzoamaka." My friend, my mother's friend groans. "She was smart. She'd not get caught up in mischief."

"Maman was brilliant. But she failed in her first attempt to free captives. Then she found success sailing with her daughter to freedom." My insides shake, but I feel strong. "To honor her, make my first attempt a success."

There's no lying to Old Jean. I begin to confess all. "I did something to help when others looked the other way. I'll turn myself in—"

"That'll not be necessary." Captain Le Basque shoves Anne up the gangplank. "Go hide on board while we grown-ups finish talking. Prison garb is not becoming."

Anne glances at me but does as she's told.

The captain stays in front of me, and I know it's him I have to convince to take Anne to Petit-Goâve. "She has family in Hispaniola. Help her to reach them. Sorry for the mischief."

"You must be slower to admit your part in things," he says quietly. "In fact, as far as I can tell, you've done nothing at all. You got up early for a walk with Captain Le Basque. I even promised to show you my frigate."

His eyes are serious.

"Do not frown, Mademoiselle Delahaye. Better to be thought of as a pirate's woman than a fantôme."

"A pirate's woman? Not sure I like that."

"You will like being my woman." He runs up the gangplank and drops into the ketch. Le Basque tosses coins to Old Jean that look gold and shiny.

After the old man bites into one, he puts them into his pocket. He climbs on board and sits down leaning against the mainmast. I see him wave and put his hat over his face.

Le Basque picks up another blanket and wraps it about Anne. "Old Jean, do you have a spare shirt for this one?"

Old Jean frowns. "D'Artigue, your father was also generous with my things . . . and my life."

Father. That's it. That is how this connects. Le Basque is the son of d'Artigue, the filibuster who was Old Jean's dearest friend.

"Wait," the captain says. "Since I'm now the financier of this venture, I haven't heard how I am to be repaid." He yanks in the gangplank then points toward the end of the dock. "Think fast, Mademoiselle Delahaye. Troops are coming. They will begin actively searching. And Fort de Rocher's soldiers are good. They're not careless like the filibusters-for-hire."

I don't look back. I keep my gaze focused on him and his laughing, sea-blue eyes. Captain Le Basque has no reason to lie. He holds the power.

"What to do?" The captain puts his foot on the pillion where ropes tie the ketch in place. "Mademoiselle Delahaye, I'm waiting."

Having already confessed about Cayonne, I don't know what to say. "Save me the trouble. Tell me what you want."

Le Basque laughs. "To celebrate our budding friendship, I request a simple walk on the day and place of my choosing."

"Oh, Jacquotte, take him to the hills." Anne's muffled voice rises. "You know the spots."

She's being funny, but I don't want to send anyone down a buccan trap who has a ship that can take me sailing.

"Someone needs to hurry up and make up her mind. The soldiers are closer." Old Jean sinks lower in his boat.

The dock shakes. The escape might be over before the ketch can launch. I hold my breath and prepare to accept blame for the deaths I've caused last night.

"A walk. I'll assume you accept." Le Basque unties the ketch and pushes off. "Until we meet again, Mademoiselle Delahaye."

He and Old Jean appear to be arguing as the boat slips away. A blind man could see the affection between them. Le Basque steps to the back of the boat and waves. He takes a crucifix from his shirt, kisses it, then begins working the sails.

"Oui, Captain Le Basque." I wave at him as soldiers stand a couple of feet away. "As soon as you return, we'll walk in the hills."

"Dress for the occasion, mademoiselle!"

Fishermen eye him and hoot. Then they glance at me wearing his coat. My face fevers.

Soldiers come to my side, but the captain's loud voice is all I hear. "I cannot wait to see you again, Mademoiselle Delahaye. Au revoir pour le moment."

His words are for the benefit of the soldiers and maybe me. By the time the soldiers start asking me questions, the captain and Old Jean are almost out to sea.

A tall fellow looks as if he wants to rip away Le Basque's coat, but before he can get his hands on me, another man, a filibuster-for-hire, stops him. "That's no wench. That's Monsieur Delahaye's daughter."

"Jacquotte Delahaye!" A woman is screeching my name. "I told you to leave that man alone."

The voice sounds familiar. I cup my hand against the brilliant sun to see who's my savior.

"Your father is furious." Sarah Sayon's rebuke rings loud for all to hear. "Come with me now. I told you to leave that man alone. Now you must face Monsieur Delahaye."

Laughing at me, the soldiers ask nothing more. The tall man signals to Sarah. "Take her to her father. He'll have enough problems. She's Captain Le Basque's woman."

They let me leave. Half the soldiers move on to check other boats. A few march toward the pens.

Sarah puts her hand to my jaw like she wishes to slap me, but she whispers, "You did it." She jerks my chin, but it's all for show. "You absolutely succeeded."

We start walking along the dock. She pretends to be fussing at me.

When no one can hear, I say, "I don't know if any more prisoners have gained their freedom other than one. Captain Le Basque and Old Jean are taking her to family in Petit-Goâve."

"You saved three others, Jacquotte." She whips her hand to my shoulder like she's hitting me. "I saw them in Basse-Terre crying about the Fille Fantôme who saved them." Her low voice is full of pride. Then her tone grows harsh and loud. "Come on back with me now. How can you be such a disgrace!"

People point at me as we walk on along the beach. I don't mind. I watch the ketch enter the sea lanes. Anne has made it. My friend will be with her cousin.

"Come on, girl." Sarah tugs at my ear. This time it hurts.

Mocking whispers of fishermen and filibusters rise to laughter. Oh, this will be hard to live down. But I'm not shamed. I made something good happen.

"Thank you. Thank you for helping me." I release a big breath and walk closer to Sarah.

She tugs the jacket, ruffling the velvety collar. "Looks like you got a lot of help."

"Le Basque was helpful. He saved Anne and I guess me."

"Jacquotte," Sarah whispers. "I wasn't lying. Your père did come looking for you. I told him you spent the night with me and ran off when we discovered my husband's body."

"Monsieur Sayon is dead?"

"Oui, peacefully, in his sleep."

I stumble then quickly right my steps. "That seems . . ." I want to say *a coincidence*, but I let the notion fade. I have enough trouble. "I'm sorry for your loss."

"I'm not. I now have a comfortable home that can hide secrets." She lifts her shawl and draws out a sack. "I have your gown. Once we find a safe place to stop in the jungle, put it on, put your friend's jacket in my bag."

"I'll wear it over my gown. There are enough who've already seen me in it. I can't hide being a filibuster's woman now."

The bruise on Sarah's neck looks pink and blue and more awful in the light of day. I think of Anne and the risks she took to get here, just to get to Petit-Goâve and try to become a pirate. I'm glad Sarah took a risk and became free as a widow.

She helps tie the corset strings of my gown. We walk together through the rest of the jungle, under branches and leaves until we enter Basse-Terre.

* * *

With three of the women from the beach hiding in an upper room, I watch from a chair near the hearth as my father and other men of Basse-Terre come to remove Monsieur Sayon from his bed and prepare him for burial.

Sarah cries pitifully, and I pretend to console her. My father is solemn.

He doesn't chastise me for leaving the tavern. He's whispered that he loves me numerous times. "Jacquotte, you look so tired. You sure you don't want to go to your room and rest?"

"I don't want to leave Madame Sayon."

He nods. There are worry lines on his brow.

Then Père scowls at Captain Le Basque's jacket draped on my lap. "Going out by yourself . . . Never mind," he says. "But I will hear about the filibuster later."

His mouth closes when two men carry the sheet-wrapped monster out to be buried.

Père holds his small cross and says a brief prayer. Then he peers at me. "You're not up to making the pottage?"

I shake my head. "Non. I'd rather keep Madame Sayon company today."

"There will be a lot of soldiers to feed. Lots of people are upset."

Sarah, on her knees warming water in a kettle on her hearth, looks at me. "I thank you for being here, Jacquotte. I don't wish to be selfish, but it would mean everything if you stay a little longer."

"Jacquotte, you stay," Père relents. "You women help each other."

"Thank you." Her voice sounds broken. Her eyes glance at me and then the flames in her hearth. "She . . . I need her, monsieur."

"Of course," my father says. He leaves with the others.

Sarah goes into the other room and brings a basin and slides it near my chair. She fills it with water from one of her pails. "Let me soak your feet. They look as if you've walked a thousand miles."

I let the water kiss my feet. Then I wash my toes clean of the dirt from the hills, sand from the beach. I scrub my fingers and nails and the hem of my shift. I wish for no stains of last night to remain. "We'll help the women upstairs get to Hispaniola?"

"Oui." She adds more water and lavender petals. "They have no family in the Caribbean. Maybe I can pretend they are relatives."

"No one will believe that. They must hide until the soldiers give up. Then we will get them to Hispaniola."

Pulling a chair close to mine, she sits. "We'll figure it out, Jacquotte. Two heads are better to come up with a good solution."

"Planning is my weakness. I promised myself to do better." I wriggle my toes in the warm water. "Sarah, you don't have to say what happened to Monsieur Sayon."

"He died in his sleep after he hit me for the last time," she answers calmly. "A pillow gave him comfort."

My thoughts center on her, that she is the one who received comfort. I sink deeper into the chair, my back supported fully by the spindles.

When she bows her head, I pray for her, and for Anne. I hope my newest friend likes Petit-Goâve and that she becomes a good pirate. Wouldn't it be wonderful to meet again on the top deck of her pirate ship?

My eyes close. I rest, vowing to myself, my mother, and my sex that this win won't be my last.

Ten

1676. The Hills of Cayonne

The wet season has passed and brought Tortuga to another year. I stand on a grass plateau, listening to a bubbling stream renewed by all the rain. It sounds peaceful here. That is very different from the past turbulent months. Gossip and accusations swirl about Basse-Terre, alighting on everything from how the disaster of Cayonne happened to who will be our new governor.

Nonetheless each week, I visit with Sarah. Père trusts her and thinks she will be a good influence. Little does he know.

Today, we sent the last woman from the beach sailing to Hispaniola.

"Jacquotte!"

I turn and wave at Sarah. She's wearing Maman's glorious straw hat. It's big on Sarah, but it keeps her skin from becoming too pink in the sun.

"Old Jean made it?" She stretches, leaning a little over the plateau's edge. "Do you see the ketch?"

"No. But everything went well when you took the woman to the docks. I wish I could go, but I'm still not allowed near the docks. Père thinks Old Jean has allowed improper influences to corrupt me."

"Oui. No problems. Captain Le Basque has not returned."

Sarah's light-blue eyes hold a soft smile. "You've been thinking of him, non?"

How can I not? His quick actions saved Anne and kept suspicion from me. And as I'm *his woman*, he leaves money with Old Jean to "accommodate my enterprise."

"He's generous. A man should be that, if I'm to think of him."

My co-conspirator smiles and takes a good long breath. "It's a glorious day to be free. Jacquotte, we don't have to be scared anymore."

I haven't been scared for a while. The talk of the Fille Fantôme died down quickly, almost too quickly. No one believed any of the captured women's stories that an apparition freed them. Everyone blamed their drunkenness. Père keeps accusing the dead filibusters-for-hire of everything that happened. Well, they say dead men tell no tales.

Shielding my eyes, I join her searching the sea for Old Jean's ketch. "What we've done with the women feels important. And the risk . . . it . . ." I touch my chest, right at my heart. "I love doing something that matters . . ."

She nods. I'm not sure if it's to humor me. "So making pottage and working for Monsieur Delahaye is not enough?"

"It's not. Père won't take any of my advice. At six, Josiah does not need to be coddled. My brother may never speak, but he's growing older. He needs—"

Sarah laughs loudly. Her voice booms. "Is the captain returning for you soon? Will you wed?"

Then I hear men talking—fine French curse words. Soon three soldiers from Fort de Rocher interrupt us on the plateau. Dressed in light-blue swinging coats with huge red cuffs, they carry polished swords. One has a musket. If not for how formal they look, I'd suspect they'd come to hunt a wild boar or to arrest me, the woman who almost got away.

Whipping off his wide felt hat edged in white lace, the lead man with sunny gold hair and grayish-green eyes calls the others to a halt.

"Monsieur Hasneau." Sarah comes closer to me, in sort of a protective stance. "We want no trouble."

"Nervous, Madame Sayon? Or is this a show of your confidence? I have always thought you were too confident."

He's taunting Sarah. Her fidgeting speaks of fear.

"Monsieur Hasneau, we are women of Basse-Terre. We must be confident." My voice draws his attention. His countenance becomes less severe as he peers at me.

He marches closer, and I maneuver myself in front of Sarah.

She tightens the bow on her straw hat and tilts it to cover her eyes. "It is a blessing to find community."

"A blessing? Like a husband dying so suddenly and leaving a house and land to his widow?" Hasneau laughs as if he's made a joke, but his threat is obvious. He suspects Sarah had a hand in making herself so fortunate.

"Where are my manners?" Hasneau continues smoothly, "Ladies, let me introduce two up-and-coming men, Jacques de Pardieu de Franquesnay and Jean-Baptiste Du Casse." The taller man, de Franquesnay, bows. The shorter, thicker man, Du Casse, does the same.

Then Hasneau stares again at Sarah. "Not everyone can be purchased quickly like Madame Sayon. I suppose some beauties are luckier than others."

Du Casse, fanning his coat, breaks in. "We need to hurry to Cayonne. We should meet Neveu de Pouancey the minute his boots touch the dock."

Hasneau rolls his eyes. "We don't know if the new governor's boat has arrived. The fog is too thick."

The men turn to leave, but my curiosity betrays me. "New governor?"

Hasneau glances back at me. "Mademoiselle, has your father not told you? Jacques Neveu de Pouancey is to be the new man in charge." He bends and dusts off his light-colored stocking. "And he will bring changes, starting with the pirates. Outsiders will have less influence in Tortuga."

Outsiders? We're a colony struggling to grow. We need outsiders. "Monsieur, all in Cayonne and Basse-Terre are welcome at the Delahaye Tavern."

"Poor, misguided young lady," he says with a snide tone. The man doesn't hide his disgust. "The buccaneers' and filibusters' days of being welcome in Tortuga will end."

De Franquesnay taps his arm. Then Hasneau steps back. His voice softens, becoming less animated. "Without the criminals, there will be more women for the men already a part of our colony. I think that's important, since we apparently cannot keep new women. And you, Mademoiselle Delahaye, have grown into a lovely flower despite such bad influences."

What's that supposed to mean? As if Sarah has read my mind, she clasps my arm. "Mademoiselle, we have detained the soldiers long enough."

With his hand holding his wide hat against his chest, Hasneau bows. "Ladies, enjoy your walk."

When the soldiers and all their weapons are far down the trail, I turn back to my friend. She's shaking like palm fronds. "What did Hasneau do to you?"

"Other than threatening me and wanting to take my home?" She grits her teeth then offers me a false smile.

Putting my hands to her shoulders, I steady Sarah. I claim her scared eyes. "Tell me."

"I have." She pushes her hat down until it's to her thin nose. "He was the guard at Fort de Rocher."

I embrace her. I don't need to ask her anything more. "He's bigger than you. As a prisoner, you had no say."

"I'm not weak." Her hat falls off, rolling on the ground. "I'm not. I'm not chattel. The Guinea women have no choice. I had a choice. I could remain in prison to be abused by him or be auctioned. So I was auctioned and became a wife. No one ever owned me."

Her harsh words sting. I remember Old Jean's warning about Blanc women. *Those Blanc women will be fine. Their children will be free. They're not us.*

Sarah wants to feel superior because she's French, not Guinea—*not like us.*

Everything aches. I can't believe my friend could say this. "Is that how you feel about the Guinea, those brought here from Africa? Your enslavement is elevated because you have an easier way to be free?"

"I . . . Non." A tear runs down her cheek. She turns her face away. This contention between us hides under the hat's wide brim. That's Maman's creation, woven with her Guinea hands.

"I didn't mean that," Sarah says. "I'm so sorry."

I hear pain in her voice. It touches my soul, drawing me away from feeling deceived.

"Please forgive me, Jacquotte. Please." She holds me tightly. "Please."

That sorry, good-for-nothing heart of mine begins to mend. "Oui, Sarah. I do."

But a sail with patched holes will always be a little weak.

Eleven

1677. Basse-Terre, Tortuga

Wet season, dry season, and a near miss of being in the eye of a hurricane brings Tortuga a new year. I stand in the kitchen listening to something I haven't heard in a while, a crowd of filibusters and buccaneers eating and drinking.

Sarah puts her ear to the slatted door. "They sound like they're having fun."

Père must be ecstatic. "There's more bluster out there than all of Mexico." The latest storm moves about like a ship following the trade winds. "Old Jean says there was so much damage to Veracruz that whole buildings were dragged out to sea. Nature is a wonder."

She sighs and begins a final inspection of my kitchen. "Fire in the hearth out. Cauldron is clean and cooling."

"And a pile of dishes in the basin." I take off my apron, proud of feeding so many, so fast. "Père will have to gather the rest. We're done for tonight."

Pulling down my tankard of spices, she shows me it's almost empty. "Not sure how we'll replace it. Only one warehouse left in Cayonne. Not certain they have spices."

Basse-Terre has changed under Governor Neveu de Pouancey. His hard stance on piracy has hurt the tavern. Most of the warehousing businesses have closed, moving on to Port Royal. Henry

Morgan lords over that city and all of Jamaica. He cares not that warehouses sell spices, cloth, and slaves.

For all of Governor Neveu de Pouancey's maneuvering, Tortuga's population hasn't increased. New businesses haven't come. These storms have ruined the tobacco crops. Nothing prospers. Some want to try sugarcane here, like that will be the answer. It's just another reason to deal in slaves.

Sarah looks out the kitchen door. "Don't hear anyone outside. Maybe it will be safe to make it to my house alone."

"From the noise in the dining room, I doubt anyone will be sober enough to try anything."

A drunk man crows about Petit-Goâve. I think of Anne. I still dream of being the Fille Fantôme. Two years since that night. I've lost count of the number of times I've looked for her on the ships that come to the docks. "Do you ever wonder about what your life could've been?"

Sarah squints at me, and I explain. "I mean, if you could choose another life. To live another life. What would you be?"

She folds a cleaning rag. "Non. I have what I want. A house, a garden, a friend." Her smile warms me. "But you are young. May you get everything that you want."

"Adventure. I still want adventure. But Josiah . . . I want adventure before I have to always care for him. He's wandering off more. It's an effort to keep up. Père has hired a fille again to watch him while we cook."

"Maybe he should wander. Wander in the garden, new places. Maybe his soul is as restless as yours. His silence just makes it seem different."

Never thought of it like that. I shrug, feeling guilty of tethering Josiah as much as my father wishes to limit me.

Père enters, grinning, but he always smiles when Sarah is helping in the kitchen.

"Tonight is good. Très bien." He puts the load of dishes onto the table. "You both go. Go together. I'll take care of everything."

"I was going to walk Sarah." I wave my rapier—well, Père's, but he's pretty much ceded it to me. "I will be back."

He begins to frown. "In fact, Madame Sayon, will you have my daughter stay over tonight?"

As soon as Sarah says oui, he's herding us to the door.

"Père, what is it you don't want us to see?"

"Men. Men acting like men." His tone seems hasty, too hasty. There's something he wants to hide. When he opens the back door and we see shadows of singing men in the garden, he takes my rapier and waves it. "Get out of there. Come to the front door. That's the only way to get rum."

The shadows leave.

"Perhaps it's not safe. I should walk you two."

Cheers and a crash shake the slatted door to the kitchen.

He turns back to seek out the disturbance, but I take the rapier and hand him my sharp kitchen knife.

"Jacquotte?"

"You want us gone. You have your reasons. Yell loudly if you need help."

He starts to chuckle then holds the door for us. "I'll see you in the morning. You ladies take care. And, Jacquotte, do not accidentally stab anyone."

"I'll try, Père."

"Do more than try. And week's end, I wish to introduce you to a gentleman who's been asking about you. He comes from a noble French family. He'll make sure that the tavern and Josiah are fine. I know that worries you."

"Come on, Jacquotte." Sarah's voice sounds calm, as though she knows how I must be raging. I leave, knowing my adventures are done. I'm out of time.

* * *

Sarah drapes her arm over my shoulder. Passing by the large open window, I see Old Jean sitting at his table with a man in a full scraggly beard.

A fellow stands on a table and commands the room. "The harbor of Surat. There I saw the golden boat of the Grand Mughal. Aurangzeb's ghanjah dhow. Masts full draped with silk sails."

"A boat of gold?" Old Jean pounds the table. "That would never float. You lie. Gold is too heavy."

Sarah tries to tug my arm, but I have to hear.

"He's talking about the land beyond Guinea. That's a place to go see."

She gives up, and we hear more.

"There's gold-laden temples and women wrapped in silk."

"Wrapped in silk? It sounds hedonistic," Sarah says. "That's what your father didn't want you to hear. He knows you want adventure. He doesn't want you dreaming of lies."

The man, the storyteller with the beard, catches me looking. He gives me one of those winks Sarah does so well when she haggles for fish. Then he beckons, like I'm going to come inside.

I jog away, dragging Sarah with me. "You were right, let's go."

"Saw too much, aye? Men being wild and drunken are a bore. Women sitting on the filibusters' laps. Soldiers throwing cards, gambling at quinze in the corner—they'll take their losses out on a wench or a poor wife. It's all too much."

I'm listening, but I'm not. My thoughts center on the golden storyteller.

She yawns all the way to her house. When she opens the door, I don't cross her threshold. "Jacquotte, what now? You will not come in?"

"I know what my father didn't want me to see, and I need to confront him."

"Jacquotte." She sighs. "Be kind to him. He's trying to do his best."

"This cannot wait."

"Do nothing until tomorrow," she says and offers a hug. "And be careful going back to the tavern. Slip up those rear stairs as fast as you can."

I raise my rapier and salute her like she's my captain. Then I turn, heading for the tavern. I should have a visitor waiting for me in the shadows.

And it won't be Père.

* * *

With my rapier outstretched, I follow the cobbles to my garden. No one is here. I lower my hand. I feel silly.

I sigh and head to the stairs.

A noise. A rustle. The heat of something close.

I lunge with my rapier. My control is perfect as I press the tip to the gullet of the man's neck. The light from my kitchen beams on the thick beard and sea-blue eyes that have darkened with mischief.

"Why are you in my garden, Le Basque?"

He swallows and puts a fingertip to the rapier. "If you draw a weapon, mademoiselle, be prepared to use it. The enemy will see your delay as weakness."

"I'm not weak. I want an explanation more than I want blood."

"Then I am a lucky man." He chuckles, pulls out his crucifix, and kisses it. The emeralds and gold catch moonbeams. "God never fails."

His voice is as rich as fresh butter. He steps away, touching his throat. "You've left a mark. I take it you have forgotten me."

"You've forgotten me! It's been two years. You still wish to have that walk?"

Captain Le Basque doesn't respond, but his gaze slips all over me. "I've been busy sailing around the world. It takes time to do so. And from the look of you, you've made the most of my absence. You're more beautiful."

As I stupidly listen, he gains the advantage and spins behind me, knocking away my rapier and pulling me by the braids into him.

His forearm is against my throat. "You've scratched me once. I'm not inclined to let you repeat that."

With my rapier gone, I have no way to defeat him, and the way his breath falls on the back of my neck, I'm not sure I want to.

"I never said when I wanted my walk, mademoiselle. So it's not I who is rude."

The roughness of his beard tickles my cheek, and then he loosens his hold so I can jerk away.

I stoop and seize the rapier, but I keep the tip pointed toward the ground.

He bows to me. "Good. You see I trust you and you can trust me, especially when I say that I would've come sooner if I could."

To believe him is folly, but I'm not running from someone with a boat who can take me anywhere. I have less than a week to escape Père's matchmaking.

"I made promises to a gentleman, one who was clean-shaven."

His knuckles rub against his chin. "A clean shave maketh me not gentle, but if that is all the lady wishes—"

"And not a walk—the pleasure of sailing a frigate."

"You want . . . to go aboard the *Marauder*?"

"Oui, captain. Those are my terms." I push past him and start up the stairs.

"Fine. In two days. I can accomplish much in that time."

Unsure if I have that long before Père draws up a marriage contract, I steady myself on the oak treads. "You do know what two days are? I won't be made to wait another two years."

"Four twilights, mademoiselle. Each day has two—one before dusk, one before dawn."

Over my shoulder, I offer him a little glance. He holds up a hand, his fingers spread wide. His gaze burns me.

"No more than two days will separate us." He gives me another a bow. "Sleep well, Jacquotte Delahaye."

I slip into my room and close the door.

My brother is asleep in his bed, snoring.

Setting the rapier on the floor, I flop onto my own straw-filled mattress, but I don't think I'll be able to close my eyes for at least four twilights.

* * *

Cayonne in the morning greets me with beautiful sea-salty air. My mission is to get fresh dolphinfish for tonight's pottage, and to see if the *Marauder* floats in the bay.

It's there, bared of its sails. The hull has new patches where a carpenter had to repair it at the waterline. The boat looks worn or aged, but that doesn't mean it went all the way around Guinea. I walk toward Old Jean's ketch. He'll know the truth. He's never lied to me.

"Bonjour, mademoiselle."

The voice sounds stronger than last night. I turn and see a clean-shaven, well-dressed Captain Le Basque.

He bows with one arm across his wide chest, over his vest of gold thread. It's long like the jackets the soldiers wear, but it has no sleeves. It takes a moment of blinking to regain my voice. "Captain, I . . . Bonjour."

Barefoot, wearing a common gown of gray with a brown corset stomacher, I feel underdressed. Nonetheless, I pretend that I am grand and curtsy. "A surprise to see you, captain. I thought it would take another day. Only one twilight has passed."

"I sobered quickly. I like to seize the morning. Old Jean has mentioned that you too are an early riser." He stops, looks one way then the other. "I don't see Josiah Delahaye. My friend says that he accompanies you often."

I sigh, even though I don't mean to. "He does. He's my responsibility, but I have risen before everyone."

The captain nods. "Do not be alarmed, but Old Jean has told me about your brother as well."

"I love Josiah and wish he did not need me, but he does. I'll always have to ensure he is well cared for. Yet, I hate myself for feeling obligated. I have so little control over my life, and to have it dictated by my younger brother . . . Sorry, I shouldn't be saying this."

"Love can be a burden." His low tone tells me he understands.

"Why are we talking of this?" Exasperated, I make to leave. "Oh, good day, monsieur."

"Non. A walk." Captain Le Basque offers me his arm. His countenance offers no judgment or pity. "Let's go toward the beach. Let us view the vendors."

"I came for fish. The fishermen are the other way. The last warehouse is that direction. I want nothing from them . . . except spice." I remember that I've run low on peppers. I should see if they have some. If they don't, maybe I can have Old Jean take me and Sarah to Santo Domingo for a short trip. Josiah might like that too.

"Well, the opposite direction has no spice, just memories of the Fille Fantôme." He winks at me. "I'm not sure I would be safe. Let's go a little farther. I can check on my men."

I agree and start moving. Le Basque looks out at the waves rolling onto the shore.

"Do not be embarrassed for being weary of responsibilities. My father was a great man, but he left me with burdens that have shaped my life."

"You were very kind to fund my enterprise to get those women to Hispaniola."

He laughs. "Needed to make sure you didn't get into any more trouble while I was away. I know you are the type to finish what you start."

"I should return your jacket. It's in my maman's trunk with my most beautiful things. I wanted to wear a much better dress for this."

"You are lovely just as you are. And keep the jacket. The pourpoint is losing favor as a fashion."

People gather in the warehouse, the open structure with a thatched roof and rows of empty spots for those vendors who will arrive later. The crowd milling inside visits makeshift tables. Breads and fresh-baked buns scent the air. Crates with bolts of fabric show a rainbow of colors. Purchases for pieces of eight happen all around me. I refuse to take another step, seeing the transactions of Guineas, the men and women of African birth exchanged for a filibuster's booty.

"Choose something. Spare no expense." The captain tugs me forward into the hateful space. "You said you needed spices." He looks around and leads me through the fabrics. He picks up the raw edge of an expensive bolt of cream-colored silk. "Does it do anything for my eyes, mademoiselle?"

"Non." I can't say more. My gaze is fixed on a man with an armful of gold platters. I watch him tell a vendor in the rear, "Quatre? Pas de dix Guinées. Au moins huit nègres."

"Settling for eight slaves. How generous." My loud voice catches their attention and makes the man increase his bargaining to nine.

"Augh. I've condemned another soul to go with the filibuster."

Captain Le Basque drags me from the warehouse. I shake in his grasp, but he speeds me away. "Just breathe, mademoiselle. Don't be a fool in anger. These men can make trouble for you or your family."

"Don't you see, I've made things worse. I want to—" I grasp my rapier, as if I can take some action.

Le Basque gently takes away my weapon—and swiftly tosses me over his shoulder.

"Put me down!" I yell as he strides along. "You will know the fury of a Delahaye!"

"I already do." He tosses me like a sack of grain into the bottom of his pinnace. Before I can get my footing, he pushes off from the dock.

He puts my rapier and its sling over his shoulder. "I usually don't let women on board, but one stubborn lady should meet another."

Anchored near the reef, the *Marauder* sits like a majestic bird, a nighthawk that has hunted throughout the Caribbean, the world.

Though awed by its power, if I find one enslaved Guinea on board, I swear I'll be the fantôme, I'll be Uzoamaka. I'll steal the ship and set everyone free.

Twelve

1677. The Waters of Tortuga

Dumped onto the deck of the *Marauder* close to the squared-off stern, I don't move as Le Basque orders his crew to set sail. I watch the canvas unfurl, strung on mooring lines. Because of the weight, two men must do this to hoist them into position.

"Before you get up screaming, know you're the first woman on my ship. Not even wenches or laundresses have been on board. Don't bring me bad luck." He scowls, but I see humor in his eyes.

The captain then motions to his crew. "Around Tortuga, men. I wish to show Mademoiselle Delahaye a little of the sea. You can all go below."

A few filibusters dressed in pourpoints or billowy shirts give me a stare, then carry out his orders. Though Le Basque says he doesn't allow women here, I wonder how true this is. His men don't seem bothered by their captain stealing a woman.

Men continue to scatter. Soon it's just the two of us on deck.

"I apologize. Mademoiselle, if I'd known the filibusters were up and trading—"

"I hate that place. I try never to go there. I want the selling of Guinea or anyone stopped."

His hands grip something that looks like a rudder, but it's long and goes through the deck. That has to be the whipstaff Old Jean mentioned. When Captain Le Basque moves it, I feel the *Marauder* turn. "Enslavement happens. You get used to seeing it."

"Never."

He sighs but keeps his hands on the staff that guides the ship. "You can't pull your rapier on everyone, Jacquotte."

How dare he be so easy with my name? I storm to him. "I'm not concerned about what booty is captured from Spain or any wealthy country. Those are fair battles. Equal opponents. Guinea men and women are *stolen.* They're not goods. They're harmed in these dealings."

Mustache sagging, he bites his lip. "I know."

Expecting more of a fight, I hiss at him. "You aren't going to try to justify this practice? Going to tell me there's no other way to be a Caribbean buccaneer or French filibuster without accepting this enslavement?"

He takes the finger I'm pointing at him and draws me close. "Put your hands on the whipstaff. It helps controls the direction we sail."

My palms are timid within his, but he fastens them about the shaft.

"Old Jean tells me that you're good at driving his ketch. Show me what you can do."

I grip the whipstaff, the same as I've steered the ketch's rudder. Emboldened, I tighten my fingers about it.

The captain begins to laugh. "You like that feeling of power?"

Nodding, I make a little turn to the left. The frigate obeys. I tremble with excitement at this, at the captain's arms about me. He smells good. The salty air frees my inhibitions. I crave this. Adventure—not a little taste of it—no way in hell can I let go.

"This is my life's calling, Jacquotte. You don't get to pick and choose what you see. Have I made trades for Guineas? Non. Have I served on ships that did? Oui."

I stiffen, but I can't close my eyes. The chance to command a frigate is rare, impossible for a woman. Yet here I am.

"Pirates commit many sins," he says. "Do you think a forty-two gun miracle was just gifted to me? I took it."

"You took a fifth-rate? Couldn't hold out for two more guns and steal a fourth-rate ship?"

He sighs, and his breath warms my brow as he steps in front of me. "No one else has had complaints about my firepower."

The wind scatters my braids. My chignon has shed pins. "I must look wild."

"You're beautiful. For two years I've had your face in my head."

Shameless, heady, I tighten my grasp. Seduced by words and power, I flex my palms about the whipstaff. I refuse to move away.

"Tell me, Jacquotte. Are you sinning, being amongst filibusters, sailing my purloined vessel?"

My lips close, forming a tight, silent line. I'd surrender everything to be Captain Le Basque, give anything for this to be my life. No manner of dreaming, scheming, or planning will make it so. At week's end, my father will put me on another path. This joy will never be mine.

* * *

We sail for hours. There's no more talking between me and the captain. Under his watchful eyes, I, Jacquotte Delahaye, command the *Marauder*, a most powerful ship. Barefoot on the oaken deck, I worship the wind, the setting sun, even the captain giving me this moment.

My mother must be looking down upon me with pride. *Maman, I was scared, trembling in a basket, when you commanded the helm of the sloop. Had I been brave, I could've crawled out and shared the twilight with you. We could've been pirates together.*

I told Anne she couldn't do this. I hope she is, even if in secret. I hope she awakens every morning to see waves cresting, splitting at the prow.

Le Basque has a boot tucked behind him as he leans against the mizzenmast. "You're a natural. Old Jean said he taught you a great deal. You know the sails, the topgallant—"

"Oui, and the main and fore courses. The halyards to raise the sails. Even the spars and braces to extend and make them square. Should I show you how to make knots?"

A deep laugh rumbles. "Old Jean is a good teacher. And he's told me so much about you and Uzoamaka."

The captain comes to my side, peering at my hands, adjusting the angle I hold the whipstaff. His are sweaty. Is he nervous?

"You're quiet, Mademoiselle Delahaye."

"It's a rarity, captain, for a man to yearn for a woman to talk."

"But, such a woman." He rubs my shoulders, and it takes all my strength not to tremble.

My cheeks warm. I swallow hard and return my gaze to the sea. "That will not work. You're purposely trying to distract me from steering."

"You need to be more relaxed. The *Marauder* will only obey a confident captain. Now close your eyes. Picture the direction we need to go. Think, *What degree do I turn the bowsprit?*"

"Umm. Fifteen degrees."

"Correct."

"Old Jean tells me to watch the horizon. It will guide me. He's taught me to navigate by the stars."

He steps close. "Orion's Belt, three beautiful stars, shine above my Port Royal, Jamaica."

"You go there often? Of course not. You're busy sailing and battling." My gaze meets his sea-blue eyes, that have darkened like water before the rain. "You've sailed everywhere. This ship can go around the world. Do you have a home?"

"I have a little house in Port Royal. From here, I sail the Windward Passage to its channel to get there. Then I see the blue flagpole that marks my land. It's heaven. I don't need to go to the ends of the earth for peace. I go to the ends of the earth for adventure, but I value home."

Seeking adventure—that's more perfume for my soul. I want adventure so badly. "Why own dry land?"

"Sometimes you want to sleep in a bed. I have a house, a place to call home, to eventually settle a wife and children. Or a brother-in-law who needs assistance."

"Josiah."

"For now, the mother of one of my crew, Gramma Nettles, keeps the place tidy. But she told me it's time to find a wife. I told your father that too. He kicked me out of the tavern."

Before I can question what he said, the *Marauder* hits a patch of rough water. I ease up, steering against the current, and point for the captain to adjust the foremast as if Le Basque works for me. "Another fifteen degrees."

Our actions curve the boat back toward the reefs where we started.

"Well done, Jacquotte." His gaze wraps about me, then he moves away. "Time to drop anchor. Those who wish to return to Basse-Terre may do so."

"I'm not leaving, captain."

"I'm not quite ready to let you go."

Le Basque drops anchor. Seconds pass before the ship lurches, then stops as the iron hook fastens into seafloor. Men have come back on top. Sails lower.

Le Basque calls out to his crew. "All ashore who's going ashore."

The men lower the pinnace. More men come from below and climb into the small boat. I hold my breath, waiting, wondering if the captain will change his mind and send me back.

When the pinnace pushes off and I remain on deck, I'm overwhelmed.

The few remaining members of his crew scoot down hatches. It's just me and the captain, the boat and the sea, and the setting sun.

Thirteen

1677. The Waters of Tortuga

All those silly thoughts I've had of Michel Le Basque for two years—waiting for his return—lively and warm, dancing in my head.

His shirt lies open, exposing tufts of black hair and his gleaming cross. "Reddish-brown tresses kissed by the sun. Deep-brown eyes that burn with fire when you are mad."

"Sounds like you like me mad."

"I like you." Le Basque steps close again, his hands pinning me against the whipstaff. "And your curves fit nicely here. But, while I have control of my lusts, I need to ask if you like me too."

Gazing back at the indecision in his eyes, I say, "I haven't decided if you're mine."

"My affections are hard to win. You must work a little. Be more enthusiastic about truly being Michel Le Basque's woman."

"More enthusiastic? I give up. I will take your ship instead," I say with humor as I reach to his side and jerk free my rapier. I whack the air, flexing the tip like a whip. "Surrender the *Marauder* to me."

"Before you steal the ship and my heart, you must know all the risks. Death is a possibility."

Is he serious? I don't want thoughtfulness or to be rational. I hold the point of the rapier to his chin. "Is it hard for you to surrender to a woman?"

As delicately as I can, I trace his buttons, skimming the tip of my rapier along the fabric of his vest. "I sharpen my weapon like my cooking knives."

His countenance sobers. Le Basque lifts the blade with his knuckle. "I have no interest in play."

"Who's playing, sir?" I move fast and slice off a button, which he catches. The mustard-colored vest opens and exposes more of the crucifix's glimmering chain.

The air crackles. Thunder roars. I sense its energy.

"Feeling powerful, mademoiselle?" He leans closer. "Does holding a rapier make you think you have the upper hand on the captain of the *Marauder*?"

Slam. He moves so quickly, I barely have time to register the motion before I fall flat on the deck. The rapier rolls from my fingers to the captain's awaiting hand.

Standing over me, he puts the tip to my neck and traces the ribbons holding my stomacher and corset. "If I were to play along and cut here and here, your drab tavern outfit will fall away. That might be a blessing. My woman will be dressed better."

Panting the humid air, feeling drops of rain on my brow, I wait, searching my feelings, knowing everything in me wishes he would free me of this corset.

He raises the rapier. "I cannot threaten my woman. That is who you are, aren't you?"

"Michel Le Basque's woman. Not his captain?" Spinning on my backside, I hit his calves and knock him off balance. He falls with a thud beside me. The necklace with the cross is flung out. I hold it, caressing it in my palm. "I don't like looking up at you when we are having a serious discussion. I like us, Michel, at the same level."

I relish the taste of his given name on my tongue. Calling him by it makes me feel as if we are the same.

He sits, takes the cross from my fingers, and kisses it. "Touché. Well done. We are equals."

"Are we? Then you should inform me, not my father, of any serious decision. I can make my own. Or must I keep cutting you down to size? Unlike you, I will have no hesitation stripping you bare."

He helps me stand, but his smirk says he's unmoved. "A child playing an adult's deadly game? This sounds like you still have some growing to do."

"Then you wish for no more mercy." I whip my blade and slice his collar. Again, I leave no mark on his flesh. The fabric of the vest falls away, fully exposing his chest—hair, crucifix, scars, and muscles.

I've seen men swim. I've seen them leave in all manner of undress from Mille's, but this—I like it. I might be grinning.

Shaking his head, Michel frowns. "The vest was a favorite. My laundress in Port Royal will not be able to repair this." He tosses the rags over the rail then marches to me. He reaches for my chin, but I graze my teeth against his thumb. He grips my hair and yanks me off balance. His mouth nuzzles my neck as his hands dip into my gown.

I lean in for him to touch me more.

Taking the hint, he jerks me into his arms and holds my back flat against him. His palms cover my breasts. "Monsieur Delahaye doesn't wish me to corrupt you. He wants you to be a virgin bride. That's an impossible request when I've thought of nothing but this . . . you . . . for years."

"If I have to be a wife, I should be yours."

He doesn't say anything, but his hold on me never loosens.

The rain that has teased its presence starts. Before it begins to pour and wash away my courage, I turn and face him. "I said, I should be your wife, Michel." I put my hands on him, on the pink of his nipples. I give him the pleasure he's given to my flesh. When the rhythm of his breathing changes, I realize I have power over him. I like power. "I said what I wanted. I'm not ashamed."

Michel closes his eyes. He leans against me and dips his forehead to touch mine. His crucifix, solid gold, feels cold on my bosom. "You should be glad that I'm patient. I'm patient because you've stolen my heart. I love you, Jacquotte."

In the steady rain, he kneels and picks up my rapier. Once he puts it into my sling, he sweeps it and me over his shoulder. I dangle down his muscular back, and he hums some sailing song and starts down a ladder. This buccan trap has a lantern, bringing light to the passageway below. If there are any doubts in my mind about what I've provoked or Michel's confession of love, they have the good sense to fade.

*   *   *

Down the corridor I'm carried. It's hot here, nothing like being on deck. Michel kicks open a door. We enter a dark room where I see nothing but his outline.

He sets me atop a barrel.

Slink. The sound of my rapier hitting the floor echoes. This room, a supply room, is small, and for a moment I fear that we aren't alone. "A filibuster's frigate has no place for its captain other than to stand at the whipstaff?"

"I sleep with my men in the crew's cabin. We are all equals here, but none is worthy to see you."

"*Equals* is the brag I hear in the tavern—how these ships are floating utopias." My hands are sweaty. I can barely see Michel and want him to speak. His voice is reassurance. So, I'll chatter about nonsense. "Then it's true, not something to make the French look like fools for having decorated rooms for their captains."

"The British and Spanish navies have such comforts for their captains, and even their officers. Those rooms are wasteful and weigh down the stern. I ripped away the nonsense. The *Maurader* is swift. We are sleek. Always ready for action."

"Oh." The sound of his boots mirrors my beating heart, meshes with the drumming of falling rain.

"For privacy, to love the woman I want, I choose a storeroom. Is that acceptable, Jacquotte?"

If I nod, I don't think he'll see my consent. Instead, I grab his outline and pull him close.

He kisses me and lifts me against a wall. The stiff oak boards demand my posture to straighten, but Michel's hands make me relax against it, against him. My skirt is tugged down to my knees. I kick it to the floor.

He hasn't taken me. I'm waiting for pain. I'm waiting for him.

"What's the problem, Michel?"

"Delaying." He chuckles. "I'm giving you a last chance to change your mind. I'm spun up, but I'll—"

I wrap my arms about him and kiss him. His lips taste of lavender and rum. "No changing your mind, Michel. I told you what I want."

A bottle rolls on the floor, one way, then another. The ship is shifting in the waves.

"There's no going back. You'll be mine, forever marked by love. You are my wife, Jacquotte."

His passion along my neck makes everything good. I sink my hands into his hair and pull his mouth back to mine. His voice rises over my madness. "Jacquotte Delahaye, you're the mate of my heart. With this act, you're mine."

The rhythm I feel when our flesh joins is consuming, natural, everything. We bang the wall. Passions build. We bump into barrels, but I can't let go. I won't let go, not until my body is broken and reborn in fire—a wife's fire.

His crucifix against my bosom sears. Everything's hot. I'm grasping flames. We burn together like kindling wood. To take this moment and stretch it to forever becomes my mission. I do so until I can't, and my soul—tired and unraveling—dies.

"Madame Le Basque." We sink, spent, to the floor. He kisses my brow. "In the morning, I will place a band of gold on your finger. Everyone in Basse-Terre will know you are my wife."

"Captain and Madame Le Basque. I'll sail at your side with pride."

He grunts like thunder and rolls our hot, sweaty bodies to a blanket, or what I think is one. It could be a sail. It should be a sail. It feels right to love Michel on the canvas that powers his *Marauder.*

Fourteen

1677. Basse-Terre, Tortuga

A gray sky greets my morning, but that is common in the rainy season. The partial sun fighting through the clouds steams the moist air. It leaves a taste on the back of my throat that's thick and salty like bouillon. I fidget, sitting next to Michel as he commands the pinnace to the docks. Going to inform my father of my marriage will be hard—hard to hear his disappointment, hard to watch him realize I've acted of my own accord.

Once he ties the boat to a post, Michel helps me onto the dock. "The dress is a little better than I thought. Seeing the intricacies of the ties, I can appreciate it more."

"Thought you liked it better off."

"True, Madame Le Basque!" His shout leads to others waving and yelling congratulations. He swings me around then sets me down on the beach. "Suppose I should've announced this to your father first. Can't help myself." He grabs my hand. "But we must head to Basse-Terre—"

I kiss my husband. On the white beach, with the wind kicking sand about us, I hold him close, towing him with my hand fisting around his crucifix. This public action shows that I claim him, Captain Michel Le Basque, as mine too.

When I release him, I point to the path to Basse-Terre. "I'm proud and happy to be your wife."

Hoots and something that sounds like congratulations follow us.

"Jacquotte, I love you." Michel laces fingers with me. "You're my beloved wife. I cannot wait to return to your arms."

My heart stops. "Return? We are to separate?"

"Oui. But I'll not be gone forever, especially after last night." Michel puts my pinkie to his lips. "And what we've done might leave you with my babe. I couldn't be happier if that is what God has blessed us with, a little lad or lass with your eyes."

My heart drops into an abyss. I just became a wife. I don't want to be a mother so soon. And I don't wish to be abandoned. "Why can't I go with you? Madame Le Basque should be with her husband."

"It's too dangerous. The *Marauder* is going east, one final time. We didn't make it to the Mughal Empire last time I rounded the Cape of Good Hope. Weather kept us in warm water too long. Woodworms and barnacles almost ate through the hull."

"Then take me to Port Royal? You can leave later."

"Non. I may be gone a long time. I want you safe with friends and family until I return." He touches my stomach. "I won't have you in a new city trying to manage by yourself."

It could be an adventure to be on my own, but I decide to save my protests as we meet up with Old Jean on the trail. His nets flop down his shoulder, like I did against Michel's back.

"Come with us, my friend," my husband says. "I must proclaim my marriage at the well in Basse-Terre."

Old Jean studies him, me. "Still going away, though? Not taking your bride? Jacquotte's frown tells no lies."

"The *Marauder* is repaired and ready to sail." I hold back tears. "Convince him, Old Jean, not to return me home debauched. I don't want to be an abandoned wench."

Michel begins to grin. "You're a married woman, not a wench."

Old Jean puts his nets down behind a group of ferns. "Fishing will have to keep. Not going to miss the look on Delahaye's face."

He follows behind us. Twenty minutes pass in silence before we enter Basse-Terre. Sarah stands at the well filling pails.

She waves. She shrieks, then runs into the tavern.

"Well," I say, "she's telling Père we've arrived."

Michel spins me to him. "I love you, Jacquotte, but I have a last mission with my crew. I promised them, but it is the last. If you say we're not married, I'll let you go. But I want you to be mine."

I grip his vest and jerk him close. "I must be bad at marriage and wifing. You're leaving."

Thunder crackles overhead as Old Jean shakes his head at us. "Here comes the in-law."

"Madame Le Basque, if you love me, you must trust me."

Looking into his sea-blue eyes, I want to see the man I adore, but this is a sea captain going off with his men, leaving me to deal with my father, my doubts, and possibly another new, dependent life.

* * *

The stony look on Père's face chills me. He steps up to Michel and tries to punch him. "You have some nerve, Le Basque."

Michel pushes him back. "Now, Monsieur Delahaye, please be gentle greeting your son-in-law."

"You bastard." Père tries to hit him again.

He shoves my father's hand away. "I told you of my intentions before. I've made good on them."

With her arm about my waist, Sarah holds me back. "Let the men do this."

I stop resisting and rest against her. Josiah puts his arms about my hips.

Père rushes at Michel, but Old Jean steps between them. "Now, Delahaye, are you saying there's a reason she shouldn't be married?"

Père's eyes go wide. "I trusted you, Le Basque! You said you understood I had other plans for my daughter."

"Plans my bride didn't know about or give her consent to." Michel laughs. "She consented to me."

"Lies. You took advantage!"

I break free of Sarah and Josiah and leap to Michel's arms. "No, Père. I claimed him of my own free will."

Many have gathered from the little circle of thatched-roof houses. Some are clapping. Others come and stare.

Michel looks at me then turns to the crowd. He takes a little sack from inside his coat and jingles it. Then he tosses it at my father's feet. "It's a worthy bride price, as Old Jean would say. It shall keep my Madame Le Basque in comfort until I can retrieve her. To all who hear my voice, Jacquotte Delahaye is my wife."

Cheers. Women clap. Even Mille, who comes from the cobbled path to the tavern, offers her applause.

Then that's it. This is all required in a place with no church. All smiles, Michel moves in front of me and crouches low to speak to Josiah. "Little man, I'm your new brother. When I return, you will come with us to Port Royal."

"My son will always be a Delahaye. Basse-Terre is his home. This tavern will be his."

I should speak up. I should—

Sarah's sharp glance makes me fall silent. With a brow raised, she wills me not to speak.

Visibly shaking, Père marches to me.

I tense for a slap or to be called a harlot. He does none of these things. Instead, he drops the sack of coins into my hands. "I need no bribe. Jacquotte, you're my flesh. You are always welcome under my roof." His tone is sour but resigned. He chooses to love me, even if I'm reckless and disobedient. "I have failed you, Jacquotte. I am sorry."

"He loves me, Père. Understand—"

"Loves you then leaves you. A pirate may not return." My father's tone is soft, but his words sting, for he is right. "I was forced to leave your mother. Le Basque goes by his own free will."

The truth hurts, but it doesn't change what I've done. "I chose him, Père. My choice is better than anyone not picked by me."

His frown trembles, and he turns away.

Then I yell at the top of my lungs. "Michel Le Basque is my husband. I claim him too."

More clapping resounds. Mille's filles shout their congratulations. A woman's voice isn't required in matters of marriage, but I want everyone to understand that I chose Michel Le Basque.

Sarah hugs me. "Go with your husband on a long walk. Do it before the rain comes. All will be well when you return. The hard part is done."

"Not really. Michel is leaving without me."

She lifts my chin. "He's here now. Walk and talk."

Old Jean claps his hands again, then gives Michel a slug to the back. "Very good."

People scatter. Sarah goes into the tavern.

I'm left at the well with a husband and a velvet pouch. I open the little sack and find ten gold Spanish coins. "Didn't know I'd cost so much."

Michel closes my hand about the money. "Let's take that walk, Madame Le Basque?"

I take my rapier strap and sling it about my shoulder.

We begin a silent trek into the jungle. Clutching my bride price to my bosom, I pray that this union proves worthy. For now, both my father and I have broken hearts.

Fifteen

1677. The Hills of Cayonne

The scent of rain grows stronger the farther we walk into the jungle. Michel cups his hand to his brow. "The clouds look dark. The afternoon will have a squall." He stops, looks left and then right. "At least this business with Monsieur Delahaye is done. We have his blessings."

"Blessings? That's what you call it?" I shake the velvet sack of coins. They make tingling sounds like a bell. "You tried to bribe my father."

"I'm providing for you. Like I did with my coat to protect you from being caught as the fantôme of Cayonne. I let every man know my claim."

My heart races as he pulls me close. The curve of his mouth makes mine tremble, but I draw back. "I didn't give myself to you for you to leave."

Seizing my gaze, he strokes my chin. "I'm selfish. That's why I'm a good filibuster. That's why you're mine. You'll not be forced to marry another fool. This fool is yours."

The palm fronds thrash in the rising wind like congratulatory clapping, but I can't celebrate. I'm going to be alone again and made more of an outcast than before. "Who did you take these coins from? Did you risk the wormwood holes and attack a ship coming back to the Caribbean?"

Michel takes one of the coins from the pouch and holds it up to the sun. It's rough, with a royal shield on one side and a cross in a quatrefoil on the other. "It's old treasure. See, Phillip III's mark. It's from the *Santa Margarita.*"

He says the name of the ship like I should know it. "This comes from the treasure that Old Jean helped my father recover. For years they were hunted for having this. Spain would hang any filibuster to get information on where the treasure is."

The pouch dangles from my wrist. "And you gave this to my father? It could implicate him—or you!"

"Your father's tavern hosts buccaneers of the islands and filibusters from Britain and France. Anyone could have paid for rum and pottage with these winnings. It will never tie him to any of my feats."

He takes my hand and quickens his pace. We are up high. To our right, the Chaîne de la Selle with its looming Morne La Selle skirt the clouds. Fort de Rocher's shadow stretches to us from the left. Michel tracks along what should be a dry path. The rains churned it into stream. We follow it to a plateau of flowering almond trees. The waters deepen, forming waterfalls and a gurgling river flowing into the hill.

"The caverns are full of water, but it's clear. See the bottom."

The copper color looks inviting, but I know this is more than a chance to bathe or swim.

"Trust me." Michel takes off his vest then unfastens my gown. "Can you hold your breath?"

With his hands on my bare skin, my dress again falling away, what else am I supposed to do? I nod.

He tears off his shirt and tugs it over my limbs. I love the feel of the warm linen and Michel's musky scent.

He fishes off his boots, slings my rapier over his shoulder, and grabs my hand and walks us into the cool water. "Adventure lies below. Come grab it."

Mimicking Michel, I inhale and drop with him below. The water becomes colder and chillier as we swim. When I think I can't hold my breath any longer, we raise our heads. We are in complete darkness.

With him clutching my hand, never letting me go, we walk out of the water into a dry cavern. The smooth rock under my feet is flat. I have no perception of how big this place is.

I lose Michel's touch. Nothing much frightens me, but this does, being alone in an unknown place. Nothingness, quiet muffling the sounds of the jungle. I trust Michel and fight with myself to turn from dread.

* * *

In darkness, standing in the damp cavern, I wrap my wet arms about the soaking linen shirt. Michel's singing reaches me first.

Quand j'étais chez mon père,
Quand j'étais chez mon père,
Petite à la ti ti, la ri ti, tonton lariton
Petite à la maison.
On m'envoyait à l'herbe pour cueillir du cresson.
La rivière est profonde, je suis tombée au fond.

"Have you lost your mind? Michel, where are you?" My voice quavers. "Michel?"

"The song helps me count my steps. I have a lamp. Let there be light." A flint strikes metal near me and a small light sparks, grows, and catches a wick. My rapier sling bangs the ground and warbles an echo in the large cavern.

"Here is my second home," he says and waves a bronze lamp that reveals an underworld of jagged indigo rocks. Light-blue sediment and purple sand fuse and form jagged dripping cones from the roof that look like they could impale us.

"Are they dragon's teeth?"

"*Stalactites* is what my father called them." He knocks open a trunk and scoops out a handful of green gems. "Emeralds. The Spanish forced the Indigenous to mine them."

He picks up a gold basin. "The soldiers melted down one of the gods of the Mexica. This treasure I share with the woman I love and trust. No one else alive knows of this place."

Dark stones under my feet seem to shift. The riches I've dreamed of fill this hideaway. Gold ingots in stacks, jewels and graven statues, and trunks of coins line the walls.

My mouth drops open. "All the treasure of the *Santa Margarita* is here. Is this safe? I know the wet season floods protect the cave, but that only lasts a few months."

"This is my father's legacy. Michel d'Artigue hid his share here before I was born." Michel kicks a pile of coins that rains down, trembling like bells. "This is two shares plus eight. The eight shares were to be set aside for the care and provision of the boat. Henry Morgan's Brotherhood got wind of the treasure and came after him. My father hid the treasure and ran the ship aground. Its blue mast is the flagpole that marks my house."

"D'Artigue couldn't have done all of this on his own. You weren't born then. Who helped him?"

"Guinea and French men worked side by side to bring up this treasure from the seabed, but the old captain turned on the enslaved men. Instead of giving the Guinea their freedom, he was going to sell them. My father resisted and led the mutiny. They helped get the treasure to Tortuga. He hid it here."

Michel doesn't seem happy. He actually sounds sad.

"What's wrong? Captain d'Artigue had the success of a lifetime. What an adventure!"

"Adventure? He won a treasure he could tell no one about." Michel picks up a golden basin. The perfectly squared sides shimmer in the lamplight. "This is worth a hundred Guinea men."

He sets it down and lifts an ingot. "This bit of gold is valued at ten men. My father swore never to deal in enslaved men. He refused to betray the men who fought with him. Each one, including

Old Jean, has spent years being hunted by the Spanish or other pirates hoping to find this. The chase nearly drove my father mad. Jacquotte, sometimes winning is a curse."

"And now his son is cursed? You can do nothing but come and admire it all alone."

Michel turns, and his sea-blue eyes capture me. Pain mars his countenance. "Am I still alone?"

He kicks at a pile of coins. They jingle and jangle and scatter everywhere. "Here's my secret. This is ours. I bring you here to a place I've shown no one. This has to convince you how much I trust you."

Standing before Michel, glancing at curls of hair and a wide chest, I reach for him, look dead in his eyes, and slap him hard. "You have all these riches, and still you risk your life to battle the Mughals. Why?"

"I promised my crew we'd try one more time."

"Michel, they only want treasure. Give them some of this."

He shakes his head. "Don't you understand? They can't use this. Questions will stir if more than a few coins reappear at once. Captain Morgan still has power. He's killed most of my father's crew." Michel picks up a dazzling statue of a woman who holds a torch and a shield in her hands. "My men follow my example, but left without options, some might haggle for pieces of eight or trade for Guinea slaves, the universal currency. I'll not let this gold feed the world's hunger for enslavement."

No one would feel so strongly about this unless this evil had touched their family. Michel is the right man for me.

He takes my hand and places it against his chest. "If I make a strike against the Mughals, the wealth they have will explain everything, including this treasure. It's legal to strike the Muslims. No one questions it. I can retire and give my wife, my family everything without fearing Spanish retribution."

"Is that why you changed your name to Le Basque?"

He gives a laugh that vibrates my fingers. "It's a bold name, isn't it? But oui, a d'Artigue caught with Spanish gold from the *Santa*

Margarita is a dead man. I'll not be hanged for my father's piracy. Spain would reward my captors with gold and honors, even political power. Then they'd use the bulk of this treasure to build more ships and finish enslaving the world."

I serve filibusters and politicians every day of my life. Michel's words remind me of their conversations.

"To have the peace my father never had, I have to be patient, Jacquotte. One win against the wealthy Mughals will make sure our family will never be hounded." Tentatively, still holding the jaw I smacked, he leans into me. "Chère, there's nothing else I'm keeping from you. Please love me again."

He flinches when I raise my hand to his cheek, but I embrace him, wrapping my arms about him so tightly he might not be able to breathe. "Aren't I a filibuster's woman? What else can I do but love you?"

"A filibuster's wife, Madame Le Basque. Keep my secret safe while I'm away. Take little bits if you need but be sparing, lest they be traced. I don't want my troubles to find you."

"I'm not touching your treasure."

His fingers tangle into my wet hair. Curls coil about his pinkie. "Say you'll wait for me."

Panic rips at my insides. Years passed before his return this time. "How long?"

"A year, maybe less." His lips press together, and he doesn't say, *maybe longer.* Or forever.

He turns and dips into a chest and pulls out a box. The hinge whines, and rust sprinkles like dust as the lid opens. Michel takes out a shiny band.

Dropping the box, he comes to me and slides the gold onto my finger. "This is how sailors wed, with a bit of gold and a promise, they have a matelotage, a union of souls who are meant to care and share and trust one another until death."

Rolling it about my finger, I can't deny how perfect it looks.

"Jacquotte, say that time doesn't matter for us. Say that what we have is greater."

I want to. He loves me and trusts me more than I realized. Nonetheless, this commitment is my prison. I'm trapped like I've fallen into a deep buccan pit. I'll die of longing, wanting his return. "You're asking for my life to stand still until you come back? That's cruel. It's selfish."

"It is. But I need you to agree. I'll make it up to you, and I will charitably bear the responsibility of Josiah. I know that duty frightens you. I'll make sure to find ways to make your dreams come true."

At least he's smart enough to know I have them. I drag my finger, the one bearing his ring, along his reddened jaw. "I'll never tell about the treasure, but I can't promise to stand still for you."

"Is that so?" His breath hitches. He takes me in his arms and kisses me, hard, then soft. "My plan will work. I'll make up the time. We will have adventures."

I wish to believe him. I have to. Can't I hear Maman's voice telling me that love is worth all?

"You're my luck, Jacquotte. Time will move swiftly for us."

I rip away his shirt from my shoulders and stand naked among his treasures. "Maybe if you kiss me right, I'll agree to anything, even waiting forever."

Michel smiles like he's taken a first real breath. "Your wish is my command, Madame Le Basque." He plants kisses down my throat and eases me to lie upon his treasures.

His mouth touches places I least expect, and we join. It's easier this time. We fit together like how I imagine love working. I want our spirits to tie strong knots, to knit us together so he takes a piece of me with him to the Mughals.

The lantern's light shows our shadows. I marvel at our love. On this bed of coins, our skin meets the coolness of gold and silver. The metallic perfume of sea and age anoints us.

Michel whispers, "I'll return fast, as fast as can be."

I catch his gaze, hold his face within my palms. "Then make this slow. Love me forever."

He nods and does as I ask.

Maybe a seed will take root and give me a piece of Michel's life if he doesn't return. That's when I realize how much I love him. I've allowed this filibuster to steal my reluctance about those things I thought weren't for me—wifing and mothering.

He takes his crucifix and slips the chain over my head so it dangles between my breasts. "I love you, Jacquotte Le Basque. Keep this for me. Think of me daily."

That pendant is his luck. I fear it not being with him when he sails. But I will pray over it every moment. To my body and heart, I pledge to hold on to this joy as long as possible. Tomorrow's not promised. Neither is Michel's return.

Sixteen

1680. Basse-Terre, Tortuga

I stand outside the back door of the kitchen, watching twilight fade into dusk. This ritual I do every night. For two and a half years, eighteen hundred twilights, I grip Michel's crucifix that I wear under my gown and wait for him to surprise me. I fervently search for my husband to appear and tell me the details of his grand adventure to Mughal territory.

Yet, for two and a half years, eighteen hundred and one twilights, I've not seen his face. I'm angry, left in Tortuga to make cauldrons of pottage or batches of foul-smelling soap.

Sometimes, I wish I'd borne Michel a babe. In the next instance, I'm grateful I did not. A daily reminder of our love without him would be hard. Everything works for the best. That's how I console myself, for I'm a woman who knows the location of a treasure that a woman and a person of Guinea descent can never use.

"Jacquotte!" Sarah rushes into the kitchen through the dining room, not from the longer, darker outdoor path to enter through the back door. "I've come to help."

She appears nervous and thin. I hurry to my distressed friend. "If I weren't so wrapped up in my woes, I might be a better friend to you."

She smiles as I grab one of the pails from her hands, and she says, "Seems like it will be slow tonight. One pot of pottage will do."

"Oui." I take the meaty dolphinfish she's brought and set it on the table. "But I could use help in the kitchen."

She nods and begins to chop vegetables as I take my sharp knife and scale the fish.

"Jacquotte, I'm thinking of going to Petit-Goâve."

My broken heart breaks more. Sarah is the person closest to me. "Must you?"

My words sound stupid, but how else can I ask her to stay for me? No one stays for me.

Done with the carrots, Sarah starts on the waybread. "You could come. You could help me find my way. It would give you a place to have adventures."

My heart leaps a little, then it settles. "You have property here—"

"In my dead husband's name. Women don't get to buy land. There was no will to truly make it mine. Monsieur Hasneau—"

"Hasneau, the beast—"

"The beast with power. Jacquotte, he's asking questions, making trouble about the legalities of my inheritance. He thinks a prominent house in Basse-Terre should be for prominent people, not a formerly auctioned wench."

I guess I know why she hides from the dark and isolated paths. The beast has confronted her, and she's scared.

"Think about it. Your père can pay Madame Mille to help with Josiah for a little while."

It's tempting. Then I think of what is keeping me here. "When must I decide?"

Barely able to breathe, she puts down her knife and holds to the table. "Soon. Hasneau is getting more persistent."

"You shouldn't have to leave to be free of him, Sarah. Your land can't be taken just because a man doesn't think you should have it."

"Jacquotte, you know what I did to get the land. The beast has guessed it. He's always hinting about Cayonne. If he brings charges, I will be doomed."

The night of the Fille Fantôme binds us together. She is my dearest friend. We saved each other. Nonetheless, a niggling question lies dormant in my head: To save herself, would Sarah reveal what I did?

Braver than I feel, I shrug off this notion. "Hasneau can prove nothing."

"You are not that naïve. Jacquotte, he will convince his governor of my guilt."

Sarah looks around as if she's memorizing my whitewashed walls, my table and hearth. Even Josiah's wash pile in the corner. "We'll discuss it later. The tavern has customers. Time to cook."

Père comes into the kitchen, a broad smile shining from his nicely combed beard. "Madame Sayon, Madame Le Basque, it is good to see the two of you cooking."

Though he says Sarah's formal name with pleasure, he offers mine begrudgingly. The man wants to proclaim himself right, that Michel was a bad match. If not for the band on my finger and the crucifix hanging from my neck, I'd have no reminders of the love I've lost. That is the cruelest thing, having so few memories of joy.

He steps over to my table. "Despite your reputation for willfulness, you, daughter, are receiving compliments. Inquiries about marriage."

Père taps the tabletop, the rhythm of his fingers matching my increasingly loud chopping. "What do I say to them?"

"Tell them to order more bowls of pottage." My voice rings with sarcasm. I'm not ignorant of what he is truly asking. Père wants me to accept widowhood to allow him to control my life again. Non. I need to do what I've wanted. I need to find adventure.

He offers me a confused scowl and turns to Sarah. "Men ask about you too, Madame Sayon."

"Non. Monsieur Delahaye. You're sweet to look after me and Jacquotte, but we are good being on our own."

Then Père says, "The governor will come tonight. He will have his lieutenants with him."

"His lieutenants?" Sarah's voice shakes and grows small. "All of them, monsieur?"

"Oui," Père answers. "Two or three of them, including his top man, Hasneau."

Offering my friend sympathetic eyes, I say, "I will wait on him. Sarah, he'll not bother you."

Père's wrinkled brow deepens. "Bother? Madame Sayon, what has happened?"

"Nothing, Monsieur Delahaye." Sarah quickly turns away and slips through the door into my garden.

He leans on my table. "Jacquotte, what did I do? Or what did he do?"

I frown at the clueless man. "Hasneau, the man you think a good match, raped Sarah when she was imprisoned. He's horrid. Every time you bring up his name, you stab her."

Wide-eyed with panicked, puckering lips, my father's countenance whips into a frenzy. "Jac . . . Jacquotte. I did not know. You win at keeping your secrets. You should have told me. I can be trusted."

Can he? Pointing with my knife, I wave him to the door. "Go out there. Apologize. And promise to keep her safe. Keep that promise. It will be hard to keep a promise against your favorite thing, politics."

He offers one of his I-almost-forgive you smiles, then goes out into the dusk after my friend.

My nine-year-old brother comes from the dining room with a basin of plates. He's a little taller but remains wordless. He moves to the stand in the corner and begins to wash and stack dishes.

"Josiah, do you like it here?"

He doesn't respond.

I stab my knife into the block at the table's edge and go to him. With arms about his shoulders, I ask, "Josiah, what if we went somewhere for adventure?"

He keeps scrubbing a soiled bowl.

"What if I went with Sarah, and then came back to you in a month or two?"

His fingers slow. He tugs frees and stretches. Josiah begins cleaning a mug. He steps back into the position he was in before. If I fold my arms again about him, it would be as if nothing changed. Josiah's trapped inside this shell.

Wiping tears away, I go to my hearth and check my cauldron. Tiny bubbles. I quickly dump in the vegetables and the fish. I would call out for a spoon, but no one in the kitchen will hear my plea.

* * *

After struggling with the hired fille to get Josiah to bed, I head down to face patrons. Short but proud, the governor, Jacques Neveu de Pouancey, enters the tavern. In a doublet of shiny patterned satin, the nephew of old d'Ogeron sticks out his chest.

The leering Hasneau and three others follow him inside and park at a table near the grand window at the front. Old Jean used to sit there, when filibusters loomed large in Basse-Terre. The table holds the best view of the well and the first houses of Basse-Terre.

Old Jean now sits in the corner. He's here tonight, shaking his head at me.

Arms behind my back, I go to the governor. "Gentlemen, what can I get you tonight?"

"Pottage for all. And rum." Neveu stretches and uses a spare seat for his big hat with white goose feathers that trail down the back. I'm reminded of Michel's hat.

"No rum for me," Hasneau says as he glances at my bosom. "Ale. I want a man's drink tonight. Nothing smooth. Just rough."

When I try to check on another table, Hasneau sneers. "Madame Le Basque. No sign of your husband . . . Any day, oui?"

I try to look calm and humble then say, "Any day."

They chuckle.

Old Jean slumps in his chair, but his hardened gaze has softened.

Older, with more gray hair and a lengthier beard, he seems as tired with their talk as I. Yet, his eyes are bright, like he still has dreams and schemes to perform. "A good many people are here tonight. More will come with the new sugar habitations."

We share a look, a realization that Tortuga will become like everywhere else, rife with slaves.

Sarah is right. It's time to get away. "I hate it here, Old Jean. I'm done. I'm ready to be gone."

My friend points. "Madame Le Basque. Your brother needs assistance."

When I spin around, I see chaos on the stairs. Josiah is wearing nothing but a shirt. He's banging down the stairs, stomping each tread at top speed. The fille runs behind him, yelling for him to slow. Hands waving, she chases him into the kitchen.

Patrons laugh and point. Others keep eating like nothing happened.

I wipe my sweaty hands on my apron. "Excuse me, Old Jean."

Though I hear the governor and his men making cutting remarks, I keep my anger inside. "I'll go get your pottage, gentlemen."

"Seems like your hands might be full." Neveu, the arrogant man, slams a piece of eight on the table. I guess it's some sort of tip or charity. "Something to hurry along our drinks."

Old Jean catches my hand, before I go the table and swat the broken piece of silver into the governor's face. "Girl, this is life. Full of wrongs. Rarely you get to do something to right things. Doing more wrong doesn't help. Eat the bitterness."

With a nod, I snatch back my hand and return to the kitchen.

"Sorry, madame." The fille is pacing. "He just wouldn't lie still. I can't make him go back."

Josiah stands in the corner, finishing the pile of dishes I made him stop at his bedtime. "Let him work, mademoiselle, until his job is done. Then he'll rest."

I fill a pitcher with ale and send her with mugs to serve the governor. Smiling, Josiah turns reddened cheeks to me. The glance grabs my full attention. I'm grateful. It's been forever, so long since my brother looked my way and I've felt as if he sees me.

Wanting in this moment for Josiah to feel loved and safe, I smile. I hold still. "Good job, Josiah."

He glances at me a little longer then turns away and scours plates. I let him work until his basin empties. Finishing something is as important a lesson as learning to swallow bitter dregs.

Seventeen

1680. Basse-Terre. Tortuga

Standing in my garden in the fading light, I gather the last of the carrots. Josiah isn't interested in harvesting vegetables or pulling weeds. He's fascinated by water, but no one trusts him near the deep well. Père will have to hire more of Mille's girls to manage the garden, my kitchen, and my brother.

As if he knows my thoughts, Josiah follows me into the kitchen, waits for me to stop moving, then puts his arms about my hips.

"You understand that Sarah and I leaving is temporary? You know, it's you and me forever." I swallow guilt. Though I love this little boy, I will relish my time away in Petit-Goâve. "I need to make sure Sarah is well. And that might be the city for us in the future."

My brother doesn't respond. He merely holds me tighter.

I will not abandon this trip. It has taken two weeks to get everything set. Sarah and I leave in the morning at sunrise. For one gold coin, Old Jean will sail us to Petit-Goâve. "A little adventure will be enough to satisfy my soul forever, Josiah. I promise."

Sarah and I will find a location for a new tavern. Serving pottage and rum is in my blood. Père will come and make the arrangements legal. He'll own the tavern, but Sarah and I will run it until I return to Tortuga. If I return.

Sarah has saved money, and I have nine more pieces of gold.

The thought of borrowing a little from Michel's cavern crosses my mind, but I push it away. I need to do this with what I have. And it might be my imagination, but it seems Hasneau has soldiers watching us.

Light-gold eyes lift to my face. Why do I read fear in them?

Something is wrong, but I can't lose time figuring it out. Nothing is stopping this trip. I put my hands to his cheeks and pull up a smile on his pink lips. "You mind Père and Mille while I'm gone."

He keeps hugging me. His little body trembles.

* * *

It's night. I've stayed in the kitchen waiting for Père or Sarah to come with the day's catch. The sun has set, and there's no fish for the pottage. It's going to be a thin soup today, but once the last of the pottage is served, I will head to Sarah. We leave Tortuga in the morning.

Cackling laughter makes me wince. Through the slatted door, I spy Monsieur Hasneau and two other men, the only people eating in the dining room. The governor hasn't shown. I prepare for these men to be beastly.

Backing from the slatted door, I welcome Mille and one of her filles into the kitchen. The young blonde is more willowy and taller than I am. "Hasneau has tried to capture Laurens de Graaf," she says in a dreamy voice. "The commander had a fleet lie in wait outside the bay, but de Graaf has a forty-four-gun frigate."

He found those extra two guns to be a fourth-rate frigate, unlike Michel's *Marauder*, a fifth-rate with forty-two guns.

The blonde saunters around my table. "Is Josiah ready for bed?"

"We have a new rule," I say. I put my knife back into its slot. "When he finishes his stack of dishes, he will go."

My brother has a few more left. He'll be in the corner for a while, but I understand now that this accomplishment matters to him. "Mademoiselle, tell me more of Hasneau and de Graaf?"

"Madame Le Basque, de Graaf sunk one ship and made the

other retreat. Hasneau failed. He and his men are in a bad mood. They have been terrible since the defeat yesterday."

My insides laugh. "Defeat is something a man like Hasneau must hate."

"The man's drunk on power," Mille says. "De Graaf raids colonies and ships everywhere in the West Indies." She looks at me. "He was enslaved in Hispaniola, like Uzoamaka. He escaped too."

"Is the pirate captain of Guinea blood," I ask, "or of the natives of the Caribbean? Hispaniola enslaves both."

Mille spins like a top. "Guinea and Dutch, they say. He's very wealthy. Madame Le Basque, the captain goes often to Petit-Goâve. Perhaps you can meet him and again become a buccaneer's woman."

The horrible woman laughs, laughs so much her wig wobbles. Père must've already told her of my plans to secure one or two of her filles to help with Josiah. Would Mille have told others? In a low, sweet voice, I say, "Mademoiselle, take this pottage out."

Shoving the tray with bowls into the blond woman's hands, I tell her, "Put them on the hungriest tables. I need to speak to Madame Mille alone."

The blonde glances at Mille for permission.

A wide-eyed Mille nods. I go to my satchel and pull my rapier out of its sling. "Talk, Madame. I want to hear what has happened."

She looks down at her jet slippers with fancy lace bows. "There was trouble earlier. Madame Sayon was taken to Fort de Rocher. Monsieur Delahaye went to see about her."

I almost cut off her wig. "Mille. Speak faster."

"Your père told me not to say anything. He headed after her. He said he would take a stand for what was right."

Oh no. All these years, I've held over his head his weak nature in times like these. Today, he decides to stand for something.

I don't know whether to rejoice or cry. I use my rapier to lift Mille's chin. "How long have they both been gone?"

"Hours." She moves away. Then she shakes a finger at me. "Stay put until your father returns. He's diplomatic. He can reason with people."

Backing away, she pushes up her sleeves and opens the door.

The wide swing lets me see Old Jean entering the tavern.

I set my rapier on the table. After pouring a pitcher of ale, I go straight to my friend.

Old Jean sits in the middle of the room with his back to Hasneau. His haggard gaze falls on me, warning me of danger.

Putting the pitcher down in front of him, I offer him a mug.

"Merci, Madame Le Basque." He gulps like he's never had a drink in his life. "Take care. They caught the Fille Fantôme today." My ears pop. I think my stomach does too, for the sharpest pain lances my gut. "That's the talk going around."

"Oh, madame," Hasneau says, fanning with his hat. "They have seized Madame Sayon's property."

Old Jean catches my hand. "That crucifix is showing . . . It won't protect you. These men will take that and the tavern."

"But my father?" I can barely talk. "Where is he? And Sarah?"

Old Jean buttons his lip, then slurps ale.

"Tell me, monsieur. Tell me before I act. You know I will."

"Non." He seizes my arm. The old, gnarled fingers have power. "You be ready to go tomorrow, no matter what. Take Josiah with you. No Delahaye is safe here. This tavern isn't safe."

Mille yells at me. "More pottage, Madame Le Basque. More for the guests." Her beady eyes plead with me to behave, to conform. How can I? I can't swallow any more bitterness.

I run back to the kitchen to get my rapier.

Mille rushes into the kitchen after me. Her arms flail as I grab the rapier.

"Act in haste, Jacquotte, and you condemn us all."

I hold on to the table for a moment. "My father might be dead, and Madame Sayon too."

"Jacquotte, you have to live. Look at your brother. He needs you alive."

Can't look at Josiah. Can't be weak. I have the rapier in my grasp. One swing and I can swipe the top off her wig. Bows and silver curls will fall to the floor.

Instead I put the tip of my rapier to her chest. "It's easier to run you through than to scale a dolphinfish. You tell me what you know. Withhold nothing if you wish to live."

"Jacquotte, you're not serious. You're—"

Slicing the lace from her sleeve makes her eyes widen. The tip came so close to her skin that she must've felt the air rush past.

"I practice every day. My next strike will end you, Mille."

"Soldiers came to Sarah's house this morning. They saw she was leaving. They hurt her very badly."

"Then what?"

"Jacquotte, they beat her until she signed confession papers. She forfeited her house. When your father found out, he took her to Cayonne."

"Cayonne? Why?"

Mille looks away.

The tip of my rapier pierces her cheek. Drops of blood dot her skin, redder than the rouge on her face. "Speak."

She dabs at the blood with a handkerchief. "Monsieur Delahaye went to appeal to the governor. He took Sarah by cart to show Neveu de Pouancey the cruelty that Hasneau sanctioned."

"How long ago?"

"Hours. Since this morning."

Mille withers and flops to my feet. Her sobbing makes my ears hurt. "I fear the worse. I think they were killed."

If I close my eyes, I'll see fire. "Hasneau is bold to be in this tavern mocking me. He's gloating, having me wait on him after he abused my father and dearest friend." I take my cross, kiss it, and stuff it under my apron.

Mille wipes blood from her face. The prick is small. It will heal in a day. "You have a weapon, but Hasneau is big. He has three soldiers with him."

She comes closer. "If you stay calm, all of this is yours. Your mother helped build this tavern. She died for it."

"Everyone must die sometime. Tonight, Hasneau will."

She catches my shoulder, and it takes everything within me not to turn and run her through.

"What about Josiah? No one else will care for him if you're gone."

I shove this wench away. "Mille, somewhere under that powdered wig is a heart. You'll find a way to run this tavern and keep Josiah to mop and wash plates."

"You know I have no heart, Jacquotte." She puts her grubby hands on my table, and I can see her mind is churning with the possibilities.

"Goodbye, Mille." Rapier drawn, clasping the handle tightly, I rush into the dining area.

Patrons jump up.

"Hasneau!" I yell and charge toward their table.

The same instant, a pail sails through the window. It lands between plates, overturning mugs of ale. Black, reeking pitch splashes on Hasneau and his men.

They jump to their feet, wiping their faces and hands.

"Thank you, madame!" Hasneau breathes heavily and flings pitch everywhere. He turns to me. "You tried to warn us," he says, in a voice dripping with false gratitude. "Madame Le Basque, I'm forever in your debt. Men, let's go get—"

Before I can gut him, my father staggers through the front door.

Hasneau backs away like he's seen a ghost. My father's so pale, he might be one.

"Père?"

He holds up his hand, stopping me.

Old Jean catches my hand, drawing me back. "Just wait, fille."

Hasneau picks up his ruined hat. The stupid ostrich feathers are inky black and drooping. "Help Monsieur Delahaye. Help him sit here."

Père struggles from the soldier's grasp. They sit him in a chair.

I try to wrench away, but Old Jean's grip is too strong.

My father is ten feet away, and I see the marks on his face. Blood leaks from his mouth. Again, he waves me away and makes the sign of the cross.

"What has happened? Père, tell me what has happened?"

He opens his mouth and points to an empty space. Someone has sliced away his tongue.

Dumping coins on the table, Hasneau waves to his men to leave. "Seems your father was punished for spreading lies. He should be as brave as you. I'll tell Governor Neveu that you are not part of the conspiracy."

He stuffs his ruined hat into the crook of his arm. Two of his men, equally painted in pitch, go out the door.

A blaze, a fireball flashes at the threshold.

Screams—the two men howl like wild animals. Burning, they slink back inside. The smell of charring flesh reeks. Their uniforms dissolve, and they collapse at Hasneau's feet.

Flames leap from them to his cape. His fine satins and feathers become fiery orange.

Hasneau tries to beat out the flames as his men die in agony. The remaining soldier tries to help, but he too becomes fire. He runs out of the tavern to the well. "The bucket is wedged fast in the well's mouth. Someone help!" he cries.

He bursts into a bright ball of flame just outside the door.

Smoke billows. Flames begin consuming everything. Mille's filles tear down the stairs and into the night. The tavern's walls burn. Père has not shifted. I can't move.

"Old Jean." I raise my rapier. "Get Josiah and my things! The kitchen. Save him from this hell. I will get my père."

"Chère." Old Jean shakes his head, his voice trembling. "You have to go."

"I have to finish this! Save my brother!" He rushes into the kitchen.

Hasneau tosses off his cape and no longer burns. He may live.

A figure, ghostly in a flowing gown, stands at the door, blocking him from leaving.

Sarah. She has a torch in her hands, hands that surely threw the pitch and set fire to the soldiers. Her face in the red light shows black bruises and purple cuts. They've tortured her to make her confess.

She told them what they wanted to hear to save me.

Her movements are slow, but she backs Hasneau into a corner. "Stop at once," he says and then looks at me. "Help me—"

"Guilty," Sarah taunts Hasneau. "You've confessed in my ear. You've tormented me. You must die."

The smoke grows thicker. Josiah runs from the kitchen straight to Père. With my sack in hand, Old Jean chases after him. Père's quivering hands rub Josiah's head. Then point to the door. Old Jean and Josiah flee.

Hasneau punches at Sarah. "Stop! Stop, you wench!"

"Y'did not stop when I begged. Beg louder, monsieur."

She swings the torch and taunts him but has not lit him again on fire. Her maddening laughter sounds as if she's enjoying her enemy's torment.

Old Jean steps back inside, waving his hands through the smoke. "Get out of there, Jacquotte!"

Père nods. He points at me to go.

Coughing, Mille comes down the stairs. "Get up, you fool," she says to Père.

He points again to the door. Père wants us to leave.

"Hasneau?" A soldier—Du Casse—rushes in. I wave at him to stay back, then trip him like it's an accident. We hit the ground, rolling in soot. Sarah ignites Hasneau. She laughs then ignites herself. I see her glorious smile. She knows what I've done. Sarah and Hasneau's bodies become living torches and disappear.

She's a true fantôme.

Du Casse's eyes widen in horror. He turns on his heel and runs out. I follow.

In front of the tavern, standing beside the well, I watch the tavern's thatched roof flare and crumble. The walls of coral blacken.

Pieces fall. People from the circle of houses, the first settlement of Basse-Terre, gather.

Some try to unplug the well, but it's too late. I wrap my arms about my brother and watch with Mille and Old Jean as the tavern and Père become ash.

Eighteen

1680. Basse-Terre, Tortuga

Waiting for the cinders to cool so that I can bury my father takes an eternity. I sit beside Josiah at the plugged well. We gaze at the stars, which have the audacity to shine through the clouds and smoke. I try to comprehend how much our world has changed.

Old Jean has my rapier and slides it into its sling. He drops it upon my sack along with some men's clothes that Mille had gathered before she fled the burning tavern. I touch a button on Père's pourpoint. Can't believe he's dead. Can't believe how brave he was in death.

I wanted to be Maman's legacy. Now I need to be my father's too.

Mille flutters about, smelling of char. Her girls, four of them, stand around. Some carry blankets. A few hold extra dresses.

"Sorry, Madame Mille." My voice sounds dry. "Sorry I cut you."

"You did nothing, Jacquotte. I was injured in the chaos." She stoops to me. "Be smart, girl. Everything depends on you."

I grab her arm and kiss her sooty palm. "Mille, you think Père knew what Sarah meant to do?"

She looks toward the smoldering thatch, the tumbled brick. "He had to, chère. He gave Madame Sayon her revenge for what those butchers did." Mille stands, her head swiveling. "I can't believe that Sarah was the fantôme, but the way she plotted this . . . she clearly had to be."

"Will you be all right, Mille?"

She jingles a pouch that hangs down her bosom. "I saved the most important thing. My money will buy new things. Maybe the governor will allow me to build something. I hear he's giving land grants." Mille cackles, for we both know those opportunities are for men. "You get out of Tortuga. Take care of you. That Du Casse has been asking about you and Le Basque for weeks. Your Père thought he was interested in you. I think it's more sinister."

Short and thick Du Casse is the soldier I intentionally tripped. "Mille—be blessed."

The next time I look up, she's standing with the governor and her girls. Mille will take care of them. Near what used to be one of the big tavern windows, Du Casse questions Old Jean.

The wind shifts. The ash in the air smells like my hearth. I'll miss the sweet, oaky char from bayahondes. I go to the well to face Du Casse directly. I turn the other way when I overhear his thin lips describe Sarah as crazed. Maybe insanity for a woman is better than being a victim.

My brother sits nearby. He stares ahead, then he drops something from his curled palm into my hand, a smooth white cobble.

"Josiah, everything our parents built has burnt. It's gone."

My brother doesn't flinch, just hands me one of maman's stones.

Governor Neveu walks over to us. One of his guards brings a lantern.

"Madame Le Basque," he says, "I offer you my condolences. Monsieur Delahaye was a pillar of the community."

"Why did a pillar have his tongue cut out by your men?"

The governor blinks, and then stares at the book in his hands. "I've not heard of this. If one of my men has acted in haste, he was not acting on my orders."

"It was Hasneau, your second in command."

"He was a good officer." Neveu's brow wrinkles. "Then there must be a connection between Sayon's underhanded dealings and

Monsieur Delahaye." The governor sighs, lowers his tone. "We've confiscated Madame Sayon's land and her possessions. They will be given to the families of the soldiers who died."

He shifts, and moonlight streaks his satin doublet. The man hasn't come to give his condolences. Dressed like a king, he comes to remind me of a woman's place. Society has given him power. He acquits Hasneau and condemns my father.

"Madame Le Basque, Old Jean and others said you tried to stop the attack. For that, I thank you. More could've died. We'll not have this lawlessness in Basse-Terre."

Swallowing my anger, drinking bitter tears, I hear his implied threat and dip my head. "Pray for us, monsieur."

He says more words that tire me. When the man is done, I keep my head bowed. Except for Josiah and a few possessions, I've nothing left to lose. This might be the most freeing time of my life.

* * *

Smoke billows from the remains of the tavern, my home. People sing, then pray, offer condolences, then leave. The governor and Mille vanish. Tall de Franquesnay, the new second in command, looks as if he wishes to ask something, but my tears make him go away. Soon no one is left but Old Jean, Josiah, and me.

While my brother sleeps on my sack, I go inside what's left of the structure. The heat or fallen beams have broken Père's precious tiles. The bird cage lies crushed by a broken chair. I walk to where my kitchen was. The pewter basin has melted. My hearth has fallen in. I kick over my half-burnt kitchen table and find my spice tankard. It's dented. The sides are blackened.

The lid still works. The insides smell like burnt cloves. The tankard gives me an idea. I take it back to the dining room and go to where Père's bones lie and scoop up some of the ash. I move to where Sarah died and take some of hers. I hope as little as possible of Hasneau comes too. I hate this, that there's no way to separate her from the evil she killed.

A small bone, maybe a finger, sits upon the ash. I scoop it into the tankard as Sarah's trophy. Her strength must be memorialized as much as my father's sacrifice.

With a final glance at what was the front wall, I remember the windows that framed my view of Basse-Terre. Then I leave the tavern forever.

Old Jean yawns. "What did you find?"

"Something to carry Père's and Sarah's ashes. Let's take them to the sea."

We walk in silence, under the canopy of leaves, but my conscience demands I eulogize my friend. "I was Fille Fantôme. Sarah died for me."

Old Jean shakes his head. "Don't say another word and condemn your life here."

"It's already condemned. I have to make something else of my life." The clapping palm leaves usher along my spirit. "Monsieur, I need you to care for Josiah for six months. I must go to Petit-Goâve as we had planned. By February, I will be situated."

He shakes his head. "No. You were to go with Madame Sayon on your father's behalf. Women can't run a tavern on their own. You're better off here. You and Josiah should keep the land."

"If Père had a will, it's been burnt up. I've no proof. And this is prized land. The governor assumes my father's guilt. He will take the land like he has Sarah's."

"Jacquotte, you're clever. You—"

"Non." I cut off Old Jean. "If I stay, I'll end up as one of Mille's girls. Or I'll have to marry some soldier to put a roof over Josiah's head."

A nighthawk screeches. Is it hunting for me or what it believes I have? "Mille says Du Casse is asking after Le Basque. He's hunting the treasure of the *Santa Margarita*. Including your share. My husband warned me that the pursuit never stops."

My friend stops moving. "How do you know I kept some treasure? Did Le Basque tell you?"

"Non, but it makes sense. You must've used part of it to buy the ketch. You live well. Maybe you are a very successful fisherman. Or maybe you got a big portion—"

"One share, mostly silver. It's easier to manage."

My hunch is right. "My brother will get into trouble wandering off while I try to find work. In Tortuga, Josiah knows his way around. People will look after Delahaye's son."

Shrugging, shaking his head, Old Jean wants me to relent. "You're not thinking clearly. Did Le Basque tell you where his treasure is? He has more than enough money to provide for you. He has a house in Port Royal."

I make Josiah sit on the beach. We listen to the waves crashing on the shore. I hold up my hands, which look black in the twilight. "Michel never took me to his house. No neighbor in Jamaica can attest to me being his wife. I'll be jailed. I won't put myself in a position to be sold."

"What of his treasure?" He fans his old hat, which has ash stains. "He left you money."

"Michel left me ten gold coins. When he returns, he has a scheme to be able to enjoy his fortune without the world hunting him."

What I've said isn't a lie. I know if I touch any part of Michel's secret treasure, I would be exposed. I'll not be hanged for a treasure I can no more disburse than he could.

"Petit-Goâve isn't safe, Jacquotte."

"Didn't ask if it was safe. I asked you to keep Josiah and to take me to Petit-Goâve."

Reaching into the sack, I jingle the pouch that holds gold pieces. "I can pay for transport and for keeping my brother."

"Keep your money. We both know I don't need it." Old Jean looks nervous. He scratches an ear. "Can he manage himself? I don't have to do nothing? Maybe Mille could do it."

The woman was making eyes at Neveu before she left. "She has no time for another mouth, not now."

Old Jean wrenches at his neck. "But he can feed himself?"

"Put food in front of Josiah, he'll eat. He's good at chores, just teach him what needs to be done."

"Hmm. Maybe help by painting the boat."

The breath I've held releases. My friend will give me time to make a new life, one that can protect Josiah. "I'm not talking about forever, Old Jean. I just need a little time to establish myself."

"What if you can't come back? I'm not looking to raise someone else's son."

"But you would, because of my mother." I straighten my shoulders and stare at him like I am a nighthawk aiming at prey. "I will succeed. You will bring Josiah to me in Petit-Goâve in six months' time. Old Jean, do we have a deal?"

He nods. "Six months. Then I bring your brother. And you promise not to get yourself killed?"

Even with all the turmoil and loss, my friend has brought me a smile. "Oui. I'll live, just to please you."

With a shake of his head, he says, "Josiah don't look it, but he's Uzoamaka's too. And I haven't done much of anything for him. You have six months. I'll have a clean boat, maybe some help painting."

I turn to my brother. "Don't be afraid, Josiah. I'm going to make something of my life. I'll prepare a place for us. It will be good. I promise."

Josiah stands and hugs me, his arms wrapping about my hips. Then we start walking the short distance to the sea. The salt—it's the first scent that doesn't smell burnt.

Old Jean hums something, then says, "At the monastery, the monks sang of their god. It was the yuletide. I didn't understand then, but now I do."

He hums louder and then sings,

O come, Thou Dayspring . . .
Disperse the gloomy clouds of night,
And death's dark shadows put to flight.

The words make little sense to me. Death's shadow doesn't fly. It swims in treacherous, glorious waters. It lights torches and burns evil doused in pitch.

But I listen to the rhythm of the sea. My mother's voice floats atop the waves.

Eke nekeng'wanso Omonene gianchere
Baba eke nekeng'waso Omonene gianchere

The sun rises on the horizon. Blond foam washes over my boots. I take them off, drop my rapier and sack. Josiah and I, hand in hand, plod into the cool water.

Tears are on his cheeks. My brother in his silent world meets mine in loss. My heart rips more. I never want pain to touch Josiah. We wade deeper into the sea and set the tankard free.

The pewter floats for a moment then sinks. Père and Sarah descend together to the bottom of the bay. They'll become another lost treasure of the Caribbean.

Nineteen

1680. Petit-Goâve. Hispaniola

Navigating the ketch past the last sandbar, I'm mesmerized by Petit-Goâve. Unlike Basse-Terre, the docks are one with the city. In a glance, I see lines of ships tethered to pillions, rows of houses, and rues leading to all sizes of buildings.

People are everywhere, strolling, working at warehouses. I get a nervous stomach until I see barrels and sacks being unloaded and stacked in the warehouses, not Guinea people.

Cupping my hands to my eyes, I hunt for the jungle, but I barely see trees. No oaks, no bayahondes. My mouth drops open at the size of the mountains. High and wide, Petit-Goâve is surrounded by them like the sides of our old pewter basin. These aren't far away like the Chaîne de la Selle. They stand boldly, not veiled, and dwarf the height of anything in Tortuga.

"Close your mouth, Jacquotte, you'll catch a no-see-um in your teeth." Old Jean laughs and swats the buzzing flies. Trusting me to sail the entire way, he's arisen from his nap in good humor.

Josiah remains quiet. I explained what I had to do, but I'm not sure he understands. Gliding the ketch into an empty spot, I jump up and tie us off on a pillion.

"You're still committed to do this, Jacquotte?"

"It's Jacques, Jacques Delahaye. The son of Pierre Delahaye."

Old Jean shrugs. I've been wearing my father's breeches and his doublet for the past day.

Gathering my sack and rapier sling, I'm ready to push out a gangplank, but Old Jean does it instead. Once I walk from the ketch onto the docks, I'll have six months to make a way in my new world.

Old Jean shakes his head. "You look like a Jacquotte in breeches."

When I offer him my hand to shake, he puts his velvet hat in my palm. "Here, this cap will make you more of a Jacques."

His voice sounds grumpy, but it's his way. I feel the love he's always given me.

Taking the hat, I risk a hug. Then I turn to my brother. "Josiah, mind Old Jean."

His light eyes are teary. My heart stings. He must think this is more loss.

"Just six months." I hold up six fingers, but the motion means nothing. I'll be his sister for a moment longer. I kiss the top of his head.

He's stiff in my arms, but I whisper I love him. For a moment, I feel him hug me back. It's everything. It means he understands.

"Go on, Jacques. We'll see you in six months." Old Jean waits for me to cross the gangplank. He draws the board back in and unties the ketch.

Standing on the docks, I watch them sail off. At the mouth of the bay, all sails extend. The canvases curve and catch the wind. It spirits them away with speed.

With my hair tied back, I put on Old Jean's pointy hat. Comfortable in a way that I was before Père decided I should dress like a jeune fille, I'm ready to start my new life now.

* * *

A breeze stirs from the bay, and it brings the perfume of seaweed and seawater to my nose. It's the end of a long workday, and I stand in line for my wages. The smells are welcoming scents, very different from the stale air and sweat contained in the warehouse. It's cooler outside, and I try not to gasp and show how affected I am by the labor and heat.

Somehow the wind stops shy of these roofs. Whether they are made of banana leaves or thatch, these buildings hold in the heat of the laborers who work all day stacking barrels and crates.

Men strip down to their breeches to keep from fainting. Sweaty chests drip with perspiration. No matter how much I sweat, I can't do the same. My breasts though bound are undeniable in close-fitting shifts. I've learned to stay low and step outside as oft as possible.

Casting my gaze to the ship I've helped empty of salted cod, I feel accomplished. Tomorrow, the same boat will be loaded with sugar, rum, and tobacco heading to London. I'd love to stow away and see the other side of the sea, but I doubt I'd be back in four months when Josiah arrives.

A sandy blonde, always the first in line for payment, Dirk Wulf laughs as pieces of eight fall into his palm. I get excited because we both worked equally hard today. Another good worker, a bald young man with jet skin, is three people ahead. The overseer grumbles and gives him his money with a closed fist. "Is this right?" he asks the man making decisions.

"Yeah." The overseer points to the rue. "Now go on, Bahati."

My gut knots. A hard worker, a Black worker has been cheated. Will I be shorted my wages? I stare at poor Bahati, willing him to fight, but he doesn't. He smiles like he's grateful and heads off.

The fellow in front me, a thick blond named Quincy, makes another rude joke. "Good wages for the Blancs, hey Jacques?" He looks at me. "Have we worked together before here?"

"Non." I try to settle down, but Quincy keeps staring. When it's his turn, he gets his full wages. He walks off jiggling pieces of eight in his palm.

Shaking my head, I try to come up with excuses of why everyone whose skin is dark is being paid less. Looking around at all the men who worked the same or even loafed, I don't understand. I got here early to help load that boat. If I am cheated, I don't know what I will do. I need my money. Holding my breath, praying for favor, I wait my turn. I'm handed a half of a piece of eight. This is less than everyone—much, much less than Quincy and Wulf, even less than Bahati.

After two months of working in Petit-Goâve, I hoped things would be different. I wrestle with saying something, because it took a month to get work. This is the third warehouse I've labored in at the docks, and it's the third time I've been cheated. Seeing more brown and black faces here, I thought it would be different.

Quincy grins. "See you around, Jacques. I'm sure I'll remember where we've met. Never forget a face." He heads off, shaking his wages in his palm.

"What do you want, Delahaye?" The overseer looks stern, but he knows what I want. I level my stance. My hands are at my sides. My sack and sling hang off my shoulder. I wish to look non-threatening. The last thing I need is to end up jailed for attacking a Blanc.

"Speak up, Delahaye." His tone is impatient, his eyes bear down like I should be intimidated.

"Is it my size? I have more strength than most. I've worked twice as hard. This was supposed be worth two pieces of eight. The amount of crates I moved, I should get double."

The man looks down. His face is pink and greedy. "That's the rate for a Frenchman. Mulattoes have a different pay."

I want to argue about my worth. "I did more. I shouldn't be mistreated for my skin."

"Go on, Jacques. Or there will be no work next time," the overseer says. "Next."

My fingers fist around the silver, and I want to throw it back in his face, but I need the money, all I can get. "I deserve more than this. I have to pay for my lodgings."

He chortles and moves on to the next man in line.

If I admit my gold was stolen from my rented room and all I have is my rapier and sack of clothes, I'll be called a failure and a liar.

No one will believe me. The innkeeper who I'm sure took my coins says he can't remember seeing me with money.

Shocked, sickened by the theft, I drew my rapier on the innkeeper. I'd have stabbed him, but he yelled for help. He accused me of being a thief, and I ran. If caught, the Blanc would be believed, not me because of my brown skin.

Frustrated, I walk away. I turn down a rue looking for a place I can safely spend the night. It will be my first night outside.

The bald man catches up to me. "Jacques, I saw you ready to spit at the overseer."

I slow my stride but keep moving like I know where to go. "I hate being cheated."

Under his jet-colored pourpoint and dark breeches, the man's skin is perfectly smooth, glistening with perspiration. Bright white teeth show as he says, "Long as you need their silver, you have to take what they give."

I stop and turn back to the fellow with the strong accent. It's guttural, it's Creole, it's Guinea. My earliest memories of the habitation where I was born sound like this. "Do you just accept being cheated?"

"I have a pregnant free sister who needs money." He laughs. His bulky arms flex. He could pound me into the dirt. "I don't give the warehouses all my strength. I do enough to be paid."

"Bahati, I need to prove I can do the job."

"Non, Jacques. You're working so hard, they know you need them. That tells them they can cheat you."

Setting my sack on the pounded-dirt rue, I peer at this man and try to understand. "At least you explain things."

His rich laughter flows again. "If you see me working somewhere, match my rhythm. That will let you know what to do."

"Where will you work tomorrow, Bahati?"

"Same place. The green warehouse is a cheat, but they let us work there." Bahati starts to go.

I motion for him to wait. "There has to be a way to make more money. Petit-Goâve is so big. There must be more opportunities?"

Looking both ways, Bahati pulls me aside as more workers pass by. "Unless you peddle liquor or flesh, you don't make riches on land. You're fit, Jacques. Look for a ship. Be part of a crew. The pay's always good. I've done it once or twice. Old Wulf too. Been more than me. He'd stay at sea if it weren't for his wench, well, now wife, running a warehouse down the way."

"A man can be buccaneer and have a wife?"

"Wife or wench?" Bahati glances behind me as if he's fearful of being overheard. "It's all the same. The sea provides for all lives."

That sounds like a dream, to be part of a crew, but Bahati can't be talking about being a buccaneer again. "Have you found a crew?"

He draws away. "I'm saying there're opportunities. Keep your head down and listen. When the next one happens, I'll be on board. It'll take a couple of years to earn a share of the treasure, but you will earn more than working the docks. My soon-to-be niece or nephew will be well off. I'm a good . . . uncle."

Bahati walks away.

I want to follow, but I don't. I'm running out of time. I've two more months to make something happen before my brother comes. If only I knew where Anne's cousin lives, I might have better luck.

Sighing, I begin to move, looking for a spot to sleep and thinking of Anne. She begged to come here to Petit-Goâve as if it were her salvation. That cousin of hers was going to help, even take her on a ship to become a filibuster.

I had hoped that Sarah and I could've found her if we'd made our original trip. In my heart, the three of us could be good at being pirates. Alone I'm a failure. It's hard being a man. Maybe it's time to be what fate designed. I've been a wife for a moment, a man for weeks. Would I still be cheated if I wenched for a night?

Twenty

1681. Petit-Goâve, Hispaniola

I take a bite out of the lime I stole. It's a sad way to celebrate the new year. I sorrow at becoming a thief, but the booty has tart, juicy flesh. Lime trees grow in the spaces between the mud homes here. The small trees scent the air as much as the sea salt. Another day of no work means stealing food is the only way to eat.

Walking past these houses, I note that they consist of one or two rooms with banana leaf–woven roofs, no thatch. Our two-story tavern would be a grand habitation home here. I begin to understand how privileged we were in Tortuga.

A new wind whips up the smell of fish bouillon and the scent of rain. My stomach churns for one fragrance as my head hurts for the other. The rainy season will soon come. I sleep on the rues most nights, but I can't have Josiah living this way. I've saved money not paying for a place to stay. I have no idea how to afford having someone to watch Josiah while I work.

I feel a sprinkle on my brow and push down Old Jean's hat. It's my only shelter. Stopping outside of the Tree Tavern, one of the biggest taverns of Petit-Goâve, I contemplate going in and finding work. Maybe they need a cook. If not, perhaps the owner will let me wash, dress in my gown, and hire on as a wench.

The trotting mule hooves knock behind me. I scoot more to the edge of the rue and let the wagon head to the stews. That's what they call brothels here. These places are busy with people going in and out.

After what my parents built with stone and tiles, seeing clapboard structures that a hurricane could tear apart is sad. Nothing is made to last. I shake myself, stopping my thoughts from falling into the past. I have to live now, not in dreams. I turn to the mountains. I worship their openness.

The scent of the bouillon is strongest from the stew closest to the water. My breath catches. The dusky light shows a two-story building like Maman and Père's tavern. It even bears a thatched roof. A rooster cackles and walks by me. I hadn't seen those running freely in Basse-Terre. I take it as a good omen and enter the Tree Tavern.

Men—all kinds and colors—fill the tables. Soldiers stand in the corner. Buccaneers going up the stairs with women catch my attention. Mille's girls wore low-cut gowns. Their faces were painted. They looked very French. These women are natural with no cosmetics on their cheeks, but naked up top. You can see every curve and every oiled breast. They wear a cloth about their waist that I can only just call a skirt, but nothing else—no tunics, pourpoints, stomachers, or corsets. The material, which might be cotton or dyed muslin, wraps their hips in bright jewel tones—ruby, emerald, garnet, and sapphire blue.

I'm nothing like these women. They are clean and beautiful and bold with their bodies. A man taunts one, the lady moves to the next. These wenches are choosing their bedmates. Their chins are up. They dance to each table, not ashamed. For the first time in my life, I realize they shouldn't be.

"Delahaye." Bahati calls to me. He sits at a table with some men I recognize from the dock. Wulf is there with a laughing woman on his lap.

"Bring your things, we have room," Bahati says. "I'll buy you an ale."

I can't. I've only known Bahati a few weeks, and I don't want to him to see how low I am. It's not rational. One man is not the whole town like Basse-Terre, but to be here ready to seek employment is to admit I've failed.

Instead, I signal to Bahati that I must leave. Turning, I dodge incoming patrons and run from the stew.

* * *

Sleeping on the rue behind the Tree Tavern, I raise my head from a discarded crate and search the night for the noise that awakened me. Cursing floods the humid air.

I blink fast and look around.

"You damned witch. I will kill you."

Jerking away my sack, I run my fingers over my sling and find my rapier.

"Calmez-vous, monsieur." This voice sounds sweet and scared.

With my weapon ready, I rise and slink to the corner. From the outlines, I discern it's a man in uniform and a woman in an elegant gown. The silhouette of her dress seems full, flowing, not airy like the tavern wenches' skirts.

Focusing, waiting for the moon to highlight the assailant, I can only see the woman. It's a noble lady with a formal overgown of purple. She rustles like lace as she backs away.

Their conversation switches from her fine French to a bit of English. The woman is fluent in both. The man struggles with anything that's not English. It must be a British soldier visiting this French colony.

I step closer. My rapier is ready.

"You stole from me," he says. "You made me a laughingstock. You owe me." The big man strikes her, backhanding her with closed knuckles. She's knocked flat.

"You've hit me. Now go."

"No," he says. "You take me for a bloomin' fool. You wanton hussy, you've embarrassed me." He pushes her flat and steps over her like he wishes to mount her.

I march into the rue and rush toward them. "Let her be."

My voice sounds sleep-warmed, full of gravel. I hope it helps intimidate.

Up close he's bigger than I am and towers over her.

Before I can stop him, he kicks at the woman. "Sir, none of this is your concern."

The moon shines on the fancy red sash on his jacket. He's puffed-up like Hasneau, but I have no fear. "Leave her alone and go on to your way."

The man lunges at me, but my whipping rapier forces him back. He spits at her. "You led me this way so your manservant can attack me, Madame Erville?"

I draw the beautiful woman behind me and go on the attack. I cut the sash from his jacket. It falls, but my precision ensures my rapier tip has not ruined his doublet. "Go, before I stop playing."

The stars shine on this man's grimace. He's older, brown hair with gray temples. "This is how you do me, Madame Erville?"

I glance behind me as the woman dusts her hands. She's tall, very tall, and angelic. There's something fragile about her, about the assessing look in her green eyes. Her raven hair makes her skin look like fine bisque. "The Lord shows mercy," she says. "I have an avenger."

Her lyrical tone encourages me. I advance on the man. "Again, I say, be gone."

"This woman," he says with a sneer, "has compromised me. Took valuable information." He turns to leave but picks up something. Then he advances, smirking like Hasneau. "Did Madame tell you what she's doing? It's treason. It's against nature and my king."

"Which king is that?" Madame Erville's voice is stronger. "There are many with their own proclivities. I guess it doesn't matter, now that I have a protector who'll dispatch you."

She believes in me. I revel, for I'm not too small, or too brown, or too new to protect her. "I said, leave with your dignity and your life."

Madame steps to my side. I take her in, admiring her, her defiance in her sex. She puts her hand on my shoulder. "Young man, thank you. Go on, brute."

Her sultry voice rallies my attention to her delicate mouth, her slim, lifted nose. Monsieur uses the distraction to punch me in mine. Smacked in the face, I go down hard.

Dazed, I roll over and see two of him. Shards of glass fly as he breaks a demijohn. "Your protection is done." When he lunges with broken glass in hand, I stab at the blur. Knowing I've pierced through his doublet, I get up and thrust my rapier through his gullet. My blade pierces him, cutting through skin and muscle and bone like my kitchen blade gutting fish.

Seeing monsieur take his last wordless breath feels satisfying, burning up some of the rage that has never left me.

Madame Erville pulls my rapier from the body. She doesn't seem scared by what I've done. "That pretty face of yours needs tending. You'll have a bad bruise."

Pretty? I'm dressed as a man . . . but her hands are about my bosom. "You know?" My head swims. "And you think I'm pretty."

"Oui. Now come with me." Madame takes my hand and leads me from the second man I enjoyed killing.

Twenty-One

1681. Petit-Goâve. Hispaniola

I walk for hours following Madame Erville out of Petit-Goâve. We pass buildings and mud houses, heading to what I hope are the mountains. My rapier's out. I cannot put it in the sling with bloodstains. "Do we need to tell the authorities?"

"Not if we wish to avoid trouble. Filibusters fight all the time. The gentleman will be found dead by morning. By then we will be far away." Madame slows her fast pace. "You'll be fine. No one suspects a woman of killing."

We keep going, journeying farther from the city. The trail widens. I see more trees, more jungle. It feels like we're journeying past Basse-Terre and somehow traipsing to Hispanola's Chaîne de la Selle.

"You are new to Petit-Goâve, mademoiselle. Why are you in hiding?"

She obviously wants to know why I am dressed like a man. "I'm strong and able. I want to work on the ships. But there's no opportunity for women."

"Have you found the city welcoming?"

I think of Bahati. He has been kind. Wulf had been sort of distant but not mean.

"Your silence tells me what I need to know. I welcome you. I am

Madame Lizzôa Erville. You'll be my guest. I will extend every courtesy to you."

I'm touched but also wary. "Because I defended you?"

She stops and looks at me curiously. In the early light, I see her face. It's youthful and bright. The heart-shaped countenance is topped by a dark wig full of curls. "A woman doesn't usually take the risks you have for me." She touches my sleeve and swats off dust. "You've suffered since being here. Today, you start anew."

She has seen my soul. I nod.

"You can trust me. And we need to keep moving. More distance from the city, especially with a sword in your hand. It could get people talking."

"It's a rapier." I lower it to my side. "I am Jacques . . . Jacquotte Delahaye."

"Please to meet you, Jacquotte. Beautiful name." Her smile becomes full. I've not seen a more angelic face. "I suspect you have no place to go."

"How? How do you know?"

"I'm observant. You carry a sack with your things. I suspect you were sleeping nearby. You follow me with no mention of stopping anywhere."

She takes my hand. "I see in people their gifts. I help them achieve their desires. You now have a new friend."

I'm mesmerized . . . and embarrassed. "I do not wish to impose, but I'd like to wash my clothes. My face. Sleep in safety for one night."

"Every night," she says with great warmth. "You saved my life. What I have is yours."

I gaze at this woman who wants to save me. I want to know everything about her.

"You have questions," she says. "I will answer those over tea."

We turn down a trail separate from the main path. A cottage sits far back, looming in the shadow of the mountains.

"This is it. My land," she says. "I grow vegetables. I hire people to harvest tobacco. But for the most part, I'm left alone."

The morning light dances on dewy haze as rows of broadleaf tobacco plantings—olive green, a foot tall—wave at us. They're ready to be cut, dried, and shipped from the warehouses where I struggle to find work. At the threshold of the cottage, I lower my rapier. "Will the master of this place mind you bringing in a vagabond, Madame Erville?"

"I own this place. I am in possession of it. You can call me Lizzôa."

"How is this yours?" My voice squeaks. I'm incredulous and fearful. Have I been led along by lies? "Are you widowed?"

"I own this place, given to me by my brother. Be at ease. I assure you it's mine. I assure you, you are welcome." She opens the door, and it's bigger than Sarah's house. The room has chairs and tables and bookshelves. A golden tapestry is on the floor. It's pristine, cleaner than any place I've stayed since leaving Tortuga.

Lizzôa stares at me as I remain by the door. I haven't moved. I feel unworthy to move. "Jacquotte, I said you're welcome inside."

I bow as low as I can. Words begin tumbling out and draw tears. I can't stop either. "I'm a widow. I'm alone. I was a proud daughter. Soon I'll have to support my brother, who'll never be able to care for himself. I fail at everything. Killing is the only thing I've succeeded at in a long time. I'm unworthy to soil your home."

With a finger under my chin, she makes me rise. "None of that. We're equals here." Lizzôa draws me inside. She takes my rapier and wipes it clean. Her delicate fingers scrub hard to remove the congealed blood.

"All that is gone." She kisses my brow, then sets the rapier down. "You are free here."

She lights candles. and I get another good look at my hostess. Lizzôa is older than me, with a delicate complexion that seems untouched by the sun. She bears a sturdy, confident jaw and thin nose. She's pretty, but not the most beautiful woman I've ever seen, not in the ordinary sense. Yet her sense of calm and elegant mannerisms make her seem the most alluring of creatures.

"I shall make us tea." Lizzôa meets me at the door and tows me to a chair. "I will have to be more direct with you."

The shine of my spotless rapier makes me almost question if I truly have killed tonight. When Lizzôa touches my face and I feel the sting, I remember everything, including how easy the act was to do.

"You are too young to be a widow. Love should not leave, not until you are very old."

But it has. I've lost everyone I love but Josiah and Old Jean. I can't hold in my tears, my exhaustion. "Love has found reasons to go."

Lizzôa makes me a fragrant cup of lavender tea. "We will have to change your fortunes."

The scent reminds me of Sarah. She made it for me after the Fille Fântome. She saved me. The lavender is a sign. Maybe she's guided me here.

Madame disappears deeper into her house. "I will prepare you a bath." Her voice echoes.

The pronouncement is another answer to prayer. I want no more trouble. I need a friend, and I need my fortune to change.

* * *

With my feet and bottom on a sponge and a white sheet hanging from the ceiling overhead, Lizzôa has me soak in a wooden tub. My clothes are in a pile dirtying the floor made of reddish-brown tiles. My new friend has threatened to burn them.

"I can clean them in this water," I offer.

Lizzôa shakes her head, offering a playful grimace. "Non. Non. A bath is not for laundering. It's to cleanse your soul."

She enters carrying a teapot. "This is fennel and mallow root." She pours this into the hot bathwater. "The fragrances will help you find peace."

The heavenly steam wafts to my nose. The heat relaxes tired muscles.

Lizzôa wears a thick linen robe that's tied up to her throat. She wears a lacy scarf wrapped about her natural brown hair. Her cheeks bear no more of the red cosmetic. She looks younger, even more helpless. My thoughts feel odd. She's mistress of this place and has instructed me on the ways of her home since I entered. No man lives here as she said.

This house becomes more magnificent the more I observe it. Whitewashed, smooth walls made of crushed shells and plaster hold up a low roof of brown tiles. I've counted four rooms: a breakfast room, a bedchamber, a kitchen, and this bathing area.

"Let me get a poultice for that eye." I hear Lizzôa dash away, but I felt her presence behind the sheet. I'm still a stranger to her, an oddity. She must wonder what kind of woman dresses as a man to find work?

I hope she's not fearful of her safety. I killed in front of her . . . for her.

Settling into the bath, enjoying the sweet mallow, I'm coming to terms with my plight. I'm still a girl playing pretend, with a faltering plan.

* * *

I awaken to Lizzôa's dainty finger massaging the sore side of my face. The sting, the pleasure of her touch, make me fearful of what I look like.

"Chère. You've fallen asleep. I will make you better."

The next I know, I smell mustard and feel something wet and cold on my face, my sore eye. I thrash around in tepid water. My wrinkled fingers feel as if I've scrubbed my kitchen.

It's been two months, two months since it all went away.

"Is the poultice burning?" Lizzôa asks. "The herbs help the swelling."

"Non. Just memories."

"Take deep breaths. I find it helps, Jacquotte." She retrieves a brush from a close-by table and scrubs my neck, working circles up to my hairline. "You are young and beautiful. You must find the right arrangement. Someone will recognize your spirit and love it. Unless, Jacquotte—"

Her head tilts to the side like it pleases her tongue to say my name. "Jacquotte, tell me, are you running from a lover? Who has made you make this change?"

"Michel, my husband, is gone." I finger the crucifix. I haven't taken it off, even for the bath. "I let him love me. I wanted forever, but I wasn't enough to keep him."

"When one finds love, one must know it's rare. One must fight for it. Defend it at all costs."

I sob now. If he had stayed, everything would be different. "Lizzôa. I am alone. I need to earn money. Help me."

"Oui." Her tone sounds absentminded. She pushes my loosed hair to the side. "I see no brand or sign of abuse. I must know if I'm dealing with a runaway. The enslaved run away all the time. And the Grand Blancs keep bringing more and more."

"I've run, but not from a master. I'm free. I am in possession of myself."

She remains close to the tub, but lines form along her forehead. "When the farmers see that the land of Hispaniola is good not just for tobacco but sugarcane, the hunger for slaves will grow even more intense. If you had a Grand Blanc looking for you, that would be a problem for me in Petit-Goâve. It could draw unwanted attention."

"Non. I have no master. My father and closest friend were killed. I will have to care for my brother in three months. As I said, I'm a widow, and I've come to Petit-Goâve for a new start."

She sighs, and it sounds musical. "And you must have a new start as a man?"

The poultice drops into the water. I need to see her to explain. "I was privileged. Living an existence that my mother and father gave me. They are both gone, and I'm left with nothing but my hands and body to earn money with. Men have more ways. You have a brother whose generosity and thoughtfulness allows you to own land and have the life you choose."

Lizzôa says nothing, but she is listening.

I raise my wet, dripping hands. "These fingers can make decent pottage, fight with a rapier, and sail a boat. Two of those occupations are not open to me. Making pottage pays poorly. I would've sold my body at Tree Tavern to get a bath, but I lost courage."

Realizing that Lizzôa has stayed without judging comforts me. "Let me dry off." I hunt for a towel. "You should've bathed before me."

"Sit," she commands in a quick, confident tone. "Let the water draw out the poison in you. How many nights have you slept on the streets?"

I sink deeper into the water. "Too many."

"So, you came to a stew." She leans close to my ear. "To be a harlot like me."

My eyes widen. "You can't be. You are too fancy to be a wench."

"Clothes don't make a woman. They only help her get what she wants." She picks up my breeches and drops them into a soaking pail. "I pay taxes. I like my lifestyle. All this requires money. I do not depend on my brother."

I'm stunned. I don't know what to say other than sorry.

"You're silent. That means you disapprove?"

I stare up at her, at her bruised bottom lip. "I don't judge. And it's wrong for me to think you to be lowly."

"Because I am Blanc? I am proud of my Portuguese and Veracruz origins, but that doesn't feed me—but it gives me an exotic allure. I take what I can. I have what I have because of my hands."

Her soft palms surround mine. "I can help these hands get what you want. I have influence in Petit-Goâve."

The possibility of this being true confuses me. I want everything. I want a future, but does that mean I have to be a wench to get it?

With a kiss, Lizzôa releases my hand. "You're in my house, Jacquotte. My rules. I want you clean. I have one bed to share, and I refuse to have a guest in my bedclothes who's not clean."

"That man with the uniform, you sure he bathed?"

A wry smile lifts her lips. "He's never been here. The dirt of the ville stays outside."

Lizzôa leans against the doorway. I see her shadow through the sheet. "You can ask me anything, Jacquotte, and when you do, I will tell you the truth."

I feel horrid to ask, but how could I not. "Why were you with that man? Why did he think you took something?"

"I was not with him . . . last night. He wanted all of my time. That is being owned. No one controls me. That upset him."

She adjusts the lacy scarf about her neck. Her shadow makes it look big and voluminous. "I listen to dreams. I listen to hopes. Men and women want that more than intercourse. Take that intimacy away, people can be violent."

When she leaves, I close my eyes. Becoming a fancy wench is not going to save me.

Twenty-Two

1681. Petit-Goâve, Hispaniola

It is noon by the time we retire to Lizzôa's bedroom. It's a small, white-painted room with brown timbers above. The thatch is thick, but I see the green of the banana leaves piercing through. The mud-clay walls make the room feel cool. Bits of light sneak in through the shutters.

And it's quiet.

I haven't ever known quiet when I sleep. Mille's brothel outside my doors, Josiah shifting in his bed. It stormed when Michel and I lay in each other's arms. I've learned to like noise.

Quiet is unfamiliar. I stretch flat on the straw-filled mattress. My host comes to bed also. I almost hope she snores, but Lizzôa will probably be a perfect sleeper—no noise or crowding.

She's given me a pale-pink gown of silk to wear. It is fine and smooth. She wears one of pure white with lace. A sheet covers us. I'm on one side, she's on the other.

Lizzôa reaches over and softly strokes my cheek. "The dead monsieur was the paymaster for the British ship HMS *Florence*. There's unrest happening. He didn't know when the admiralty will send money to pay the sailors. Monsieur did not want me to know this."

"Why?"

"The truth might cause a mutiny. Men on board may take command from the British officers. They could seize the HMS *Florence* and try their luck at piracy."

That knowledge is worth killing over. Bahati's looking to join a mutiny. "But who would you tell?"

"You would be surprised what that type of information is worth in the right hands." Her palm smells of sweet lavender. "If a mutiny happens, and it can be traced back to the paymaster, he would be court-martialed. Monsieur didn't want to take the chance, I suppose."

I turn and look at her. Angelic eyes, dainty lips. "How can he look at you and find you a threat?"

"Because I can be. I've caused mutinies. I've aided rebellions."

Her tone sounds so innocent, but her words aren't. Who is this woman?

"Sleep well, Jacquotte. You'll not be able to work as a man for a week. Not until that eye heals. The next time you're in Petit-Goâve, you must appear as if you've never been in a scuffle, and you must leave your rapier here."

"That will leave me unprotected, Lizzôa. I'm not sure."

She touches my nose, and I take a deep inhalation. "You must trust me, Jacquotte. Until we are sure that paymaster's death has caused no stir, we must be cautious."

Only one person knows I have a rapier. Bahati. Would he figure it out? Would he turn me in? "If anyone asks, I'll say that the rapier was stolen."

"Good. You're thinking." She lies flat and closes her eyes. "Logic is a woman's weapon."

I've never envied anyone in my life until now. Lizzôa is beautiful. She lives on her own terms. She has the best of things. More importantly, she brings reason, not mere emotion, to a problem. I want that. I crave it.

I watch her fall asleep, trusting a stranger in her bed. How does Lizzôa know which risks to take? I close my eyes, knowing now why

I'm here in Petit-Goâve. I believe I've found someone to teach me what I've been missing, how to plan for my dreams.

* * *

The docks of Petit-Goâve are a sight to behold. The bay is always busy. The largest ships can only float so far. They put down anchor beyond the sandbars. They have to use longboats or pinnaces to move men back and forth to the docks.

I step away from the water's edge and trot down the docks to the open barge. My head's up. My face holds no bruises. Lizzôa has been a great friend, getting me good-paying jobs. I've worked in two warehouses and a storeroom. Each one of the overseers is Lizzôa's personal acquaintance. I'm paid fully for my labor. I'm not cheated.

Madame Erville is quite popular in Petit-Goâve. Every morning we walk to the ville. She introduces me to everyone as her dear friend, Jacques Delahaye. She brags of my strength, and I work doubly hard to make her proud.

Bahati is here. "Fellows," he says, "Jacques is faster than anyone." Everyone laughs, but I begin lifting two sacks at time.

I like rote, mind-numbing work. It keeps me focused. I use my time to study the boats in the harbor and learn or relearn the language of seamen. Old salts here help repair frigates. Others are just old filibusters or buccaneers with stories to tell. Grinding through jobs keeps me from fretting about how Old Jean's doing with Josiah. Blessedly, it also stops me from thinking so much about Lizzôa.

While I'm in town, she's here having her meetings. Somewhere she's being charming and lovely and conducting her business. This morning, I awakened to find her out of bed, dressed and meeting people in her garden. The talk with the strangers seemed intense. I'm still fretting, wondering what Lizzôa has promised to do for them. Her safety concerns me.

From the corner of my eye, I see someone walking toward the

docks. The way the lilac fabric drapes and moves with her hips, I know it's Lizzôa.

I can't help but stare, even as I lift more grain.

A man steps into her path. They chat. She touches his arm. My heart races. It becomes clear it's a social interaction, her business. She clasps his arm, and the two walk in the direction of the inn by the Tree Tavern.

Bahati pulls me to the side. "Jacques, be careful. The last man that lusted for Madame Erville ended up dead."

I keep my expression even and nod at Bahati's warning. I try to offer an expression of mild interest. "Do people link the death to Madame?"

"Non. What I'm saying is take care. Madame Erville is meant for someone with power and wealth, not a dockworker."

* * *

I return to Lizzôa's house early. It's a sunny afternoon. Her fields and gardens are in bloom. I carry my package of fresh fish and vegetables into the house.

Lizzôa lets me stay, continues to help me find work, and never asks for money. Every night when our routines are done, I tell her stories of Tortuga. She knows Maman and Sarah, Père and Old Jean. Haven't been able to talk of Michel. When I do, I get tongue-tied. I didn't realize how angry I am at him.

My thoughts are less and less of Michel and more of Lizzôa. She said she knows how mutinies are started. That surely would include how someone could become part of a rebelling crew. If I want to become a pirate, Lizzôa must know how.

I go to the hearth and run my hands along the surface of the bricks. I can't believe it's almost been four months since I've cooked. Lighting logs and coals, I start a pot of water to boil. I will make my friend a pottage. Scaling the fresh dolphinfish and chopping carrots and potatoes brings me to tears. This feels good to do. If I had a tankard of spice this would be perfect. Lizzôa only has salt.

A taste says my pottage needs peppers. It will do. I set the cauldron on the back of the hearth to stay warm. Then I begin to boil water for baths. The house darkens. I look out at Lizzôa's garden. I hope my friend will appear before twilight.

* * *

It's very late when Lizzôa drags in. I try not to appear anxious, but the last time she was out at this time, she was attacked.

"Bonjour, Jacquotte," she says. She looks beautiful and unharmed in an over-robe of cream and inner gown of sea blue. Her gaze catches mine, but then flits away as she looks around the newly cleaned house. Her eyes close as she takes a whiff of the lavender.

She dances to the hearth. "I am famished."

"You walked here by yourself?"

"Non. A friend brought me in his dray." Her voice sounds so innocent. She gives a smile that makes me hold my breath until she turns away. "Jacquotte, you are so thoughtful."

Her green eyes are shiny. "I must bathe before I can enjoy."

She goes to lift the kettle and exposes a bruise on her wrist.

I don't say a word, for Lizzôa's eyes beg me not to ask. *Her business*, I say to myself. "Why don't you get ready to bathe? I'll fill the tub with fresh water. It's no trouble."

Lizzôa wraps her arms about my neck. Though she's inches taller than me, she seems so small in my arms. "Thank you," she says.

The hug lasts another minute, but when my sleeve catches on her collar, she flees to the bedchamber. "Thank you, Jacquotte."

Why does she run from me as if she has something to hide? Were there more bruises about her throat? I take the pail and walk out into the night.

With more confidence in myself than I've had in a long time,

I walk in peace. Not everything is what we wish, not all the time. The fact that I am here, able to see someone else's light—to feel light when it shines on me—is enough. Absolved of thinking or feeling more than I should, I fill the pail and then step into the cold waters of the mountain stream.

Twenty-Three

1681. Petit-Goâve, Hispaniola

Lizzôa tells me her Portuguese father insists that strangers be treated as family. "We sleep in the same bed. Quem boa cama faz nela se deita. That is to say, he who makes a good bed sleeps well on it. I've made this bed very well. It was the first thing I purchased. I like nothing better."

She's had another of those long days. Though I finished up at the docks early, I waited for her outside the inn near the Tree Tavern. "I could sleep on the floor, Lizzôa. I don't mind."

Her sleepy eyes flicker open. "Non, Jacquotte. I have my best dreams when you are beside me."

I don't have to look at her to feel the brightness of her smile. "I only want you to be comfortable, Jacquotte. Don't you want to be here?"

That's not the problem at all. I am here, with Lizzôa. Lizzôa is with me always. "I don't want to wear out my welcome. But this time with you . . . I love that you listen."

"Good," she says. Her voice is buoyant. "Jacquotte, my love, tell me of your best dream." Though it is a hot and sticky day, she lies beside me in her lacy scarf with her thin body bundled in a muslin gown. "Tell me."

"I'm not sure, but it would have a boat." I sit up. I need to confess. "I want to be a buccaneer. I want to command a ship. I want to have adventure and sail the seven seas. I want to earn treasure."

She pulls me back down to lie with her and snuggles into my chest. "How will you survive on a ship? You are small like me."

Slowly, carefully, I fold my arm about her. "I'm stronger than I look. I can control a whipstaff. Michel taught me. I know how to string sails. I could command any third-rate or second-rate that I see in the bay."

"You rarely talk of your husband."

I begin to pull away, but Lizzôa won't move. "Tell me," she says. "I want to know the man who broke your heart."

When she says it like that, my throat grows thick.

Lizzôa's fingertips stroke my lips. "Speak, Jacquotte."

The plea, the touch unlocks my tongue. "I loved Michel Le Basque's kindness and his principles. But his crew came first. His mission was more important than love. I begged him to take me with him, but he believes women on board is bad luck."

"That is just an old tale. Almost all boats are named after women. We cannot be bad luck."

"He believed it, and if he thought it, it was so for him. He never came back for me. No one has seen the *Marauder* since it set sail from Tortuga."

Lizzôa is quiet for a long time. I hear her soft breaths, but I know she's not asleep. She grips my hand, and I stare off into the dark trying to find the words. The touch says more than words.

"If I'd gone with him, we would've died together. But there would be no one to take care of my brother. I'm all Josiah has. Old Jean will bring him here in three weeks. I have enough to rent a place—"

"You'll not rent anything. Your brother is welcome here. There's room for him."

I'm touched by her words. I take her hand and kiss it. "That takes so much off my mind. My money can go to hiring someone to watch him. The land here is beautiful. Josiah will love it."

My chest feels so free. My worries fade. I have a plan that will work.

"Jacquotte? May I ask you something?"

"Oui, Lizzôa, anything."

"If you didn't have to mind your brother, would you want to be on the sea?"

"Having adventures? Oui. Not a night goes by I'm not at the helm in my dreams. That would be my life."

She says nothing, and I wonder if my enthusiasm has frightened her.

"Lizzôa, once my days at sea are done, I'd love nothing more than making you pottage and swabbing your tiles. I'd be content in this world you've built. You are my dearest friend."

She clasps my hand, dragging it to her stomach. The muslin is so soft, soft as her skin. "I'm going to think of how I can help you have your dreams."

Her breathing slows. Lizzôa drifts to sleep. I kiss her brow. She's had a long day. I think she wept in the tub.

I wanted to come in, interrupt her privacy and hold her. Selling her flesh can't continue. If I could free her from this life, I'd do it.

* * *

Dawn has come, and I awake alone. Peeking out the window, I see her in the garden. My pulse slows then speeds again. She's not alone. Two men have joined her. One Blanc man and one Brun. Who are they?

My hand fists on the sill.

The Blanc stands up and points at Lizzôa. He grimaces. The other man pulls him back. They both look young and strong. They could hurt her.

I take my rapier from the corner and watch. I'm in a gown. My hair is out, and I look more like a woman than ever. I can't intimidate anyone, but these men will be slaughtered, and they'll know a woman did it.

Lizzôa stands. She's arguing back. Can't make out her words, but her tone sounds harsh. The angry person backs away. I shouldn't underestimate Lizzôa. I look around at this house, this gorgeous land. Lizzôa has done well. She's a survivor. It's obvious she doesn't need me. I am the one in need. The sooner I convince myself of this, the better off I will be.

I take a breath and look outside again.

The aggressive Blanc is shaking Lizzôa's hand, seemingly content. The two men walk away. Lizzôa returns to her chair. She sits looking up at the mountains, taking in the calming, clear view of the peaks. I have a feeling she will finish her tea before she comes inside. The face she shows me is always calm.

I need to focus on me, my plan. This situation is temporary. Josiah will soon be here. I have money to pay someone to watch him, but I still do not earn enough to be independent of Lizzôa's kindness.

I think of Michel's treasure. If I were able to go back and retrieve some of it—the gold plates or the ingots—would Lizzôa, through her connections, be able to exchange it for silver?

But how do I bring gold out of Tortuga? I'd need help. I couldn't risk Old Jean by asking him to retrieve it.

Even if Lizzôa's connections are able to exchange the *Santa Margarita*'s gold for silver, someone might figure out the pieces are part of the larger treasure. I can't risk it.

The world hasn't changed. Every day I see frigates bring more slaves to the port. Exchanging a lot of gold means it will pass through many hands. One of those hands will be raised to auction men.

If I had no conscience, I'd be wealthy. I could pay for Josiah's care. I could take care of Lizzôa and keep her away from a life of dealing in information and peddling flesh.

I hear her coming and put my rapier away. I prepare to greet her and pretend I'm not anxious or concerned. My brother will be here in weeks. He's my concern, my responsibility, not my friend who can manage with me or without.

* * *

Walking away from the docks, I jiggle the reales and pieces of eight in my pocket. My reputation and work ethic have raised my pay, but I know it is also due to Lizzôa's influence.

I stop and look at the HMS *Florence.* It has shifted positions in the bay, but the fourth-rate frigate is still here. I wonder if the sailors have been paid yet. Is the ship still ripe for mutiny?

Bahati comes up to me. He's counting his coins from a job down the way. "She's a beauty," he says.

"She is. Look at the oar ports in the lower deck. All those cannons. I wonder if it slows her down. The second deck would need to be lightened to bring up the oars' line. She'd be a dream to sail, fast and free."

Bahati eyes me with what seems a new respect. "You are full of surprises."

"I've learned a thing or two. Captain Le Basque's *Marauder* had such modifications. It was a fast ship to sail." I turn to him with my chin high, and my chest puffs out. "And when I controlled the whipstaff and sailed the beast around Tortuga it moved like the fastest dream."

A look, a nod, one simple glance burns between us like a pact. But I want this silent deal clear. "I've some personal issues to settle, but if I can, know I will go, and you can count on me."

A brow cocks, and my friend says, in the deepest, darkest tones, "You want to be a buccaneer?"

I laugh and drop my voice an octave. "Can't be a filibuster. My blood is here, from the Caribbean."

"My blood is Guinea, but my heart is here." Bahati extends his hand, and I take it. "I understand complications. My sister has had twins. I need double the money now."

We go our separate ways. I pray the HMS *Florence* is still here and still ripe for mutiny when we both have our houses in order.

A gunshot. I curse under my breath. The mutiny has already started.

Yet the HMS *Florence* looks peaceful. I see a sea frigate pulling into the bay. On the top deck, I see a sailor holding a flintlock. Did he shoot his gun?

"Dang fools." Wulf ambles toward me. "Hey, Jacques. Wait up. Oh no, it's time."

My curiosity gets the better of me. "What is it I'm about to see?"

"That boat's slave driver has to keep his commodity under control. The gun's a signal he's letting 'em come up for air."

I focus on its deck and the Black heads crowding around the white masts. My stomach drops. I can't turn away when the dots sing. *Yo-yo-yo.* All-male voices moan those notes. The mourning hits me in the chest.

Wulf rubs his blond hair that's now cut short and curses, then wipes his hands on his sweaty pourpoint of linen or wool. "That's one of the British West Indies ships," he says. "They trick them to get them on board. It's not right. My Margaret won't have those trades in her warehouse."

Quincy who finished up at the end of the dock, runs to us. He's laughing, saying, "Stupid Guinea. Tricked by painted rocks. You see that, Jacques. Your people are singing. They are stupid but can sing."

This man picks at me and only me, and I'm tired of living so carefully. "Monsieur, if someone put shiny trinkets on the dock, you'd gather them hoping to get rich, wouldn't you? And that's what they did to my mother. She never saw her land again."

The man keeps looking at me, and recognition lights his face. "Your name is Delahaye. And you're from Tortuga. You know, I thought there was only a half-wit boy and a daughter in that family."

He steps up to me, and I knock him flat. My arms have new power from weeks of hauling and lifting. "Who are you calling a half-wit?"

Dockworkers start gathering around. Bahati has circled back too. My livelihood is on the line. I'll be my father's son from now on.

"I never forget a face." He thumbs his chin. "But you're the fille.

I've seen you in gowns in Basse-Terre." I drag him to me with one hand and slug him with the other.

"Hey, Jacques, Quincy," Wulf says, "cut it out."

Bahati looks like he wants to step in. "You both need to stop. You'll ruin work here for us all."

"Monsieur Delahaye." Lizzôa is here. I turn toward her voice. The distraction gives big Quincy a chance to strike. He hits me hard in the chest but slams his knuckles into the metal of my crucifix, then shakes his hand like he broke something.

I step toward him and punch him in the nose. The bones crunch under my knuckles, and the fool goes spiraling to the dock.

Lizzôa takes a fan and whips people aside until she stands by me. "Monsieur Delahaye, fighting for me again? So soon."

She puts her arms about me. The crowd now whoops in pleasure, but when her lips meet mine, there are cheers. We kiss for show, for curiosity, for pleasure maybe, and it lasts more than a few heartbeats.

"That's Madame Erville. Jacques Delahaye is doing all right!" Bahati laughs.

Wulf claps and hoots. "Let's send the lovebirds off."

Lizzôa blushes, then clasps my hand. My head spins as she leads me from the docks. I'm ready to follow her anywhere.

Some distance from the docks, walking down the rue, Lizzôa kisses my wrist. "Jacques, I see you had some trouble. Did that man hurt you?" She's in lilac, glancing at me with soft emerald eyes that steal my breath.

With a quick shake of my head, I look forward. "No. Quincy's a fool. I let him get to me."

"You defended yourself like a champion," she says.

I did, didn't I? "True, but Jacques still has the same problems. My brother will be here soon, but I'm thinking daring thoughts. I want to join the next mutiny and become a buccaneer. Help me figure this out. I'm not good at that. I'm impulsive. I just attacked a man twice my size for telling the truth."

"Jacques, are you serious?" Her soft palm goes to my face, my brow.

"I know I can be good at being a buccaneer. I just need the chance." I ask, "Do you still have access to information on the HMS *Florence*? The ship's still here. I see it. I study it every day. I count oar ports and dream of how to streamline the beast."

"They are waiting on pay." Her eyes are wide. "What are you planning to do?"

My heart beats wildly. I focus on the one thing that's true, the one thing I've earned: an opportunity. "I need you to find out how to put me on the HMS *Florence*. I'll mutiny for the ship."

"So, you want to leave me to be a buccaneer?"

In public, everywhere outside, I have to remember I'm a woman and only hiding as a man. And I shouldn't have thoughts of wanting Lizzôa. Of touching her, as I do after that kiss. "I cannot leave a friend, a true friend, forever."

She smiles, but her eyes dim.

I wasn't pretending before to want her, but now I am pretending that I don't want to put my lips to hers again.

The way our fingers entwine, and have been entwined at night in her bed, says: Oui, there's enough between us to make us more than friends. Maybe there is enough to forge a love that lasts forever. But I'm not Michel. I won't commit to Lizzôa and leave my heart with her while I take my body to sea.

Twenty-Four

1681. Petit-Goâve. Hispaniola

I work all day, rising before Lizzôa and staying late at the docks. But when I return, there is light coming from her garden. The torch makes the rear of the house glow.

I take a deep breath and then march to her. "Lizzôa, good evening. Have you had a good day?"

"It was a day." Her voice sounds strained. She gazes at the smoky torch. The distant look in her eyes sends shivers down my skin. It's a humid night. My clothes stick to me from hauling crates. And I tremble with thoughts of her.

"Go in. Water is on the hearth. Take a bath."

I come to her and stand between her and the light. There are bruises on her face. The delicate curve of her nose bears a scratch.

"Did a customer do this?

"Go inside."

She winces a little, and I want to protect her. I'm strong. I still practice with my rapier. With my fist or a weapon, I'll equal the score. "All I need is a name. I'll humble the man who did this."

The mug clangs on the table as she tries to pick it up. "And ruin your chance to mutiny, to become a buccaneer? Non. A bath, Jacquotte. I made a request. Honor it."

"Did this happen because you asked about the HMS *Florence*?"

She doesn't look at me anymore.

Does she know how much I care? How my heart breaks for her suffering? But I turn away. She's right. I lust to become a buccaneer. So, I walk away and go to bathe.

Sighing, I climb into the tub. The water is tepid on my skin. I loosen my hair. It falls to my back. I dunk my face and let the warmth caress my breasts.

The longer something steeps, the stronger the flavor. It's better on the tongue. But I'm not tea. I am bitter dregs. I must become satisfied with the dreams I can grasp and wait for sleep to give me the fantasy of Lizzôa's love.

* * *

The bedroom is dark when I come from my bath. Lizzôa is here. I hear her breathing. Easing into the bed, I get comfortable. The straw seems fresh in the mattress. It has a heady smell of ferns, reminding me of the hills of Tortuga.

I shift and stretch, and Lizzôa wraps her arms about me. Moonbeams penetrate the thatch roof and reflect on her face. My eyes adjust and meet hers.

"Are you frightened, Lizzôa?" I gently put my hand to her cheek. "You can tell me anything."

"What if I say I don't want you to go?"

"Lizzôa?"

"There, I told you." Her tone sounds like a pout. "Now what?"

I stroke her hair. It's soft and free. "What if I say I'll be back?"

"Like Michel? He said the same to you."

My husband is an unhealed wound, and she's poking at the scab. I turn away. "If I say it, I mean it."

We are silent, but no one is sleeping. It's quiet away from the ville. The mud walls, the roof block most sounds. It's rare, but sometimes I can hear a trogon.

But I need to hear Lizzôa. "What happened today?"

"I met with people who can help with Josiah. They can care for him when you are away."

I roll to her and hug her. "You have made my dreams come true."

Rubbing her arm, I kiss her cheek and inhale lavender and roses. "This eases my mind. But I had a picture in my head of you caring for him. It's selfish to think of the two of you being here when I return from my adventure."

My enthusiasm sobers. "I'm too full of vanity. You have your own life and responsibilities. You're not committed to me like a—"

"A wife? A lover?"

"Lovers are not permanent for you."

"Oh." Lizzôa stiffens. She shifts, making space between us.

After hurting her with my careless words, I have to confess. "Lizzôa, I can't stop thinking of you. I want you. I'm going away for me, for Josiah, but also for us. When I'm a success, I can take care of you. I want to keep you in silks and satins and lacy collars. I don't want anyone to be . . . The dust of the ville will never be on your skin."

The distance between us melts again. "What are you saying, Jacquotte?"

"I don't know what I'm saying. I don't know what this is. But I'm not afraid of it."

I feel like a fool. I'm saying too much. I sound lovesick. Maybe I am. But just because something isn't said doesn't make it less true. "Lizzôa Erville, I've only loved one person. That was Michel Le Basque. Now I love you."

Holding my breath, I wait for her to say it too, that I'm in her heart.

Lizzôa puts her hands on my shoulders. It's something she often does. Her fingers massage the muscles and the tightness that forms at my neck. "You talk a lot at night. Talk is cheap. It means nothing in the next moment. Love is actions."

"Does that mean—"

She leans into me and kisses me. Our mouths find each other perfectly fitting together. The ties on my night robe open, and Lizzôa's fingers trace my bosom. The soft hands slipping against my skin build sweet tension in my body. "Refuse me, Jacquotte, if that's what you wish. Or let *me* give you pleasure."

I nod like a fool. I don't know if she sees my face. "Oui."

My mumbled plea draws her laughter. Her breath smells of chamomile. She's a garden of strength. And swift. She's stripped me bare, as I try to figure out how to please her.

"Do nothing, Jacquotte." She fingers the crucifix that has sunk in the valley of my breasts. "Give me control."

"Oui, but Michel gave that to me. He slipped it onto my neck."

Her kiss demands my passion, my earnest attention. She tugs at the crucifix and frees me from the chain. I hear it fall to the bedclothes then glide to the floor tiles.

"Tonight, I want all of you."

The kisses we share are different than the one at the docks. Everything is deeper than yesterday. And better because it's true. Her fingers stroke. . . . I groan with pleasure, but don't understand the sensation. My heart spins. I have no control.

Of course I don't have any. I gave it to Lizzôa.

I want to stroke her, mirroring what she's doing, but she pushes my hands above my head. "You're leaving me, remember? I'll not let myself get used to you loving me."

I'm panting, barely able to reason. "Don't treat me like the rest. I don't want to be selfish. I want your love. I want to love you too."

"Jacquotte, if you don't know that this is different, I'll have to be at you all night until you do."

It's unfair, but Lizzôa muffles my complaints with kisses. She makes me noisy, questioning me for the longitude and latitude of what I like. Her passion leads me to paradise, and waves of everything hidden in my flesh release. I break and speak her name. "Lizzôa. I love you, Lizzôa."

"I think we will not see the ville tomorrow. I'm not convinced you know this love is different, not yet." Her laugh is that of an angel, but she's wicked. How am I to leave something this good? I will crave her forever.

Twenty-Five

1681. Petit-Goâve, Hispaniola

Every night is the same. I return here, to Lizzôa's home, our home. I bathe and then head into the dark. My love is typically in bed waiting for me.

"I missed you today," she says as she welcomes me into her arms.

"I think of you constantly. You're a fever." I burn as my body reacts to her breath on my skin, but I want her to feel this heated.

It's dark. I'm naked, while she's clothed. I am free, but she seems bound. "We are unequal." I make my tone as gentle as I can. For maybe, like Sarah, Lizzôa was scarred or abused by someone when she didn't have control. "Nothing will make me love you less. But I want light tonight. I want to touch you."

"Non. You will leave."

I sit up and hold her in my arms. "Non. I am yours. You are mine. What we have is true, but I'm not selfish." With my hands to her face, I say, "Love is actions, but it is also trust."

Reaching over, I light a candle. "I want you. You're beautiful. Where there is no shame, there is light."

She looks down at the bedclothes. I finger her gown and lacy collar. "Let me see you. Let our bodies touch. Nothing between us."

Pure panic crosses her light features, but I suckle her thumb. "Trust me. You do, don't you?"

Lizzôa nods. She takes the lacy collar from her neck, exposing creamy skin and a rounded Adam's apple. She peels layer after layer, and her bosom is small, almost flat. She hides in the sheets as the rest of her clothes fall away. I snuggle with her, and she's trembling. "You are beautiful."

"Hold me," she says. "Hold me tighter."

I oblige. I am so pleased. "You trust me. Lizzôa, I love you."

She takes my hand and pulls it to her sex. I am ready to show her the pleasures I've learned, but my fingers find something unexpected.

My head spins. I think of every moment past. Nothing has prepared me for Lizzôa's truth. Outside of this house, I am a woman pretending to be a man. Lizzôa has been pretending too.

"There's no brother who bought this land far from Petit-Goâve," I say slowly.

"Non," Lizzôa says. The voice I love, I crave, is soft and full of tears. "I bought this land. Then I became me and invented a story to have my life. I am Madame Erville.

"I deal in secrets, Jacquotte." Lizzôa's voice is low and wet. "I always have been a secret that hides in plain sight. No one understands."

"I'm listening. I will understand."

"I grew up in Veracruz, very close to the Pánuco River. I am the bastard of a Portuguese explorer and his Spanish concubine. I wasn't happy being who my father wanted me to be. One day my father caught me in a vestido and ripped the gown off me. When I tried to tell him how I am, how natural it felt to be womanly, he beat me. He chased the abomination away, hoping I'd die in the jungle. The Zapotec people found me. They took me in, as I am. They loved me as me. They became my family. For the first time ever, I could live my true nature."

Lizzôa begins to weep. I hold her tighter. "Keep talking."

"I watched the Spanish raid those sweet people. It was my fault. I knew I had brought this evil to them and hoped to sacrifice myself to Cocijo, the god of rain. I jumped into the sea. I would've drowned, but sailors fished me out and impressed me to a Spanish ship. I served. I rose quickly in the ranks and watched how secrets flow from within a command, and from city to city. Dealing in secrets saves lives—saved my crew. Then I abandoned them for Petit-Goâve. Here I use all my talents to makes dreams come true."

"You lived on a frigate. You know that life. You can come too. We can be pirates, buccaneers."

Lizzôa touches my throat. "It's not that simple. As a sailor, you do as you're told. I have helped transport captives. I've had to enact trades. A pewter bowl for my captain, fifteen Guineas. I've been forced to do raids in Veracruz. When the navy look for slaves, they don't always go to Guinea. Anyone with Indigenous blood can be taken. I'm ashamed of that. There's no guarantee that the HMS *Florence* will be any different."

I don't know what to say. I force myself to breathe. "But to stay in this life . . . I don't mind backbreaking work, but for you it means to continue being wenched."

"The need for sex and females is a desperate fever. I've turned desperation to my advantage and kept my living safe. Brutes in the dark don't care. Then there are some who like men more than women. And men pay more for what they perceive as rare. Men in high positions pay the most and are ridiculously careless with secrets." Lizzôa's laugh is forced.

She's hurting, and I don't know what to do.

"Well, there you have it. I'm not ashamed of what I've done. I've stopped insurrections. I've sunk ships bent on dealing in slaves. I tell filibusters when shipments of gold are transported, the number of accompanying vessels. Information pays handsomely, so much more than sex. Men who believe themselves in high company sometimes will talk all night. Often that's what they truly want." Lizzôa sighs. "Now you know. Someone else in the world knows my story. Maybe that's all I wanted, for you to learn my truth."

I steady my embrace. "Truth means more than anything. You mean more. I love you."

We lie like this, and I want to reassure her that I love her, love her soul. She must love me too to be so open. My actions, my hands will prove it. I caress what I can without relaxing my hold upon her. My touch is light. It takes time, but comfort and ease grow between us.

Oui. Soon, with abandon, Lizzôa kisses me. Then I willingly put my hands above my head. "Take control."

Her glinting eyes sparkle with tears. "I love you, Jacquotte. I can say it now. I will love you forever."

We consummate this vow in the ways she's comfortable. I touch her where she leads me to do so. We slip against each other, allowing love to define a rhythm and a pleasure that's our own. The truth has changed nothing. I have the love I've been seeking.

* * *

The sound of her soft breath nestles against my ear. It's peace, our peace. I look at this woman in my arms. She's awake and listening to rain softly tap the roof.

"Jacquotte, the new paymaster has received information. The delay in the pay for HMS *Florence* will end soon. Once that happens, the ship will leave port. No mutiny will happen. The time to strike is now. We shall be on the ship. We are not separating. We shall be buccaneers together."

My arms tighten about her. I bury my face in her warm, soft skin. "How will you do it?"

"I can pretend to be a sailor again, if it means staying with my love."

"If you are only going because you think I cannot be faithful or that I will forget about the woman who brings me such joy—non. What we have is true." Lifting my hand, I slide off my gold band, Michel's band. "Wearing this on your hand will prove I mean it. If there was a well on your property, I would take you there and proclaim that you are my mate."

Lizzôa leans back. "Does that mean you are done mourning?"

This isn't breaking vows. It's making new ones. Michel is always in my heart, but he's dead. Lizzôa is life. I find her index finger on her left hand and slide on the band. "You are my mate, and I'll be true to you. You don't have to come. I'll come back for you."

Lizzôa doesn't say anything. She admires the ring on her finger.

I hold my breath. Maybe I should have said that part about her not having to come before asking her hand in marriage. "My love, please understand."

"I do." Lizzôa smiles. "My mate, my mate forever."

So relieved. Lips to lips, we sink into the bedclothes. I'm not hollow anymore. Lizzôa loves me and fills me. The rain picks up, but my mate's whispers are the adventure I didn't know I needed. Unlike Michel, I won't keep tempting fate. I will win my share and leave. I know what I have here. When my time at sea is done, Lizzôa will be here waiting for me. This time, this love will last. As much as she says she would come with me, I know the hard sea life is not for her, not now, not again.

* * *

I wake up reaching for Lizzôa, but the bed is empty. I won't go find work today. We need to firmly agree about the HMS *Florence.* I dress in breeches and a doublet, but when I go to the window by the hearth, I see that Lizzôa is in our sanctuary with three men.

Though it looks peaceful, I don't like it.

I clasp my rapier but put it in my sling. I calm and take a breath. Lizzôa can handle herself, but I still go outside.

"Oh, Jacques. Good, you are up, come join us."

Two men I recognize. Bahati. And Wulf. I shake each's hand. "You're a long way from the docks."

Bahati says, "This will save me the trouble of telling you about the next mutiny."

Wulf grins. "This is the best of all worlds, then, to undertake this with people I trust."

"Oui," I say. "Men I trust."

Bahati's smile fades. "For trust to be complete, we must be transparent. I am not a man. I am a laborer. A former buccaneer. And I am a woman."

Wulf doesn't look shocked. Neither does Lizzôa, but before I can respond, Wulf says, "I am Dirk De Wulf, but Dirkje De Wulf. I too am a woman." She stares at me and says, "Margaret is all women. My wench is the best for she accepts all of me."

I'm dumbfounded but say, "I am the same. I'm Jacquotte Delahaye, daughter of Uzoamaka of Kissi and Pierre of Tortuga. I can fight with my rapier. I know my knots, can repair a sail, and have commanded a frigate. It was but one day, but it was life-changing."

"And this is Celia Chilango," Bahati says, "She is from Veracruz."

"My grandfather is of Spain," Celia adds. "My mother is Indigenous, but my great-grandfather is also of Guinea descent."

The hard expression in this third woman's face reveals her resolve. Her close-fitting indigo pourpoint gives nothing away. I offer her my hand.

She takes it. "I will be called Chilango when we are there, but Celia is good for now."

All of us pretending to be something else—it's hard to fathom, but what choice do we have to live the lives we want?

"The HMS *Florence* is still in the harbor," Lizzôa tells us. "Jacques and Bahati can attest to this. The British have not paid the crew. The men onboard have been given promises and excuses. My sources say they've been told that the scrip will be here by month's end. No one believes it."

I don't glance at Lizzôa. We're outside the house with our outside truths. I wonder if her recent bruises came from gaining this information. She shares nothing else. I doubt if anyone but me knows Lizzôa's complete truth.

Celia rubs her hands together. "Then our mutiny must occur before the pay comes."

Lizzôa says, "You were taken in a Spanish raid. You and your mother were sold off to Santo Domingo. You can't let that influence what we say or do on board the HMS *Florence*."

Celia's face darkens. "My enslavement ended two years ago. I made it end. I ran away. I'm ready to go to sea and earn my fortune. I want revenge on the bastards who hurt my mother."

Wulf waves her hands at Celia. "Don't need no emotional creatures getting killed or ruining this for me. Bahati, I know. The others . . ." She sucks her teeth. "Under Lizzôa's influence, Jacques seems steadier, but any volatility will ruin the plan."

Nodding her shiny bald head, Bahati glares at Celia and then me. "We've waited for the right opportunity for over a year. You can't bring your anger. We may be forced to do things we hate. When we sign on board, we take a blood oath to the captain. We have to depend on one another to comply with our shipmates."

"Especially for things we hate." Everything Lizzôa told me about being impressed into service echoes in my heart. She turns to me. "But most things come down to a vote. Our numbers staying unified can sway most decisions go our way."

Puffing up her chest like she wants to spit, Celia curses. "You mean if they want to traffic Guineas you'll stand for it?"

"Look at these hands." Bahati pulls up a sleeve. Scarring from lashes are bulbous and purple black on her arms. "I will try to persuade the crew, and the captain to be righteous. But if the vote happens, we are crewmen first. My goal is the same goal I've always had. Get gold, don't get caught, come back to Petit-Goâve alive for my sister and now her girls."

"I will stay on the mission." Celia slaps on her cap. She starts walking through the garden.

Lizzôa motions to Bahati. "She's volatile. Will we be able to handle her?"

Bahati shrugs. "I know Jacques can." She raises her fists and punches the air. "Can fight and sail. Good combination."

I nod. "I'm ready."

"And I'll have no problems dunking Chilango overboard. You too, Jacques. I've done this too many times. Margaret expects me home."

"We will be fine, all of us." Lizzôa sips her tea. "I will be prepared to ensure it."

Wulf nods, then bows and leaves. Bahati remains with us. "And now you want to come with us?" She laughs. "I thought you got seasick, madame."

"I will adapt." Lizzôa glances at me. "I've grown ginger in my garden. It helps with the sickness. I will bring my knowledge and skills to give us every advantage. I too have my reasons to make sure Jacques comes home."

Bahati grouses. "You will be a target, Lizzôa. Of all of us, you will look the most womanly. Long stretches at sea make men look for targets."

"And lovers." Lizzôa smiles and blows me a kiss. "That's why Jacques is essential. She can fight. She's good with a rapier. We'll have protection at sea. If necessary we'll make it known that I'm her matelotage, her special mate."

Glancing at me as if she's weighing the risks of a matelotage pirate marriage, Bahati shrugs. "It's a lot to ask Jacques to protect you and herself at sea. Guess I'll have to keep an eye out for you, Jacques." She punches my shoulder and then walks out of the garden and heads to town.

Turning to Lizzôa, I begin to panic. "But Josiah will be here this week. I can't go until his care is settled."

"I have it all arranged." Lizzôa sets down the mug on the small table. It wobbles then comes to rest. "We will be buccaneers next week."

She stands and puts a hand to my arm. Her touch is delicate. Then I feel a hard squeeze. "Jacquotte, I love you, but I'm not Le Basque. I won't give you my heart and then wait here, hoping you don't die. My expertise will help us both live."

"I don't know, Lizzôa. I'm scared for us."

"My looks won't last. My expertise and influence will dwindle.

I'd rather choose to be with my love and have an adventure that will make us wealthy. When you find love, you keep it. I will keep you. You will keep me."

I hold her hand, but I'm raging inside. I'm afraid. I'm hopeful. I don't say a word of these feelings. "Tell me about Josiah's arrangements."

She taps my hand. "The boy will be safe with the monks. Madame Erville is a great supporter of the church—L'Église de L'Assomption." Lizzôa turns to look out at the stream and her garden. "I'm giving you the chance to live the dream that you have wanted. We will go to the sea. You'll make a name for yourself, Jacques Delahaye. You'll be a buccaneer supreme."

Heaven must help my brother. He will come to Petit-Goâve and be left by his sister. I hope the monks at the monastery will teach Josiah how to forgive me for abandoning him again.

Twenty-Six

1681. The Bay of Petit-Goâve, Hispaniola

The sun sinks lower in the sky. Twilight and dusk arrive just as I finish my last loading job. When I heave the last tobacco bundle onto the longboat, this arduous labor is done.

Wiping my brow, flexing my shoulders, I wait for my pay. I hardly notice the pieces of eight falling into my palm as I stare at the HMS *Florence.* The British frigate hasn't moved, hasn't raised their flag in days.

I look away and hunt for a different ship, one with two masts. I thought Old Jean would be here by now. Time is up. This is four months to the day. If he's delayed, I might miss my opportunity to be a buccaneer.

Pretty as a rose, Lizzôa meets me at the dock. "I am assuming that your brother has not arrived."

I want to lean my head against her shoulder. My frustration and fear knit together. "Let's—"

A ship with two masts with the sail I have patched enters the bay. "The ketch, Lizzôa! You will meet my brother today." I embrace her. Lizzôa doesn't pull away. It's Jacques and Madame. I look at her and know that we won't have this freedom for much longer. Once we step onto the HMS *Florence*, we must be all about the job.

If I didn't feel that my destiny was to be on that ship, I'd change my plans. "I'm glad that we will be doing this together, Lizzôa."

She lets go of my hand. "Go get your brother. The monks are ready for him. It's all arranged."

I swallow hard. "Let's walk out to the ketch."

"Non. I will stand here. Go to your old world. Greet them without having to explain me, our situation."

The lump in my throat grows bigger. Pretending to Old Jean that Lizzôa is just a friend would be a lie. Explaining that we are lovers probably isn't a conversation the dear man needs to dwell upon sailing back to Tortuga. Especially now that Lizzôa has stopped shaving. It's part of her morning preparation I did not know she performed. The shadow on her jaw is barely hidden with powder.

Shoulders leveled, I go to the spot where Old Jean heads his ship. I catch the rope he throws to me. Then I jump onto the gangplank he puts up.

The man smiles at me. "Jacques. You've survived."

Extending my hand to shake his, he pulls me into a hug. "You lived six months. You look good. You've been eating. You can do this."

He releases me and tweaks the hat he gave me. It's clean and smooth, and one of the dearest things I own. "My brother looks well too."

Josiah sits silently at the back of the boat. His dark mop of fine curly hair flutters in the wind. He's clean, a little tan. I see him looking at me, but I don't know if he recognizes me. I wait and wave, then I say, "Josiah. It's me. Come."

My brother dutifully gets up and walks to me.

I kneel and hug him. I feel better when he finally hugs me back. I lift him up in my arms. With the greatest balance, I go across the gangplank. The feel of this little boy, his arms about my neck, is wonderful and heartbreaking.

When I set him down, I hold his hand with one arm and then

untie the ketch. Together we wave goodbye. "Old Jean, you're the best. You've saved the Delahayes."

"Just repaying Uzoamaka. You keep paying her too." He pulls in the gangplank. "And you were right to leave. Governor Neveu de Pouancey is feckless. De Franquesnay and Du Casse convinced him that you were helping Sarah. He's hunting you. They confiscated the land where the tavern sat. Basse-Terre's getting a church."

"Du Casse is looking for Le Basque's gold. Mille's convinced he thinks I have it." I pull at my father's doublet. "Doesn't the wealth show?"

Laughing, Old Jean adjusts the sails and goes to the rudder. "Gold makes men crazy."

"Be careful, my friend. You need to stay a free Guinea with your own means."

The wind starts the ketch moving. When I tap Josiah, motion him to wave goodbye again, he hugs my hips. This is a temporary balm to my soul. It will be broken again when I surrender him to the monastery. I'm forsaking my brother's care for my dreams. I pray this adventure, this calling, will be worth every sacrifice.

* * *

At the iron gate, I stand outside waiting to be let into L'Église de L'Assomption, the Capuchin monastery. The estate is lovely, a garden and high walls of gray limestone at the top of the rue. I don't understand why an iron gate is erected to keep people out. Does God require an appointment?

My hand clenches around the slender iron pole, then slides to a half-rusted lock. I'm drawn back to breaking a similar one on a pen on Cayonne. If I had a knife, I'd be tempted, for I couldn't sleep last night. Willing away tears, I've come at the first of the morn to see Josiah, to make sure that he is well here . . . the pen of God.

Monsignor François Robilere approaches. A pointed gray capuche covers his head, but I see his grimace as he looks at me. I know that stiff walk. When Lizzôa and I brought Josiah here yesterday, he didn't like the look of me. He wouldn't talk to me, just to Madame Erville, and I must beg him now to see my brother.

Standing on the other side of the gate, he shakes his head. "Monsieur, may I help you?"

"I must speak to Josiah Delahaye. Monsignor, please."

"The young monk came to us yesterday, already committed to his vow of silence. You know he'll not break this commitment for anyone." His head lowers. His mouth twitches beneath his white beard and whiskers. "Hasn't Madame Erville explained to you that you must not disturb a priest in contemplation?"

He talks to me like I'm a stranger to my brother. Well, that is deserved. Only someone estranged from decency would leave a dependent brother to the church.

"I came with a whole reale, another offering for the monastery. Just five minutes. I want to make sure that my brother is well. I owe it to his father and all those who have cared for Delahaye in Basse-Terre."

Monsignor Robilere doesn't take the silver coin. I think if he did, he'd bite it to ensure that it is silver. "He cannot be disturbed."

"I just need to see that he's fine. He spent his first night here. I'll be bringing the money to pay for his continued training and edification. I must lay my eyes on him this one time, so I can faithfully report to those in Basse-Terre."

I repeat the lies that Lizzôa has given me to gain Josiah's admission. The truth has been stretched and twisted so much I barely recognize it. My brother is humble and mute since birth, but she described him to the monks as a devout follower called to a vow of silence since his youth. "The believers in Basse-Terre want him well cared for. Please, Monsignor, I must report his condition."

He nods and takes the money. His grasp is cold and quick. I barely feel the silver slip from my fingers. "Step back."

The monk drops the silver into the pocket of his brown cloak, then fishes a key from the same pocket and opens the gate. "Follow me."

I do and startle when the gate clinks shut behind us. Entering the monastery, my boots pound and Robilere's sandals make a dull slap as he walks down the long whitewashed halls. Our echoes sound like we are in an underground cavern. My eyes whip up, searching for stalactites. I find expensive bronze fixtures bearing down, holding the tallest tallow candles I've ever known. Paintings of the saints hang on the walls, watching us . . . me . . . like I'm about to steal something.

I feel dirty and don't dare touch my crucifix. I've sinned. I lied to give my brother to the priests so I can become a thief at sea. To them, my love is illicit. They would want me to burn and become ashes like Hasneau.

The monk stops and opens a door. "He's in here."

A little shadow in a brown gown sits on the floor. A pile of books are near him, which he stacks like dishes.

"His commitment to silence is to be honored. He's never wavered, even when meeting the other monks." Monsignor is proud of my brother's curse. "Silence in our order is special. Brother Delahaye will achieve great honor. Go in, but don't disturb him from his mission."

I nod and put my finger to my lips and enter the room.

Josiah doesn't look at me. I wait. I try to be patient, but his eyes are on pages of scriptures. He doesn't read, but he has not closed them. They lie pristine in a stack. Maybe God is allowing him to absorb the words. Maybe touching them feeds his soul.

Stooping, I say, "I'm leaving for a long time. I wanted to say I love you again." My throat clogs with tears. "It's for the best."

His head tips up. The capuche falls back. His eyes move to my face.

Then he turns back to the scriptures.

This is the rebuke I should've received yesterday. He saw his sister for an hour, after months of being away. One hour. When he hugged me, he gave me a chance to be his sister again, but instead I chose a ship in the harbor and a dream that has chased me since Maman and her pirated boat.

Shoulders slumping, I rise. "Though I want to return, I might not see you again. Michel had the best of intentions but never came back."

I wait. I hope. I pray for Josiah to rise and wrap his arms about my hips, but he doesn't move. Josiah saw my face, my eyes. He knows I'm Jacquotte and is unmoved.

Sorrowfully I give him a promise that I don't know I can keep. "I'll be back for you, Josiah."

His hand reaches for the scriptures. He shuffles the pages.

I turn and creep to the door.

"Merci. I will give a good report. I will urge the delegation to send money as often as possible."

"Good. But you must go." The monk smiles and waves at me with the hand that grasped my silver. He walks me back down the hall and leads me to the gate. "Many think we are beyond material things because of our vows of poverty. Though we grow our own food, the parish would not be sustained without tithes. Our enslaved do grow extra tobacco on our fields. That helps too."

Keeping my face tight and smooth, I trudge away from the monastery. The gate clangs behind me. "Go with God, young man," Monsignor Robilere says.

Blinded by tears, I head out of the ville to meet with the others. Tonight is the mutiny. I will finally have what I've wanted—to man a ship and become a pirate, a buccaneer of the Caribbean.

My hunger and my lies are in league. There's no turning back. I'm a man ready to commit to Lizzôa's plan. Winning is the only way to redeem this body, this flesh, and make things right with Josiah.

Twenty-Seven

1681. The Bay of Petit-Goâve, Hispaniola

Now or never, that is the rhythm pounding in my pulse. My gut burns as I stand in the dark with Lizzôa, holding hands in the garden. My stomach fills with tightness. I'm in Maman's basket, waiting. The sounds, the flintlock shots trying to stop all who fled, repeat in my mind. This escape from the habitation seemed successful, but the dead we left behind made the victory bittersweet. That twilight morn right before sunrise, we stood on the docks. I hid, waiting for Maman to take command of the sloop.

"Jacquotte." Lizzôa's voice booms louder than my beating heart. "Our plan will keep your brother safe. The capuchins do good when you pay them silver. We've paid them well."

Our hands are still locked together. The torchlight illuminates Lizzôa's face. More stubble, but the same gorgeous eyes remain. Loose fitting breeches that hang well to the ground replace gowns of satin.

I straighten the collar of her linen doublet. "It looks good on you." I try to offer encouragement. The changes haven't been easy.

"In the future, we add color." She tugs on my matching loose sloppe breeches. "But these disguises will help us blend in with the sailors, our future comrades." Lizzôa's heart is in her emerald eyes. She's silent for a moment but then says, "Staring at my plantings and herbs is peaceful. Ships are noisy and dangerous. We'll never truly be safe."

This is true. "Our enemies could be someone else on the boat, any soldier who wants to be king. It could be nature. A hurricane could sink us."

"Hurricanes aren't until June." Lizzôa's chuckle eases the tightness in my chest. "We have a good number of months to go. It's barely March."

I lift her hand to my mouth. I put a kiss to each finger to prove that nothing has changed between us.

"Jacquotte, I've made arrangements to ensure the property is kept up all year, for several years. We'll not have to rush back."

If she thinks I'll rush through being a buccaneer, she's wrong. I will be one until I can't. I have to fulfill my destiny. "The others will be here soon, and then we will be off in a canoe to join the HMS *Florence*."

I draw Lizzôa into my arms and glance up at the unveiled mountains that we never had the time to climb. That will be the first thing we do, when we retire and return to Petit-Goâve. Then I, with my love and my brother, will shout to the whole world, *I, Jacquotte Delahaye, have taken my destiny into my own hands.*

* * *

At the edge of Lizzôa's land, the river seems incredibly calm. The five of us—Celia, Bahati, Wulf, Lizzôa, and I—gather to board the canoe. I concentrate on the details of our cover story as Lizzôa recites them.

"I am a retired British physician," she says. "A surgeon is what they'll call me." Her soft voice is brusquer. It sounds clipped and strong as she explains. "I've herbs and wads of cotton and other medicines. One of the herbs, shepherd's purse, can lessen or stop menses. The cotton will be used if it can't."

My menses ceased months ago. I thought it was because I've grown too thin. But now I wonder if the tea Lizzôa gave me every night has helped.

Wulf laughs. "The hard labor I do has made me barren."

Bahati nods. "My season for uncleanness is long gone. My sister wishes me a speedy return and has given me a list of what to get her twin daughters. She knows that piracy is good for our future."

Chilango looks nervous. "I . . . ah . . . My menses are light. I tie rags about me."

"You'll begin chewing a little of these dried flowers. And you will stick cotton wads up into the womb. It's more comfortable than wool and won't itch. It's most effective. But a sailor's diet and the labor will soon make the problem rare."

Lizzôa's resourcefulness and knowledge are unmatched.

"We won't be able to plead the belly if we're caught." Bahati's laughter is dark. "The Brits hang women pirates. They wait a few months to be sure there's no child."

Lizzôa waves her hand dismissively. "We must try to sleep together or close by. Hammocks are shared, but a close group will be less likely to be discovered." She closes up her leather satchel. "I speak multiple languages. I know Jacques does too. Look to us if there's confusion. But the quicker you learn more than French, the better off you will be."

She hangs her satchel across her shoulder and holds a telescope. My rapier sling loops across my chest. I sharpened and oiled my rapier. Bahati strapped two flintlocks to her back. She pushes the canoe into the water. With a tether, I hold the boat steady and let everyone climb aboard. Once they paddle and start it moving, I chase it and climb into the rear position. We sail along the tributary heading to the bay of Petit-Goâve.

"You any good with that thing?" Celia taps my sling. "I've known Lizzôa forever, Bahati for three years and heard of Wulf. You're new. I want to know what to expect."

"My rapier will defend us all tonight," I say. "Even those who doubt me."

My bold words make Bahati laugh. The slap of our paddles grows louder as we row against the current. The air feels hot and sticky the closer we get to the bay.

We're a good distance from Lizzôa's land now. The outlines of the jungle and mountains give way to the flicker of torches. The buildings of the lively shore loom. I think I see the Tree Tavern. "I wonder how many of the HMS *Florence*'s crew are in there begging for something to eat?"

"Hopefully a good many, Jacques." Lizzôa aims her scope toward the mountains. "The fewer people on board, the better our chances the mutineers will let us join."

Our craft becomes unsteady, rocking with the fast waves. I use my paddle to steer like a rudder, holding it, angling it at the back like I'm controlling the ketch. "Keep paddling. Keep the rhythm steady."

I shift us to the right. We float for a moment. With everyone following my orders, the rocking calms. "Smooth and easy," I say, "and we might just live."

"Good boy, Jacques," Wulf's voice booms. "You just guided us around some rapids."

Then she peers at Lizzôa. "You're going to miss this place."

"I'll be back with a fortune. And I'll live a quiet life of luxury. I'll have my silks, my teas, and my quiet days again." Lizzôa's gaze makes my cheeks warm. "And a family."

The last part is a whisper meant for me. It means everything.

"I won't miss this place." Celia grunts and clicks her teeth as if she's spitting. "I want a chance to get the bastards that enslaved my family in Veracruz. That and gold."

Bahati chuckles. "You better put those grievances away, Chilango. We're about to join a boat of people who'll commit the exact same acts for money. But don't worry. Since you have your menses, you, like your mother, will mate with one of them and mix more of that blood and procreate and make creatures lighter than Jacques. Another generation, they'll blend into whiteness. Then your children will become the enslavers. The circle of life for colonizers."

"So why do you want this?" Celia stops paddling and squints at Bahati. "You want gold, or you want to be an enslaver too?"

Bahati's paddle slaps water, kicking up a spray. I think she wants to splash Celia but changes her mind. "I want to be an equal. I want to come back richer than anyone. My family is here in Petit-Goâve. Wealth will keep us safe and free."

"Focus, everyone." Lizzôa's voice sounds strong. My doubts about my love surviving diminish. "We are about to pass Pointe Antoine. We'll be in its direct line of fire."

Looking up into the hills, Wulf says, "The fort will rain grapeshot down on us if they see a mysterious craft too close to the HMS *Florence*."

"Then we must be as silent as possible." Bahati shows us all how to stroke the water.

We settle and take greater effort to paddle with no noise.

I keep looking back toward the cannons. A rapier or a flintlock can do nothing to protect our canoe from heavy fire. In a way, this is how we've all lived our lives—silent, unprotected, disguised, and hiding in plain sight.

In an hour or more, I see the silhouettes of the three masts. The poles rise into the night sky. I make out the extended arm of the bowsprit. No jib sail or any others hang from the masts, just spars. The halyards are slack, the lines probably wrapped about cleats. A few lanterns hang off the deck or the arm of a sailor. We're almost there.

Twenty-Eight

1681. The Bay of Petit-Goâve, Hispaniola

Lizzôa motions for us to stop. "On Pointe Antoine's mountain battery, men with lit torches, a patrol." She curses and puts down the scope. "They know. Someone has made them wary. We must assume that all the forts and batteries around Petit-Goâve have soldiers on alert."

"That could be dozens of cannons," Celia says. "They'll rip us to pieces."

"It's the twenty-four pounder of Pointe Antoine that we must fear." Lizzôa sighs.

Wulf offers a low curse. "The twenty-four pounder has the range to sink us until we flee the bay and are out to sea."

That means we have a very short time for the mutiny to succeed and to escape with the HMS *Florence*.

My heart beats harder. The crucifix knocks against my bosom.

"Don't panic." Lizzôa's voice remains calm. "I've studied and planned. We can't wait for the men on board to begin it. We give the code word, and let human nature do the rest."

No one is better at getting secrets than Lizzôa. No one would know how to use them better either.

I straighten up and urge everyone to keep paddling. Slipping a hand to my chest, to my crucifix, Lizzôa settles the cross for me. “We’re so close to having it all. Let’s have it all.”

Those are words to fight for. “Lizzôa, Bahati, look for shifts in the current. We need to know where the sandbars are. We can’t maroon ourselves tonight.”

Celia, Wulf and I, power the canoe. Slow and steady, we mark the sixteen-foot depth of the bay. I’ve studied the depth maps Lizzôa has.

The breeze picks up. The smell of fish and salt covers us. The full outline of the frigate is ahead. The hull of the HMS *Florence* has forty-six guns. I counted them every day I labored at the docks. To be so close to this fourth-rate vessel makes my blood boil.

The wind stirs and brings a baritone voice’s sea shanty to us . . .

Sailor, stop dreaming.
Don’t think about home.
Sailor, wind and waves
Call you out.
Your home is the sea.

The last thing I expect is a man singing about dreams. This is rhythm. This is home. It’s a sign. Lizzôa passes me the scope. “No lookout in the crow’s nest on the mainmast. Don’t see much activity at all.”

Peering up to the deck of the HMS *Florence*, I see a few sailors pacing. “There are three on the bow. They’ll spot us any minute.”

Lizzôa taps Bahati to give the mutiny signal.

In a deep voice, she says, “The sailmaker is out of cloth. You’ll have to get underway.”

The English words sound right, even close to their accent. Didn’t know Bahati was such a mimic.

One of the lookouts comes close to the rail. A hand cupped to his face, and in low tones he asks, “Is the sailmaker here? I thought the drunk was onshore till tomorrow.”

Bahati answers, "The brave make our sails ready now, for our home is the sea. And the batteries are on alert. The hills say now."

The silence that follows is maddening. It's now or never.

A clap sounds.

Sparks of flints scatter like fireflies. "Then we should get the sail-maker more cloth." This time the answer is as strong. Boots begin to pound. More lanterns light.

Men fill the deck.

Someone shouts, "Now!"

Another yells, "Who's with me?"

Bahati raises her flintlock. Lizzôa, Celia, Wulf, and I paddle backward toward the stern. Closing toward the quarterdeck, we hear the battle—the fighting, the killing.

We're quiet waiting for the right moment to join the mutiny.

* * *

The clink of swords. The shouts of sailors. The screams of death. The fight is intense. I have Lizzôa's scope, and I witness chaos on the HMS *Florence.* So far, the batteries and forts seem asleep, but the minute they suspect a mutiny, they'll awaken. The frigate may be sunk before it makes it out to sea.

"Steady, men." Lizzôa's words are soft, but they're a rallying cry. We are men. We are about to become buccaneers, if the crew wrests control from their British commanders.

"Any movement from the batteries, Delahaye?"

"None, but fog is rolling in. It will be to our advantage."

"If we can't see them," Wulf says, "they can't see us."

"The fight is heaviest at the waist of the *Florence.*" Bahati's tone sounds tense. "The battle is evenly split between the fore and aft sections."

"That's where the sailors do most of their work. They'll battle there until one side overwhelms and wins." Lizzôa glances through the scope. "Right now, I can't predict who that will be."

Swords clang. Jeers reverberate. My quick glance at Celia reveals shaking hands.

"Grasp the oar tighter," I say. "Let it ground you."

She does. "What do we do if this fails? What do we do?"

I shrug. I've done too much to turn back. Who knows when another opportunity would arrive.

A flash. The boom of an explosion. The air turns ferrous.

Splash. Jeers.

A voice cries out. "Lower the pinnace!"

Lizzôa takes the scope, and I pull my rapier and get ready.

Lights begin to flicker. The warm glow of fire casts brightness on pale and tanned faces.

A man jumps onto our canoe. "You're part of the mut—"

My rapier goes through his gut. His flesh slices easily, like the belly of a wild boar. My movement is all instinct. I draw my weapon out of the man and ease him into the water. This, the way my rapier slips smoothly in and out of his flesh, confirms how to target the enemy.

"Guess Jacques knows a thing or two about that pointy stick. Aye, Celia?" Wulf makes a joke of it, but the newest woman of my acquaintance nods.

"Oui."

Lizzôa motions us to paddle closer. "I see a rope dangling from the quarterdeck. Move nearer to the stern. This is our way onto the frigate."

We paddle to the rear of the ship and hear groans from sailors working on the pinnace. The boat's strapped on its side near the quarterdeck, and the capstan, a big, grooved drum with ropes, is being hooked to it. Pure brute effort lifts the large boat over the side of the ship. Three men turn a handle and begin lowering the pinnace into the bay.

Bahati catches the dangling rope and holds it steady. I climb first. Once on board I lift my rapier. I'm to provide the signal that the mutiny has succeeded. I peer around the corner to the quarterdeck.

Men with fine uniforms, fancy doublets and hats, are backed into a corner. One sailor shouts at them. "Where's the second in command?"

The English jars my ears, but I understand it. My gaze is pinned to his sword. He waves it in the faces of the fancy men.

"I'm the commander," the fanciest fellow says. "Let us go. We'll overcome this adversity. Don't do this, lads."

"Lads?" Another sailor steps up. He fingers the fine jacket and takes the feathered hat. "This will settle the bill for my pay. We were promised wages for our families. We'll take no more lies."

The gathered men in uniforms murmur. Their pale skin flickers in the torchlight. More men choose to surrender to the mutineers. The uprising is winning.

The cranking of the pinnace is near complete. I glide back to the stern, balancing along the tight gangplank, and wave to my team. "Come to our new home."

Everyone takes turns to climb. Dangling, heaving, even slipping a little, everyone makes it, though I had to stretch and pull Lizzôa up a third of the way. She takes a glance at the main deck, holding a finger up, waiting, counting, then jabbing the air. I know that signal. I cut away the rope tied to our canoe.

At the same moment, the pinnace splashes into the water.

"When they set the officers off in the pinnace, we join the crew." Lizzôa points to Bahati to get flintlocks ready for Celia and Wulf. Then Lizzôa turns to me. "The sails must go up as quickly as possible. We won't have a moment to lose. Don't let the ship be sunk before we flee the bowl of Petit-Goâve."

This is the moment of a lifetime. We stand at the ready, waiting, watching the canoe, our last chance to retreat, drift away.

Twenty-Nine

1681. The Bay of Petit-Goâve, Hispaniola

The winds ramp up again. They blow southwest, moving my hair in the direction of the sea. That's favorable for the frigate's escape. My frizzed curls blow in my eyes. I flick strands away and watch as the last of the men loyal to the British Commander climb down ropes into the waiting pinnace.

Lizzôa jerks her head toward the cabin on the quarterdeck. "Someone's hiding in the stores."

I glance at Bahati. As Wulf readies to fire to protect us, Bahati and I move in rhythm, like our work at the docks. We head to the place stocked with provisions and possibly explosive powder. The door is cracked open a sliver. I smell sweat.

"I'll show myself and knock. If I'm not killed, or even if I am, grab the person inside. But don't shoot. If there's powder in that room, it will burn."

I glance back at Celia. She's looking out for Lizzôa. She looks stronger, attentive. She may just be able to do this.

With her finger on the trigger, Wulf signals she's ready.

The sailors and the mutineers on deck are preoccupied. I wait for Lizzôa's signal, and she flicks her hand.

I hit the door, then I drop low. A gun blasts, ripping through the wood, sending splinters everywhere.

Bahati pushes through. She grabs a man in a fancy uniform and drags a flintlock away from him.

Mutineers run toward us, but we have the man in in our custody.

"Who in the devil are you?" an older gent demands. He wears a sailor's uniform and has graying blond hair and a beard.

"Does it matter?" I say. "I think we found your second lieutenant."

The prisoner laughs but stops when Bahati chokes him with her forearm.

Lizzôa steps in front of us. "My man misspoke. But we captured Boatswain Hackney, the man responsible for your stores. He's also responsible for informing the commanders in the French forts of a possible mutiny."

Hackney tries to jerk free. "That's a lie." He looks toward one of the mutineers. "I'm with you, Dender Smith."

Lizzôa doesn't back down. "If that were true, you'd be fighting. Not hiding and protecting the powder."

Celia picks a splinter from my hair and points to the door. "He wasn't trying to help."

"He would've blown you all away with the powder saving the boat for his King George, the one not paying you," Wulf adds and still has her gun raised.

The man who seems to be the head of the mutineers steps close. "Hackney, I thought you were with us?"

"He's not. Or he wouldn't have mouthed off in the ville . . . in town." Calm, cool Lizzôa moves in for the kill. "Look, there's not much time. The forts are active."

I point. "See the lights in the battery. They're being lit. They are on alert. When the fog lifts, they will realize what's happening."

Men behind Dender start grousing.

"Give up, mutineers! Those lads are speaking the truth," a fellow yells up from the pinnace. "Every battery will fire on the HMS

Florence if she mutinies. We can work through this. The pay is coming, Smith, believe me."

The headman leaves us and goes to the rail. "Nickels, I told you I don't believe you." He's pointing and pounding his fist on the rail. "We've heard these lies for months. We came on board for money. Haven't seen a pence. We don't have to wait anymore. With me as captain, we can go out onto the seas and get rich."

"The man talking about the forts is right. Ensign Dender Smith, you try to sail, they'll cut down the *Florence*."

Hackney hits Bahati and wiggles free, but I catch him with the point of my blade.

"Captain Dender Smith." Lizzôa steps toward him. "They've probably noticed that the pinnace is lowered. They just don't know if you're merely taking a party to the taverns and stews."

Hackney laughs. "The coloreds and the Blacks come here with all this talk. But we don't have money." He turns and leers at us, especially me and Bahati. "Well, all have a say here. Somehow, they've snuck on board to cause havoc. Maybe they're here to steal. They've come to take our deposit on our future. They'll ruin our prosperity."

With a shake of her head, Bahati's calm breaks. She charges Hackney, punches him, while Celia, Wulf, and I force everyone else back.

With one hand on his beefy neck, the other on the man's wiggling leg, Bahati has him in the air, spins him, and drops him into the bay. "I just made a deposit into the bay. I choose Captain Dender Smith. I am on Captain Smith's side."

Lizzôa's face remains calm, her voice reasonable. "Captain, add us to your crew. You're down men. We come with knowledge and skills."

Lizzôa walks to the mainmast. "Let's get the sails extended, cut the pinnace away, and go the sea. We have to string these fast and get out of here before they can aim their guns."

Smith rubs his chin, but it's obvious the others on deck want us to join their side.

Hackney swims to join the pinnace. The men aboard pull the soggy soul into their boat.

Smith turns to his mutineers. "What say you?"

Lizzôa bows with a dip of the chin. "We came here to become buccaneers. We'll not fail you."

"Give up!" Nickels yells from the pinnace. "Don't do this, lads!"

A man comes up to Smith, whispers in his ear. This one is young with brown hair. I can't hear what he says, but he's passionate. Then he turns to the crew and raises his voice. "Our new captain, Dender Smith, should make the decision."

Smith pats the man on the back. "Zuth Danseker, good man. Where's our helmsman?"

Danseker shrugs. "I haven't seen him for a while. Maybe he's not loyal."

"But he has to navigate." Smith's face burns like fire. "How—"

"Get ready to steer, Jacques." Bahati looks at me and then the rest of the crew. "He has the experience we need. What say you, Captain Smith?"

The man wipes sweat from his brow but nods. "Do it. Get the *Florence* out of here."

"Let's get the sails up. All of them," I say. "We need the mainsail first." I put my rapier in its sling and head to the mainmast.

Men start moving. Colored, ebony, and Blanc hands get the largest square sail unfurled. Quickly attaching the halyard, I make sure these ropes are tight. Pulling and pulling, we get the mainsail up and fully extended.

Yelling from the pinnace gets louder. The men on the pinnace are starting to climb the ropes tethering the small ship to the frigate.

It's a race to see who wins—the mutineers raising the sails or the sailors bringing a renewed fight to retake the ship.

* * *

Thicker fog rolls in from the sea. The humid air feels dense. I uncoil the halyards for the next sail we must raise. Smith goes to Bahati and Wulf then points to Danseker to help. They cut the pinnace free.

Every remaining person joins me pulling on ropes. We continue our coordinated dance of lifting the foremast, setting the fore course and topsails in place.

With halyards tight, we hoist the topgallants—three sails on the three masts. Our rhythm is smooth. The men that stayed are true sailors. Their experience shows.

The sails billow, catching the wind.

I stand in front of the mainmast with my back to the stern. My hands claim the whipstaff. I look to Lizzôa, but this time I give the directions. "Raise the anchor. I'll tell you how to trim the sails."

I hear splashing. Water slaps the frigate as the anchor gives way. Then we move. I motion to tack the sails slightly until the *Florence* slips faster toward the open sea.

"Stop!" The old captain and his twenty men stuffed into the pinnace scream at us. They're trying to signal the forts. Bahati shoots a hole in the boat.

The men stop yelling and start bailing.

"Nickels," Captain Smith shouts, "I do hope you make it to shore."

Smith strides around to me, his boot tapping near the whipstaff. "You got this, son?"

A cannon booms. Smith's face changes. His jaws tighten as he looks toward the forts.

I exhale like this is my first breath tonight. I tweak the whipstaff and feel the vibration of the rudder beneath us. This is freedom.

"We did it," I whisper.

"Non, not yet," Lizzôa says, her eye again glued to the scope. She turns in the direction of the frightening battery with the twenty-four pounder. "Not until we are in the sea."

The fog splits with fiery flashes. *Boom.* More of the cannons begin to fire. The air smells of gunpowder.

Boom. Boom. Boom. Splash.

Sails billow. *Boom.* I'm almost blinded by the brightness of the cannon blast, but I aim the prow at the curtain of blackness, where the sea and the sky meet. I turn the whipstaff to harness all the wind.

Boom.

Iron whips through the air. You can hear, feel it cutting its way to us. Smoldering grapeshot hits the mizzenmast's topgallant. The sail smokes, but the fire is just at the tip. The flapping of the canvas extinguishes the flame like blowing on a candle.

Boom. Boom. Boom. Splash. This blast falls short. Nothing can reach us. The HMS *Florence* has escaped into the sea! My smile is so wide it hurts. My praise is so loud I feel my lungs burst. "We made it!"

"We're out!" Danseker yells. "We are out of the bay!"

Cheers go up. Others jump with pure joy.

Smith taps my shoulder. "Well done, son. Who taught you to sail like that?"

"I sailed under Captain Michel Le Basque and Captain Jean, but my first teacher was Captain Uzoamaka." She showed me how to keep my eyes open and live outside the basket, that one where the world of men with power put women and outsiders. "I was born for this day."

He nods like he knows these names. "Head us to Jamaica. Port Royal. I've friends there. We'll need to get some more men. It's a good place to hide when the Brits try to find us."

"This is the calm before the storm." Lizzôa points to constellations. "That's Centaurus. We follow that and head to a latitude of 18° and a longitude of 77°."

Why does it feel like Lizzôa is speaking a completely different language? "I think you need to translate."

A smile peeks out. "Just wanted to remind Monsieur Whipstaff, he still needs me." She shows me a map. "You will follow the coastline of Hispaniola heading to the southwest tip. From there, we'll catch the Windward Channel. Then we'll look for docks. Smith should be able to give you more help."

Looks like I'm going to have to learn quadrants or be able to sail by the stars.

"The first order will be to recruit an experienced navigator." Lizzôa folds up the map. "But you can do this, Jacques. I wouldn't risk it all if I didn't believe in you."

I want to smile again, but I keep my eyes on the sea.

Men go into the stores where we found Hackney. Bahati, Wulf, and Celia stay close to me and Lizzôa.

Danseker and Smith chat away. I don't like how Danseker looks at Bahati and Lizzôa. We'll have to sleep with one eye open. Makes no difference for me tonight. I'm on watch, looking for a star to follow as I sail a frigate, a fourth-rate ship along the Hispaniola coastline.

Thirty

1681. The Caribbean Sea

The most terrifying, wonderful moment of my life has come true. I've stood all day at the whipstaff commanding the mutinied frigate HMS *Florence*. At last, I'm a buccaneer.

The glorious sun that I've clung to since daybreak begins to lower. There are about three more hours of light. Waves slap the bow, lurching over the rail, sending foamy water and seaweed onto the deck.

I had the topgallant furled to slow our speed. Our new captain didn't fight me on it. A glance to the left shows him sleeping in the old captain's cabin. Danseker is in charge right now, but he knows nothing of navigation. I'd overheard he was the former bosun, the man in charge of the deck crew and maintenance of the *Florence*.

He's in the storeroom with Lizzôa, counting munitions. At least with Lizzôa, we'll know what we have and what we'll need to acquire in Port Royal.

In the latest patch of water, the spray reaches as high as the rails. The ship weighs at least five hundred tons. That's equal to forty of the barges I loaded, stacked on top of each other. One wrong move of the whipstaff, and I could sail this beast to the middle of nowhere or topple her by choosing the wrong direction to counter the waves. Betwixt my palms lies the power to sink us and drown everyone's hopes.

Breathe, Jacques, breathe. Thinking of the responsibility makes my fingers tremble.

Celia comes over. "Twenty men left, not counting us or the captain."

"Not enough to man all the cannons and sails. We need sixty for a full crew."

"They weren't at that number before."

The lack of pay made the crew abandon the *Florence.* "The ones who stayed want adventure. Stay alert, Chilango. Check the ropes along the prow."

The sails of the mainmast whip overhead, casting long shadows over me, a woman in hiding, steering a fourth-rate frigate. I must grow into this job. Forty-six guns of power, and I revel at what we've done.

The *Florence* shimmies again. The vibrations creak the boards beneath my feet. My breath falters. Then I see the sun slip lower. Once it dips into the sea, all sense of direction dissolves. This grand attempt at being pirates could end in one day because of me.

Danseker and Lizzôa step out of the stores.

"We'll need more water, foodstuff, and powder." Lizzôa's voice is loud. Her usual soft tone is gone.

Bahati leaves Wulf at the mizzenmast and pounds over to me. Presenting me my rapier, she says, "All clean and sharpened, Jacques. Good as new to kill again."

Too afraid to take my hands from the whipstaff, I dip my chin. "Merci. Can you put it in my sling?"

I straighten and look Bahati in the eyes. "I'm scared. I can't read the sky. I don't know where Jamaica is. The moment Hispaniola's curve leaves view—"

Bahati pries my stiff fingers from the whipstaff. She fights to take hold of it. "Walk around. Look at the waters. You did good so far."

"It was the mountains. The range all along the southwestern bottom of the island guided me here."

"You guided us into the Windward Channel," Bahati says, "It's time to get out and go south. We'll run right into Jamaica."

Realizing I have someone else to trust, I let go and flex my hands. "You know a great deal more about sailing than you let on."

"I know some things. Change the sails to tack out of the channel." She smiles at me. It's rare and brief. "We will be arriving in Port Royal after sunset."

"We will?" My voice sounds light.

"You will see the land, the Blue Mountains and hills." A second smile lights her face. "See, not so hard, Jacques, to depend on someone."

"I'll yield to your wisdom and experience any time."

"Aye, Jacques. Together, our strengths are greater." Bahati begins to release the whipstaff, and I put my hands to it—a perfect exchange.

Thirty-One

1681. The Caribbean Sea

Two hours of fear fade with the first sighting of clouds. Puffy and white against the orange and red of the sky, they make my heart race with joy. We've sailed in the right direction.

In another hour, right before the light fades, I see stretched vertical clouds, similar to the ones that I've seen from the hills of Tortuga, the ones that veiled the Chaîne de la Selle.

I whisper a prayer to Maman, to her gods, even to Père's and Josiah's monk's too. The sight of clouds confirms what Bahati said. The outline of Jamaica becomes clear. "Land ho."

My celebration ends as the captain gathers the crew to the waist of the frigate. Captain Smith gestures to silence everyone. Below the billowing sails, he says, "We'll be in Port Royal in a matter of hours. It's time to make a vow to our manifesto. Any man who doesn't agree can leave the ship and find your way in Jamaica. There will be no ill will."

Heads nod. A man says, "Get to it."

Captain Smith looks left and then to the right. His gaze falls on Celia. "Does everyone here speak English?"

People are affirming, as Lizzôa steps forward. "Sir, as I've been discussing with Danseker, we'll need to increase the crew. That means buccaneers from all over the Caribbean. I speak all the essential languages—French, Spanish, Portuguese, and English. I can translate if it's needed." Lizzôa's tone is a polished version of the captain's brusque voice. She sounds like a Brit.

The captain looks at Danseker, who says, "Yes sir. Lizzôa is right. We'll need a full crew. We can't just have everyone from Bristol."

Chuckles resound. Wulf laughs the loudest. "Or Rotterdam of the Dutch Republic."

The captain casts a look in her direction, then shrugs and adjusts his hat, black with satiny ribbons. "Very well, but our first act is to rename the ship. I'm partial to the constellations."

"Little Dipper!" someone in the back yells, drawing many laughs.

"What about Mawu-Lisa? Goddess of the Sun and Moon." Bahati stands behind me. Her voice sounds deep. "Those are good stars."

"Mawa? What?" The captain looks confused. "I was thinking *Canopus*. It's the second-brightest star in the sky. It's one of the brightest that can be seen in the Caribbean." He pivots and glances directly at Bahati. "It will guide us to Africa and many other places. The *Canopus*."

Bahati seems pleased, but I'm fretful. The only reason pirates sail to Africa is to capture and steal people. Does Captain Smith intend to participate in the slave trade?

Smith waves his hat. The ribbons flap in the breeze. "Signify that you want the new name to be the *Canopus* by saying aye."

A round of hoots and stomps thunder. Even I agree.

"Good." Smith claps and says, "Very good. Now—the old ship divided the booty with shares for the crown, for the ship, two shares to the captain, share and a half to the paymaster, et cetera, et cetera. I propose, for the *Canopus*, four shares for the ship's stores, two shares for me as the captain, one share for everyone else."

"That sounds fair," Danseker says and holds up his pencil and ledger. "The ship will be in need of repairs, especially as we engage in battles. And the captain will be hanged if we're caught. I think it fair."

Nods and ayes all around, again. For a moment, I think of Michel and all the treasure his father collected for the ship. "Maybe the ship's portions should be allocated after every fight."

Everyone stares at me, but the captain agrees and says, "That is a good notion, as long as every man understands that the provision for the *Canopus* can go up too."

No one responds, and the captain moves closer to the crew on the other side of the waist. "When we have votes, every man has a vote. If anyone defrauds our company by stealing, I shall personally maroon them."

Bahati's full lips break into a grin. "I've missed this."

Wulf, who's stepped closer to her, nods too.

"Hold up your hand if you can read."

A few men do, as do Lizzôa, Wulf, and I.

"The candles shall be put out at night. No leeway in that. A man must get his rest. Tonight, we sleep below. Get a mate for the hammocks."

A skinny fellow in the rear yells, "But there's plenty of room to spread out now."

"But there won't be for long," the captain says. "I'll use my old contacts. Samuel Axe will have people ready to join. These hammocks will be full soon enough."

"Lastly, the drinkers," he says. "Every one of you raise your hand, or I'll know you are lying."

Everyone lifts up an arm. One fellow, a portly man, stands with both hands high.

"If any man desires to drink after eight, they shall sit up on the open deck out here beneath the stars with no lights." This causes a little grumbling but no direct complaint. Then he waves Danseker forward. "This is Zuth Danseker. He's my first mate."

Danseker, with his big, muscled arms, comes forward. "Honored to serve you, captain."

This is no surprise. He's been acting as if he's in charge. Lizzôa slips beside me. The movement is so quiet I don't notice until I hear her whisper, "Danseker is a Dutch last name, but the first name I can't place."

"Take all the names of our crew, first mate," Smith says to his number two. "Assign them positions and bunk but let them partner up. I don't want no squabbles. We'll save that for the fighting. Lastly, I need everyone to hear me. No young boy or woman is allowed to be amongst us. Any man found seducing a woman and convincing her to disguise herself shall suffer death. They will be marooned. Is that clear?"

As Danseker begins to form a line of the crew, the captain turns and heads to me. "What's your name and your age, boy?"

"Jacques and twenty-two, sir."

"Good. You have a soft look about you, Red."

I keep my breath slow and even. "I have a baby's face, but I kill with an angel's touch. People do badly, underestimating me."

The captain claps my shoulder. "Just get us to Port Royal, lad."

"Aye-aye, captain." With one hand on the whipstaff, I raise the other and salute. "Lizzôa, I've known you the longest." My tone is manly and forward. "Go sign us up to bunk together."

Brow raised, smothering a smirk, my love goes to the line.

Bahati points to Celia and Wulf to do the same. Then glances at Smith. "Where do we sail to, captain, after Port Royal?"

Fanning himself with his fancy hat, the captain says, "Well, we need to avoid Hispaniola. News of our theft will be all over the island. We're not ready to sail to the East. We don't want to get caught in France's war with Algiers, though Zuth wants to head that way."

He paces a little. "We'll need to stay in these seas until we build up strength and have attacked a few vessels. I don't know what we are working with. If we happen upon a Spanish galleon, we need to be ready to meet her in battle."

Bahati's face settles into a peaceful grin. "I've heard a few men talking about attacking the Mughals."

Smith pops his hat on his head again. "We may go fight the

Mughals. It would put us out of range of the Brits. I hear their King Aurangzeb has too much wealth."

The way the captain looks at me and Bahati, he's already counting the number of pewter mugs selling us would buy.

I take my hands from the whipstaff. The deck creaks as the sails fight the drifting.

"What are you doing, Delahaye?"

"I need to know if everyone is equal on this ship." It's not wise to threaten my new captain, but I'm not risking my life on a Blanc who'll turn on us when we can't defend ourselves. "I don't want to be part of a slaver crew."

"No slaving. I've never dealt in chattel. I see no reason to do so now." He turns to the lined-up men. "I need a vote. No dealing in chattel. Say aye."

Celia's yell is the loudest, but the ayes outweigh the silence anyway. I guess that's all we can hope for, for now.

"Now take us to Port Royal." Smith starts to leave, but then says, "You're the new helmsman. Bahati is the quartermaster."

He steps away. The shadow of those flapping feathers lengthens. The second in command keeps taking names, and I bring the new *Canopus* back under control.

The sun slips into the water. Its last gasp sends orange and pink into the sky. I can still make out the outline of Jamaica's mountains. Bahati stays with me. We have new positions and an alleged vote of confidence from the crew and captain that the ship won't deal in chattel. Yet, as I glance at my friend, and she at me, we wonder which truth will be revealed first—that we aren't men or that Blanc men will always trade slaves when there's money to be made.

Thirty-Two

1681. Port Royal. Jamaica

As the *Canopus* follows the curves and mists of Jamaica, we sail for four more hours in the dark.

"Jacques, you still awake?" Bahati taps me. "You've been on your feet all day."

"I can make it until we set anchor. Then I'll sleep."

"You think so? We're sailing a stolen British frigate within firing distance of the Brit's Fort Charles."

I glare at Bahati and assume I've been punched. "Did we risk everything for only a day and a half as pirates?"

"Don't be glum. Danseker has the Union Jack flying off the stern."

Looking over my shoulder, I see the red, white, and blue crosses flapping. I must be exhausted, for I didn't notice it being raised off the stern on the ensign staff. "This foolishness is getting worse."

Bahati sits on the deck boards. She crosses her long legs and holds her hands together. I hear a whisper that sounds familiar. The song is just beyond my ears but I feel the rhythm in my chest. I let her worship. I've never seen her do this in the months we worked together. I know it's sacred.

Turning my face to the sky, I focus on the stars. Over Port Royal are three bright stars, Orion's hunting belt. A little way up is a red-burning star. That's the warrior's sword or maybe the shoulder or both. Below all this is a tiny blue star, glowing and blinking at me. That's Orion's foot.

I suppose it grounds the hunter.

A few of the crew are near the bow, drinking. Lizzôa has gone below to sleep in our assigned hammock. The captain and Dansेker went off to talk in the captain's cabin.

Everything has calmed; even the waters have settled.

Bahati points off the bow to the lights burning in the distance and hands me Lizzôa's scope. "Torches illuminating the bastions of Fort Charles."

Bastions? I stretch my tired eyes. The fort spreads the width of my hand, as if I can pluck it from the shore. I look through the scope and see torches illuminating a twenty-four pounder. "The fort's thick walls will never be breached by our guns. There's probably stockpiles of iron balls waiting to rip the *Canopus* to shreds."

"They're not expecting a stolen ship to come to a fortified port."

It's a twisted logic, but possibly true. I refocus through the lens. For a brief moment I find a pole, a tall pole, like the mast of a ship. I can't breathe.

Right under Orion's Belt is a house on the water with a pole. It could be blue. It could be blue and be that other life—where I am the wife of a retired filibuster, caring for children and a beloved brother.

"Jacques, you'll slip us in easily . . . Jacques?" Bahati's calm voice, praising me, speaking it into existence, can't quite shake me from seeing my past, and what could've been.

Her words switch to my mother's tongue. I don't know what she says, but I feel the blessing. I remember that I am where I am supposed to be.

"Jacques, why are you crying?"

I wipe my face on my sleeve. "Someone promised to take me to Port Royal. But then he went to fight the Mughals. He and his filibusters never came back."

Bahati is silent for a moment. Then she says, "Well, you've come to Port Royal on your own. That's something."

Oui. I'm grateful for that. Grateful that Lizzôa is below, with me on this journey. Lizzôa will not leave me. "Get ready to drop anchor, Bahati. We'll get close enough for the captain to go ashore."

"Smith's no fool. He'll send Danseker or Lizzôa to do his bidding, and not leave the ship until he feels we're all united." She points to the men drinking and lying along the bow. "They've joined because they're tired of no money and lies. Until Smith has their confidence, he'd be a fool to step off this ship."

My gaze sharpens as I count the number of vessels anchored at the docks and the frigates lining up near a sandbar. "We'll take our place with the other frigates. Go get our captain. Ready the riggers. We're here."

"Yes, Helmsman Delahaye." She salutes and heads to Smith's quarters. Soon, men are running. Chain drags off the stern. Ropes sing and zip. Sales furl as the anchor digs into the seafloor.

* * *

Port Royal during the day is a sight to behold. Morning adds hues of warm reds and oranges to everything, including the sparkling water. The sun will soon beat down on my weary brow. Alert, but fatigued, I yawn at my post, waiting. Can't shake the feeling that everyone on board could be attacked.

So I stand guard at the whipstaff. My eyes examine every rope of the halyards and rigging. If we're struck, I'll get this ship underway and out of the fort's range as fast as I can.

But how could I do all this if Lizzôa is not on board?

Can't leave her. We're in this together.

Wulf comes to me. I see she has questions, even before her mouth moves. "So you sailed with Captain Le Basque. How come you didn't say anything? I thought this was your first time."

The way she stands is directly in my view of Michel's flagpole. "It is my first time. But I was in a worse state. I was married to him."

Her light blue eyes grow wide. "That's something to mention."

I want to slap the whipstaff for speaking it, but how could I not? Here, of all places? "It happened. He left. Never came back. Never heard from him again."

"Still mad at him for doing what you're doing now and having the misfortune of dying."

Mad at him? No. Maybe. I shrug my shoulders, then work the knot forming in my muscles along my neck. "I have what I need now. I have love and adventure. Hopefully, I'll be able to say that when the day ends."

She turns from me and glances at Port Royal. "I was in a matelotage once."

Now, it is my turn to look at her like she's spinning lies. "I don't understand. You and Margaret—"

"When you're a smaller man on the crew, it's better to have a mate than be a target. We all say we're equals here. This is a damned meritocracy. But this utopia is nothing more than winner-take-all at sea. The strongest survive, and I found safety in Frederick. I kept him safe, too."

"Did he know your true identity?"

"He might've. He might not have. Most folks don't care on a boat as long as you can pull your weight and fight."

She's silent for a moment as some crew pass by. Then she says, "I must thank Frederick because that's how I met Margaret. Before he died in a battle, we went to Petit-Goâve to share a whore. He went first, and I was supposed to take what was left. Margaret was special. She'd seen a lot. She'd been hurt a lot. We struck up a friendship. She kept my secret. Then, she became a reason to belong. I'm devoted to her. I'll always be devoted to her."

"Then why keep risking everything and being away from her?"

Wulf grins for a moment, then sobers. "She knows I like adventure. She'll never take that from me. That's why I love her so much. But one day, I'm gonna know when it's time to hang it all up. And when that comes, I will be her devoted servant."

This old salt is saying all this for a reason. "You're telling me to stop, now? We just got started."

"Lizzôa is here only for you. Just wanted to let you know how special that is."

Wulf walks away, and I'm left with my thoughts. Lizzôa seemed good now, but there would be a moment when she'd need to return to her garden. I hoped and prayed that it would be the same day for me, for us.

* * *

From my post at the whipstaff, I examine the docks, searching for Lizzôa. Long, sturdy, wide, and gray in color, the pier of Port Royal moors all kinds of boats. The numbers of vessels here is greater than Cayonne by a factor of two, maybe three. At least five frigates and three sloops anchor like the *Canopus* at the sandbar.

Captain Smith comes up to me. This time he's wearing not only the fancy hat but a British officer's blue uniform. I must admit, with his cocky chin raised, he looks the part today. The man even shaved. "Captain, what may I do for you?"

He looks tense. "Well, Fort Charles hasn't sent down the militia. I suppose that's something."

The fort is an impressive sight in the daylight. The high stone walls are decorated with ports for soldiers and guns to peer through. The holes give troops a better ability to defend the harbor.

"Do you see any activity preparing an attack, Delahaye?"

"Sir, I have no worries about the soldiers in the fort. But their big cannons can strike us. I see two twenty-four pounders on the battery to the right of the fort. Either can sink the *Canopus*."

"Let me look."

The captain has followed Lizzôa's advice that the crew dress in the military sloppes. Since we look no different than any other British ship, we will continue to hide in plain sight.

Of all the things I've ever worn, this disguise—these baggy

pants and the tunic that hangs to my knees—feels the oddest. I do keep on Old Jean's hat, no British covering for me. Bahati is below finally getting well-deserved sleep, but only because she'll not easily pass for a sailor under British command. She'll never pretend to be the captain's slave either.

"Any signs of Lizzôa or Danseker?" Smith asks.

"No." I try to keep my voice even, but I'm fearful. Their visit seems to be taking too long.

The captain huffs and lowers the scope from his eye. "Was there any talk of deserting?"

"No, sir. They'll be back."

"They're dawdling, Delahaye. We need water, not a tour report."

"You have no faith in your number two?"

Smith eyes me. A smirk forms on his thin lips, confirming he's wary of Lizzôa.

"Son," he says and hands me the scope, "not sure if you've ever visited Port Royal. Plenty of distractions can be found and paid for with the coins I sent with them to buy water."

Hmm. Maybe he's concerned about Danseker, too. I put the scope to my eye and whip across the dock and beyond. The rues of Port Royal stretch forever. People are everywhere. I see stews and taverns, but my gaze goes to a blue pole, and I groan. "Knowing Lizzôa as I do, if there's a delay, it's for a good reason. The information retrieved will be well worth it."

Smith looks like he wants to say more. Yet for some reason, he won't. He lingers by the whipstaff. Then I realize that he must be hoping to gain some kind of deeper allegiance with me. He needs me. "Captain, who was to be helmsman? You wouldn't have dreamed up a mutiny and then be unable to navigate the boat."

"Binkler. Captain Nickels's second in command. He was supposed to be loyal to me. He could navigate a frigate, even a first-rate ship of the line."

Binkler. At least now I know the name of the second man I'd struck down with my rapier. "Since he's not here, I guess he wasn't so loyal."

Smith nods and clenches his fists at his sides. "It was a blow to my heart. And if we'd waited until the end of the week, or even another twenty-four hours, Nickels might've been better prepared to stop the mutiny. We'd have all been hanged."

That's true. "If you want my allegiance, you must give me something."

His brow furrows. "I already have your allegiance. You're on my ship."

"If you want the kind that means I'll die for you, that you'll never have to question my loyalties, I need a promise from you."

"You want more gold?"

"Non."

His bushy brows rise. He must want to dismiss me, but since I didn't ask for gold or a bigger share of the treasure, he remains. Finally, he asks, "What is it?"

"That the *Canopus* never deal in slaves."

"We voted as a ship on that. We said no chattel."

I step closer to him. "I'm not asking the whole ship. I'm asking you. You call me young, but you don't mention my mixed blood. I want your word as my captain that you'll not lead our men into temptation if the chance to enslave comes along."

Like a boar gnawing at scraps, the captain chews on something in his mouth. "Fine, Delahaye. I promise you that. And you'd better hope that Lizzôa and Danseker are able to use Lizzôa's forged letter of marque to get provisions. The men are restless. We have a career as filibusters to start."

The captain walks away, and I want to trust his word. Turning back to Port Royal, I pray Lizzôa is as smart as she needs to be to succeed at this theft.

Thirty-Three

1681. The Caribbean Sea

Standing on the raised quarterdeck, I have the ship underway with all the sails fully extended and its belly full of provisions.

Lizzôa continues to wear the officer's hat with feathers, but the rest of the British uniform has been stripped away. A tailored oxblood coat has replaced the baggy doublet. "Captain, I assure you, we can seize the sloop and take its silver."

Smith looks like he's considering it. "Hmmm."

"It's risky," Danseker says. "We still don't have enough men."

Lizzôa laughs and in the haughtiest British accent I've ever heard says, "The surest way to get caught is to recruit men from a British colony. We still have the old Union Jack flying off the stern."

Captain Smith straightens up, puffing his chest. "We need money."

"The ship should be streamlined." Bahati's voice is low. She's at my side, teaching me to look at the sun's position to the horizon, another thing that Old Jean barely mentioned in his lessons. I make a slight shift and ensure we are tacking north-northwest. "The captain's cabin?"

"Should be removed," I agree. "It will reduce the weight and make us faster."

She eyes me. "You are Captain Le Basque's boy, all right."

"Captain Le Basque streamlined his *Marauder.* He was a great filibuster."

Lizzôa glances at me as I'm praising Michel. For a moment, I feel ashamed. I haven't said his preferred name aloud to her in a long time. "He was a great filibuster," I repeat.

The captain points at me. "Steady as we go, Delahaye. I want silver. We're going after Lizzôa's mark."

Danseker's stance stiffens. "Sir, if we fail, we risk everything. We've done too much to make mistakes now."

"We need money, first mate. Money's not coming to us. You and Lizzôa came back with good intelligence."

"And the water." Lizzôa's jaunty tone sounds as if antagonizing Danseker brings her pleasure. "We did get a good amount from our letters. Shouldn't we remove our British markings now?"

Captain Smith nods. "Yes. Danseker, get the Union Jack off the stern. But bring the flag in with care. We're still British, after all. That's our flag."

Danseker grunts. His frustration's obvious, but he's not the sort to disobey an order from his captain. Well, at least not now. Having mutinied against his last, the man does have the ability to disobey. What could push him to do so again?

Lizzôa looks amused.

"If there is one thing I know," I tell the captain, "it's that if Lizzôa says there is a sloop with silver, it's there for the taking. Bahati and I will get us there."

"I'm going to review our cannons," he says. "I'll get the gunners ready."

"That's Wulf and Chilango's specialty," Lizzôa says, that smile growing larger. "They've got good aim and can load fast. Good thing you accepted us as part of your crew."

Captain huffs and glances at us. "You five truly wanted to be pirates."

"Some of us have been pirates before." Lizzôa steps closer but stays in the captain's sight. "We count ourselves lucky that this ship came along."

* * *

Two hours later, we round the Tiburon Peninsula of Hispaniola heading to the eastern tip of Jamaica. The water is calm, rippling every so often with white foam. The sky bears bluish-gray hues. The clouds that point to land have disappeared. Soon, my view of the mangroves and treacherous flowers will disappear as I guide the *Canopus* into the Windward Passage. Those flowers, the yellow dots on brown, stretching limbs, wave at me—hopefully, not to say goodbye to the girl about to traverse open water.

I tack whipstaff and adjust the sails to head us northeastward. Bahati, the old salt, slyly instructs me, offering tips about the speed and flow of the waves.

The way the *Canopus* shimmies into these waters reminds me of sailing Old Jean's ketch around Tortuga. I wonder about him and what he'd think if he could see me now.

Bahati grins for a moment. "Such ease, Jacques. You're masterful at moving the ship."

"Your teaching has helped."

"Jacques, you are gifted."

Celia comes running, pointing to an abandoned ketch. It's tilted to the side, cocked up on the coral reef. One of the two masts has fallen away. She says, "Look at that wreck."

A terrible foreboding darkens my vision. When it clears or I can see clearly, I am witness to Old Jean's ketch . . . his wrecked ketch.

"Half the hull . . . is sheared off," Celia says.

With my heart pounding so much that I want to vomit, I can't determine which mishap befell his boat first, the reaching arms of the mangroves or the abrasive grind of the coral reef.

"Should we stop to see if there's anything here? A few of the sailors said that Spanish ships have run aground here and lost treasure."

My mended soul shreds into a thousand pieces. Old Jean wouldn't have sailed this way, not from Petit-Goâve. Was he chased then attacked?

All I can do is will away the lump in my throat. I can't go any closer to the ketch to investigate. "Non. An unexpected shift of wind would run us aground, too."

Old Jean was too careful to let mangrove sink him. Could someone have stolen Old Jean's craft? I blink away a tear. Doesn't matter. The results are the same. If Old Jean crashed his ketch or a buccaneer who stole it did, then my friend is no longer in this world.

"Lizzôa's signaling, Jacques. We've spotted the sloop. We can't stop for bones, dry or wet." Bahati's scolding is true. It shifts my focus from grief to the concerns of our ship.

Lizzôa climbs down from the poop deck. The captain and Danseker come too.

"Straight ahead." Smith grins. "It will be ours."

I blink fast to clear the tears from my eyes. "We'll keep up with the sloop through the passage. We'll catch and overtake them in the channel. It will be easier."

"Yes," says the captain. "Man the cannons."

Danseker nods and runs to get the crew in place. Everyone seems excited. I'm numb as I guide the *Canopus* away from Old Jean's watery grave.

Thirty-Four

1681. The Windward Passage

The *Canopus* rushes at full speed through the Windward Passage. The western skies look radiant in pinks. The sun starts to descend. We have two more hours before the sea swallows the light.

Captain Smith has the scope. "It's about ten to fifteen miles ahead. Son, can we catch them before nightfall?"

"No, sir." I look to Bahati. "It's about five hours before either ship hits the fastest currents."

Bahati educates me about the maps. She's so much better at reading them. She should have the position of helmsman. "The channel, the waters nearest Cuba, are slower. We don't want to chase the sloop there."

I cough and swipe my eyes. Not taking a moment to say a proper goodbye will haunt me. "Do we take the sloop now in the light or follow through the night and strike first thing in the morning?"

Lizzôa stands quietly outside of the circle surrounding me. I long to hear her voice, to tell her of Old Jean.

Danseker takes the scope. "We're not close enough."

The captain clicks his tongue, then turns around and glares at Lizzôa. "I know you have an opinion. And since you've been right before, I want to hear it."

Lizzôa clears her throat. "At this distance, it may take five hours to catch up to them. It will be dark then. First light will give us the advantage of surprise. I like surprises." Her gaze settles on me. "But I think the helmsman is the best one to answer. Delahaye knows how fast he can close the gap."

All eyes are on me. "If I had my druthers, I'd get closer through the night while the crew rests. We attack at twilight. By the time the sun fully rises, the sloop will be ours."

The captain nods. "We attack at twilight. Get us into position, Delahaye. Close but not so close that they spy us and prepare to attack."

"Aye-aye, captain," I say.

He dismisses everyone, but Lizzôa stays.

"Something has happened."

Of course she'd notice.

Before I can stop myself, I have water streaming down my face. I wipe my cheeks with my hat—the one my friend and mentor gave me, the one I always wear. "That was Old Jean's ketch we passed on the sandbar. There's no way it sailed without him unless someone killed him for it. But he was old. Maybe it was his time, after bringing Josiah to me."

Lizzôa steps closer, close enough that I see the new growth of her beard along that feminine jaw. "Jacquotte. I don't know what to say."

"Don't say anything, just stand near."

I take Lizzôa's hand and pretend I'm showing her how the whipstaff works, but I need to feel her pulse against mine.

With a squeeze of my hand, Lizzôa moves away. Her eyes become distant and veiled. "One day, we'll be sitting in a garden, will be proper people and think of all the people we've lost and mourn. But we're not proper. We're pirates. We will lose people all the time. We go on. We must."

Her words are harsh. I feel stung.

"Jacques. This is us, here. I need you focused on the tasks here. That way we live. Don't forget that."

Those are her final words before Danseker waves Lizzôa into the stores.

Rebuked, I toughen my heart and set my eyes again to the sloop. The distance between us slowly dissolves. By twilight, my favorite time of the morning, the *Canopus* will, I hope, engage in its first combat. I pray that the five of us survive. I'm not good at pretending nothing hurts.

* * *

Twilight. The sloop looks sleepy and still. They're barely going a knot. We've been sailing at seven knots, and I had to furl the topgallants to slow the *Canopus*.

Bahati's up. "We're a mile out." That's still over five thousand feet away. "We need to be under a thousand feet for our cannons to be effective, and avoid theirs."

"Oui . . . Yes."

"Jacques, you ready for this?"

If I say I was born ready, I think she'll laugh. Instead, I sing,

Eke nekeng'wanso Omonene gianchere
Baba eke nekeng'waso Omonene gianchere
Ntwe ntobwati kende kobua ekio
Omanene Otwabere ebibe biato bionsi
Omonene Otwabere ebibe biato bionsi
Ekio nekeng'waso twakoire rero.

She joins with me, humming with a deep, low voice, repeating Maman's song until Captain Smith gathers everyone to the main deck.

"Get into positions," he says.

The crew divides and goes to the cannons. Lizzôa and Wulf will be a runner for munitions. Celia is the loader for a cannon on the starboard side of the *Canopus*.

"These sixteen-pounders," Danseker says, "are good for long range and can devastate forces close up."

I tack the whipstaff and use the position of the fading moon to set the *Canopus* on course to intercept. We head perpendicular to the sloop, cutting through the inky waters. The sun hasn't risen, but the lightening sky makes the outline of the ship's hulk more visible. Our firepower will have a clear shot.

I wave to Bahati, and she gets the fore and aft mainsails angled. We're going for a broadside attack.

The sloop doesn't hear us. It drifts along, as if they have left the boat for the taking.

When I see that the guns are ready on both the larboard and starboard sides, I wave to the captain, letting him know we are in range.

Smith charges to the quarterdeck. "Prepare to fire. Gun crews, stand at the ready!"

Our sparse crew loads the cannons, stuffing them with gunpowder and iron shot. The captain shouts, "When I give the order, aim to cripple the sloop. Shoot at the masts. Fire on the riggings. Don't waste a ball trying to hit the crew." He takes out a sword and waves it. "We'll take them alive or dead."

I point to Bahati to lower the aft-most mast to slow us. Smith looks at me. Then he signals to Danseker. "Fire!"

The broadside shoots seven cannonballs, one after the other. Fire launches into the sky. *Splash.* Some balls fall short. Some are flung past overhead. But most hit the sloop. One cuts through the mizzenmast. Another catches a sail on fire.

The sloop's crew pull down the burning canvas. The fire is out, but the smoke is choking.

Smith turns to me. "Go closer, Delahaye."

I do as the light of dawn breaks, but they fire back. All their balls splash into the water, spraying the air with soot and fire and sea salt.

"Surrender!" Captain Smith shouts at the sloop.

The sky lightens more. The deep blue of the hulk, the white of the bulwark contrast against the dark water.

Smith turns to me. "Pull closer, Delahaye."

The smoke clears, illuminating the carnage of this second round of cannonballs. The mizzenmast has completely fallen.

Spanish sailors fire back. Balls drop close but one lucky bullet from a flintlock grazes Bahati's shoulder.

She stumbles but I prop her up on the whipstaff. Lizzôa scrambles over with the medical sack and stops the bleeding.

Our side fires again. Screams and curses echo. We're so close now that none of our pounders miss.

"Fire." Danseker has taken over from the captain. He has our crew launch another barrage that takes another chunk out of the mainmast and knocks a hole in the sloop's remaining sail.

"Surrender or we will board!" They don't answer, so the captain signals, "Get us closer. Sailors, prepare to board on my mark!"

"Matad a los esclavos! Se unirán a los bucaneros!" At the order, sailors take out their swords and rush below.

The look on Bahati's face, on Lizzôa's, tells me what that order means. My soul cries. The Spanish would rather kill their chattel than let these men and women go free.

I motion to Lizzôa to take control of the whipstaff. "Just hold her steady until I come back."

Wide, scared eyes turn on me. "Non. You don't have to—"

"Oui." Pulling out my rapier, I nod. "I must."

When the captain gives the order to board, we throw ropes to the sloop. The lines pull their ship closer. I hook a hand into the rigging. I take a run along the deck and swing. My feet hover above the sea. Then I land, almost tumbling, with my sword raised.

Immediately, I start on the attack. I defend the deck, allowing the rest of my buccaneers to land on the sloop. We rampage.

Clang. Clang. I strike with my rapier, cutting through men. From the corner of my eye, I see Wulf swing over. Then Celia. We line up and begin chopping our way through the sloop's crew.

Footsteps pound. Our side continues to come aboard.

Splash. The smoke is thick, and I can only hope it's the Spanish falling into the sea.

We advance. We've taken more of the deck.

Captain Smith yells, "Surrender and my men will let you live."

Curses sound in multiple languages, but the crew of the sloop sing out in Spanish, "To hell. Take them to the doors of hell."

Close to the mast, I hear the crackle of flames. Another sail has caught fire.

Clash. Clash. The *Canopus*'s forces edge forward. The deck beneath us spins. Someone's trying to ram the sloop into the *Canopus.*

Clouds of smoke and bursts of fire erupt all around. The boat shifts, like it's trying to dance to a new rhythm. I give up trying to get into the cargo and save the prisoners. I have to stop this burning wreck from touching our ship.

I jump to the stern and fight my way to the tiller. My blade goes through a man. I rejoice when I drill it through another. I have the tiller. I make the sloop turn the other way.

Splash. A body has fallen into the sea. *Blam.* One tumbles in front of my boots.

Footfalls rush. In the smoke, I can't tell if those are men of the *Canopus* or the sloop. Doesn't matter. I keep fighting, protecting the tiller.

Clang. Clang. A brute sees me and runs at me with a shiny sword. Sparks fly as our weapons meet. He swings a cutlass. The curve of the blade is larger than anything I've seen—it slices through my hat, ripping it to pieces, severing a braid, and scattering them to the wind. I'm not hurt physically, but inside, I boil at the destruction of my treasure from Old Jean. Hair loosed, I fight back even as he uses his strength to drive me to the rail.

Celia screams.

It's a feminine scream, and loud. It will reveal her.

Wulf gets to her first and begins defending her, swords clashing. The noise makes my foe look to them. The distraction is enough to dispatch him. I stab him through the heart and hurl him to the sea.

Cannons sound. Our cannons. The *Canopus*'s sixteen pounders. Why fire? We can't be losing. Why risk hitting our crew?

One shot strikes the sloop's hull. Everything beneath my boots shakes. We have to gain control or we'll all die.

Our men beat them back. Victorious, we gather at the waist of the sloop. I leap up to signal to Captain Smith and Lizzôa or even Danseker that we have possession of the ship.

A gun blasts.

I feel the impact knock me down. The rest of the mast falls.

Pain. Darkness drops upon me like the closing of a basket's lid. And I hear Maman singing. *Eke nekeng'wanso Omonene gianchere. Baba eke nekeng'waso Omonene gianchere.*

Thirty-Five

1681. The Windward Passage

There are voices all around me. Père's. Maman's. Old Jean's. Sarah's. *Get up. Get up. Get up.*

It's hard to move. Hard to do anything, even breathe. The basket's hot, stifling.

Maman—she shakes me as I lie in the darkness. "You can't hide your light for anyone."

She shoves me harder. I push at her hands and try to punch back.

Then I stop.

Why fight Maman? I want her to be proud of me. And I can't achieve anything if I stay in darkness.

My hands lift; I push at the lid above me, pressing with all my strength until I see the light.

It's bright to my blinking lids. The sun warms my face, but I'm blinded. I sit up and see nothing, but I hear my buccaneers.

"All run through in the hull. Pity."

When my eyes are fully open, I see dead Spanish sailors lying all around. A piece of fallen mast is propped up on a smashed barrel. That space was the difference between me living and dying.

My ears perk up. Wulf points and cheers. Others do too.

"Back from the dead, Red!" The buccaneers from the *Canopus* chant this over and over.

"Back from the dead, Red!" Bahati's voice is close. "Back from the dead, Red!"

"Bahati!" Lizzôa yells. "Get Delahaye. Take him back to the *Canopus*. I'm almost done with Chilango. These men need rest. Good job."

Lizzôa's on the sloop giving aid to Celia and our men who've been hurt—either in combat or by the *Canopus*'s final cannon blast.

"Come on, Delahaye." Bahati stoops to me. Her ripped doublet exposes a scratch on her arm. It smells of rum, which must've been used to clean it. She reaches out with her big arm. "Put your weight on me."

We pass by the port leading into the hull. I slow my steps. "I want to go look."

"Why? You don't need that in your head. You'll not be able to trust white skin if you see the worst of what they do."

But I have.

All those years ago, I saw the slave drivers beat and kill those caught trying to escape. I witnessed how they punished and scarred Maman.

Bahati jerks me away. "Trust me, Jacques. You tried to fight for them. That's the most you can do. While we sail the *Canopus*, you have to be blind to some things."

"People, not looking for traps, fall into them."

She tightens her hold and walks from the port to the gangplank. The sloop is fastened to the side of the *Canopus* like the pinnace was. The board allows men to go back and forth.

My head is woozy. I can't fight her. Resigned, I lean on Bahati, and she helps me to stand on the gangplank.

More men cheer.

"The mast fell on you. That damn Danseker shot the cannon when everyone could see that we were winning." Bahati's voice is tight. "He could've sunk the sloop before we got the treasure and killed the only helmsman we have. But the Blancs will handle him. Even they can sense he's trouble."

From atop the gangplank, halfway across, I try to release my fury. The water below stirs, brightening to a striking blue. But its magic can't help. I'm not that girl running to the beach to be calmed by the sea. "I want to kill him."

"Shut up, Jacques. Your skill will keep making a difference if you live." Bahati readies for us to jump off the gangplank. With a huff, she helps me ease onto the *Canopus*'s deck.

She rolls her shoulder. "Stay here and be good."

Bahati goes back to the sloop and works at Lizzôa's side. They exchange whispers and looks, but I whip around, hearing my captain calling my name. His face is cherry red like Père's when I first stayed out all night.

* * *

The afternoon sky burns. The air remains thick from the smoke of our battle. Across from me is a Spanish ship filled with the dead. Here, on deck of the *Canopus*, I face a man who, like my father, has control of my life. I'm twenty-two years of age, still fearing what a man can do to me.

"Delahaye," Smith says. "You left your post."

That's true. I could give him a hundred excuses, but it will change nothing. "I'm back now."

Members of our crew again yell, "Back from the dead, Red!"

Wulf waves her hands, making the chant grow.

Captain Smith claps and repeats it. Then he waves his hands and silences the crew. "Men, go on. Finish getting the silver from the sloop. Get clothes. Weapons. Provisions. Anything not nailed down. We need it all."

More men go over the gangplank. A few still sing the chant, *Back from the dead, Red.*

"Delahaye," Smith says. "I'm glad you're alive, and that you're an expert with a rapier. But you didn't have permission to leave your post. You're the helmsman. Your loss would impact the *Canopus*."

"Captain—"

"Next time, don't leave the quarterdeck." The fierce frown on his face disappears. "But it's good to know you're handy with that rapier. And that you said you'd kill for me."

He chuckles, and we watch men bring over ingots of silver. Danseker has an armload. The fool passes me and can't look me in the eyes.

"It's a good haul." Captain Smith looks to the gangplank. "Lizzôa will now be my third in command. The intelligence he's culled is the sort of thing we need. We have to be smart. We have to go about things rightly."

"Does that include firing when the *Canopus*'s sailors are at risk?"

Captain Smith nods. "I spoke to Danseker. He says he thought he'd been signaled to strike."

I fume. That's a lie, but even in my rage I can't be stupid in my response. "He should've been more careful. Who's going to teach him this lesson?"

Captain Smith clicks his tongue. "I will discipline him, but do you understand my orders?"

"Yes. I'll get your permission to lead an attack."

Lizzôa helps Celia cross. Bahati follows, carrying Lizzôa's medicine sack.

"Captain, the Spanish sailors are dead, all but one. No survivors in the hull." Lizzôa's face is stern. "The survivor does not wish to join our cause."

Motioning to Danseker, Smith says to him, "Tie him to what's left of the mast. We will leave him to drift. Hopefully another Spanish ship will rescue him."

With a shake of her head, Lizzôa looks at me. "Sailor, put your arms about my shoulder. I'll help you to your hammock."

I do as I'm told by the new third in command.

In the depths of the hull, Lizzôa wraps her loving arms about me, holding me to the ladder. I take my time descending. I miss being close.

At the bottom, Lizzôa blows out the light in the wall sconce. For a stolen moment, I'm in the dark with my lover. For three fast heartbeats, I press hard into Lizzôa's embrace. A kiss feels so nice. I've risked death, why not risk life?

"Nothing is safe," Lizzôa whispers in my ear as boots echo above the tight passage.

"Danseker wants us dead."

"He just hates the color of my pretty skin." I murmur from exhaustion.

Lizzôa's small, perfect hands take a risk at finding me in these baggy sloppes. They wriggle beneath the bandaging of my bosom to that small valley holding my crucifix.

Then everything stops. We're not in Petit-Goâve. No bath in weeks means we carry the filth of every nautical mile.

Still, I want the closeness. I want the risk. I want Lizzôa.

"Someone's coming." She starts us moving. "We can't be caught. That's an order."

"Yes sir." I agree reluctantly, trying to cool my blood. "You're right."

"I am, but you're getting wiser and more daring. I'm proud of your courage." The words feel heated. "You're swaying, Delahaye. I said lean on me. You're so stubborn."

Lizzôa catches me again and I do sway against those enticing arms. People run past us.

"Back from the dead, Red," the sailors cry out as they pass us.

There are no windows, only brown walls in the bow where we sleep. I count the boards that slot together to form the ceiling as she tows me to our hammock. These quarters smell of sweat, of men living in close proximity.

"Pèrc had us scrub the tavern every day so this odor wouldn't linger."

Lizzôa laughs. "Soap won't save this."

Bahati and Celia are here. Poor Celia is changing her shirt with Bahati to shield her. Luckily, everyone else is above counting the silver.

Bahati gives Lizzôa her satchel of supplies. She hands a wad of cotton and wool to Celia. "That wound should stop bleeding, but keep a bandage on it." Bahati says this loud, as if other sailors are near. I look and see that Celia's menses are also a problem.

When Bahati glances in our direction, a smile paints her full lips. "Jacques. You're crazy." She comes to me and fluffs my hair. It crackles. There's even a spark.

"Knew you were a witch." Celia laughs. "How else could you kill five men, then survive getting hit by a mast falling from a misfired cannon." She slaps my back, and I fall over.

Bahati lifts me up. "You did good, and you lived. Well done."

Celia seems relieved. "I don't mind if she is a witch. Your skills saved us all."

"I hate to stop the celebration." Lizzôa's tone is serious again. "We are lucky Jacques is alive, but it was no accident. Zuthimalin Danseker is dangerous. He's Dutch, but also part Algerian."

Wulf enters. "He does not represent the Dutch. We are smarter. Give him to the Algerians."

"Most of us are part something," Celia says as she slips on a dark pair of breeches, as Bahati lifts me into a hammock.

"Algerian? Why does it matter?" Bahati asks.

"They are Muslim." Lizzôa digs into her sack and offers me a fresh ebony ribbon for my hair. "Danseker wants to steal the wealth of the Mughals to help Algiers aid the Muslims of Barbary Coast."

"So he's part Muslim but wishes to attack other Muslims to help a different group of Muslims?" Wulf scratches her head. "Just doesn't seem right. Corsair logic, I suppose."

"So he's a corsair, you say?" I mock Wulf's British-sounding accent, then touch my crucifix. "Alas, he's not the only man I know who wanted to steal the Mughal's treasure."

Lizzôa's eyes flick to my chest. Something in her face changes then disappears. "Our growing influence is a threat. Danseker had Smith convinced to do that until we came along."

The world moves about us, but the hammock feels gentle. "Lucky us."

Bam.

So much for gentle. "Is the anchor down?" I try to sit up.

"Yes," Bahati says. "Once we knew we'd won, we lowered it."

A loud creaking noise, followed by another bang, rocks us.

I glance at Bahati, and she says, "That's the sloop. It's bumping the hull. They need to hurry and cut it free."

Lizzôa turns to her. "Can it be repaired? Perhaps we should keep it. Our pinnace is gone."

"If they keep it, they need to empty it of the prisoners they've slaughtered." Bahati crosses her arms. "I'm not touching it until it's cleansed."

I close my eyes. "Let the men do it."

Then Lizzôa pulls a belt out of her bag. "Instead of your sling, use this for your rapier. The leather stamping has bandings to hold it. I think it will be much more convenient."

It is beautiful, and my rapier fits securely. "I'll keep it always."

Lizzôa smiles, and for a moment, it is just the two of us here in the crew's quarters.

Bahati coughs. "We should be going up. Celia, you're injured. Stay here. Come on Wulf."

"Shadow Lizzôa, folks. We have to watch out for our own safety."

Celia already looks asleep, rocking in the hammock next to me. My eyes follow Lizzôa, Wulf, and Bahati. I can't close my eyes, not until they're back and safe.

Thirty-Six

1683. Port Royal, Jamaica

On the quarterdeck, I signal for the anchor to be dropped. I've guided the *Canopus* into Port Royal's harbor. There's a glorious blue sky hovering over hot, humid air. "We've arrived ahead of schedule, captain."

Smith nods. "I think you could steer the *Canopus* in your sleep. Two years and you get better and better."

Two years at sea as a buccaneer—I've fought, explored, battled, and kept my position.

"The winds have shown us favor today, unlike yesterday when they impeded our assault on the Portuguese frigate, captain."

"Delahaye, don't beat yourself up over that."

Our iron shots hit dead on. But the wind caused a raging fire, and the frigate went down, taking man and treasure with it. No one considered diving into the sea and trying to recover booty. No one is Old Jean. "It's still a shame."

Bahati, who's been standing at my side, says, "I think we should revisit making modifications to the *Canopus*. If we're more streamlined, we move faster. Then we wouldn't have to use so much firepower to slow down our target."

Captain Smith rubs at his mouth. It was his call to bombard

the frigate when I couldn't catch it. "Danseker thinks that the *Canopus* is just fine. I'm beginning to agree. We need to keep our risks low."

Smirking, Danseker steps away. He orders Celia and another deckhand to lower the new pinnace.

As the captain and his first mate go to oversee this, Lizzôa comes up to the top deck, cheeks a little green. I know she needs to go into Port Royal to get more herbs to battle her nausea that returns every so often.

Bahati fumes. "Their contact will be able to take the gold and silver from our two last successful campaigns and exchange them for provisions, reales, and pieces of eight, yes? You sure about that?"

"That's the plan." Lizzôa turns toward us. For a moment, I see vulnerability and sickness etched in her delicate features.

"Lizzôa, are you well?" Bahati steps a little closer. "You don't . . . I feared the seasickness would catch you."

Lizzôa tips up her chin, and any emotion disappears. "You figure out how to make us faster, Bahati. Or we will see less success in the future." She catches my eye. "Or we'll have to go try our fortune in other parts of the world if we stay on the *Canopus*."

"No," Bahati says. "Fools like Danseker are just waiting for the opportunity to trade in Guineas. I'll figure out something."

She storms off to pray or study the waves breaking against the hull. These activities bring Bahati peace. Mine erodes more with the growing discontent.

* * *

Alone on the quarterdeck with just the two of us, Lizzôa twists the gold band about her finger. "Can't change your mind, Jacques, about going into Port Royal? We could visit the inn. It has the highest discretion."

My pulse races. Anywhere else, I wouldn't fight my feelings. In other ports we've escaped hand in hand to be us, to soak in baths, to be scented in lavender and love. Lizzôa shaves. We enjoy nakedness and lotions and heady teas.

But love and escape aren't enough, not anymore. "Lizzôa, you go. Get our business done. Send money to Josiah's monastery. Maybe you'll get us a lead, while I think of a new way for the *Canopus* to attack. We can't leave the Caribbean."

Emerald eyes run over me, scanning for something else. "You haven't been the same. Since that second visit to Port Royal."

It feels as if the sun is in my eyes, burning truth from me.

I want to reach for Lizzôa, but I can't, not on deck. I take the scope from my pocket and give it to her, pointing to the big blue pole.

"Your favorite inn is near Captain Le Basque's property."

"Yes, I love Port Royal's King's Haven Inn."

"Lizzôa, I'm not in the mood to hear of his and his father's exploits. Port Royal is Michel's town. He had a whole life here."

She puts down the scope. "Perhaps it's time to be done with all this and have our life. If the *Canopus* can't attack faster, it will lose and be captured. We will be killed."

"Non, Lizzôa. We can't quit."

"It's been two years, Jacques. Two. We've won many battles, a lifetime of them."

"Not enough wins. Bahati's right." I panic. My chest pounds too hard. "The ship must be modified. If you get a chance, convince the captain. Danseker is a lost cause."

"Jacques, you're not listening. We need to return to Petit-Goâve. I fear if we keep at this, we'll lose ourselves. I do not want that. And I don't want either of us to die in these clothes, hiding our true selves."

But I'm not hiding anymore. This is me—a buccaneer and her lover.

"Lizzôa," the captain calls out. "It's time to go. The pinnace is lowered."

"Coming, Captain Smith. Was trying to get the helmsman to come ashore."

Danseker laughs. "Delahaye is married to the whipstaff. Never seen him look at a wench, and there are plenty to choose from in Port Royal."

"Exactly," Lizzôa calls back. "Plenty, Jacques. I could show you a madame who'd be perfect."

"Leave Delahaye alone." The captain yells for Lizzôa to come. "The lad is dedicated. I like how dedicated he is. I know he's preparing for the next battle. Right?"

"Yes sir. Go, Lizzôa. The faster the exchanges are made, the sooner we can get out to sea."

Lizzôa rolls the gold band, gives me that sorrowful look, then joins them.

Two years at sea and Lizzôa can no longer pretend to want to be here. When we share a hammock, I hear her groan, yearning for her peace—her safe garden and cottage by the stream and the unhidden mountains of Petit-Goâve.

* * *

Night falls in the bay of Port Royal. Clasping the whipstaff, I feel the wind blowing through my curls. The docks of Port Royal have been busy all day. Boats are tied everywhere, even more than when I first sailed into this harbor.

The music of taverns and stews filters from the shore. Filibusters and buccaneers are here converting their stolen goods to reales and pieces of eight. Dozens of new warehouses have opened along the shore to service all the incoming pirates. Once that's done, men go into Port Royal and spend their gains on wine and song. Some buy a woman for the evening. Some share one. Others, like Lizzôa and me on past visits, carry on their matelotage in the privacy of an inn. Those in the know keep their heads down, guard the secrets of their relationships, and live quiet truths on land.

Port Royal is special, accepting everyone's gold or silver or life choices. No one questions anything. The taverns and stews delight in paying patrons.

So accepting, the city endures the great sin of enslavement. Slave ships, four of them, are anchored three frigates away. "Supplying demand," their captains claim. Danseker has renewed his quest for the *Canopus* to become a slave ship. Then he says speed wouldn't be an issue. The next moment, I hear him holding court on the bow, waxing eloquently about Muslim gold and the righteous fight of the corsairs. Madness.

One might say I'm picky in my sins. Piracy is stealing, but it's fair combat. I shrug to myself and lift a demijohn of rum to my lips.

I try to find something to look at before the liquor gives me bad dreams, but my gaze stops at the pole. Right now, it's a black silhouette. But I know it's blue. Michel's dreamy cottage on Lime Street is abandoned but treated like a Le Basque shrine. Even from here I can't see past it.

Should've went with Lizzôa, but I couldn't do it tonight—hear another story about Michel and his father told by the many denizens of the ville, pretend to Lizzôa that it means nothing. How do I tell Lizzôa, after all she has done and risked, that I could toss away this crucifix and there'd still be a part of me that's Michel's?

Soapy water streaks the planks. Mel, one of our new buccaneers, swabs the deck. His arms are thick, and yet he moves the mop with elegance. The fellow is young, with brown hair and chubby baby cheeks. He reminds me of Josiah.

"Hey, Delahaye," Mel says. "Can you teach me how to fight?"

"I'd rather teach you about the rigging or how to make knots. That will make you a better sailor."

He smirks and wipes his hand on his pourpoint. "I'll learn all of that. But your swordsmanship . . . Delahaye, everyone knows you're the best."

"That's good, Mel?"

"Yes, that makes you indispensable."

Indispensable? Guess I am. I let my hair loose today. My fears of my curls giving away my sex has disappeared. The rapier at my side has cut down enough filibusters, buccaneers, Spanish sailors, and upon occasion a Brit or two, that no one will risk calling me womanish. I'm safe because of my skills. For their gifts, Bahati, Lizzôa, Wulf, and Celia are also untouchable on the *Canopus*.

"You seem trapped in your thoughts." Mel's looking at me with inquisitive brown eyes. "Maybe you should go rest. We're anchored in place."

"I'll stand guard. I'm fine."

He shrugs and keeps mopping. That boy will make the *Canopus* sparkle like the three bright lights forming Orion's Belt.

I crouch down on the quarterdeck and pick up my demijohn of rum. I love that it offers that good burn. The sweetness overwhelms my guilt and drowns the urge to admit how selfish I am. But the stars blinking above shine on my hands, the hilt of my blade. It's picked me, picked me.

The sky, the heavens are right. I should be picked. Maybe it's not so selfish to want this life? My desire to be me—the best me—that's a worthy life.

* * *

The cloudy sky overhead feels ominous. The winds have picked up. From my post on the quarterdeck, I search the seas for signs of doom. A hurricane killed over four hundred in Florida a month ago. We need the *Canopus* to be away from here if the sea and sky begin to rage.

"Delahaye," Mel cries out. "The pinnace has launched."

With a hand cupped to my brow, I see the ship. It was supposed to return at midnight but didn't.

I take the scope and see our crew on board, but the captain, Danseker, and Lizzôa sit at the rear. No one appears to be speaking.

Bahati comes from below. "Jacques, that frown. What has happened?"

Lowering the scope, I say, "Nothing yet, but I have a bad feeling. Thought it might be the weather. I fear it's worse. The pinnace is returning late."

"But it's returning." Bahati stands at my side. "Wulf sort of mentioned . . . just to me, you were married to Le Basque. He's a hero to many here."

Why would she do that? I grouse but admit it. "Yes, Bahati, many talk about him here."

"He's a legend. Pity he sought the lands beyond Guinea. I heard he and his entire crew were held captive by the Mughals then tortured to death for desecration of the Muslim holy land."

I clutch my gut as if Bahati has kicked me in the stomach. "Tell Danseker this. He's determined to get us all killed by going after them."

"You drunk, Jacques? You've been sipping the rum more and more."

My head shakes. "Maybe, but I sober quickly." My hand fists, then I ease it to my side. "I hurt for Le Basque and his crew. It would have been better if they were lost in a storm."

Bahati extends an arm to me. "Aurangzeb, the Mughal emperor, is a brutal man. He killed his own brothers and even imprisoned his father to secure power. Boiling men in oil, gouging eyes, any manner of torture. Oui. A storm would be better."

My heart drops down into a buccan hole. I'm sure I'm bleeding.

Bahati's grip on my shoulder tightens.

"Jacques?"

My friend's more spiritual, and she will kill at will like me. But I know her to be a better person, a much better one. "The *Marauder*, they didn't deserve that." I push away. "Our crew's back. We have jobs to do."

Hooks drop. Men climb up rope, then raise the pinnace along the starboard side. The clacking capstan turns forever. Wulf leaps in. She catches my gaze.

Our three leaders come to the quarterdeck, heads bowed low like the devil kept them captive.

Bahati points to the empty pinnace that's being strapped to the waist of the *Canopus*. No provisions, no water, no gold. "Captain, what happened?"

Smith wipes at his mouth. He huffs and puffs his chest and says,

"Samuel Axe is dead. My connections to him are gone. Lieutenant Governor Henry Morgan and his associates have confiscated our winnings."

Confiscated. "We've been pirated by the king of the pirates. Is there nothing to be done?"

"Take us under way, Delahaye, before he turns the guns of Fort Charles on the *Canopus*."

Danseker's face becomes fire red. "You're such a smart man, Lizzôa, you'd think you could've seen this coming."

Lizzôa sneers at him. "I didn't cheat us."

Danseker pushes his way to Lizzôa, but in a flash my rapier is at his neck. "I dare you to move."

"Men, stop. This is my fault. My connections have been good up until now." The captain pats my back. "Everyone calm."

Hands up in the air, Danseker backs away. "Well, we need to fix this."

"Captain, I'll take us underway, but I think we must act differently." I have the attention of everyone on the quarterdeck. "We aren't the fastest ship in the line. Sloops are now being guarded by frigates."

"We should attack settlements," Lizzôa says.

"Yes." Bahati claps her hands. "That's what the old lieutenant governor did himself. As a filibuster, Morgan attacked Panama Viejo and won a ransom of a hundred thousand pounds."

"That's exactly what I mean." Lizzôa nods and smirks at Danseker. "That's exactly what we need to do. Find the right settlement. Plan the right attack strategy."

Captain smacks her on the back. I bet that stung. "Good idea. There's a prime target waiting for the *Canopus*. Jacques, get us underway."

He walks off, and Danseker follows like a limp puppy.

"Good idea, Lizzôa." Bahati rubs her hands together but stops when the rhythm of the enslaved takes over. The frigate farthest from us has made their chattel come up to sing.

Yo-yo-yo.

The chant continues. A whip snaps in the air.

I close my eyes to it and bark out orders to change our sails.

Lizzôa's lavender hits me. I look at her with her fine clean shave. "Glad you had a moment to enjoy a good rest. We need you to plan our best attack."

"Yes. New risks. New dangers. Jacques, going to a new settlement keeps us out of the main ports. It could be months before we can be back."

I want to say . . . I need to say . . . I say it. "Lizzôa, maybe you should go back to port and take the next ship to Petit-Goâve."

Emerald eyes assess me. They seem a little hurt. Then they show nothing. "I want us both to leave the *Canopus* alive. We must do it together. Nothing else. No separating. You chase happiness, but when you find love, you keep it."

"Lizzôa, this is my dream, not yours. You need—"

An index finger with a band touches my lips. It's a mere second, but it's everything. "Together. That's the only way."

Danseker coughs. He's come back, and I'm not sure what he's seen or heard. "Captain wants you, Lizzôa. Or should I tell him you're busy?"

My love trudges away, heads to the captain's quarters and disappears.

Danseker stays. "There are other plans, Delahaye. You keep stalling, but you will run out of time."

"We do things right, Danseker, or not at all."

"Perhaps not at all. You and Lizzôa should think about retiring." The hate in his eyes can't be unseen. But I meet his gaze with a stony countenance that makes him retreat. Danseker trudges away, barking orders to the crew. The first chance I get—the moment I sense him coming for me or Lizzôa—he's dead.

Thirty-Seven

1683. The Caribbean Sea

After poring over her maps, Lizzôa identifies the settlement of St. Andrews. Celia takes exception to the British name and calls it San Andrés, as it's under Spanish control. Doesn't matter. We have a target and something for the men to believe in.

Sails engaged, the topgallant fully extended, I guide the *Canopus* toward the fast-moving Windward Passage. Storms have slowed us. It will take another day before our frigate hits the strong waves. Bahati doesn't care about rain. She stands beside me and helps me use the sun's position to guide our frigate.

Bahati reports to me. "Any adjustments to the sails?"

"Not yet. You have them extended perfectly for this wind." A few men and Wulf are busy behind us. The leaders are in the captain's quarters.

"Have you attacked on land, Bahati?"

She cranes her face to the sky. Water flows down her cheeks like tears. "It's very different. It can be chaotic. We have to protect *Canopus* at all costs. It's our means of escape. Blancs get dangerous when they are fearful."

Wulf comes over with a rope bundle in her hand. "I read lips very well. And yes. Men and land combat can be difficult."

Bahati sighs. "Hand-to-hand battles are very bloody."

I start feeling bad again. "Is it going to be worth it?"

"With all of our treasury gone," she says, "it's going to have to be."

Wulf nods. "Yes, the crew is restless." She tips her hat and leaves us at the whipstaff.

"Our shares this time haven't been distributed," I say to Bahati. "Everyone's owed at least twenty reales." In a few more months it will be time to send money to the monks, money I don't have.

Bahati glares at the officers' quarters behind me. "And Smith knows we can't outrun these frigates and their accompanying vessels, not without modifications." She twists my hair that the wind loosed.

"Did you shave your head to become a pirate?"

"Non. The first time a man dragged me by my hair, I decided no one would control me again."

When Bahati has finished plaiting my tresses, I have two fat braids down my back. "You must do well with your nieces."

"Aye. But I can't go see them with nothing." She sighs like she sprung a leak. "We need to take as much of value as we can, but in silver, in reales. A poor haul from this settlement will make Smith desperate. Danseker could get the crew to go after Mughal, or convince everyone to be slavers."

"Smith promised me. I told him he'd have our allegiance."

The low, bitter chuckle that falls from her thick lips chills me. "Jacques, a Blanc man says what he needs to control you. If not by hair, then by lies. He'll use you up and then toss you away. You have to control you. And you have to know when to say you're done."

She lifts her fists like she's waiting to be bound. Then she hits them together. The crunch, the impact of knuckle on knuckle, echoes, lodges into my chest. "Tomorrow, Danseker will have Mel shadow and learn from you. They've picked your replacement."

* * *

Two and a half, almost three days later, we arrive in the waters surrounding San Andrés. "Captain, I suggest we anchor the ship here, two miles from shore."

He and Danseker are off to the side, whispering about the settlement's potential as if we can't hear them.

"Why not move the *Canopus* closer?" Mel asks. He stands by Bahati. They both report to me. The young man has become stout. Bahati is tall and muscular. It's an odd, almost amusing, match.

"Not sure we want to run aground on a sandbar. Lizzôa's maps are not current, but they are better than sailing blind."

Mel nods then quiets.

"We don't know what type of cannons San Andrés has. We can't put the *Canopus* at risk. Delahaye's approach is correct." Though I like the praise, Lizzôa's tone is curt. She mentioned us leaving the ship again. I can't abandon this vessel or the crew. In the dark, my feigning sleep made her angry. In the daylight, neither of us concedes on the notion of quitting. We're in uncharted territory.

"We need to explore the island." Lizzôa brushes at the sea spray that has wet her skirted Spanish doublet. The silver satin over the dark breeches looks valiant on her small, lithe frame. Her cheeks are thinner from worries and seasickness, but her tone remains confident, even strident. "I'm sure the captain is not just going to risk manpower or the *Canopus* without a solid plan."

"Yes." Smith has the scope. "Lizzôa, Mel, Chilango, and Wulf head the scouting party."

I want to yell out that I should go, but Danseker and Bahati are glaring at me. The only navigator leaving the ship is too much of a risk. Resigned, I order the mainsail furled. The more we blend into the horizon, the more time we have for reconnaissance.

The quarterdeck empties, leaving just me, Lizzôa, and Wulf.

"Yes," Wulf says, answering the question I hadn't asked. "I'll be Lizzôa's protection. I hear the way some people talk." She brushes her blunt-cut bangs aside. "I'll protect what matters, just like I'd do for Margaret. I wish she could be here with us."

With that, she walks away, heading down to the hatch. I'm left speechless, realizing that the life Lizzôa and I have bolsters others.

"I need to prove my worth, and show that I do wish to be here. I need to prove it to you, Jacques." Lizzôa takes the scope and views the tropical island. "Combat is dirty business. And I can be in the dirt like a pig like Danseker and then I can glory in my baths at Port Royal." She puts down the scope. "He followed me last time. It was good that you stayed behind."

"If he'd caught us, I'd declare out loud our matelotage. Then we could do the customary thing. Share a wench at a stew."

We laugh, as we haven't in forever. "I love you, Lizzôa. I will still love you if you go back to Petit-Goâve. You're my dream at the end of my days."

"Jacques." She points her scope at me like she can look into my heart. "It is hard out here."

"You're handling it well, Lizzôa. I once told a girl she couldn't be a pirate, because the world said so. Anne Dieu-Le-Veut wanted this life. I'm sure she made it. Hope she did."

"Anne is a pirate. I helped her join a ship back in eighty."

A year before my coming to Petit-Goâve, Anne's dream came true. "Lizzôa, that's your gift, planning and making dreams true."

She bites her lip. "Then how can you want us to be apart?"

"I've never loved anyone the way I love you, Lizzôa. And I'm starting to think of the life in Petit-Goâve ahead for us. Us and tea and quiet except for the rustle of palm leaves in the roof. And Josiah's with us. But I'm going to carry on here. Make as much money as possible. Then I'm coming home to us."

Tears are in her eyes when she lowers the scope. "Then I'm not done yet either. And you still can't plan worth an arse." Laughing, Lizzôa turns from me, taking my heart, too. She joins Mel and Celia on the starboard deck boarding the pinnace. I don't stop her. That is love, believing and letting go.

* * *

It is almost sunset before I spy the small boat rowing toward us. From my scope, I see Wulf, Mel, Celia, then Lizzôa. A long, happy sigh leaves my chest. All looks well and safe. Then my eyes narrow as I notice how Lizzôa leans on Wulf.

When the boat comes closer, I notice my Lizzôa's hunched over, rowing with one hand.

My heart lurches, and I help man the capstan's drum and ropes. Mel and Celia climb out, but Wulf and Lizzôa stay in the pinnace as it's raised.

I swing down and grab Lizzôa. "Hang on. Can you do that?"

I ease her over my shoulder. I feel a wince ripple through her. I climb with the strength of two men and carry her to safety.

"Lizzôa got hurt," Wulf said. "Won't be able to go on the next mission."

Mel and Celia take Lizzôa from me and lower her onto the deck. "What happened, Mel?" My voice is harsh, like this is his fault. I soften my tone. "I'm glad you all made it back in one piece."

"Lizzôa saved my arse. The townspeople knew we were buccaneers. They threw rocks and he pushed me out of the way. I'd have been miserably hurt."

"Missed your head," Lizzôa says, "but took out my knee."

The captain and Danseker hurry to us.

Celia looks distraught. "Should we abort? The colony's aware of us."

Wulf shakes her head. "No. It can be a good strike."

"The settlement is vulnerable." Lizzôa sits up. "Twenty-two thatched cottages, eight huts, and a church. Prime targets, captain."

Danseker folds his arms. "Well, there you have it. Prime targets, says the person felled by a brick."

Even Mel grouses. "You get hit with a brick dead on, Danseker, see how you like it. Matter of fact, I'll find one now."

Wulf glares at the second in command. She's ready to fight, too.

"Stop. Everyone, stop." Lizzôa winces. "We made it back. San Andrés is worth attacking."

"Thatched cottages, huts, and a church doesn't sound like much." Danseker huffs. "I'm not sure. We should look at other ways to get the silver flowing."

Pushing up from the decking, Lizzôa stands. Her small face

bears a tight grimace. "We're here. It's worth the effort. We can outrun a colony as long as the cannon is disabled. Jacques, they have our old friend, a twenty-four pounder."

Danseker steps closer, and Celia puts a hand on my rapier. He backs up.

I shake free of Celia and step up to the captain. "If Lizzôa says so, it's worth it. Finish the report, Lizzôa. I know you have more to add."

"Not much more." Lizzôa's typical breezy tone shows no urgency, even as she struggles to balance on the wounded leg. "There are no forts, just the cannon. The houses and the church will have plenty to plunder. Just be sure our people disable the cannon. There are three balls by its side, but we don't know if they have more elsewhere. Jam the barrel so there will be no resistance. Once it's disabled we'll get away easily."

The captain speaks up. "Anything else? You always have more."

Lizzôa nods. "To the left of the settlement are hills and jungle. That's where I'd gather our men, then go en masse and attack at full strength."

Captain Smith's face bears a slight smile. "Good work, Lizzôa."

Now I interject. "Come on, Lizzôa. Don't hold back. Tell 'em the rest."

"Glad you asked, sir." She offers a prideful grin. "There's more. I didn't see many weapons other than six or seven flintlocks. There's decent powder stores. We should take that to replenish our own. The church has Spanish crosses. I'm sure those have been made from melting down the gods of the Indigenous. It's fitting we steal what's been stolen."

Celia straightens up with pride. "Captain, I'd love to ransack their church."

The Brits on board seem fine with that too. Now even first mate Danseker seems interested.

Wulf beams, then sobers like she'd made a feminine action. "Tell the last bit, Lizzôa?"

A radiant smile sweeps over those rare, elegant features. "Just one more thing to add. Many colonists are British emigrants. They typically possess heirlooms of value." Lizzôa flicks a feather on the hat that Danseker sports. "What Brit goes anywhere without finery? Have the men take sacks. Snatch, grab, and get out."

"I've heard enough." The captain gathers everyone. "We strike at twilight. Danseker, form up the parties. I want men to be fast and on target."

"I want to lead the attack," I say. "I'm not staying on the ship when I know my rapier can ensure we win."

Captain Smith looks hesitant. He won't answer. He shifts his stance.

Danseker snickers. "The soft helmsman gets to play soldier."

A few others grin like they're sharing a joke—a joke told by a fool. My grimace silences everyone. I glance at the captain, "What say you?"

"Fine," Smith says. "But you get yourself back to helm our ship in one piece. Take the second mate below now."

With Bahati's and Wulf's help, I scoop Lizzôa up. My heart calms when I feel a strong pulse. The thought of losing her wakes me up. It's time to take control. "You're going back to Petit-Goâve. I'll take you home."

Wrapping her in my arms, I tell my mates, "I have Lizzôa. Go listen in on Danseker. Make sure he doesn't ruin the raid."

Then I take Lizzôa below. She's in pain but smiling. Her arms are about my neck.

I haven't said the rest. When I step from the ladder and head to the crew quarters, I say, "When you're better, I will come back to the sea. I'll join another ship. I'm not done. That's what we're doing."

"Well, a wounded leg on a ship will never do." With a tight hug to my neck, Lizzôa says, "I like it when you're forceful."

Lizzôa faints as I tuck her into the hammock. I loosen her doublet and then take a good look at her knee. It's purple and swollen. The morning will show us for sure if it's broken. I lean in close and whisper, "Love you."

Panting, Lizzôa rouses. "Give me my satchel. There's laudanum. It will help me sleep. That knee is badly hurt."

Before I let her drink, I risk a kiss. Then I stay at her side, waiting for the medicine to give Lizzôa deep, restful sleep. It's silent here, but the noisy footfalls of our crew walking along the bow boom above. I wonder when this fool Danseker will rile up the men and cause the next uprising.

* * *

At twilight, that moment before the sky starts to brighten, twelve of us from the *Canopus*'s crew of sixty-five set out in the pinnace. A haze slightly covers Orion's Belt.

"Low clouds can help us." My whisper reaches Bahati and Danseker. We each are leading a party. Three parties of four head to the island settlement.

We launch onto a blond beach. The urge presses to take off my boots and feel the sand on my toes. It's the first and only time I miss Cayonne. Danseker and I stand watch while the rest secure the pinnace. He gapes at me with narrowed eyes. "It's not that I don't like you. You hide your proclivities well. I don't like Lizzôa. I'm wary of men who are obvious with their unnatural urges."

"What?" I'm rarely shocked by someone's prejudice, but this confounds me. Lizzôa is the most discreet and the most competent. "You don't have to like us, Danseker." My hand is on my rapier, and I know he sees it. "But respect us. We get things done."

He chuckles. "You have spirit," he says.

Wulf in the back nods. "Smarts and pride too."

I chortle at her kind words, but I suppose Danseker's trying to offer some sort of compliment. I urge the fool forward. "I'm going to let you lead." I want to see any bullet coming for me. "But with the captain's permission, I will steer us to Petit-Goâve on our return. Lizzôa's hurt and needs to retire. When we're gone, you won't need to fear our love."

My voice is loud. Others can hear my declaration. I don't care.

I'm not ashamed. I'm lucky to have love. There is so much to hide of me, I can't keep doing so with my heart.

The rest of our crew has caught up. I take charge. "We have the plan. Danseker will disable the cannon. The rest of us get the booty, get out, come back here. Watch out for one another."

The first mate jerks, realizing I've just given him a command. Nonetheless, he starts moving, slipping from the beach into the thick jungle.

The canopy of coco palms covers us. Smells I haven't known since Tortuga are all around—the clean ferns, the sweet flowers, which I pray are almond blossoms.

A bird screeches. It's not a trogon or nighthawk. Whatever it is, it's hunting for a last treat, just like me—a last battle on the *Canopus.* I'll join a new crew in Petit-Goâve if I have to. This feeling, the need to win, is not satisfied in me. I need the battle. I need more wins.

At the edge of the forest, we look down at the village. Like Basse-Terre, a ring of thatched-roof houses circle a well . . . and a church. Don't see a tavern. Maybe God, liquor, and wenching can't exist side by side.

In the middle of the settlement but close to the beach stands the cannon. The light of dusk highlights a shadowy bronze sixteen pounder, not a twenty-four pounder. Fear isn't the word for what I feel when I see it, like when I feared the cannons of Fort de Rocher. This one with a worthy gunner has the range to strike the *Canopus.*

"Danseker, before your party takes the houses on the far side, don't forget to disable the cannon."

"Yes." He nods. "For the *Canopus.*"

* * *

Our teams spread out. Danseker heads to the cannon. From the corner of my eye, I see his men already at the far houses. Wulf and I stop at the first house. Mel and Bahati are two doors away. We all wait for Danseker's signal.

Whhhhhhooooop. Danseker blows the conch. I kick in a white-washed door. The house is modest inside. People run screaming from our guns. "Don't hurt us. Don't, please," they say in English.

Silver candlesticks from a mantel. A pewter plate. Wulf grabs these and tosses them into my sack, and we run, hollering like demons to another house.

At the next house, a woman, older, with a scarf on her head, wraps a child in a blanket. She's tossing books, even a basket, at me. "Don't hurt us. Please."

I'm stealing from a mother and child? Is this my legacy? Non. I put back the silver teapot I grabbed and retreat.

Others of my crew have bulging sacks full of possessions. "Head back to the boat." We've taken enough. I've no more appetite to steal from these people. It's not the same as fighting Spanish soldiers.

Bahati has a barrel of powder. I join her and take the other end of the barrel.

We head back to the jungle. "We're done!"

As our crew leave the circle of houses, I see Mel's in trouble. Villagers with swords chase him, keeping him from joining us. He's dropped his flintlock. "Wulf, go to the landing."

"Jacques??" she questions as I run toward Mel.

I toss her my sack. "I got 'em. Go." I run and take on the villagers. "Mel, head to the boat." I keep my rapier raised. "Back away."

They laugh and charge. I strike one man on the wrist and blood flows over his black doublet. The others flee.

Mel stayed. He disobeyed me, but we head off together. Celia comes out of the church. She has heavy sack with silver and gold sticking out. "I feel these are from my ancestors, taken from the Pánuco River."

She's babbling. Don't know if she is right or wrong, don't care. "Run, man. We have to get out of here."

Shots fire at us.

We escape, dipping into the jungle. The canopy of emerald

bayahondes and lush palms keep us in the dark until our feet reach the blond sand.

Danseker waves to hurry. Wulf rushes to us and helps drag Celia's and Mel's sacks to the boat. We've done it. We've acted as a team. Together, we push the pinnace into the sea.

A few men chase us to the water's edge. They fire but their flints miss.

"Buccaneers!" an old man in a dark brimmed hat shouts. He raises a flintlock and fires. Celia goes down into the pinnace.

Leaping out, I run at them with my rapier and beat them back. I kill the one with the gun. I snatch it up and swing it onto my back.

The crew has the pinnace in deeper water.

"Come on, Delahaye!" That's Bahati yelling for me. Hitching my rapier in my belt, I run into the waves. It's cold and knocks the breath from my lungs.

The water turns from indigo to blue to clear. It's dawn. The crew doesn't speed up the pinnace. They've slowed for me. Soon, Bahati grips my hand or I grip hers, and she pulls soaking me into the boat.

We've done it. I want to laugh or cry. We possess a boatload of stolen goods. The majority is from the church. It seems oddly right. It will make the next payment I send the monks easier.

Checking Celia, Wulf and I find that the shot has gone straight through her leg. We pour liquor on it. It'll heal. I tear at the cuff of her sloppes and use the wide band to tie off the wound right above her thigh. "You and Lizzôa will both be out of action."

Celia closes her eyes. "We still did it."

Bahati takes her oar and swats waves of salty water. "What's so funny, Jacques?"

"My town of Basse-Terre, we wanted a parish." I raise a silver communion plate. "Maybe it's safer not to have one." I laugh and pray to the gods, all of them, that none of the men of the *Canopus*—

Boom. A cannonball flies wide over the pinnace. "Danseker?" I gape at him. "You didn't plug the cannon!"

"I took the balls." He lifts one out of the sack.

Boom. This one splashes close to the *Canopus.*

"They have more! You idiot! You were supposed to disable the cannon!"

The man looks shaken. He begins to paddle faster. A sixteen pounder can sink the *Canopus.*

"Take up the anchor!" The captain is waving at us, yelling for defensive actions. "Get the ship ready to go out to sea."

I see men running about on the deck. I'm paddling as fast as I can.

Boom. The ball sails over the top of the mast. That's close. Too close. The anchor goes up like it's a snail.

"Get the ship farther out!" My heart drums. It wants out of my chest. I don't know if Smith can helm the frigate. "Just get her moving."

Miracle of miracles. The ships shivers and heads away. All the sails are raised. It's brilliant. White ghosts swell, leading the *Canopus* from danger.

The pinnace heads to the stern. Sailors are there. They have ropes and hooks.

Danseker looks up. "We just need to get tied to the *Canopus.* We can be towed until it's safe to board."

Captain Smith looks in our direction and calls out, "Come on, lads!"

Boom. We're almost to the rope when the cannon blasts a fourth time, crashing into the mainsail. The topgallant is in flames. It drops to the bow, which also catches on fire.

Panic ensues. I see men screaming. Some, fully engulfed in flames, jump into the sea. Smoke billows everywhere.

I leap out of the pinnace and swim to the *Canopus.* Bahati and Mel follow. The bow burns. It rages and smokes. We climb up and help to put out the flames. We drag buckets of seawater to douse the inferno.

It takes forever for the fire to be quenched. Once it's out, Mel drops to his knees by the port that leads to the crew's sleeping quarters. I look down and see dead men, men strangled by the smoke.

Mel chokes back tears.

Bahati tries to stop me, but I jump down.

One swabbie, two cannon loaders, one rigger are dead. I jump around them and go into the crew's quarters. The fine brown slats that circle and flare with the prow are jet black and smoking. The flames must've been so hot here. It became hell.

Coughing, I move farther in. The floorboard seems solid. No water's coming in; there's great damage to the beams above me. The fire moved fast. It couldn't have blazed more than twenty minutes.

My steps fall on a hammock that has been burnt to ash. Another smolders beneath my boots. I pass a man half burnt, not breathing. He was the cook. Nothing was wrong with him and still he couldn't escape the smoke.

Tears flood my face as I get to the blackened corner where our hammocks remain as burnt black webs. There's a charred husk on mine and Lizzôa's. Small and thin and delicate, the occupant now sleeps forever.

Bahati has followed me. She sinks to her knees. "Lizzôa. Lizzôa. No!"

The laudanum I gave Lizzôa . . . She couldn't awaken. Maybe she felt no pain. All the pain is mine. I feel it all, every bit of our love gone.

"One of the gods has struck down my angel, Bahati. Lizzôa was to return to Petit-Goâve, back to her teas and her garden. Lizzôa would be waiting for me when I was done with being a buccaneer."

Big black arms wind about me. "Jacques, let's get some air. You can't help Lizzôa, not now."

With a shake of my head, I push her away and take back the gold ring. My love doesn't resist. Her ashes flake and give up the treasure. I take it and hold it high.

Bahati stands next to me. She finds a piece of silver satin that fell away. It's from Lizzôa's doublet—perfect and raw, stained with Lizzôa's ashes.

Bahati hands it to me. My trembling fingers grasp it. I stuff it in the binding about my chest, next to my crucifix. The ring I slip on my finger again. Then I let Bahati lead me up top to the salty air.

Thirty-Eight

1683. The Waters of Tortuga

For two weeks, I stay in a drunken rage. No one dares talk to me, not even the captain. I have plotted Danseker's death a thousand times. If I'd killed him the first time I felt the urge, Lizzôa might still breathe.

The crew dealt with the dead, wrapping bodies and ashes in canvas and weighting the bundles with iron shot and sliding them into the sea. Wulf, Bahati, and Celia took the ashes of our dead crew, of my Lizzôa, and scattered them off the bow.

Inebriated out of my mind, I'm still the only who can helm the *Canopus*. Our ship is badly damaged and in need of repairs.

"Jacques," Bahati says. "How many of the sails should be replaced?"

Looking up from the whipstaff, I blink at the bright noon sun. I count white ghosts and lose track. "You know, Bahati."

"The upper part of the hull and the bow are in need of new wood. I have to get under the charred sections."

"I don't . . . Do what you must, Bahati."

Celia comes to check on me. Mel and Wulf too. "We brought you some soup, Jacques," Celia says.

A glance at the clear, weak broth sends me back to my rum. "Danseker killed off our cook too."

I take the bowl and hurl it into the sea. "Go."

Mel shakes his head and draws Celia away. Wulf stays.

I feel bad, but I again don't care. As I raise my demijohn to my lips, Bahati grabs it and pitches it into the waves. "Life is abominable for everyone. The tally for this misadventure is six dead. Six. Each one didn't deserve this."

"And for what was this sacrifice?" Wulf looks out at the water. "A silver cross, some candlesticks, a chalice, and a golden frame." She looks at me. "I want out. First stop, first chance. Let me go. Being with Margaret is worth more than a stick of silver. You should go too, Jacques. Those like us will never be safe."

Bahati steps closer. "Go to your duty sailor," she says to Wulf.

When she leaves, Bahati looks as me. "We have nowhere to go to convert these to silver reales. We need money to buy timber to fix the *Canopus.* Unless you've had enough too?" She folds her bulky arms. "Old Wulf there. I've sailed with her before, but I've never seen her frightened like this."

"Maybe she's the smart one. She knows this life isn't worth losing love. Didn't I know this? Didn't Le Basque teach me this?"

Bahati shakes me until I want to vomit. "Delahaye, snap out of it. Lizzôa is gone. Others can quit but not you. People here still need you."

"Oui, 'cause I'm the helmsman."

"Non. 'Cause you have principles. You fight for them. And right now they're voting."

My mouth tastes like ash and sawdust. "Why are they voting about me?"

"Non, Jacques, you fool. They're changing the rules. Danseker's pushing for slaves."

I sobered instantly and grow more furious. I follow Bahati to the waist of the *Canopus.* We join the crowd under the hanging pinnace. Thirty-one men plus me, Wulf, Bahati, and Celia. Since our run of bad luck, some have abandoned ship. They were the smart ones.

Smith sees me and he looks like someone about to be stabbed.

He wears bandages on his hands from trying to put out the fire.

"Lads, we're desperate. We need to convert what we've taken from San Andrés. Tortuga is where we'll head and make the trade. I need a vote." He looks at me. "I know I promised some of you that we wouldn't deal in Guineas, but we've no choice. We can't abandon the *Canopus.*"

Smith stops in front of me. "I don't think that those who gave their lives for the *Canopus* would want us to quit."

"Lizzôa detested slavery. You promised the *Canopus* was different."

"You drunk, Delahaye?" Danseker comes from the shadows. He's been out of sight since the disaster. "You going to sober up before you—"

My rapier is at his throat. "I chose this spot, because I want to feel you dying. I want my blade to rip your through your skin, cut out your voice so you never utter another stupid word. If you still twitch, I'll use both my hands to push this through your spine."

Bahati pulls me back. My rapier dislodges from the fool's throat. Blood spurts, but he's not dead.

Smith steps between us. "Stop. Now."

I try to break free from Bahati's grasp. "Next time, I'll just do it. No warning."

"Delahaye, you've been brave and dedicated. I need you on my side regardless of this vote." Smith turns to the crew. "We are a brotherhood, even when we err."

He can take his brotherhood and shove it up his arse. I start to turn away.

"That's why Jacques Delahaye is now second in command."

I stop and turn back. "What, captain?"

"We need you. I'm demoting Danseker. You're second in command. Bahati is now third, but you two must abide by this vote. We need pieces of eight. We have gold to trade, but it's from a blasted church. The Spanish will know. They will come after us. Since we're not dealing with Port Royal right now, Tortuga will do."

Celia looks at me, then Bahati. "Just one time. After, we can figure things out. But you two will be our leaders."

Danseker's face is bright red. He holds his neck to plug the leak. "Captain. We don't need them. I can—"

"You damn fool." Captain Smith turns to him and pokes him in the chest. "You can't navigate the *Canopus.* You said you knew how. You lied. Then you ended up killing six of my men. So you're lucky we're low on men, or I'd maroon you."

Danseker looks small, diminished, but he's a Blanc man. Arrogance lives in his veins. He'll get over this humiliation soon enough and come up with a new way to get us killed.

Wulf looks resigned. Her eyes keep going to the water. Maybe she spies ashes, ashes on the sea, floating along the waves.

Captain Smith pounds back to me. "Jacques, I'm asking you. You need a new purpose. Being my second is that. Don't you see it, son?"

A glance at Bahati reveals that she's nodding. I don't know what her plan is, but we are stranded with no port in sight. I don't have much choice. "Yes, I'll be number two. And I will abide by the vote. But I beg of you all to vote no. We're buccaneers. We're not slavers. Vote no."

Danseker claps. "Delahaye is right. We aren't slavers. And we don't intend on keeping them in bondage. It's a mere transaction. For a moment in time, the chattel will be in the hull until we get to Petit-Goâve. That said, when you see how lucrative the practice is, we may have to vote again."

Smith wipes sweat from his face. "This is for one vote only. To trade the winnings from San Andrés for chattel. Then we can get the *Canopus* fixed and pay you all. Let's vote."

"Aye-aye," thirty-two of them sound. Only Wulf, Bahati, and I dissent. Celia votes with the masses.

The captain pounds his fist into his palm. "We have our answer. First mate Delahaye, set a course to Tortuga."

I want to spit and curse him. Instead, I grumble, "Aye, captain." I turn and walk the short distance to the quarterdeck with Bahati at my side. Neither of us says a word as I head the ship back to the Windward Passage.

"Tortuga is where you are from?"

"Oui. It was home until I met Lizzôa." I stand up straight and almost try to stare into the sun. Blinded by success, I sailed into the ball of flames and burned up my wings. I am Icarus. I am Uzoamaka. I am a fool. "My legacy is ashes. Everyone I love dies by fire, reduced to nothing but charred dust."

"We all become dust. But don't blame God. Blame Danseker. While you've mourned, he's been politicking. I think he's surprised that the captain has demoted him. Actually, I am too."

"We can't do this, Bahati."

I adjust the whipstaff and wait for answers. Right now, all is silent in my head but the crying of my soul.

* * *

As soon as night falls, we catch the prevailing winds. The *Canopus* heads to Tortuga.

It's been three years since I've been to the island of my youth. I was so different then, younger and filled with desperation and rage. Now I am returning less desperate, wiser, but still full of rage.

"The damage to the bow and the crew's cabin is extensive." Bahati has a habit of speaking low and in quiet tones to me. She must sense I'm a cannon waiting to fire.

"Is it fixable?"

"Yes, but it's going to take a lot more than selling some stolen candlesticks." She comes to my side. "I don't ask that many questions. I've seen a lot. Know this, Lizzôa helped many people, many women in particular, to join pirate crews. Not once did Lizzôa ever want to be a pirate. She came for you."

I take a deep breath. "Is this to make me feel better? I killed Lizzôa. If we'd left the ship months ago, we'd be in Petit-Goâve. She'd be alive."

Bahati touches my arm. I ball a fist. "Jacques. There's no changing the past. We have to live a future worthy of the ones we've lost."

"What if you had a cavern full of Spanish gold? How would you change it into something useful like a ship?"

Bahati scratches her ear. "You really need to stop drinking."

I do sound ridiculous.

"Mourn, Jacques. But there's a time to weep and a time to build. This is a time to build."

"Build 'cause I have nothing left?"

"Build because *you* are left. No woman has had the position of second in command, not in the Caribbean." She steps forward, casting her gaze to the charred prow. "This matters, Jacques. Do you know how many have come and told me to thank you for staying?

"Without you, we'd all have to join a new ship, but our ruse here has worked. It's still working."

"Wulf is gone the moment she can be. She's going home to Margaret."

"Then be a leader and get her there safely. We're in leadership. There may never be another opportunity like this one. This is Lizzôa's legacy, putting women in positions of power. The success we make of the *Canopus* honors her."

* * *

I find the brightest star, the North Star. Alone on the quarterdeck, I trace it to the Southern Cross, a beautiful collection of lights that form a crucifix in the sky. These celestial jewels will help me sail north, then northeast and make steady progress with our limp vessel.

Over the next few days, Bahati, patient Bahati, teaches me more of the sky. We pass the eastern coasts of Nicarao. Then a collection of islands she calls the Mosquito Coast. It looks like a thin slice of Cayonne beach but covered in dense jungle. One coco palm is bent and stretched so far I think we could grab a coconut if the water by the shore were deeper.

The following day we reach Jamaica and her mountains. I defeat the urge to pull into Port Royal to fire cannons at the ville. I look again at the sky. The belt that Orion wears guides me to the Windward Passage. A little way north, we'll be at Tortuga.

Bahati comes up from below. "Jacques, can you sleep? Is there anything you need?"

I slap at the whipstaff. "I'll need you to adjust the sails. Fifteen degrees. That will head us on to Tortuga. And tell Celia she is safe. I know she's afraid of me."

Her sigh is long and hard.

"Bahati, I'm still praying that we don't do this."

We're both quiet for a long time. Then I hear her or she hears me. We sing the song of our mothers until Tortuga comes into view.

Omonene otwabere ebibe biato bionsi
Ekio nekeng'waso twakoire rero.

But this time, Bahati translates it into English and sings, "Lord, forgive us all our sins. That is the sacrifice we have given today."

Is that the answer, to merely ask forgiveness for what the *Canopus* is about to do? Will I be forgiven, the woman God allowed to steer this frigate and send its crew to commit the worst sin?

Thirty-Nine

1683. The Waters of Tortuga

Nearing Tortuga, I guide the *Canopus* to the deepest waters. In the years I've been gone, they've cut back the jungle and expanded the docks of Cayonne. I'd cheer for this progress, but I count four warehouses. The island's slave trade has grown too.

I glance up to the hills where Fort de Rocher looms ominously. My gaze locks on the sixteen pounder I see near a battery to the left of the fort and the twenty-four pounder on the right. How many times had I looked up into these hills and not realized how deadly those weapons could be?

Stretching, I turn to Hispaniola. The cloud-veiled mountains of Chaîne de la Selle greet me.

The moment sours as I hear the capstan whine. Men lower the pinnace. Mel slaps his mop about the deck, swabbing.

Wulf and Celia mend sails. I haven't spoken much to Celia since the vote. Not sure Bahati has delivered my message. Because her skin doesn't reveal her Guinea ancestry, I think she feels she can ignore Danseker's threats. The betrayal hurts, but being in Tortuga reminds me of Sarah. She taught me to forgive scared women. In her honor, I'll have to give Celia grace.

Men are laughing.

Danseker and his closest associates on the *Canopus*, armed with swords and flintlocks, haul the sacks of relics into the smaller boat.

Bahati comes to me. "So this is your island, your home. You are not getting off?"

"This is the place where I came of age. If you call that home, so be it."

She leans against the rail. "We've come a long way, Jacques. Seems wrong not to visit."

That's the problem. There isn't anyone to visit. "Non. I'm not leaving the boat. Do you intend to go back to Guinea one day, Bahati?"

Shrugging, she says, "I'm there sometimes in my dreams. The heat wraps me in such warmth. I see the fruiting trees. My belly's always full. My mother takes red clay and dyes fabric. Then I open my eyes and know that world is gone because of invaders, the colonizers."

I glare at the busy beach. "Maybe we jump ship and join another crew? One these crews in this harbor could use us."

Bahati offers a bitter chuckle. "Better to be with the devils I know than to start over with new devils. We have respect here. We earned it." She slaps at the rail and lifts her jet-black hand to the sky. "And as long as we are the universal currency, this will happen again."

* * *

The fishermen of Basse-Terre haul a catch of dolphinfish to the beach. As they struggle with their nets, the battle wafts the tang of salt and fish to the *Canopus*. From the quarterdeck, I watch Celia and Mel struggle with their lines. I try not to gawk through Lizzôa's scope at Danseker, but I'm curious at how many Guineas those relics are worth.

Captain Smith takes the scope. "Delahaye, we've enough lumber and provisions on board to fix the *Canopus*."

I glare at him. The next load the pinnace brings will be Guinea men. Goodness, I hope it's just men. "Will you consider Bahati's modifications now? We need the *Canopus* to be faster. Losing the captain's quarters and having our stern flush will do it."

He lowers the scope from his eye. "Perhaps. Let's get underway. Then we'll discuss it. But you know I rather like my quarters. That distinction is important."

So, he likes being set apart from the crew. Our ship is slow because he likes being king.

Captain Smith's lips are pressed together. "The exchange is going well. This may be the first of many dealings with de Franquesnay."

I want to warn him that all the governors of Tortuga have been untrustworthy and self-serving. But there's no reason to help him with this miserable business.

Smith's light-blue long coat flaps in the breeze. His buttons are wood, not brass like Michel's. But this is the finery of a would-be British officer, not a proud filibuster. Michel kept to his principles and became famous like his father. In my heart, I know it has to be possible to dream and be righteous.

I walk to the rail and stand next to Bahati. At the starboard deck, she prays aloud. The language she uses is foreign but familiar. It's not Maman's Kissi. My friend's head is bowed. Her voice rings out over the water. Wulf stops doing inventory in the stores to listen. Others on deck do too. The rhythm is pleasant even if one can't understand her words.

Captain Smith aims the scope toward the pinnace and Cayonne. "Danseker has made an excellent trade. I count twenty slaves."

Bahati's prayer becomes louder as the pinnace is pushed into the sea. The waters of Tortuga are the clearest I've ever seen. On a day like today, one can see into the deep. The pink coral teems with fish near where we've dropped anchor.

When Smith hands me Lizzôa's scope, he glares at me like I should silence Bahati.

He tugs me aside. "Jacques, one day you'll be a captain. I see the fire in your belly. When you get out of your own way and stop feeling sorry for yourself, for that Guinea blood in your veins, you'll inspire men. You're French too, after all."

My *fortune* is in having a Blanc father?

"And you keep your hands and your proclivities to yourself."

The fire pent up in my bones smolders. My race isn't the captain's only complaint today. My grief for Lizzôa has been so visible, I should expect even fools to notice. I roll our band about my finger. "I'm not ashamed of being loved."

"Calm down." Smith crosses his arms. "It's about the crew. You do what you must for them. Like I said, someday you'll have one."

If I ever became a ship captain, I'd not yield to temptation merely to gain a private cabin and laud my stature above my crew.

Bahati chants louder as the pinnace slips past the sandbar and heads to the reefs. Soon it will be in the deep waters near our anchor.

"Are you with us, Jacques? I promoted you and Bahati. Be ready to help load the captives."

I don't answer. Instead, I run to the rail. "Captain! The pinnace."

He turns, and his expression mirrors mine—full-on shock. The boat is bucking. The enslaved men are fighting our buccaneers.

"The fools are going to capsize!" The captain turns to me, but he knows the *Canopus* can't get to the pinnace.

"Stop them!" Smith yells to Danseker, who's fighting hand and fist with a Guinea man in chains.

Danseker stands and tries to wrestle the slave backward, but the fellow overpowers him, wrapping his black arms and rusty links about Danseker's white neck. Face ashen with fear, he's dragged below the water's surface. The two men disappear.

The struggling flips the pinnace. It's belly up, bobbing in the churning water. Bahati prays louder. The crew on the *Canopus* yell for Danseker, yell for their friends who are being drowned by the chains they use to control the chattel.

I catch Bahati's quick smile. I think her prayers have brought a solution. Like scorned women, men can choose when to be free. And they can take as many slavers as possible with them to hell at the bottom of the sea.

Forty

1683. The Waters of Veracruz

I steer the *Canopus* away from Tortuga toward the cayos of Florida. For the past two days, Captain Smith has sent emissaries to Governor de Franquesnay to try and get back our relics or some measure of compensation.

I hear the governor laughed at these attempts and had the cannons of Fort Rocher turned on the *Canopus*. I guess those guns aren't so rusty, but I gloat on the inside. Danseker met his end because of enslavement.

Celia comes with a report on the stores. "Wulf's counted the stores. We're low on ale and bread, but we have enough salted dolphinfish for a few weeks, and we have enough water."

"Thanks, Chilango," I say. I can't look at her. I stare at the sea.

But she remains.

"Yes, Chilango?"

She adjusts her brown pourpoint. Her sloppes look freshly washed. "Don't hate me. We're in this for the wealth."

"At what cost? You said you wanted to avenge your people in Veracruz. How can you abide enslaving someone else?"

"I survived it. I—"

Bahati laughs. "You weren't put in the fields, were you? You're light enough for the Blancs to forget. But trust me, they don't truly forget."

"This argument isn't helping. The complexities that make us chattel or not don't matter. We're still women with colored skin on a boat of Blanc men. We must stay unified to survive."

Mel comes up. "Reporting to duty. Calico Mel here. That's my new name. Wulf thinks it's a strong name. He's great at names."

Mel and Bahati take turns learning the whipstaff. They're both pretty good, but Bahati knows the stars better than anyone. I step out of the way and let Mel have at the helm. "Bahati, you assist him. Chilango, go inspect the sails. I need us to be ready for anything. We're a leaner crew."

"Will do, first mate." She starts to leave but turns back. "We good, Jacques?"

"You're part of the crew of the *Canopus.* Oui. We're good, Chilango." I put my hand out. "You're with us, right?"

Relief whips across her features. Her high cheekbones become part of her smile. Celia shakes my hand hard then returns to duty.

With my scope, I surveil the sea. Then I see it, an answer to prayer. "Buccaneers, we have a ship with Spanish colors ahead of us."

I give the scope to Bahati. "Confirmation, vessel spotted. I see blue and white. It's Spanish."

"Is it a frigate?" We can't take on a frigate or a galleon, not now.

Bahati takes her time. Mel looks anxious. It's been a while since we've engaged a ship.

"It's a sloop bearing Spanish flags." Bahati lowers the scope. Her face looks jubilant. "How do we proceed?"

Well, we have a new opportunity for plunder. "Get the men ready below. We must catch the sloop. At thirty men, we'll have to cripple the sloop quickly with a broadside attack and then board and fight hard.

"Chilango," I say, "adjust the sails to ten degrees, then go wake the captain."

She offers a nod, then runs.

I wave Mel away from the whipstaff. Leading the attack renews my strength. A win will restore unity. We all need this. I'm not sure if anyone knows who to trust anymore—or how to let themselves be that vulnerable.

* * *

Captain Smith climbs up to the quarterdeck. His coat is only half on, but the black hat with feathers is on his silver hair. Those tail feathers flap in the wind. "Good boy, Jacques. You found one of the Armada de Barlovento. Must've lost its way to be so close to Florida."

I rub my hands together. "If it has payroll, it will be in reales and pieces of eight. That's what we need."

Grumbling, Bahati lowers the scope. "I was mistaken. It's not a sloop. It's a flat-bottom boat, but it's loaded with crates. If it has payroll, great, but I bet it's got provisions and maybe more things we need to fix the ship."

The captain looks anxious as I ease the *Canopus* into position. "Their guns are too close to the waterline. If they try to open 'em, they'll flood. That reduces their firepower. But if we are too aggressive, we could sink them. We must be careful in our approach."

"Let's get it." The captain's chest puffs out and he beams, taking pride in my success. In truth, he can't have it. I stand on the shoulders of the lady pirates who've come before me and the mastermind who made it possible.

Bahati is again off to the side praying. Please let her voice call down favor.

* * *

Dawn comes, bringing a dusty-pink sky. We've followed the flat-bottomed boat through the night. The vessel makes no defensive maneuvers nor attempts changing course. Having passed the Yucatan Peninsula, it's obvious its destination is the port of Veracruz, a heavily fortified Spanish city.

The port of Veracruz teems with galleons. Fortaleza de San Juan de Ulúa is like Port Royal's Fort Charles, well-armed and highly regarded for its military. Their twenty-four pounder guns will strike terror in a weakened frigate. We need to strike now or risk a counterattack and sinking.

Captain Smith comes up from his quarters. "How's it look, Delahaye?"

"There's no movement up top. But we haven't done anything aggressive yet. We look a poor sight, so they're not frightened. We should strike soon, well before the ship gets to Veracruz."

He chuckles. "Pull us into position. Let's engage in the broadside attack."

I have Celia and Wulf adjust the mainsail. Mel and the rest of the crew ready the guns. I favor our starboard side, which has less damage. Soon, I have the *Canopus* ready—parallel and a mile out.

Captain Smith goes to the waist of the frigate near the gunners. "Get ready to fire on my command."

Our gunners prepare iron balls. My heart pounds as we wait for the signal.

A shift in the wind moves us closer than I want. I wave to the captain that all is well. We're three quarters of a mile away.

The captain signals the command. "Fire broadside. Give 'em all you got, lads. Aim for the rigging, the helm, take the mast."

Balls of fire leave our cannons. Smoke fills the air. *Boom*. We have a hit.

The captain looks through the scope. "They're scrambling on board." He waves his arms. "Focus on the sail. Fire."

The *Canopus* shakes, the reaction to a second volley launched. We make holes in the flat-bottom boat's sail.

Flintlocks belch, but at this distance they're powerless. None of their cannons fire. I was right. They're too low in the water.

"Delahaye, get us closer. It's time to board."

I point to Bahati. "Adjust the sails, give ten degrees more."

Everyone is working together. The crew is smaller, but this is more coordination than I've seen in a long time.

I sail the *Canopus* within a hundred feet of the boat. I read their name on the stern: the *Honduras.*

The captain orders another round of cannon blasts. "Fire."

At close range, we hit everything. The mast is down. We've wrecked the helm. Men are scrambling. Some pepper us with shots from flintlocks. In the time it takes them to reload, we have grappling hooks engaged. Our crew swing over.

"Delahaye, stay!"

Captain sees me getting ready to go to the fight, but men from the *Honduras* have swung over to the *Canopus.*

Clang. Clang.

Our men fight the *Honduras* crew, here and over there. I drop the anchor and defend the *Canopus.* My rapier is as deadly as ever.

Clang. Clang.

Smith has a sword. He's fighting poorly. When I kill the sailor attacking him—a quick stab through the chest—the captain cheers and claps.

Bahati is on the other boat. She's fighting, pushing people into the sea. I take one of the enemies' hooks and swing over. Like a pendulum, I take down one man here, another there, before I drop onto the *Honduras*'s deck.

"Surrender!" I yell and wave my rapier. "Surrender and live."

"Nunca," someone replies. He's big, wearing the fancy skirted doublets. He waves a big sword, yelling at his men to fight. He shouts at me. His tone is fiery, a blaze. "Mátenlos!"

But I am fire too. Sparks fly when our weapons strike. I don't take prisoners.

The man is not easy to kill. There's wild strength in his blows.

From the corner of my eye, I see a cannon being dragged from below. It's only a six pounder, but at this distance, it can sink our vessel, our men. "Mel, Wulf, get our cannons ready!"

I hear the movement on our side. Our crew obey my order.

Three men are getting the *Honduras*'s cannon ready at the ship's waist. Bahati and our men are near the bow. The *Canopus*'s strike won't hurt them. Only I am in close proximity. "Calico Mel, fire at will."

I step up my fight with this big man.

Then I hear two rapid explosions.

One ball rips through their gunners like the men are paper. They are dead before they hit the water. The other, from the *Honduras*, rips through our mainmast. We have a blackened hole, and a fire. My men scramble.

Smoke pours from the *Honduras*'s deck. Someone here is throwing demijohn bottles turned into torches. They're trying to make explosions with good liquor.

I finish off the man, jabbing him through his eye.

A flintlock fires. It takes some seconds for the deadly cloud to clear. One of our gunners is down. The scent of blood and gunpowder wafts in the breeze. We need to end this fight. I'm tired of fire destroying what I love. I love the *Canopus*. I'll die for her.

My fighting becomes more fierce. I strike down anything that moves.

Clang. Clang.

Celia's fighting at Bahati's side. They're winning too.

Soon, Wulf gets the fire under control. But another bottle tosser hurls a flaming demijohn. With rapier extended, I rush toward him. I'm ready to run him through, but he turns and fights. His sword's blade is twice as wide as anything I've ever seen.

Clang. Clang.

The dull sound when his blade hits mine vibrates my arm. I stab his own arm. It doesn't slow him down.

Clang. Clang.

He turns and slashes at me. The sharp edge of his sword scales me like a fish, cutting through my doublet. It hits the crucifix and tears away the bands around my chest. For the first time in a long time, I can breathe. The breeze chills my chest, but I'm renewed. I fight harder than ever.

Clang. Clang.

I advance my position, but the man starts to laugh. "You sent a wench after me!"

While he laughs, I charge and keep going until my hilt is in his ribs and my blade slides out his back. For good measure, I twist, then shove him toward the sea. His palm grabs my shredded doublet. He takes all of it with him as he drops to the water.

Naked from the waist up, but unafraid, I cut down three more men. I'm exposed, but the *Canopus* will be saved.

All is quiet when the last man of the *Honduras* is dead.

The smoke clears. The unified crew of the *Canopus* is victorious. We have command of the *Honduras*.

Yet, instead of a celebration, everyone is mournfully silent. I glance about to see if any of those closest to me are dead. Wulf's good. Bahati's alive but wide-eyed and still. Celia points, then gasps at my bosom as if she's surprised.

I look down. My rapier drips with blood. My breasts bear my shining crucifix. It's a shield between them. I bend down and take the shreds of Lizzôa's jacket that had been in the bandaging and stuff them into my breeches.

Mel jerks off his doublet and tosses it to me. I grab it, but I almost don't care to put it on. I'm done hiding. Let my sex finally kill me.

After shrouding myself with the doublet, I take a rope and swing back to the *Canopus*. My boots thud on the deck. I march to the quarterdeck, my quarterdeck. I climb up and present my captain my rapier.

"Yes, captain. I'm not a lad. I'm Jacquotte Delahaye, daughter of Pierre Delahaye and Uzoamaka. I'm your first mate and a woman. I give you today's victory."

The disgust on his face tightens his jowls. "You broke the rules, Delahaye. You must be marooned."

He kicks away my rapier and summons two members of our crew. "Take her to the brig."

With my head up, I go with them. I put up no fight as my crew takes stock of the booty won and my disgrace.

Forty-One

1683. The Waters of Veracruz

In the darkness of the hold, I sit with shackles on my arms. Oar holes nearby let in dampness and the blessed scent of sea salt. It tamps down the ever-present smell of char. I don't know if the sourness is from today's battle or the devasting fire on the *Canopus*'s bow.

My epitaph must be: *She went out fighting.*

Waves slap against the hull. Oddly, it's peaceful. I know my fate. We voted for the punishment for a woman found on board long ago. I'm more curious about where I'll be marooned. And will they give me my rapier, so I can choose the moment of my death.

Mel and Bahati can capably steer the whipstaff. I'm not irreplaceable. I wonder if Captain Smith feels angry enough about my deception to sell me into slavery. What's the bride price for a woman buccaneer, a Guinea woman pirate?

Wrenching at the chains, I feel my humor dissipate. I decide I want a quick death or a long life, nothing in between.

I close my eyes. I've had the best adventures. I've loved hard twice, lost twice. I was, until this moment, second in command of the *Canopus*. Maman, is that enough of a legacy?

Boots pound. The ceiling trembles. Noises echo. The door to my prison opens. Captain Smith has come down with Celia and

Calico Mel. "Delahaye, it's time to face your fate in front of the crew."

Spittle flies when he says my name. I offer no resistance and allow them to lead me into the corridor. A torch shows Smith's face is red like blood.

"You of course know Chilango," he says in mock introduction, "and my new first lieutenant, Calico Mel."

"What about Bahati?" I almost stop myself from asking, but a doomed woman still can fight for women.

"No, Delahaye." He sighs. "Bahati wants the crew to reconsider your fate. Says you have a brother who needs you. But that's probably more lies."

"Josiah." Now I panic. My resolve begins to crumble. I've forgotten about my one responsibility. "My brother is true. Give my share to the monastery, L'Église de L'Assomption. I support him with my pay. I always have."

Smith folds his arms. His blue coat flaps at his thighs. "How long did you think you could get away with this?"

"As long as I could, captain. You have to admit I'm a good sailor. That should be all that matters. And I saved your life today."

He chuckles, but the laugh is bitter. "And Lizzôa, all this time I thought you two . . . a matelotage, sodomites . . . but you . . . are just a woman he brought on board the ship."

I step closer to him. "I came on board with Lizzôa, but I fooled you all. I willingly deceived everyone but the person I loved. So don't try to place blame. I own everything I did. Every man I saved, every mile I navigated, every sailor I stood up for, trained, and lifted—I own it all."

"That you did, Delahaye," Mel says.

Captain Smith raises his arm like he wants to backhand me, but Celia steps in front of him. "Captain," she says, "we're to finish this on deck."

At the ladder, the captain climbs up first. Then I go, followed by Mel and Celia.

Wulf and Bahati stand among the crew, which is down to thirty, including them and Celia.

"Captain," Mel says, "before we decide Delahaye's fate, can I remind you of how lean we are? She's been teaching me how to helm the *Canopus*, but it's her boat."

"No, it's mine. It's ours. A liar has no rights."

Wulf yells, "Let Delahaye speak."

Another echoes the same. He's not a woman pretending, but one of the original British sailors of the HMS *Florence*. "For what Delahaye has done for us, let her speak."

I glance at the captain, and he nods. I step forward, lifting my shackled hands. "Captain Smith gave us rules that we're meant to abide by. I broke the rules. I am a woman. Many of you saw that today."

Chuckles resound.

"But Captain Smith forgets how capable a buccaneer I've been. I've advanced our cause. I've saved lives and acted with no thought of preservation of my own. It shouldn't matter if your comrade in arms is a woman, not if you know she will fight to the death to protect you."

My eye catches every person I fought with today. Then I say, "I should be allowed to stay and do my job. It's the fire of my heart."

A fellow by the mast claps. Then another sailor. Then a gunner. Then they all do.

Captain whistles through his fingers. He regains order. "It's against the *Canopus*'s rules. The rules we all agreed to."

Calico Mel coughs and holds up my rapier. "Rules are meant to be changed. We all voted and changed the rules on trafficking Guineas. First Mate Delahaye and Second Mate Bahati tried to tell us not to. They tried until it was too late. Changing the rules cost us more men." Calico Mel looks around, and his voice becomes louder, more angry. "Delahaye has saved my life. She's always been all about the ship. The ship needs to be about her. Captain, I say we vote again."

Celia steps forward. "Captain, you said we live by the vote. Vote now to see if any care that Delahaye is female."

The captain rubs at his face. His cheeks look raw, like he's rubbed them off. "You think we should vote, even though she's a liar?"

"Who among us does not lie?" Bahati's voice booms. "We're buccaneers. We do what we must to win. That's what Delahaye does—win."

"No vote," the captain replies. "This is a matter of honor." He shoves me to the starboard side. "There's a sandbar. If you can swim like you can lie, you can make the fifty miles to Veracruz."

"I request my sword be left with me. It's my father's."

Captain nods. "We'll toss it to you. Say your goodbyes. God help you."

On the surface of the water the sun is about to set. The flat-bottom boat smolders in the distance, but it's still afloat.

"Captain," I say. "One last bit of advice. You can't sell these goods to Veracruz. They're marked. When the flat-bottom boat doesn't show, they will know that it's been attacked. Go back to Port Royal or even Petit-Goâve and recruit more men. Don't get these who are loyal to you killed for nothing."

"We're not going to Veracruz for provisions. There were no reales or pieces of eight on board the *Honduras*. We still need silver. We will raid Veracruz as I've done in the past. We'll sell slaves to Petit-Goâve."

Bahati comes out from behind a large sailor. "You mean you'll gather people from Veracruz to sell?"

The captain grimaces. He knows he's said too much.

Celia's hand shakes. "Captain, you didn't say we'd be doing that again. After Tortuga, aren't we done with trying to deal in chattel?"

"Chilango, I've been on these raids before. When Samuel Axe stopped pirating, I had to find other ways to earn as a privateer. It's quick. The browner men and women fetch a good penny, sometimes more than a full Guinea. You'll see. It will be easy."

Celia shakes all over, her eyes a flaming demijohn. "No. We're not going to do this."

Grabbing my rapier from Mel, Celia goes up to the captain. "You are a liar and unfit to lead."

"Put down that sword." Smith edges closer to me as if I'm going to help. "Mel, Delahaye, hold her back."

Mel simply shrugs.

Bahati takes the rapier from Celia. "Control yourself, sailor."

Captain Smith moves close to Calico Mel, his new first mate. "We need a currency that everyone understands. If we go to Veracruz and capture twenty, we'll have enough pieces of eight to buy provisions and powder to get us ready for battle in the Red Sea. Every man will have a thousand reales for defeating the Mughals."

Mel tugs me by my chains to the waist of the *Canopus*, where the crew stands. "How shall we beat the Mughals without our best swordsman?" He shakes his fist. "No. Not without Delahaye."

The crew comes and stands behind me. It's like a line has been drawn in the sand, like Josiah drawing a mast, to divide the *Canopus* between us and the captain.

Unlocking my shackles, Mel says to Wulf, "Since we can't vote on having a woman on board, I say we vote on a new leader who will let women on board. I vote for Delahaye 'cause she won't get us killed."

"A mutiny?" The captain's eyes grow big. "No! Let's talk this out."

Celia laughs and runs to my side.

Smiling, Bahati says, "Here's my vote." She tosses my rapier toward me.

Celia catches it, runs at Captain Smith. She stabs him in the gut. The big man hits the deck with a thud.

"What have you . . . you done?" Smith breathes hard as he bleeds on the deck.

After giving my rapier a twist against his innards, Celia retrieves my weapon. "That's my vote."

My dripping blade shines in the dusky light. It's been a long day. A long day of killing.

Celia kneels in front of me and gives me my rapier. I take it and lift her up. There's so much I want to say. So much gratitude to her and for all these buccaneers who've stood up for me.

Mel closes Smith's eyes. Then he returns to me. "All those in favor of Jacquotte Delahaye being our new captain, say aye."

"Aye. Aye. Aye." The ayes go around the deck. The rhythm overpowers me. The unanimous vote brings tears to my eyes.

I look out at our men. "I say we vote for true freedom. Some of you bear disguises. You've sacrificed so much to be here. I say, be here in truth. No one shall fear being who they are. Everyone here, be true to themselves. No more hiding. I say oui."

"Aye."

"Aye." Again the crew sings these affirmations.

Mel and Wulf roll the body of Dender Smith, former captain of the *Canopus*, off the starboard side of the boat. It hits the water, sending up a splash.

I don't watch Captain Smith sink. I have a ship that needs repairs and a crew to rebuild. "Mel, Bahati, second mate and first mate. Set a course to Port Royal. We'll make modifications to the *Canopus* to make her the fastest ship that has ever sailed."

"Yes, captain," Mel says, and Bahati too.

"You're each brilliant, and when you are ready, you'll command your own ships. But for now, we've got work to do."

Mel salutes. "I'm going to organize these crates. Wulf, come help."

"Make a list," Bahati says to them. Then she comes to me and clasps my hand. "Told you you'd be a captain one day."

"Well, you were right. Now it's time for us to lead the *Canopus*."

Bahati salutes and goes to her position by the whipstaff. After putting on my belt and cleaning my rapier, I join her. Standing on the quarterdeck, I seek Orion's Belt to lead us to Jamaica.

An hour ago, I was ready to die. Now I've been reborn. I'm the captain of a frigate. I lead buccaneers who no longer have to hide or be ashamed of anything.

Whether we head into the light or dive into the heart of the darkest storm, the *Canopus* will be unified. Together, we swim or sink. Together, we go to heaven or hell. I cannot wait to find out which we will earn.

I'm unafraid. I found my destiny.

Forty-Two

1691. The Waters of Florida

The sun in the glorious blue sky begins its descent. I, Jacquotte Delahaye, the captain of the *Canopus*, have my frigate in the hunting grounds off the Marquesas Islands. Laurens de Graaf, one of the shrewdest buccaneers I've ever met, has given me a tip. It's a reward for helping him in a skirmish with a British frigate.

De Graaf, the legend, is a good man and an excellent sailor. Over the past eight years, the *Canopus* has fought side by side with his frigate, the *Neptune*. As a formerly enslaved man, he hates anything to do with chattel slavery. As far as I know, he's never compromised his principles like the Captain Smiths of the world.

Unlike me, de Graaf's father had no use for him. The Dutchman abandoned him and the woman he wenched. My friend had to claw his way to freedom and then leaped to the top of the world. De Graaf has never made it clear if his mother was Guinea or mixed with Guinea and Indigenous roots. I'll say she's Guinea. Either way, strong-willed women raise strong seed.

My mixed crew of men and women has grown in numbers and wealth. We embody freedom. I even dress for me, not as a man or a caricature of one. I'm a buccaneer not hiding her femininity. I wear a red hibiscus–colored doublet with buttons undone, exposing the flesh of my neck and a bit of bosom. Once freed of binding, my breasts will never see bondage again.

Phipps, the new surgeon on the *Canopus*, comes to the quarterdeck. "Captain Delahaye, will we be heading to port soon? We need more bandages and medicines."

"Yes," I say, "we'll go to Petit-Goâve. It's our next stop. One of my old crew, Wulf, runs an excellent warehouse." Wulf stayed on board five years longer than she'd wanted. Yet, when she returned to Petit-Goâve with armloads of wealth, it was time. She retired for Margaret. Theirs was the first wedding ceremony I performed as captain, where both mates weren't members of my crew.

"Shore-bound, a businesswoman, Wulf always gives us the best prices. I like an honest seller."

Phipps smiles and then heads away. Our revamped *Canopus* has a wider hatch and more light for the corridor, and the crew's cabin has ports to let in fresh air. All of us, officers to swabbies, share those bunks. Whitewashed and clean without a speck of ash, soot, or love, the tragedy's gone from the walls. But my mind has trapped the loss inside me. My flesh mourns. Years matter not. My hell shall always be with me, as heavy and as present as the cross on my chest.

* * *

I turn my attention to the land. Coral reefs sit close to the peninsula of Florida. Lush mangroves grow here, stretching their arms at unsuspecting supply ships. Today, a beautiful sloop filled with rum and sugar has run aground. "That booty will pay handsomely in reales."

Bahati grunts a yes. She and Calico Mel stand at my side on the quarterdeck. Mel's eager for battle.

Though Bahati and Mel have learned to navigate the *Canopus*, I'm at the whipstaff. I'm always guiding us on this journey, trying to ensure a win. Eight years of battles have made me more cautious, have focused me more on my mortality. I still have a brother to care for—one who needs me to live and be his family. And I will gladly do so, for I have earned adventure, and my motherly bosom has nurtured a crew.

"Calico Mel, adjust the topgallant. I want to be within a mile of that sloop before the sun goes down."

He nods and heads down to the deck. His new boots sound like a nighthawk's squeal. He's become a stylish dresser like Michel, like myself. Today, he wears a maroon-colored doublet with jet sloppes. His hat looks very French. It's wide brimmed, just missing feathers.

My first mate perks up. The silent competition between the two continues. "They are loaded and stuck, captain."

She lifts her scope from the strap at her side. All my officers have one. I keep Lizzôa's original scope safe in a sack with my dearest possessions.

"It's going to be a good haul." Bahati nods, her head still shiny and smooth like a fine black pearl. Her style of clothes hasn't changed much. She's in a close-fitting pourpoint and dark breeches.

I don't care how any sailor dresses or what they do off duty. No one fears marooning or being thrown in the hold for existing. We've pledged our lives to victory—sweet, sweet victory.

"Captain, there are seven men," my first mate says. "Seems an odd assortment for just silver."

"Tell me why, Bahati."

"If it's a typical transport of goods, the ship wouldn't have so few men or be trying to travel so close to the cayos. They're carrying pay in those barrels, or guns."

"Excellent." Bahati always has good instincts. She's as good as me at picking targets.

"I'm curious," she says. "I suspect we will return to Petit-Goâve with even more wealth. Will you take more than a day off, or will you rush from port as always? Wulf says you don't dine with them anymore."

"It's hard seeing them so happy. I mean, I'm glad for Wulf and Margaret. It's the path not chosen for me. Sometimes, I just want to curl away in an inn and drink."

Bahati's black eyes settle on me. "Stop with drinking. Go force a visit with the brother."

Blast it. When did Bahati get so good at understanding me too? I blow out a breath and stare at the foaming water that kisses our sprinting bow. "Josiah refuses to see me. I pay for his care with more alms than those priests have ever known. And all I get are letters from Monsignor François Robilere."

"Try again, captain."

Josiah and I haven't locked eyes for seven years. I told him what I'd done. I talked of Lizzôa's death. Josiah looked at me as if I were nothing. I deserve this. "Last time I was at port, Monsignor Robilere shamed me. He takes my silver and makes me feel like the lowest of the low. But at least they revere Josiah's commitment to silence."

"You are not a quitter. Try again."

Mel runs back. "What next?"

"Patience," I say, watching him fidget. "We're closing in, get the gunners ready. We're moving in for a broadside attack."

The *Canopus* cuts through the crystal waters. The mangrove flower blooms look like yellow dots. They fly into the air when the sloop breaks free. The trapped rats try to escape. The sloop extends a sail.

"They'll try to slip past us, captain." Bahati crosses her arms. "Do we raise all the sails and intercept?"

"Yes. We go on attack." My crew of forty stand at the ready. Bahati yells commands to adjust lines, change the angle of sails.

The waves get choppy. The distance between ships is cut in half. White, billowy sails whip like they're gasping for air. Soon, they fill and stretch, and like a fantôme floating above they push our ship into position to strike.

The breeze tastes salty and sweet. The rosy patchwork of jasmine-scented frangipani florals battle the strong sulfur of the mangrove and the acrid scent of gunpowder.

Blam. The bow of the sloop flips up. Water and waves spill into the stern. "The mangroves did the hard work for us. Cut the topgallant, Bahati. Mel, fire on my signal. Let's see how foolish the sloop's captain is."

I glide the *Canopus* closer. Half a mile from them, our nine pounders aim at the mast and the now-raised hull. "Try not to hit the bottom. I want save the boat. Fire!"

Our cannons shoot a volley of iron balls. Nothing answer this but a flag waved from their bow.

"A white flag, captain," Bahati reports. "Do we trust it?"

"Fire one cannon. Get close to the mast but I want our shot to fly over. Let them sit in the shadow of our power. Ready a second to cut through the waist if their captain decides to test us."

"Aye-aye." Bahati and Mel both go to our guns. Competitive as they are, they work well as a team.

Boom. The *Canopus* shimmies. The black ball streaks through the blue sky. Men scream. Chaos. Their crew leap off. I tell our guns to stand down.

The white flag, a lone miserable ghost, waves in the wind. With swords raised and flintlocks brought to bear, Mel brings us close enough to board the sloop.

Grappling hooks shoot into their rigging. I swing over, leading the assault. The resistance is nothing. It doesn't take long to have a chest of silver reales meant for Veracruz brought on board the *Canopus* along with a load of freshly minted Spanish gun barrels from Catalonia. These miquelets are more accurate than English flintlocks.

Back on the *Canopus*, I hold one up, marveling at the sleek silver finish. "The Spanish tried to hide this in plain sight."

We gain more powder and some medicine, but I leave the sloop's sailors food and water. "Good day, gentlemen," I say to the sailors marooning themselves in the mangrove. "Celia, cut our lines free. Bahati, steer us into the wind.

"Set a course two hundred fifty degrees southwest to Port Royal. We need rest and supplies and to meet with de Graaf. Mel, distribute the silver. I want everyone to have a good time in the ville."

My crew cheers. Celia, our bosun, salutes then heads to the bow.

Hair out and blowing in the wind, she leans on the low prow to ensure we avoid any uncharted sandbars.

Bahati shakes her head at me, knowing I've delayed our trip to Petit-Goâve. "We will go home sometime?"

I swallow the dregs that word brings. "De Graaf knows everything in the Caribbean. He'll know why the Spanish are smuggling guns. We need to be prepared. That's how we protect home."

"Get the topgallants going," Bahati calls out. "We know our captain hates to waste an evening breeze." I laugh and take her place at the whipstaff, and seize a final glance at the stranded sloop. In a spirit of goodwill, we also left tools to repair their ship. We've given them a chance to live, which is more than another pirate crew might do.

A legacy isn't a legacy if it's not spoken of broadly. I want to be known as a valiant, honorable captain, not the angry, jealous woman with nowhere to call home.

Forty-Three

1691. Port Royal, Jamaica

Three days sailing in decent weather puts the *Canopus* in Port Royal at the twilight before dusk. The graying sky lets the sun sink into the sea. The place keeps growing. Tonight the city seems crowded, with boats covering every inch of the bay. We'll have to anchor farther out near seven other frigates. I'm in luck. De Graaf's *Neptune* is one.

His third-rate frigate with at least seventy guns has a white-and-blue painted hull. That's a telltale sign of his *Neptune* being a former Spanish vessel.

"Bosun, prepare the ship for anchoring," I yell to Celia, who proceeds to check the lines and gathers her team to drop our heavy iron anchor. "All hands, stand by to lower the pinnace."

My crew works diligently. Bahati will stay on board while I will go into the city. It's rare for me to leave the *Canopus* overnight, but I want a bath and a bottle of rum. Some habits never die.

The pinnace is lowered. I, Mel, Celia, Phipps, and ten others climb in. Soon, we're zipping through the crowded harbor and tying in at the docks.

My sailors scatter except for Celia. That's Bahati's doing. God bless her—someone should be my keeper when the weight of the *Canopus*'s responsibilities aren't on my shoulders.

"Come on, Celia. Let's go catch up to de Graaf. I know where the devil holds court."

A big smile settles on her face. "He's nice to look at."

I laugh and have to agree. "This way."

We head down familiar rues, past the looming outline of Fort Charles. To save time, we cut through the yard of St. Peter's church. Her footsteps slow when we reach Palisadoes Cemetery.

"Captain, uh, must we go this way?"

I want to roll my eyes so badly they hurt. "After all the people we've battled, you can't be afraid of fantômes?"

Her chin juts up. "No. But this makes me think of the people we've killed. You ever think of them?"

"No, Celia. I don't." I start walking, and slowly she catches up.

"How is that, captain?"

Rubbing my tense neck, I glance up. The night sky becomes brighter as it unveils itself, ripping away clouds, showing truth of the stars. If I cup a hand to my eyes and squint, I can see Michel's blue pole in the distance. Lamplights glow on the property. Life has moved on. The house has a new owner. "Orion's Belt is above."

"You didn't answer, captain."

"Celia, I've killed too many to think about any of them. The men and women who I've lost, who meant something to me, they occupy my thoughts. Bahati says I should give them less room too."

She shrugs and clasps her hands behind her. "Still, we shouldn't linger in a graveyard." Her tunic and baggy sloppes seem white in moonlight. Celia could be mistaken for a ghost.

We keep going until we stand beside a big marble crypt. "They gave this bastard, Henry Morgan, a state funeral. In eighty-eight, they offered amnesty for every pirate to attend. I hear they put him in this tomb with a twenty-two-gun salute."

Celia laughs, and I do too. We didn't go to the funeral. "I haven't forgiven him for stealing the *Canopus*'s treasure and making our crew so desperate. He still owes me."

"But you forgave me?" Celia's face bears a deep frown. "I need to hear that you have, captain."

"Getting rid of Captain Smith helped, immensely." My tone is light, but even in the growing darkness, I know she's hunting for my truth.

"The ancestors, before becoming bastards of Spain, believed differently, that all enslavement is wrong. Captain . . . Jacques . . . I wanted adventure and fortune and to belong more than I wanted to be right. I was good as long as it was only others who were hurt. Should've realized, a wrong hurts us all."

I put my foot on Morgan's grave. "I forgive you. You're a damn fine bosun, a good buccaneer, and a friend. We can be weak sometimes, but then we must step up and do right."

Celia hugs me before I can stop her, before the part of me that fears losing people rears its awful head. I feel her arms, and it's like she touches my soul, but this is friend to friend. Captain to sailor. Even mother to daughter.

Forgiving, truly forgiving anyone means I should start with myself. I embrace her, and I embrace me. "Now we have to leave the dead alone. Come on, sailor. I know a place that serves the second-best pottage in the world."

A quick swipe at her eye, a sniffle, and then we two salts start to move on.

Click.

I whip around with my rapier drawn.

No one is there.

But then I see two of my other sailors. They came to me early this morn. At my whipstaff, I gave the brave men what they wanted, a blessing on their matelotage. I suggested they go to King's Haven Inn. They'll be cared for as they express care for each other.

Again, I feel the loneliness and weight of my responsibilities. "Can't wait to see de Graaf. Few know the burdens of being a captain like him."

"You're the best, Captain Delahaye."

Sheathing my rapier, I quicken our pace. Celia is right about lingering too long in a graveyard. Can't take a chance on which of the souls tied to me may rise and haunt me in this place celebrating the dead.

* * *

The Fair Weather Tavern is close to Lizzôa's favorite inn. I decide to treat Celia to a meal before going off in private with my bottle. I don't drink on the *Canopus* anymore. She demands my sobriety, but my thirst is heavy when I'm alone and on land.

At the front of the inn sits an unusual young fellow. With short, straight, jet-black hair and beautiful olive skin, the boy in scarlet silk pourpoint sketches under a pitch torch. No one bothers him. I hope some wealthy person hasn't stolen him to be a scribe. The Brits do that, dressing up enslaved boys to be pages.

Celia tugs me away. We find seats in the crowded dining room. Filibusters and buccaneers from every part of the Caribbean have gathered. Celia and I have stumbled into some sort of meeting. With so many captains present, it's obvious my invitation was lost.

Someone mentions de Graaf. I wonder if the sloop in the cayos was a gift or a way to keep me away from Port Royal.

Plunking down by the window, I worship the full moon's light. My temper rises at the notion of being excluded. A serving girl comes up, no more than ten or twelve, wearing a stained apron. I remember working at that age in Père's tavern. She eyes me. Her smile blooms. And I want to tell her it's possible to escape this life.

After ordering ale and pottage, I spot de Graaf. He enters the tavern and heads to the center of the room. Sandy-brown hair, tall, muscular in a jet doublet and tight, tight breeches, he saunters with great confidence.

"Gentlemen . . . and captains," he says in a deep, booming voice. "The War of Grand Alliances has been raging three years with no end in sight. Trade lines continue to be disrupted. More guns are being smuggled in. That means fewer single-ship missions and more heavily armed convoys."

That's exactly what we found in the Florida cayos.

He stands on a rickety stool that makes the tall man a giant. "Letters of marque are being offered from all the governments. More rival marques from the Dutch or the Brits or the French, and even Spain, weaken their alliances. These actions are akin to sanctioning all-out war on our waters. Ours. We rule these seas."

"Why is it bad?" A ragged voice arises from the other side of the room. "Doesn't that mean we can attack with impunity? There's safety in sanctioned piracy."

I can't get a good view of the questioner, but his voice sounds . . . familiar.

De Graaf turns in the direction of the voice, then smiles. The man must be someone he knows. "That's a fair question. These nations want our help to defend their sovereignty. At the first signs of peace, these same countries will declare us the enemy. It will be the same chaos that brought Governor d'Ogeron to power. He turned on all pirates from Tortuga. It's not wise to bed fickle friends. I propose we don't give in to their inducements. Let the imperial powers fend for themselves."

"Why run from money, de Graaf? Are we just to disappear when money's to be made?" This skeptical voice sounds younger than the previous one.

This is no time to disappear. I must remain visible. The world needs to see what women can do.

A fellow to the right of Celia stands up. "My friends, we should turn our attention to the Far East. Spain is fighting on all sides, depleting their treasury. Let's go after the one power who's smart enough to stay out of it. The Mughals. They grow wealthy from trade while others lose treasure and men fight amongst themselves."

I grumble. This delusion has chased so many to early graves. Frustrated, I slap the table, almost spill the fresh pottage, and unintentionally gather the attention of the room.

"Yes, Captain Delahaye?" De Graaf jumps down.

Celia looks at me with a sideways grin. "He is handsome."

De Graaf comes to our table. "Please, Captain Delahaye. Have your say."

Slurping ale, I stand. "Everyone talks of the Mughals, but whose boat has actually made it to their empire? How many have been sunk by worms in the wood or downed in storms about the cape? It's a dream that makes the dreamers pay."

The room goes silent. Not sure if that means they agree or if they are stunned that a woman is in their midst. I take my seat, but the fellow I challenged charges toward me. I put my hand on my rapier.

The aggressive man slows his steps.

"Tew and Delahaye," De Graaf says, "stand down. This is a discussion."

"Why is a woman here?" Tew says.

De Graaf blocks my path, standing between me and Tew. "Delahaye, no one here in their right mind questions your ability. Mr. Tew needs to rethink his stance."

But I don't need anyone to fight my battles. "Tew, go find a ship. Then do your best to prove me wrong. Bring back silk and gold from the Far East. And stay alive."

The room laughs. Tew almost leaves the tavern, but sits at a table near the entrance.

Moving back to his position in the center, de Graaf begins to explain developing strategic blockades to attack vessels bringing arms to the West Indies. "It's simple," he says. "These governors will not invest in building their own defenses. We will grow fat in riches. Our presence will not be questioned."

Celia leans closer. "Captain, if all the buccaneers work together, this plan might work."

I don't disagree.

"De Graaf!" Tew yells. "You're the richest one of us, and your plan will only gain us a moderate income. Some of us want more. Let Le Basque tell us about the Mughals. His *Marauder* made it to the Far East. Tell them, Le Basque."

My heart stutters, then seems to stop. I pinch my leg beneath the table. I check my full mug of ale. I'm not drunk or dreaming. I see a man with smoke-tinted spectacles that hide his eyes. He wears an oxblood coat with fine pearl buttons, glossy shined boots, and dons a wide hat with long feathers.

My late husband, Michel Le Basque, is still stylish and still alive.

"Tew, you're a braggart," Michel says. His voice is a bit deeper, a bit more gravelly, but it's the voice I remember in my dreams. "You're always talking too much, stretching the truth with your mouth."

"Tell them, Captain Le Basque." Tew sounds desperate. "Tell them what you saw before you lost your eyes."

"The riches are true." Michel sighes and faces straight ahead.

How can he be alive? How can he sit here like he hasn't heard my name?

De Graaf goes to Michel. "Le Basque, you don't have to be party to this. I can have your servant take you home."

Michel's hand flutters in the air until he catches de Graaf's arm. "No! I don't need a nursemaid."

Trying to contain all my emotions, I swallow my ale and wish it were stronger, to dull the pain trembling my soul.

Older, with a scar running from one dimmed eye to his jaw, Michel's face tells a truer story than the flowery words he uses to describe the East. That's how all the lies began in Père's tavern. Michel says names like Grand Mughal, Aurangzeb, that sound regal and grand. Then he speaks of torture and the killing of the *Marauder*'s crew.

My gut feels punched through. I want to scream.

I don't. I can't.

As angry as I am that I'm hearing these pitying words, my heart also breaks for Michel. He looks tired and old. The stern posture that I've always admired, even emulated, slumps. "Tew is right. The riches of the Mughals are on the magnitude of my father's trove from the *Santa Margarita*," he says. "But Aurangzeb is ruthless. We're infidels to him. My eyes were put out because I refused to pick which one of my crew to slaughter first. My story should've ended in the Far East. But I'm here with a warning. Aurangzeb's ghanjah dhow travels well-armed, just like the Spanish Armada. Only an entire convoy of pirate ships should ever consider taking him on."

I stand up. "Captain Le Basque." His back straightens, and he turns toward my voice. Now I am sure he knows it's me. My throat closes a little, but I force it, command it to work. "If Aurangzeb ensures his fleet is well-armed, how do you expect an attack by a band of ships to succeed? Everyone remembers your exploits, your fast and sleek *Marauder*."

He takes a breath. "I'm advising everyone to not go. Mughals have riches, but they have no mercy."

My hand trembles. "So, it's a mistake. A suicide mission."

"I would stop no man from his pursuits. I'd love for someone to avenge the dead lost to Aurangzeb, but revenge is no reason to sail to the ends of the earth."

I toss coins on the table.

Celia looks at me, confused. "Captain, are you well? You look pale."

"Need to go. I remembered something. See you on board tomorrow." I start walking away. "Gentlemen, I'll let you fight this one." Passing Michel, I drop my hand to his shoulder. I feel velvet and flesh and bone. The scent of clean soap wafts up to my sniffling nose. "Still like that soap? Try ones made of lavender. They are superb."

He says nothing. When I see his fingers reaching for mine, I lift my palm and leave into the night.

My wobbly legs hold me up. With tears wetting my face, I stumble into Lizzôa's inn, grateful to be in the King's Haven.

At least I saw Michel again, met captain to captain. We are equals, more than equals. I hold a powerful command. I have crew who depend on me. I'm not nor ever will again be the wench Michel left behind.

Yet, in my prideful heart, I know that him being injured and needing help has kept him away. I'm no caregiver. I'm an arse.

My sobbing stops long enough for me to sink into a steaming bath. I wallow, drinking rum, wishing I didn't know my first love is alive and would rather spend the rest of his days letting me believe he's dead.

Forty-Four

1692. Petit-Goâve. Hispaniola

For the rest of 1691, I stay away from Port Royal. I even avoid de Graaf at sea. I'm not sure what he knows of Michel's and my history. My marriage to Michel died a long time ago. The band on my finger I wear for Lizzôa.

I walk the rues of Petit-Goâve, trying to ignore the anger I can't release. A wife deserves to know her husband's fate. Leaving me to wonder, is this to punish me for becoming a successful captain? Wishing I had a demijohn of rum, I avoid the warehouses, even Wulf's and head up the rue to the monastery.

Josiah, I must see him. He's twenty-one years old, and I've laid eyes on him once, eight years ago. My hand trembles when I shake the gate. Without a whipstaff to hold, the tremors are harder to ignore. Some sailors kill their demons by smoking tobacco until they wheeze. Rum is my medicine. I'll have it morning, noon, and night once this visit to the monastery is done.

I shake the gate again. "Father, have mercy."

Hours go by, but I keep making the same racket. The dead in their graves behind the monastery should awaken. When the sun starts to set, Monsignor Robilere in long brown robes comes to the gate.

He glances at me. My curls are free, not pinned up under my wide-brimmed hat. I've styled my ebony velvet vest like a corset. The black lacing over the scarlet satin lifts my bosom. My indigo breeches are probably too snug for his celibate tastes. He says, "What can I help you with?"

"I've come to see Brother Delahaye. I must see him."

A long, exaggerated sigh releases from his big nostrils. "Brother Delahaye does not wish to see anyone."

"He'll see me. It's very important, monsignor." I dig in my pocket and pull out a satchel of coins. "Please."

He practically drools when I shake it. But then he resumes his righteous stance. He shakes his head. "Non. I'll not disturb him for the likes of you. Go sleep off the rum, Jacques Delahaye. Clean yourself up. Decide if you are a man or woman and then come back."

The monsignor turns.

My knees weaken. I can barely stand from this sharp rejection. "Aren't we all God's children? Isn't the church a place of refuge, even for those who you think are lost?"

With a shake of his head, he keeps walking. The monsignor enters the monastery and shuts the door. I rattle the lock. I want to tear the gate off its hinges.

I wait there at the iron bars until darkness falls. Then I must accept that the church has turned me away.

All my life I've prayed to all the gods, even Père's. No one wants my soul, not even me.

* * *

Petit-Goâve is a busy town like Port Royal. Full of people going to and fro. I think about going back to the *Canopus*, but I know I've drunk too much rum. I can't let Wulf and Margaret see me like this. I won't let anyone lose more respect for me.

So I wander. The rues are familiar. Stews and taverns have closed or reopened with new names.

Music. I hear someone singing. A sea chanty. A hymn? I find myself outside of a stew. The name says Twilight Tavern, but it's the same brothel I tried to work at in eighty-one. That night I met Lizzôa and she changed my life. I barge inside.

An old man sings and eats a hearty loaf of bread. By the window, the best place in the tavern, stands an empty table.

Thud.

A slatted kitchen door swings open. Someone inside shouts like Père. I look up at the dark beams and think fondly of our tavern. I remember swabbing the floors, cleaning my kitchen until every speck of dirt disappeared. Josiah would be in the corner, washing bowls and mugs in the pewter basin. That basin today would only fetch five Guineas, not fifteen. The demand for slaves, especially Guineas, has driven up the value of their bodies.

A little miss with sandy-blond curls, maybe four or five years old, follows an older girl around. The babe toddles behind, picking up a dropped spoon. "Wash?" she asks. The little voice sounds light and innocent.

The older girl, a young brunette, comes over. Unlike the former establishment's servers, this one wears a dress, not merely fabric draped at the hips.

"We have pottage," she says as she comes to my table. "It's made fresh."

"That and rum. I'd like rum."

"You sure you want more?" She waves a hand about her nose. "You smell like you've had enough, Captain Delahaye."

She knows my name but says it with respect. "Never enough. Bring it and a bowl of the pottage. Maybe it's as good as what I cooked in Tortuga."

"The new owner says it's the best."

New owner? Hmm. That must be why the women are modestly dressed. The server scurries away and soon returns with a steaming bowl. I smell garlic and onions, even carrots. The stock is beef, not cod or dolphinfish.

Nonetheless, the serving girl hasn't brought the rum. "Have you forgotten my drink? If you're out, fetch ale."

"Not out, but Maman says to check back when you have food in your gut. Please don't fight with Maman."

This girl is brave and protective of her mother. I chuckle as I dip my spoon into the bowl. The pottage broth tastes good. The bread at the bottom seems crisply toasted. Pretty good. "I'm eating, now fetch the rum."

She runs into the kitchen.

I hear a man's voice asking, "Is she a buccaneer, dressed like that?"

"Joseph," a sweet tone answers. "Watch your mouth and your temper. She's good people. Let her be. Go on to bed. You have a meeting with the council tomorrow."

"Very well, my dearest wife. I must make my speech with care. Things will change in Petit-Goâve."

Out of the kitchen comes a man with a black beard. A blond woman about my age kisses him. He heads up the stairs, leaving this pregnant woman and the girls to clean the tavern.

At first, I feel pity for her. Then I think I recognize her. "Do I know you?"

She gazes at me and smiles, and her eyes brim with tears. "I told you you'd make a good filibuster."

That voice, it sings through my memories. I picture the hills of Cayonne, hiding with the young woman I rescued from the pens. "Anne? Anne Dieu-Le-Veut?"

She nods and aims for the chair next to me, but that big belly's in the way. Doesn't matter, because I'm on my feet. "I looked for you when I came to Petit-Goâve in eighty."

"That was years ago." Anne clasps my hand. "I'm so proud of you, Jacquotte."

I grab her and hold her like she might disappear. For someone who doesn't think she's sentimental, I'm a sobbing wreck. There are very few times in my life where I got things right. Rescuing Anne was one.

She holds me. I hope she won't let me go either.

"You saved me, Jacquotte. I've heard of your exploits. There's talk you're a man pretending to be a woman. Whenever the *Canopus* comes to port, I pray you'll visit. I wanted to go meet the ship, so many times."

She's babbling. I hold her tighter. She feels real, true flesh and blood. "Anne, please be here. Let this not be a rum-sotted dream. Please be true."

"I never forgot you," she says. "You saved my life that night. I did become a filibuster on a ship. I lied and wore disguises. Madame Erville helped me get on my first ship."

I cry harder. It has been years since someone said Lizzôa's name aloud. "Madame Erville died on board the *Canopus*. Lizzôa Erville was the best person I've ever known."

Plopping into the chair, I'm blubbering. I hear Anne chase away the other patrons. She's giving them their meals for free. When all are gone and it's just us, I give her a satchel of coins. "They wouldn't take this at the monastery. You take it. This will pay for the coin you're losing on me tonight."

She doesn't take it. Instead, she hands me a napkin. "Non. I owe you more. I have a life, two beautiful children." Anne rubs her stomach. "About to have one more. I'm happy. I'd not have anything if you hadn't risked your all to save me."

Anne takes my hand in hers and tells me her story, the highs and lows. I feel the pulse in her thumb, the warmth of her sweaty palm.

So much to take in. She's happy but lost one husband, a pirate she met on the ship. "When I could plead the belly, Pierre Lelong and I left and married. Then he died. I married Joseph soon after. I don't like being alone, not with children."

Her blue eyes are wet, but she smiles. "I hoped you'd come into my tavern."

"Anything you need, Anne. I have means." I swipe at my eyes. "I am glad to see you, Anne."

She finally sinks into the chair I pulled out for her. Her gown is pink and light. Her bib collar is lacy. Her sleeves are rolled up, exposing hands chapped from dishwater.

Anne's face becomes wistful. "You saw my husband, Joseph Chérel. He owns this tavern but wants to be a politician."

Politician? Nothing good can come from that, but I keep my face even. No dampening her happiness.

"Joseph loves Pierre's children as his own, and he's excited about the new babe to come."

She looks over at the light-haired four-year-old following my server. "He adores my daughter Yvonne. The older is Jacqueline. Every time I say her name, I think of you."

Smoothing her skirts, Anne waddles to her feet. "Whenever the *Canopus* comes to port, we have rooms upstairs for you. I want you to take one tonight."

Does she know I no longer have a home here? I had one once. I had a life and love, but I was too restless to appreciate it. "I don't want to inconvenience you."

"My tavern is yours. I'd love it to be a place that's safe for you. Let me do this."

Lizzôa's cottage near the mountains has become another sugarcane field. Not sure when it was sold off or by who, but it's no more.

Anne smiles and disappears into the kitchen. She shouldn't have to work so close to her time. The littlest one comes out. She looks at me, this little Mademoiselle Yvonne. "Maman says you sail boats."

I nod to the moppet. I see Anne's eyes in this one. For a moment, I think of Michel. That time in the cave on a bed of gold, I wanted his babe. I wanted something to hold on to. Anne and I are close in age. She wanted to be a pirate but has taken well to motherhood. Her dreams changed. I wondered if mine would've if Michel had stayed, if we'd had a son or daughter.

Yvonne climbs up into the chair next to me. She fingers the chain of my crucifix and yanks the cross up from my doublet. "Treasure," she says.

"It is." I smile at what might have been, but I'm thankful for my ship, my marriage, my matelotage, my crew. "Tell your mother I'm an early riser. I'll probably be gone before she rises."

"No go." The moppet jumps down and goes into the kitchen. The door swings, then stops. I rest hearing the noise of pots being cleaned. Perhaps the little one has a basin in the corner like Josiah.

Forty-Five

1692. The Caribbean Sea

The high, wispy clouds in the graying sky are the first indication of oncoming inclement weather. The second is a throbbing in my knee. I've wrapped it in linen bandages so I can stand without limping on the quarterdeck of the *Canopus.*

"Like a red morn that ever yet betoken'd," Calico Mel says, sounding like a priest. "Wrack to the seaman, tempest to the field, / Sorrow to the shepherds, woe unto the birds, / Gusts and foul flaws to herdmen and to herds."

Bahati groans. "What does that mean?"

"That's Shakespeare," he says, lifting his nose into the air. "I'm trying to become more learned."

"Show-off. I should quote the prayers of the Kissi." She says this with a shrug, but I hope she doesn't sing any death prayers, like in Tortuga.

"First mate, how about we agree that the weather is turning for the worst?" My tone is stern. I'm not looking for more trouble. I need to get to Petit-Goâve to Anne.

Bahati looks over at me, her nose twitching. "You all right, captain?"

"Just fine." I'm lying, and she knows it. I'm not even sure why she's asking.

Leading the assault on a British sloop in my favorite Florida hunting grounds gains us a boat in great condition and a bothersome dilemma.

"Chilango, how are the lines towing the sloop?"

She signals that they're fine. Celia has taken ropes from the capstan to tow the sloop, keep it close to the stern, and reduce drag on the *Canopus.* The choppy water churning beneath us whips the sloop. If it looks likely to ram my ship, I might have to cut it free.

The wind picks up. I tug the collar of my pourpoint closer to my neck. My stomach knots. I may have to make a decision that's been on my mind sooner than I'd planned.

I turn to my two officers, Bahati and Calico Mel. It's time for them both to fly. I clasp my hands behind my back. "First Mate Bahati and Second Mate Calico, I couldn't be more proud of your service to the *Canopus.* Bahati, your bravery is unmatched. You're a great navigator."

Then I move to Calico. "Your instincts are superb. You've learned to command the whipstaff with elegance and authority. You too are a great navigator."

Calico's frowning. "Captain, why does it sound as if you're saying goodbye?" His face is tense. His lips thin to a line.

My visits to Petit-Goâve have become more regular, particularly as Anne's time nears. It puts things into perspective. "Sailors, I have no intention of quitting." I point to the sloop that's slowing our progress. "One of you should take command of the sloop and become its captain."

Bahati's black eyes go wide. "You think we're ready for that?"

"Yes—yes, I do. I learned by fire. You've both learned in battle. You've been at my side observing how to lead. You're my legacy. Tolerance and diligence are something I expect on each of your ships."

I turn to Bahati. "You have the greater rank and more experience; the sloop is yours."

Clapping her hands together in a big slap, she smiles. "I beat the Blanc. Beat you fair and square." She laughs then sobers. "I don't want it. I'm with you for life, Captain Delahaye." She rotates to a stunned Calico. "You. You're good. Take it, Mel. I've enjoyed our battles. But you, my friend, are the sloop's new captain."

Calico's mouth drops open. He dances around and dares to try to kiss Bahati's cheek. He leans toward her and gets slugged. The two laugh as she helps him up from the quarterdeck.

Signaling with a gesture, I gather my crew together. "Calico, go to the waist of the *Canopus*."

He does and stands by the mainmast. All the sails are out except the topgallant. The extra weight makes my ship shimmy.

I give Bahati the whipstaff and go to the main deck. "Calico Mel will be the new captain of the sloop we captured. He'll need a crew of ten to help him get started. If you choose to go, it's no slight to me or the *Canopus*. You're all brave. You can return to the *Canopus* at any time, but Captain Calico needs to be sent off in the best possible manner."

My sailors look stunned. A couple of congratulatory words are offered. We've been a team for years. We are many nationalities and skins, men and women. All are unmasked, being who they wish. Fifteen have been enslaved at some point in their lives. At least seven are original members of the HMS *Florence*, and thirteen served with me on the *Canopus* under Dender Smith. Ten are women. No one asks about their fellow sailors' private affairs. They just care if you can load shot fast or have a steady hand for a sword fight.

I look around my crew—*my* crew—painting a picture of everyone to keep in my heart. "Congrats, Calico. I wish you well. I look forward to when our ships fight together."

"Three cheers for Captain Calico." Bahati pumps her fist and whoops up the crew. Clapping and hoots abound.

I feel good letting a baby bird fly the nest. And Celia is looking at Mel with proud eyes. I believe I'll need to train a new bosun as well.

* * *

Calico Mel's sloop follows behind the *Canopus.* It's our own convoy. The rain beats down. My scope feels slippery in my hands. I fumble but manage to put it in my jacket pocket. My long-skirted coat, though thick, doesn't repel the rain when the water falls like a rushing river. The quarterdeck is soaked. I push my beaver-pelt hat down on my head. The Brits do make a nice hat. Water beads up and rolls off the wide brim.

"You think the hat will survive a hurricane?" I ask Bahati, who wears a matching one. "I need you healthy."

"I'm strong, captain." She comes and looks me over. "I need you healthy. All that rum will give you gout. They say Henry Morgan's last days were awful and sickly."

Been trying to hide my habit, but Bahati knows all.

"It's the no rum that's causing my hands to shake."

"It will pass, as will the craving. If not for yourself, do it for me. I'll always choose you, Jacques. I see the power in you. But you're killing your light."

Killing my light? I've killed a lot of people, a lot of things, but never light. Light is that bit of Lizzôa in me, that shining part of Maman. "For you, I'll suffer. Can't kill the light, Bahati. It's the only good left in me."

"Pain enslaves us to the worst notions of ourselves." She taps her skull. "We do that up here. We let darkness chant at us in every failing. We must stop. That's how we keep the light."

I take off my hat and get a good faceful of rain, of tears, and I beg the god of clouds to unveil in me my hidden light. "I guess I need a plan for the rest of my life. Lizzôa would want that."

"Yes, she would." Then Bahati smacks the hat down on my head. "Now take us into the Windward Channel."

Chuckling, I catch her gaze. "You sure you didn't want to command that sloop? You give good orders."

I look out at the roiling sea, gray and foamy, turning indigo. "Go position our sails another ten degrees. I'll try to get us past Jamaica as fast as I can."

"Port Royal is a closer port, captain."

No, it isn't. It is the furthest thing I need for my peace and sobriety. "We're heading to Petit-Goâve. That's my plan."

Forty-Six

1692. Petit-Goâve, Hispaniola

In the upper room of the Twilight Tavern, I hold little Jean-François Chérel. The healthy boy cries a bit, then goes to sleep after unsuccessfully trying to latch onto my buttons for milk.

The oldest girl looks at me. "I don't think I've ever seen a buccaneer holding a baby."

"Just pretend it's a cannonball, Jacqueline. And make sure I don't pitch your brother away."

She rolls her eyes. "You always act so tough. You're a woman. You can be motherly."

As if she's cursed me, I almost lose my grip on the babe. "Perhaps you should take the cannonball."

The girl just looks at me. "You could be a mother. Probably a good one."

"Jacqueline, stop teasing Jacquotte. She gets enough of that from Joseph." Anne winces as she mentions her husband's name.

Joseph Chérel isn't as bad as Hasneau, but he's no friend to my kind, buccaneers. He wants us all gone from Petit-Goâve. The man's business is hurting due to this stance.

Unlike most, Anne's husband has principles. Unfortunately, his principles will probably make her a widow for a second time.

She groans as she tries to find an easier position to lie in.

It was a hard birth, almost breech. I thought I saw Maman coming for Anne. I'll stay in the ville to make sure death doesn't still take my friend.

I give her a little more of my last bottle of rum. This demijohn is Barbados rum, distilled in copper pots, aged in oak barrels, and infused with hints of vanilla. I pour her a small mug of the dark liquor and make her sip. If no fever comes, death won't trouble us.

Yet, the darkness is all around us. Joseph can't sit still. Too many filibusters and buccaneers have come into port, a bunch are downstairs eating pottage. The hurricane has made everyone dock.

Lightning crashes outside. "Daughter, go check on Yvonne." Anne sits up a little. "The storm must terrify her."

Jacqueline nods and dashes out the door. When it shuts, I still have the little thing in my arms. "You need to learn all your words, little one. You need to tell the stories of us. You and your sisters must remember us."

"I tried to call this one Jacques." Anne lets out a big yawn. "My Joseph wouldn't agree."

My friend lies in the clean bedsheets that we've laid out. I've washed her with lavender soap.

"I like that name. I tried." She sounds exhausted.

My fears ramp up. "Well, I appreciate the effort. But my friendship doesn't depend on a name."

Her smile lights then fades. "I'm glad you've come back, Jacquotte. I think you needed me. Now I need you again."

"It was time. As odd as it may seem, I have delivered a baby before, on the *Canopus*. That's the trouble with having a crew of men and women. Women aren't bad luck at sea, but we might have a tendency to give our hearts away. That can lead to horrid luck."

"Like I said, I always knew you'd be a hell of a pirate."

Coming closer to the bed, I kiss Jean-François on the forehead and hand the babe to his mother. Sensing the change, he wakes up. Anne presses the little face to her bosom and begins to feed her newest babe. "I don't know what I would do without you."

"You'd find a way. You've always been smart like that, Anne. You're a survivor."

She glances at me with a wavering smile. "Jacquotte, I worry about my husband. He wants to be involved in politics. Political men enslaved me. They enslave your people. There's not a person I meet in the ville with a hint of color to their skin that's not been impacted."

That's the truth. When will it all stop? "Politics is evil, but maybe an honest man can make change."

My voice sounds hopeful. I forgot to add *liar* to my many accomplishments.

"Jacquotte, they won't let him. The French won't heed to a mere tavern owner. Grands Blancs, and only Grands Blancs, hold power. A Petit Blanc is doomed to service. Joseph wants to make changes—"

"—but he doesn't have the stomach for the fight." Anne's husband is a kind, dull little man who lacks real political savvy. Nonetheless, he's treated her well and her daughters too. "Everyone wants to be remembered for doing something. Someday he'll realize his legacy is the family he made."

She cradles her hungry little man and starts to cry.

I pour fresh water on a towel and press it to her forehead. "I need you to live, to care for this brood. You know I can't."

She grasps my hand and pulls it to the crown of her babe's head. "Promise me if anything happens to me, you'll look after this one."

"Anne—"

"Promise. Let Jean-François be your nephew. You be his aunt. We are sisters of Tortuga. This is your family."

My throat is thick. I haven't had a family to come home to when I leave the ship. Bahati is with her nieces, and the rest are with family too. I like this thought. I slide my other hand atop Anne's.

When she looks up, probably seeing a sparkle in my eyes, I say, "Smoke from whale tallow candles sometimes makes me misty."

She grins a little, then stops when the sound of loud voices interrupts us. Curses muffle Joseph's shouts.

"Let me go see what's going on. You have a full house downstairs." I put my rapier on my belt and go down to see if I can keep Joseph from dying in a tavern brawl.

* * *

Stairs creak as I come down to the dining area. I don't see Joseph but hear his voice.

People lounge on the backs of chairs, sipping mugs of ale. Others spoon bowls of pottage into their mouths. For a moment, I see Père's ghost, robed in a white silky pourpoint. He's in the midst of these men, like always. Politicking, camaraderie, and a clean floor were his joys.

"Thievery, murder!" Anne's husband bellows about law and order. As I reach the last tread, I see him sneering. One of his regulars tries to calm him.

"It's not right," Joseph responds. "It's wickedness. You slaughter families, and for what?"

The fool keeps railing. "Have you forgotten the commandment? Thou shall not steal or kill or covet. You daily break divine laws and expect to come into town like heroes. The heroes are the planters—"

"You mean the ones importing Guineas? Taking other men's freedom to become rich in tobacco or sugarcane?" Laurens de Graaf is here. I thought I recognized his voice and reasonable words.

Jacqueline goes to Joseph. "Père, please. Let's serve these men and let them be." She shows him the silver coins she's earned, and he swats them from her hand. The child runs to me.

"Little one, get to your sister. Stay upstairs. Don't bother your mother about tavern business."

The young girl scampers. Her slippers on the stairs are light, barely audible under the next crash of thunder.

"Joseph Chèrel." I call his name. "Go to Anne. She's just birthed you a healthy son."

De Graaf nods to me and makes people sit back in their chairs. "The entertainment is over. Let's clap for the opinionated new father."

People do, and I begin to breathe easier. I hope everyone will let him be, take pity on a man who has children to feed.

Noisy conversations begin again. Laughter rolls through the dining room.

"A zealous fool. It's not a fair fight." De Graaf speaks to a crowd of his mates. I recognize his bosun and first mate. He waves at me. "The storm has us irritable. Let's respect the little man's establishment." De Graaf puts three reales on the table. "I'll pay for the next round. We'll celebrate the new birth."

"Half-breed." Joseph utters the slur. One I've heard about me and Josiah when men think no one is listening. But I'm not sure if Anne's husband means me or de Graaf.

De Graaf doesn't have the patience of a saint. No one in our profession does. He stands again, putting out his hand to keep his men in their seats.

Wanting to keep the peace, I'm about to jump in when I see Michel. He and the fancy little boy from the Fair Weather Tavern are here.

I shake my head and try to calm the situation. "Keep your silver, de Graaf. I'll get you gents the next round."

De Graaf doesn't look at me. His gaze is trained on Joseph. His fingers flex on the sword at his side.

"Monsieur Chérel." My voice becomes loud. "You should go up and see your wife."

Thunder pounds outside. The shutters flap.

Joseph doesn't flinch. It's like he's picked today to risk his life.

I try again. "Please, Joseph. Go upstairs to your wife. I'll handle things here." I turn to the crowd. "Who needs ale?"

De Graaf flexes his fingers.

Joseph grabs a demijohn and smashes the end of the bottle on a table's edge.

Shiny diamond bits fall away, leaving a sharp, jagged-edged

weapon. "I want you to leave, de Graaf," he says. "If a half-breed like you can't respect my point of view, you can go drown in the storm."

De Graaf can't back down. Too many in the Twilight Tavern know him. A reputation for weakness is fatal to a pirate.

I can't let this happen. Unsure of my target, I go for my rapier.

"Wait, Jacquotte."

Michel's voice distracts me. "Fille Fantôme, you can't save everyone. Sometimes, you have to watch and hope."

The distraction wins. Joseph swings the sharp glass at de Graaf. The master pirate trips him. Anne's husband flies headfirst into a table and falls onto the broken bottle.

He screams as blood spurts. Stooping close, I try to no avail to stanch the bleeding the shards in his neck have caused. Red flows onto the floor, a floor that had been freshly swabbed. It might've shone like Père's before the pirates arrived. Now it holds blood instead of ashes.

Unlike my père, Joseph doesn't get to motion goodbye to those he loves. He just dies.

Forty-Seven

1692. The Caribbean Sea

The *Canopus* and I set to sail to Port Royal because de Graaf asked me to. Favors and filibusters go hand in hand. The use of his frigate as support in a future battle might come in handy, but I know this is his way of getting Michel and me to talk.

De Graaf himself is staying in Petit-Goâve. He's racked with guilt over Joseph Chérel's death. He is distressed that Joseph had just become a new father. De Graaf has been acting strange since he saw my grieving Anne. I've never witnessed him like this.

Anne, my poor Anne—she mourned briefly in private then returned to being the most practical of women. When I left, she seemed more concerned about the tavern becoming hers than where de Graaf intended to bury her husband. She has three mouths to feed. That tavern is her primary means. Women inheriting anything isn't guaranteed.

Bahati comes to my side, and I ask, "Are we drawing close to the Tiburon Peninsula?"

"Yes, captain, close to the Winward Passage." She puts down her scope. "When were you going to tell me the man you were married to is alive?"

Never. "Does it matter?"

She shrugs. "Depends. I take it Le Basque is the reason we are sailing so soon after violent storms. We don't know if these winds will swirl into another hurricane. If you weren't so high-strung, you might've waited a little longer in port, especially with your friend grieving the loss of her husband."

"De Graaf asked me to do this. I didn't feel the need to say no. And the sooner Captain Le Basque is where he belongs, the better off he'll be."

"Him or you?"

I cut my gaze to her. "Go get him and his eyes, as he calls the boy. I need Le Basque to know something about our mutual friend Old Jean."

"Yes, captain." Her footfalls pound away as I keep the whipstaff steady. Bahati knows me too well. I jumped at the chance to put Michel Le Basque back into his separate world, to keep him far away from mine.

The past is done. That's another of those lies I tell myself.

Bahati leads Michel and young Tomás toward my quarterdeck. The smoky lenses of Michel's spectacles hide his gouged-out eyes. They do nothing to cover the scar that runs from his eye to his jaw. It's more red today. Somehow, I doubt his sight was taken by a broken demijohn.

"Captain. Captain Le Basque and his ward."

"Bahati, you have control."

I step down and stand beside Michel. "Take my arm."

He does, and his grip is strong. I lead him to the starboard rail. "The little boy looks a little green. Lizzôa would give him . . . ginger. Sit with Bahati, young man."

"Tomás does feel a little seasick. He's a son of my caregiver from Surat and one of my crewmates. His father died in Aurangzeb's courts. The mother felt he'd be better off as my ward. He's Portuguese and Mughal."

I'm stunned that Michel would offer to care for someone when he needs help himself. Then I remember, that's who this man is. He would do anything for his crew.

The waters hitting the *Canopus* are a soup of seaweed. It looks horrible and disturbed, not the clear, blue-green waters that I know. My insides stir, the past roiling the present. I glance up at Michel, looking into a face that I once prayed every day to see, and I patiently swallow my bitterness.

"I brought you up here . . . to see where . . . to know where I found Old Jean's ketch."

Michel takes a deep breath. "I feel the sun in my face. I know directions, but all I have are memories of how things once were. Your ship is near Tiburon, close to the Windward Channel. I remember it vividly. But this is not the way to Tortuga. Why would he—"

"Old Jean had just brought Josiah to me in Petit-Goâve, in eighty-one. Michel, I'm sure he was attacked. I found his boat abandoned, hung up on the mangroves. I was on duty. I had to hold in my grief. I pretended it was just another wreck."

I swipe at my eyes. Old Jean's been gone eleven years. But I look at Michel and know I'm weeping not just for the loss of our friend. This is mourning for us too, our lost marriage and friendship.

His long, thin fingers swipe tears from my cheek. "I'd like to think I was once good at comforting you."

"Tell me what happened, Michel. You must know how awful it was for me. You left in seventy-seven. By eighty, I'd lost everything. Why did you never come back for me?"

He swallows. "I was imprisoned until ninety. I assumed by then you'd have found a new life."

"You could've looked for me. De Graaf knew me." I stop myself from beating on his chest. "If you hadn't gone, you'd still have your sight."

"And my men would be alive. You want to hear about my damn pride?" Michel points at himself. "The *Marauder* made it. We sailed around the Horn of Africa. We took all the precautions against the worms. She was ready to fight."

His hip bumps the rail as the *Canopus* hits a big wave.

"Lower the topsail," I call out. "Slow us down, Bahati."

"I'm not delicate, Jacquotte," Michel assures me.

"Michel, I can baby the *Canopus* if I want to. I'm in command." I soften my tone. I hate how defensive my words are. "You're my guest, Captain Le Basque."

"A mere guest? When you're ready to talk, Jacquotte, let me know. I have a story. I know you have one too."

He walks away, counting his steps like he knows where he's going. Tomás grabs his hands and heads him toward the hatch leading to the crew cabin below.

"When you are ready, captain, I am ready." His head dips. His lips press into a grimace. Then he climbs down.

For a moment, I look back at the waters where I last spied Old Jean's ketch. "My friend, help me make peace with your friend. Tomorrow's not promised. I know that. I can't hate a man who had dreams, and I don't want him to hate me because I lived mine."

I take back my whipstaff from a saluting Bahati. Gently, I coax my baby, my *Canopus,* forward, urging her onward.

* * *

It's late when I come to the crew's quarters. The men and women not on duty are curled into their hammocks. About to get into my bunk, I see that a body's already there.

"Michel?"

"Oui. Lie with me, and I promise . . . I'll tell you everything."

In the dark, I see nothing but outlines and shadows. I'm curious. I've only lain in his arms for a week when I was a girl. And I miss lying next to someone, feeling their warmth.

I climb up and balance at the edge. Off balance, I start to slip, but Michel reaches for me. Even without eyes, I know he still sees me.

Propped against his shoulder, I settle. My face falls into that space beside his neck, and I wait. I want to hear how his great plans went wrong.

Time passes. I'm impatient. I put my hand to his chest and say,

"Captain Le Basque, confess. Say it all. I'll give you only questions, but I'll listen and not judge."

"Oui, Captain Delahaye. The *Marauder* was outgunned by *Ganj-i-Sawai* in the Arabian Sea. I surrendered my ship. Ten of my men were slaughtered on deck after we'd put down our weapons. They were the lucky ones."

The hammock rocks, but he steadies it with his foot. "Aurangzeb's royal guards put us in chains and took us to the Red Fort. Oxen transported us in a covered wagon. When we could see out onto the rues, there were people of elegant dress. The textiles looked woven of gold. Spices scented everything: sweet black cardamon, yellow turmeric, and golden saffron."

His voice wants to focus on the pretty sights, but I wonder how it felt as a man, as a Blanc man, to wear chains subjugating him to the whims of another race.

"I think we were in some sort of procession. Elephants paraded and trumpeted. A horse wearing gold ribbons in its mane led us into the fort. I understand why foreigners call it the city of gold. I saw gold everywhere."

He draws a breath. I hear a rattle in his chest. "We were taken from the wagon and led to the Takht-Murassa, the Ornamented Throne Room. Never had I seen such beauty. Peacocks, jeweled inlays, and embroidered fabrics were everywhere. Gold and silver swords. A crystal dagger. Curtains and pillows in the finest silks. Rubies and emeralds studded everything—belts, the eyes of statues. The wealth in that single room was equal to what I have in the caverns from the *Santa Margarita*."

"But you were in chains, taken from your ship?"

"Oui. The waiting was the worst. Not knowing what the Mughals said in our presence was maddening. Then my first lieutenant touched a royal shield. For that sin, they cut him in two with a tulwar. The curve of the blade was so sharp. It tore through his guts like he was paper."

A shudder rips through Michel, as I remember the close call I had with a Spanish cutlass. I know this was worse. I hold him for a moment. He's solid but lean.

"Then in the madness of my lieutenant's death, musicians began to play. I'm not sure of any instrument except a drum. Officials in bright colors and long robes entered the room. Then Aurangzeb came. His jama was made of crimson brocade. The finest embroidery I've ever seen. His turban was jeweled with a giant ruby and bore a perfect white plume. They treat him as a god on earth."

The tremor in Michel's arm increases. "You can stop. You don't—"

"But he was no god. Aurangzeb and his officials claimed we'd desecrated the royal *Ganj-i-Sawai*. Another said we looked at their veiled women. Others blamed us for incursions that other filibusters had committed. The devil Aurangzeb sentenced us to death. I was to pick who died first. I told him to kill me, for I couldn't watch them suffer. So he had his officials take my eyes. I was made to listen to every punishment, every death."

Michel shakes as if the ordeal is recurring. I hold him tighter, and he says, "I was released in a trade deal with the French East India Company. Seems my father's name still means something. De Graaf brought me back to Jamaica. I've been living in my house in Port Royal since ninety."

Two years. "I have sailed by Port Royal so many times. Had I known, I would've looked for you. I could see the blue pole every time I drop anchor. I know that's your house." My throat feels full. I swallow hard. "Sorry. This isn't the time to blame anyone but Aurangzeb. He's a monster. He tortured and enslaved you in the Mughal Empire for twelve years."

"Is he a monster? The *Marauder* sailed to his world to steal. The pirates who came before raped Muslim women. They burned mosques and killed innocent people. Why not inflict torture on the next infidels to arrive? That's what we are to them." He sighs. "Aurangzeb did take pity on me. When I learned his language, he made me his translator to the world that kept coming. I've lived longer than I should have and heard too many die."

For a moment his sobs are violent. Then he's silent, wiping at his cheeks. "Joseph Chérel was right in so many ways. How many have we killed because they were on a ship we suspected carried silver ingots or barrels of cod?"

I touch his face, my pinky settling on his scar. "Michel, I'm sorry."

He lifts my hand and threads his fingers through mine. "At least you didn't say you told me so. You told me back then it wasn't worth it. It's I who am sorry."

The regret in his words reminds me of mine. I have many. "At least I know what happened."

"Never thought I'd hear your voice again. De Graaf told me of Captain Delahaye. You did it. I'm so proud of what you've achieved. Your ship is amazing. You sail well too."

"I had great teachers. You were my hero. The first man I loved." I take a full breath, filling my lungs until they might burst. "But you weren't my life. I found my way in Petit-Goâve and on the *Canopus*. I love the life that I've shaped. I love how I've been shaped. And I haven't been alone. I loved again, and it was almost perfect . . . if she hadn't died."

Waiting for the questions that don't come, I remain silent. I hear him snore a little. He mumbles something about olives. The missing years of his life are now mine, but there's still so much of my life Michel doesn't know. Not sure I have the words to tell him.

Then I decide it isn't necessary. We'll be in Port Royal by morning. I'll see him off to the house with the blue pole, and that will be that. Another chapter in my life will be closed. I'm not volunteering to give up my life to take care of a man who chose the sea over me.

* * *

The *Canopus* gets closer to Port Royal. I'm at the whipstaff. It's about twenty minutes to noon. It's a beautiful morning with a clear blue sky. It's a sign. It's the perfect way to say goodbye to Michel.

Ships crowd the port. From my scope, I see rows and rows of boats. Dot-size people walk along the docks. Fishermen work their nets or cast lines for cod or dolphinfish. My stomach rumbles. Maybe Bahati and I will go into Port Royal, and I'll take her for a fine meal. They know how to cook in Jamaica.

Six frigates sit in a row near a sandbar. I don't see any slave ships. I put down the scope, knowing those beasts are out there. The fever for sugar is an uncontrolled contagion. My appetite sours.

Brrr. The breeze becomes stronger. I pull my velvet coat tighter about me. It's sunny. It should be hot. Bahati joins me on the quarterdeck. She rubs her hands together. We look at each other.

"Why is it so cool?" I cup my eyes and see the outline of Fort Charles. With the scope, I locate the cannons. I sigh when I spot the house on Lime Street with the blue pole.

Michel, led by Tomás, comes up onto deck. "Captain Delahaye," the young fellow says, "I want to learn to sail. My père sailed. He explored the world like Monsieur Le Basque. I cannot wait to tell Gramma Nettles of Petit-Goâve."

"That's my housekeeper. She cooks too." Michel has a smile on his face. His head is cocked back, and I imagine he's sensing the view, picturing it from the many times he sailed his *Marauder* into the harbor.

Tomás is an adorable, well-mannered boy. He walks up to me and asks, "Can Monsieur Le Basque come up onto the quarterdeck?"

"Oui, and you are welcome too." As soon as they step up, I see them shiver too. "So, we aren't the only ones who are finding the weather odd."

The joy in Michel's face disappears. "The change in temperature could be a resurgence of bad storms. What color is the sky, Captain Delahaye?" He keeps his balance, grasping Tomás's arm as the boat shifts a little.

"It's blue. Nothing unusual." I know he's asking about the dreaded red sky, but there is none.

I have the *Canopus* about a mile and half from where we'll dock and then lower the pinnace. But the water looks agitated. There are bubbles, like a monster is breathing underneath.

The sea isn't clear. It looks as if it's churning.

Bahati yells to a gunner in the crow's nest. "Anything unusual?"

"There are eddies rippling everywhere. It seems quite choppy even near the shore."

A rumble sounds. It's low but strong. I don't know where it's from.

Crash. I pick up my scope. Dust puffs up. A building onshore falls.

"Eddies?" Michel tugs on his collar. He pulls out a small cross. It's a match to the one he gave me. "An earthquake on the ocean floor. That's the noise. Captain, you might want to slow down."

I know better than to ignore Michel's instincts as a sailor, and yell out, "Lower the topgallant!"

Bahati instructs my riggers. Soon the *Canopus* slows.

"Everyone, stay vigilant." I don't like this. My stomach is queasy. The *Canopus* lifts as the sea swells underneath us.

"Something's happening!" Bahati points to boats close to the dock starting to sway. They collide as they slip their mooring lines.

The next thing I know, the *Canopus* lurches forward as the sea rushes away from the seabed. Sunken ships caught on sandbars become visible. Pink coral is exposed. A graveyard of dead ships looms before us.

I come to my senses. "Reverse the sails! Reverse now!"

My crew keeps their head. They run, catch lines, and change the position of the main and topsails to change our course.

Our speed reduces. I grip the whipstaff, readying to tack the rudder against any force drawing us to the shore. The air smells of seaweed. Salt pelts my skin.

A deeper rumble sounds. Port Royal! A massive gray cloud rises over it into the sky. The docks break apart and fall away. Boats moored at the shore go down.

Darkness sinks upon us, but not before showing stews and taverns crumble.

We're slowly moving backward, but I'm dumbfounded. Bahati's mouth opens as wide as mine, but I wager we're each too scared to pray.

The strong scent of freshly dug dirt blows across my bow, like a grave, like our own grave has opened. More ships disappear.

The raging waters slow our escape. We've moved away from Port Royal, but the sea changes course and rushes at us, pushing us back.

"Jacquotte!" Michel yells. "Have your crew tie down everything."

"Do as Captain Le Basque says. Tie down everything immediately."

The sea rises before us like a wall.

I'm struggling with the whipstaff, but I get the *Canopus* farther away just as a wave, thirty feet tall, speeds toward the shore. The height of two *Canopus*es stacked on top of each other, the water swats at the city. Buildings that hadn't fallen . . . do.

A noise like a whistle vibrates the air, my skin.

Part of Fort Charles explodes. Through my scope, I find the solid-bronze cannons are gone. The dots that were walking through the busy city have disappeared. The *Canopus* is rocked. Ropes tie every person and thing to the ship. Bahati and I have strapped ourselves to the whipstaff. Michel and Tomás and my crew are lashed to the masts.

Water breaks over the bow. The *Canopus*'s deck floods as waves wash over us. We straddle the turbulent water. My ship quivers, and wobbles but stays upright.

Other ships are not as lucky.

People and barrels and broken masts float in the water. No one is swimming. The impact has crushed them, beating the air from their lungs. Hulls, blue and brown, bob upside down.

Two buildings on the edge of the newly pushed-back shore teeter and fall. Flames erupt. A reddish glow fills the sky. The house with the blue pole vanishes.

Water drains from my deck. Dead silence envelops my crew. The sky around Port Royal darkens to the colors of twilight, the one before dawn. Indigo bursts at the top of the world. Purples and dusky pink smear the horizon. Gold hues float above the leveled city. The sun, the judge of the world, wants us to see the destruction. So many ships float upside down or in broken pieces. Not a frigate, longboat, pinnace, ketch, or sloop anchored in the bay survived.

"Look for the living," I say. "We can't be . . . Just look."

We hunt, listening for any souls that live. I see none—none with my eyes, none with my scope. The water calms. The sea gloats over the dead it has swallowed.

"Most of Port Royal." Bahati unties us. "The city's washed away."

"We barely escaped." Tomás's voice is small.

Michel signals to undo his ropes. When freed, the young man embraces Michel about the waist. Michel hugs him back.

It stings as much as it warms my heart, the sight of them. I'm reminded of that other life we might've had with Josiah. Then I feel a gnawing truth in my gut. I would've found joy as Michel's wife, as a family with my brother. Yet, I'm filled with joy being tethered to my ship, and my ship remaining tied to me.

Dead livestock and lumber drift in the water. A beam comes close to hitting the *Canopus*'s hull, and I decide it's time to move farther away. I take a final look at the ville. Lizzôa's secret inn has fallen. The taverns we supped at have vanished. Part of the steeple of St. Peter's is missing.

Flames continue to sprout. I put down the scope in disbelief that something can burn after all the flooding. But this shouldn't shock me. Fire finds a way to live. Fire is a sword even to the sea.

Bahati looks through her scope too. "Thousands and thousands of people lived there."

Tomás guides Michel to the quarterdeck.

"Your house is destroyed, Captain Le Basque." I hope my tone is gentle. "I am sorry."

He bites down on his bottom lip. His voice breaks. "My housekeeper. She stays there. . . ."

Michel can barely finish the words. The loss hits Tomás. The boy weeps. Then, in the warmest way, Michel says, "I'm here with you, and Gramma Nettles will always be with us too, like our fathers."

He turns his weathered face and tinted lenses to me. "You've saved us, Captain Delahaye. I suppose we serve you, now."

My jaw drops. His words . . . they are just words. I've no response to him. I need to look after my crew. "Be on alert. This might not be over."

"If we hadn't delayed to see Old Jean, the *Canopus* might be sunk in the harbor," Michel says. "I know Tomás and I wouldn't be here. Thank you, captain." He lifts a fist to the sky. "Thank you, Old Jean."

He's right.

But there's no way to comprehend the magnitude of this tragedy. A simple shift of time makes the difference. If Michel hadn't left. If Sarah and I had left sooner. If Danseker had disabled the cannon. If Lizzôa hadn't decided I was worthy of my dreams.

I cough from the haze in the air and sink into my coat, hiding like I don't know what to do. Then the captain in me arises. "Everyone hold positions until we are clear."

My crew plus two does so. We stay in the area hoping to help a distressed ship or someone who might've survived the impact and floated into the water. A couple of other lucky frigates join us in the search. We pass in silence. No one is a filibuster or navy man now. We all are Port Royal.

Forty-Eight

1692. The Caribbean Sea

We aren't in any hurry to go anywhere. The destruction of Port Royal is too fresh. I let the *Canopus* float within two miles of the harbor. For hours, I fear destruction will follow us or that we might miss a soul to save. Bahati, Phipps, all my crew scan the water for hours. We find nothing but death.

The tragedy of fishermen and pirates, of slave and free, of sons, daughters, families must be written. It's still so hard to accept.

I slump over my whipstaff. Bahati shakes me. "Captain, go below. Rest."

"No, I need to see if the governor of Jamaica will come from Kingston to help his people. Who is it now? Beeston? He followed Morgan, running the island. Morgan was corrupt, but he'd be here. He'd be a filibuster, searching for sailors."

"Go. See about Le Basque. He and Tomás went below hours ago."

"No. I need—"

"You aren't alone in this tragedy." Bahati grabs my arm and turns me to the crew hatch. "We are all here. Your crew can manage this."

"I need to do something."

"You can do nothing. We all knew someone in Port Royal. And each of us feels how close we came to being at the bottom of the sea."

Bahati is right. I ease my arm free and smooth my wrinkled doublet sleeve. "I'll go down for a little. Search the waters another hour, then head the *Canopus* to Petit-Goâve."

"Aye-aye, captain."

I leave Bahati and go down to the crew's quarters. The ladder creaks. The sound of footfalls is muffled. The corridor sits in shrouds of dark.

I find my way, unstrap my rapier belt, and head to my bunk. Again, Michel has claimed it.

After facing my mortality again, I don't complain. Easing my weapon to the floor, I let him have my hammock and climb into Bahati's.

The stretched ropes of the floating bed start to swing. Michel reaches out. His hand grasps them and slows the hammock, then it stills.

"Thanks," I say. I want to ask what's going through his head. He has no home. I'm not sure if he has money other than what's in his pockets. His treasure, as far as I know, remains in Tortuga.

He takes back his outstretched hand and folds it behind his head. "Rest, captain."

"How's Tomás?"

"He's a tough young man." Michel's voice sounds weak. "He loves this new world. Gramma Nettles . . . I wish you'd met her. If I wasn't such a coward . . . I should've gone after you after de Graaf's meeting."

"Why didn't you?"

"I'd been back a year. I never wanted you to pity me or think me another burden. And I didn't know how to say I was a fool. I've earned every disappointment in my life, including losing you."

I turn in the netting, feeling like a fish staring at the fisherman who caught her. "Hard to care about a week of marriage."

His breath blasts out his nostrils. "It meant—"

"Please, Michel, I've relived that week every day for years."

I hear him shift. His hammock rocks. The outline of movement flutters in the dark.

"For what it's worth, I wouldn't be me if you'd stayed." I keep my voice low. "I'd be Madame Le Basque, not Captain Delahaye. I'd be in your shadow. Shadows exist where light is blocked."

Michel's quiet for a long time. Then I hear a whisper. "Jacquotte, how did you find your light? How did you become a buccaneer? You're not even hiding who you are. Your hair is loose. Your bosom too. Tomás is good with describing things. Corseted waist, broad hips, strong, muscular legs. Gramma Nettles would fuss and bundle you up in a bib gown."

I laugh, and he says, "The men at the meeting said quite a lot about you when you left. Tomás thinks you're very pretty."

"Well, thank him. Tell him captains only wear gowns on special occasions."

"I'm serious. How did you do it? How did Jacquotte become Captain Delahaye?"

"Madame Erville. I met Lizzôa in Petit-Goâve at the lowest point in my life. I . . . I was mourning Sarah and Père. The tavern was gone. I needed to earn a living in a place where no one knew me."

"So from Tortuga to Petit-Goâve."

"Oui . . . oui." The room is quite empty. Tomás is sleeping just below us, but I'm not ashamed of my life. "Those gold coins you left were stolen almost as soon as I arrived. I spent nights on the street. On the eve of deciding to sell my sex, I ran across a woman, Lizzôa Erville. I killed her attacker."

I ease onto my side, chuckling. "Didn't feel much. Thought there should be more remorse. Today I feel the sadness of lives lost."

"Well, a buccaneer has to be able to do what he . . . or she must to survive." Michel's voice grounds me. It's sleep-warmed and thick like molasses. "It's either you or them."

"I didn't . . . don't mind killing."

Funny thing, the faces of most of those gone seem erased from my mind. Maybe because I'm trying to hold on to ones who mattered.

"You mentioned Madame Erville, Jacquotte." His tone sounds kind and curious. Of course, he knows. I wasn't secretive about my loss of her.

"Lovely Lizzôa changed my life. She helped me get good-paying jobs. She dealt in information, and when she heard rumors of an impending mutiny, she formed a team to join the crew. I wouldn't be a buccaneer or a captain without her."

"Then it's good you loved her. And she loved you."

I bite my lip. I'm lying so close to where Lizzôa died, and it feels good that our truth, the union of our souls is known. "Madame Lizzôa Erville loved me. It wasn't sisterly affection, though I did adore her as a sister. It was passion. As a lover. She will always have my heart."

I barely hear a breath. Then I feel his hand reach for mine.

I don't flinch or turn away.

"I was dead to you, to everyone. My arrogance destroyed us. It's only right that you live and love again."

His resigned tone makes me angry. My life isn't the result of his failure or his bad luck. My life is a miracle born of fire, sword, and sea. I own my luck and my failings. "You think it nothing, loving a woman? You're not threatened by our mere week of marriage compared to years of love?"

He curses. His voice lowers and he curses again. "I cannot begrudge you anything. And who wouldn't love you?"

His hand on mine never wavers, never draws away. "I prayed to see your face again, to ask forgiveness. When Aurangzeb took my eyes, I knew the sad look of being abandoned would be the only image of you I'd ever possess. Then I prayed to die. Then I prayed to live for Tomás. Now . . . I pray for you."

He's heard me. He listened. Somehow, it's still not enough.

I sit up. "I'm not tired. I'll go relieve Bahati."

"You should rest, Jacquotte. Your first mate seems quite capable."

I free my hand and jump down. "I know. That's why she has the job. You rest. I need to see the twilight."

"Then be about your duty, captain."

Alone, I make my way through the darkness. I know who I am. I'm Jacquotte Delahaye, the helmsman of my fate, the maker of my peace.

Forty-Nine

1692. Petit-Goâve, Hispaniola

Night surrounds me on the quarterdeck. Storms have delayed us from reaching Petit-Goâve. We're weeks off course, but there was no way in hell I'd try to ride out a hurricane. "At least the sky is clear."

Bahati yawns. "Navigating by the stars is pure pleasure. With all sails extended, the *Canopus* will be in Petit-Goâve by morning."

Footfalls sound behind us. She heads away. "Captain Le Basque. You shouldn't try coming up alone."

"Tomás is my eyes, but he needs to sleep. Permission to come up, Captain Delahaye? You've been without your rapier for days. I think it must be an oversight."

I nod to Bahati to bring him up, then she disappears.

Snatching my rapier from him, I say. "You should not be carrying weapons. You could put out an eye."

I cover my mouth at the awful retort, but Michel laughs. "You don't need to treat me like an invalid. I appreciate it when you don't." His head swivels, like he can see the blackness of the night and sea. "I grew up on frigates. I merely needed to count the steps from the hatch to the quarterdeck."

Michel puts his hands on the whipstaff. We hold it together, under the unity of our palms, our fingers lacing together like we did on the *Marauder.* "I need your help, Jacquotte."

"I'm quite well off now. I can give you any money you need."

His lips purse. "That's generous, but I have wealth. I need you to get it."

My hands fall away from the whipstaff. "No, Michel. Take my money. There's no need to compromise your principles. D'Artigue's treasure can still get you hanged. It will still be traded for slaves. I can't let you do that. The *Canopus* won't be used for it."

"Let me? I didn't come up here to ask permission." Michel looks upward. He feathers his graying hair with his fingers. "I'm still the same man I was. That will never change."

He sighs and points his face to me. "But a friend can ask a friend for help. You, Tomás, and de Graaf are the only ones in the world I trust."

I strap my belt sling to my waist. "Keep talking."

He faces the wind. "My last idea was an utter failure, trying to pretend my father's treasure wasn't Spanish, so that Carlos II wouldn't hunt me down. But the longer that treasure sits in one place, the more likely someone will find it and use it for buying Guinea slaves."

He turns back, adjusting his lenses. "I've heard men are searching. One approached Gramma Nettles before we left."

My pulse speeds up. Men who want treasure can be ruthless. "What do you propose, Michel?"

"I'll do what de Graaf has done. His connections have allowed him to exchange his wealth for silver. He's received fair exchange rates. Treasure for coins. Not one of his trades adds misery to the world."

Now I'm intrigued. Laurens de Graaf is cunning and wealthy beyond compare. "How has he done that?"

"De Graaf contracts with certain governors. He makes private transactions with them for silver. I can disperse my holdings the same way. My treasure can be made clean and safe in the hands of moneylenders."

I want to laugh, but he's serious. "I've never met an honest governor. When Morgan ran Jamaica he confiscated all the cargo we'd captured. And I could tell you horror stories about the crooked dealings of all Tortuga's governors."

"De Graaf works with the governor of Curaçao, Johannes van der Bosch, and Captain Nicholas Trott, the governor of Nassau. Van der Bosch has the strongest ties to the Dutch West India Company, which gives him access to silver, more so than to flesh. De Graaf was on his way to take me to Van der Bosch. But I asked him to stop in Petit-Goâve so I could see you."

"This sounds too good to be true, Michel . . . trading for silver reales. Are you sure it will work?"

His lips flatten to a line. "I trust de Graaf, like I trust you. His connections are using his plundered wealth to fund a bank. The Brits are using booty gained by pirates to create a legitimate bank."

He steps closer. "I need a friend with eyes, a boat that can haul the weight, and trusted sailors. I will give half to you and your crew. The rest will educate Tomás to be a gentleman. We'll start over in the Americas, the land of adventure."

Michel picks up my hand. He tucks it against his chest. "What do you say, Captain Delahaye? Will you be my business partner?"

A stumble. Noise comes from behind us. I turn and see Phipps. "Sorry, captain. Forgot to put out my lantern."

"Wait," Michel says. "Your voice. Do I know you?"

"No, captain, but everyone knows you." Phipps pauses by the hatch. The even-tempered physician regards us. "If you ever need me to look at those eyes, I will."

"Good evening," I tell the doctor and wait for him to go below.

When we are alone, Michel leans toward me. "Do we have a deal?"

A partner and friend—that sounds like a role I can accept. Yet with him holding my hands, I get lost in his warmth. "Going back to Tortuga poses some risks. Jean-Baptiste Du Casse was looking for your treasure. He's one of the reasons I left. I hear he's governor of Tortuga now. If he gets wind that your treasure is there, he will confiscate it . . . after he kills us."

"Then we'll have to plan how not to get caught. I have ideas, but

Du Casse is a fortune hunter and slave trader. You are wise to be wary of him."

"We both need to be wary. He'll take the *Canopus* as a trophy for Louis XIV." Michel has lost so much trying to protect the treasure of the *Santa Margarita*, do right by his father, and adhere to his principles. I have to make sure this transfer goes well. "I accept."

He shakes my hand, and I revel in the strength of his fingers. Older but still strong—I like that. "Before we do anything, I must check on Anne. De Graaf should still be there, and I'll verify what you've told me. The weather's been slowing us down."

"I fear God's not done pounding on Port Royal."

The loss of his smile means it hurts that I don't fully trust him, but I have a crew and a ship to protect. "If everything checks out, then I'll make plans to help you."

With a kiss to my fingers, then a hearty shake of my hand, we agree that Captain Le Basque and Captain Delahaye will go into the salvage business together.

* * *

Avoiding the horrid weather and what seems to be the tail of a hurricane, we arrive to Petit-Goâve weeks later. The rocky sailing makes it easy to decide who to release from my crew—the ones that seem unsteady or spooked by Port Royal, I dismiss. I hate it, but I must. I can't have untested men for this mission.

Bahati comes to the deck. She's stretching and perhaps worshiping the clear blue sky. "How long will we be in port this time? I'm wondering if I'll have a chance to see my nieces."

"See them, Bahati. Let them know you love them. Then come back ready for battle."

Her black eyes stare at me. Her full lips lift in a smile. "Always ready when you are, captain."

"Oui, but keep Tomás close."

Now she gives me another look. Big, tough Bahati has to babysit. But I know my formidable friend has a soft spot for children.

"Then you'd better hurry back before I show him how to steal a frigate."

Michel and I get into the pinnace. The salty sea smells of fresh rain. Olive-colored seaweed stirs in the water. Petit-Goâve has had bad weather too. When we dock, Michel holds my arm as we cross the gangplank. His steps are solid. If I didn't know better, I'd think he could see.

When we are away from the docks, he whispers, "Did you have to let so many of your crew go? Their disappointment sounded awful. The more the merrier when hauling the treasure out of the cave."

"Your father moved the treasure all by himself. We can do it with fewer. I need battle-tested men and women. I have a feeling this won't be as easy as we hope."

Phipps follows us. My surgeon has been with me since '91. Has patched up broken bones and knife wounds. Still doesn't believe in the use of herbs. He turns toward a stew.

With a shrug, I lead Michel toward the Twilight Tavern but stop at the rue that leads to the monastery. I want to go see Josiah. He might want to see Michel. My brother must remember him.

"What's the matter, Jacquotte?" Michel's tone is light, but curious.

"My brother's monastery is close. He refuses to see me, and the priest won't admit me because of the way I dress. I don't know what to do."

Michel pulls me away from the route to Josiah. "Some men, even in hallowed positions, will never care how brave you are."

Three matrons in dark gowns of green and deep blue stroll on the other side of the crowded street. One hides behind a fan and whispers, while the others point at us. "Hear the shrews over there, Michel. Perhaps they are nuns at the monastery."

"They are jealous of your legs. I'm jealous I cannot witness this." His chuckles ease the tension in me. "Ignore fools, captain. Later, if you must dress as the Queen of England to see Josiah, what's a little sacrifice? You'll be beautiful in a gown. You always were in everything you wore."

When he says it like that, with his voice rich and warm, it doesn't seem so awful a compromise. "Let's go see about Anne and the children. Josiah is happy and safe. It's been two months since I last laid eyes on her. We'll visit my brother later, once we've taken care of our business."

"We?"

"Yes. If I have to dress as a queen, you should come along as my royal attendant." My chin is lifted high. I saunter along a few steps but cling to Michel's arm.

He smirks. "At least you didn't say jester."

The air is humid. A breeze whips up. Coco palms clap their leaves along the water's edge. I hear people talking of Port Royal. Over a thousand or more they think died in the tidal wave. My heart hurts for the people, for Michel. Someone says it was hit with a hurricane. Earthquake, fire, rain . . . I can't believe the ville's luck.

In silence, and maybe a little reverie, we march into the Twilight Tavern. The scent of meaty tallow candles and burnt pottage hits me. Expecting customers, I find it empty, with two figures locked in a horrid feud. Anne has her hands on her hips. She wears a jet gown. A dark veil covers most of her shiny blond hair.

She takes a mug from a pile on the table and throws it at Laurens de Graaf. The man ducks as it hits the floor and shatters. "You wily woman," he says. "I'm trying to help. Let me explain."

"Explain, murderer!" She tosses a plate at him, but he catches it. "You kill my husband, now you help yourself to my son's property."

Anne throws more things. The arm that pitched a pod into a buccan trap seems to have lost its accuracy. Objects scatter all around de Graaf. No direct hits.

"The taxes are due, madame. And if something isn't done about it, you'll lose the Twilight Tavern."

"Madman, you want me to thank you for robbing me? Thank you. Thank you." She aims again and this time strikes de Graaf 's shoulder.

"Anne." I wave at her to get her attention. "Anne, please calm down. You had a baby only a few months ago."

"I had a husband then! Don't forget that part, Jacquotte." Anne starts to weep. She puts her face in her hands. "I've children to raise and must do it alone."

Swiping at her eyes, she comes to me. "Can I borrow your sword? I'm not a wife, and I won't wench; I'll go back to being a buccaneer."

"No, Anne. And it's not a sword." I jiggle the hilt in my belt. "It's a rapier."

"Then give me the rapier."

"Madame Chérel," De Graaf says, "we are embarrassing ourselves in front of your children and our friends. We need to be rational."

He looks at Michel and even me for help. Michel struggles not to laugh. I don't know how to feel, but I say, "He didn't kill Joseph."

"The fool came at me with a glass bottle. He fell and cut himself." De Graaf rubs at water stains on his scarlet coat. Anne must've hit him before we arrived.

"Blast it. There's nothing rational about you, Anne Dieu-Le-Veut, or how I feel when I am near you." De Graaf's tone begs. "I've known you since your first husband, Pierre Lelong."

Wait. What?

Anne puts down the plate she's about to hurl at him. "Sweet talk will not stop me from hating you."

"I must do the honorable thing." De Graaf steps bravely up to Anne and her throwing arm. "Anne, marry me."

The tall man with sandy-brown hair bows before Anne. "Marry me. You don't wait long between husbands. Barely four months between Lelong and Chérel. Feeling as I do, I must insist you marry me."

Everyone stops. Jacqueline had started to come downstairs. The girl also stands still. Her ruddy face is painted with shock.

Michel goes over to de Graaf. "You mean it, don't you?"

"Absolutely. I didn't intentionally kill Joseph Chérel." De Graaf rises and takes Anne's hand. "But Chérel took too many risks without considering what it might do to you or your children. He didn't deserve you. I don't, either, but I'm here. I want you."

Anne's cheeks flush like she has a fever. De Graaf is a man of the sea. Is he going to change his whole world for my friend?

"I bought the tavern," he says, "to keep it safe for you. I know you have three children you must care for. I will take them on as my responsibility. Will you have me?"

Anne shakes her head and runs into the kitchen.

De Graaf looks at us. "I meant it."

"Then go talk to her in private," Michel says. "We'll come rescue you if we hear knives chopping."

Shaking her head, Jacqueline comes the rest of the way down the stairs. "They've been strange like that since you left." Her head swivels toward the kitchen. Pots bang, but no one has screamed. "Is Maman all right?"

"Reasonably so," I say and tap my rapier. "If not, I'll protect her. Now, go upstairs. Sit with the baby and your sister. I'll let you know how things go down here."

She nods and says, "Captain Le Basque, the jars of olives you ordered have arrived."

"I'd forgotten about them. I sent some treats here for you, Jacquotte, as a peace offering." Michel grins. "It's the only taste I grew to love from the East. Olives, pickled with lemons and salt."

Noises sound in the kitchen. Something drops to the floor with a clang.

"Oh, no," I say, "the proposal's off. Things are being thrown again."

"Jacqueline, run along," Michel says. "Your mother's fine. She's negotiating."

I wait for the girl to leave. I don't want her frightened when I draw my rapier. "Step aside, Michel."

"Jacquotte, you may want to hold on that."

I hear the pounding of a fist on the table. Pushing past Michel, I throw open the slatted door.

Anne and de Graaf are quite engaged. She's in his arms, and they're kissing like fools.

I close the door and back away. "Guess that means we'll be seeing a wedding before we leave on our partnership. That is assuming your story is confirmed, by the soon to be groom."

"It will be." Michel laughs. A smile spreads from ear to ear. "Sounds like de Graaf found a way to convince Madame Chérel." He taps his ear. "Other senses have sharpened. I thought that sounded like a man making a passionate argument to win the woman he wants."

Working with Michel was supposed to be no trouble. I suspect now that it will be plenty of trouble. Nonetheless, I will focus on the plan, one of action and contingencies. I take a deep breath and pray for favor. Without some goodwill, I know everything shall go wrong.

Fifty

1692. Petit-Goâve, Hispaniola

The noon sun burns brightly above the docks of Petit-Goâve. We take on additional provisions—barrels of water, bread, cod, and powder. Once we collect the treasure, we cannot stop until we hit Curaçao.

The capstan whines as the pinnace rises. Sweat glistens on the arms and brows of my crew. I've reduced the *Canopus* to twenty-five, almost the same number as when I became Captain Delahaye.

Michel strides to me. He's using a long reed to guide him. "I guess you believe this will work."

"Yes, de Graaf confirmed everything. Going into the bank-funding business sounds good." Then I glare at Michel—freshly trimmed beard, his black hair with hints of gray combed and curled. "Never had a problem believing in you. But I have to make sure that my decision is wise for those who follow me, wise for the *Canopus*."

Tomás ushers him from the quarterdeck back to the mainmast where the little boy is helping with the stores. The animated chatter between the two warms my heart. They aren't a bad addition to my crew.

With my scope, I look at the forts surrounding the bowl of Petit-Goâve. The mountains are visible, lush with pines and mahogany, open and waving. "You've been good to me."

The usually even-tempered Bahati comes to me and parks herself on the quarterdeck. My friend looks like she wants to punch something.

"Speak, first mate."

The cranking of the capstan catches our attention, but I draw her back. "Bahati, what is it?"

She takes a moment, folds her hands in prayer. "We saw the act of the heavens, captain. We saw judgment at Port Royal. The dead now number over two thousand."

Bahati shivers with rage. "The governors of the French colonies are recruiting buccaneers to Jamaica. Tortuga's governor has personally led attacks against Port Royal . . . what's left of it. Du Casse is a monster."

"That bastard is obsessed with glory and treasure. He thinks ransacking a fallen city helps his reputation. He's a coward."

I smell molasses, and it makes my grieving soul thirst. Someone is passing around mugs of rum to celebrate going to sea. "Don't tell Captain Le Basque about the continued misery of that city, not today."

I turn and face my crew like I'm not wishing to destroy Du Casse.

Phipps comes to me with a tankard. "For you, captain. It's a celebration."

He holds out the rum, and it almost steals my will. "No, you enjoy, Phipps. I have duties. You know how I love making official those that find a union worthy of fighting for."

"Yes. Unity," he says with a smile.

"Go with the rum." Bahati growls at him, and the poor man flees.

I glance into her dark eyes. "Get us extra firepower. Make sure we have more than enough powder. We need to expect a fight, especially if other governors are in league and somehow alerted to what we are doing."

Wulf and Margaret stand near the waist of my ship. They've both joined my crew for this special mission. Wulf shows her about. Arm in arm, they smile at each other, Wulf in breeches and a silver pourpoint, and madame in a flowing emerald robe similar in cut to the gowns of the mean *nuns.* I wonder if their warehouse supplied the horrible women with those outfits. Never mind. My heart warms seeing Wulf and Margaret, holding hands, as much in love as ever.

"Captain de Graaf is coming aboard," Bahati leans closer to my ear. "Should we ask him to help? He does owe us."

"No one asks to collect on a pirate's debt. It's paid when the opportunity is right." De Graaf the hardened buccaneer holds baby Joseph while Anne and her daughters board the *Canopus.* This side of him, the softer side of many of us who choose this, is rarely exhibited. Yet, I witness two examples in him and Wulf.

I think back to the matelotages I formalized here at the prow of the *Canopus.* Lizzôa in spirit stood with me every time. We offered our blessings mate to mate. I gave what hope I could to celebrate the love they found. Any who judged my sailors for trying to keep a little joy had long been banished from our community. We were a damn utopia.

De Graaf takes his bride-to-be's hand, her small one in his . . . the hardened fool I am, I smile a little inside. I'm happy for Anne. Finding a partner and holding on to care and intimacy were blessings.

"Captain? Let's hurry this."

"No, Bahati. I won't take this time from them." Time is the only thing that matters when it comes to happiness. One never knows how much is allotted to the saint or the sinner.

She rolls her eyes. The woman is happy by herself. She is her comfort. Nothing in her jet eyes says she misses a thing.

I reach up and straighten her new hat. The beaver pelt of her wide brim has a streak of white. "Lovely to see you spending silver on you."

She laughs, and I leave her and welcome everyone for the wedding.

Showing the girls about, I glance at Michel and see the fury on his face. He's standing next to Phipps. The surgeon must have told him about the new attacks on Port Royal. My gut twists. I ache for Michel and all his losses.

"You should think of retiring." Phipps's voice becomes loud. "You and the boy should become fishermen. You've no need of money. I've heard that Captain Le Basque has a fortune set aside from his long career."

"What boat do you suggest I get, doctor? What's good for someone without sight?"

"A canoe or maybe a sloop. Or something more stable, like a ketch. Just have to teach your ward to be your eyes."

Michel turns, so his back is to me. The man can't stand pity and nursemaids. I shouldn't have asked the ship's doctor to check on him. *Sigh.* I pray everyone on board savors this moment of peace. It's the calm before the *Canopus*'s storm.

* * *

Officiating a wedding while planning for war presents challenges. In addition to barrels of cod, I had to make room for bushels of almond blossoms and a few good-luck fern fronds to scatter along the deck.

De Graaf hands out bottles of something he calls champagne. He seized it on his last raid. The Benedictine monk Dom Pérignon supposedly makes the best. Some of the demijohns have bubbles. It's odd, seeing wine with bubbles. I refrain from a taste. My sobriety will be needed to win the battle I sense ahead.

After offering more blessings to the couple, I kiss Anne goodbye. She's truly happy. Her fears about how to provide for her daughters and infant son have disappeared.

Laurens de Graaf is wealthy, handsome, and smitten. Anne draws her fingers through the curly hair that he's slicked to the side with some coconut-scented pomade. "Captain Delahaye," she says, "you throw a beautiful gathering."

I smile and dip my chin and gaze at the hibiscus strewn on the *Canopus*'s rails. I've married them on the bow with the power vested in me as a ship captain.

Michel stood at de Graaf's side, close enough to me so that, just in case there is some law preventing a woman captain from marrying people, Michel could pretend he did it.

"De Graaf, congratulations." I speak with him at the starboard side. "You're confident that the governor of Curaçao will give Le Basque a fair deal? The last time I dealt with a governor, it was Henry Morgan, and my captain was cheated."

The affable de Graaf is distracted. His gaze shifts from looking at his new bride chatting with Michel to the extra cannons being loaded from Calico Mel's sloop.

"Oui, like I told you before, Back from the Dead Red," de Graaf says. "Governor Johannes van der Bosch of Curaçao will deal fairly with Le Basque. He'll pay handsomely in silver for rare Spanish artifacts and then give you a writ after the fact to make the recovery and sale legal. I've given you a letter with my personal recommendation. You'll have no troubles."

I nod, grateful to him for presenting us with a new path.

"Le Basque and his ward can retire in peace," de Graaf continues. "I hear he's looking at Louisiana. Might consider land there myself."

"Retiring to America? You, de Graaf?"

"Oui." He grins at Anne, who's engaged with Tomás and Margaret near the mast. The young boy is dressed in a fine silver doublet and dark breeches. His thick, curly hair has been freshly trimmed by Bahati. "We can't be on the run forever. You have to know when the mission changes."

Not necessarily acknowledging this truth, I bump de Graaf's shoulder. "Take care of Anne. She's special."

A dimple shows. "We'll be in Petit-Goâve for a while. When little Joseph is weaned, we will sail the world."

He goes to Anne and takes the babe from her arms. Anne's daughters hold on to the rail. Their creamy ivory gowns trimmed in silver ribbons blow in the wind, and their eyes are as big as reales. They see what I, their unofficial aunt, commands for a living. Not a wench, nor a wife, but another choice for a woman—that's a pretty good legacy.

With a look of delirious joy on her face, Anne comes to me. "Husband number three. I think he'll be the best of them all." She sighs. "I've been a filibuster, and I've married two buccaneers. I can tell you, Jacquotte, it's not defeat to be a wife."

"Everyone's path is different." Then I give her my blessing. "May this union keep you happy and healthy."

She embraces me. "If anything happens, remember you promised to take care of Joseph."

I grip her hands, and with tempered strength I say, "I'll care for them all. I know I can, now. I've cared for a crew. I'm not afraid."

She hugs me, and I walk her to de Graaf. I take her palm and place it in his. This is their troth, according to God's holy ordinance. In the look the two exchange, I feel the heat and the power that will keep them in sickness and in health until death.

My gaze grows misty. I hear Michel talking with Bahati about soot. That's what I'll blame for these tears.

Michel is still a nice dresser. The cranberry coat looks very similar to the cut and color of his old oxblood one. He's strong and fit, hiding behind his smoked spectacles. Maybe too strong. Two bulls will butt heads, even if nine years of loneliness makes one dream of finding someone to hold.

"Goodbye, everyone." Anne waves from the pinnace. De Graaf is by her side. He has the babe. The girls are at his feet. Two officers that came with them have boarded. Phipps, Calico Mel, and others of my crew will take them to the *Neptune* and then return.

The pinnace gleams. Its good condition is integral to my plans.

I walk to my quarterdeck.

"You need help?" Michel, with his reed pattering before him, comes to me by the prow.

"Oui, toss the flowers into the sea. It's time for the *Canopus* to be ready for battle."

He nods and yells for Tomás. The two begin ridding my ship of the wedding decorations. It's time to get my frigate dressed for war.

Fifty-One

1692. The Caribbean Sea and Tortuga

After a day and half of steady sailing, we near the waters of my youth. With the topgallants furled, I steer the *Canopus* northeast following the curves of Hispaniola. The sun lowers to the horizon. At ten knots, we will get to Tortuga in the dark, a few hours before twilight.

A strong wave breaks against the bow. Bahati tenses, and so do I. Port Royal's tidal wave still haunts us.

Michel and his reed move close the quarterdeck. His shin, the part unprotected by his boot, hits the raised platform.

The less light, the less he can see. At least that's how it seems. "Can I help you, Captain Le Basque?"

"Why not go the long way around, captain? This way Fort de Rocher may detect us."

His voice is unusually loud. I want to ignore him but he's not moving along. So I answer, "We arrive at night, they won't see us. The longer way, if the winds prevail, would add about five hours to our journey. That would be dawn. I don't want the *Canopus* seen in the morning light by a twenty-four pounder."

He chuckles.

And I hear Phipps laugh too. "She's got you there, Le Basque.

Maybe you need to sit this out with the old fellows. I know I've told a few men when they need to."

Michel asks for my rapier and passes it to Bahati. "Phipps's questions have been very specific about the *Santa Margarita*, tonight. More so when he thought I was drunk."

Bahati looks at me. I don't know what Michel wants.

"Phipps, tell the captain who you told about our quest to Tortuga. Who did you meet on the docks when taking the wedding party to the *Neptune*?"

The surgeon looks nervous. "I don't know what you're talking about."

I nod to Bahati, and she points my rapier at Phipps's chest.

"Whoa there, Bahati, Le Basque." The man coughs nervously. "You trying to kill me?"

"Probably," I say.

Then Margaret and Wulf come up from below. Margaret's jet free hair waves in the wind. "Did we miss the theatrics?" she asks.

"Non," Michel says. "But tell Captain Delahaye what your friends have heard."

Wulf half bows and brings Margaret closer to us at the quarterdeck. "The wenches at the stew," Margaret says, "tell me Phipps is after the *Santa Margarita*'s gold."

The doctor takes a step back. "A wench's word is nothing."

"It's something, all right." Wulf pokes him hard in the chest. "And sweet Margaret has great hearing and many friends. I think she's discovered a problem."

Michel laughs. "And I thought I recognized Phipps's voice from when I was recovered by the French East India Company. This confirms things for me. You're a traitor."

Beads of sweat form on Phipps's upper lip. "I don't know what you're talking about. You sound insane."

Michel grimaces at Phipps. "Come now, doctor, confess. I may not be able to see your lousy face, but I know voices. I heard a fool talking about retiring and sailing ketches. You wanted me to know you killed my friend."

The surgeon shifts his stance. "A canoe is good for fishing. A sloop too, if you can get one. But a ketch, a ketch would be nice. That doesn't make me a killer."

"I think it does." Michel's statement is monotone. I don't know if he's bluffing. "Our old friend had a ketch. His boat was sunk somewhere near Jamaica."

"Yes, Old Jean had a nice boat," Phipps says. "Hung it up on Tiburon Pass. Terrible."

"He didn't mention a name." I take the rapier and put it to Phipps's throat. "And how do you know where Captain Le Basque was talking about?"

"A guess." Phipps shakes his head. "Everyone knows how close the two of them were. A free Black and a French filibuster."

Michel's fists clench. "The whispers I've overheard from you make sense now. Captain Delahaye, this man is a threat to our mission."

Wulf clasps madame's hand and says, "I will leave you to this, captains. Wife, this will be ugly."

Margaret chuckles and lets Wulf escort her back down into the hull, like the princess she is.

Michel sneers at the villain. I see his temper release. "Why, Phipps? Why did you have to kill an old man who meant no one any harm?"

"I didn't—"

I shift the blade closer to the doctor's gullet. "Speak up. I don't have time for lies."

"Wait, Wait." Phipps's doublet has a growing red spot. "We thought he knew where your treasure was. He said he didn't know. Things got out of hand."

"Who is *we*, Phipps?" I increase the pressure and draw more of his blood. "You and who else killed Old Jean?"

"Not me, I swear. But others."

"You joined my crew in ninety-one, after Michel was freed." I bite my lip. "I thought it wise for the crew to have another physician after Lizzôa died. I thought you were loyal."

"I am, but . . ."

Michel finds my wrist and steadies the hilt. "Phipps joined your open crew because he knew we were married. He knew that sooner or later we'd reunite and hoped the union would lead to the *Santa Margarita*'s treasure."

"That's mad, Captain Delahaye." Phipps touches my rapier and then immediately draws back, licking his fingers like they were cut. "I've been a faithful member of this crew."

Bahati's voice booms. "Tell us who you're working for."

My gut fears the worst. I voice it. "Du Casse? He knows we're coming."

His lips clamp shut. I press the rapier forward, and begin to feel it pierce Phipps's skin

"Wait. Wait." He whimpers. He sinks to his knees. "Please. Maroon me. Have mercy."

Michel growls. "Answer the captain."

"Yes." Phipps rubs at his throat. "Fort de Rocher's on alert. Once you secure the gold, they will attack. They'll sink the *Canopus* if you don't surrender."

"And they will kill us if we do." I adjust my fingers along the hilt of my rapier. "What were Old Jean's last words?"

"I don't know." Phipps bends forward, cowering, his palms against the deck. "He was singing."

"Singing? Like: *Eke nekeng'wanso Omonene gianchere*?" My pitch is low like Bahati's, like dear Old Jean's.

"Yes. That sounds like it." Phipps sighs. "Now let me go."

"Oui, to hell." I start driving the blade through him. Michel helps until the point of my rapier hits the deck boards.

When Phipps twitches no more, we withdraw my rapier. He heaves a tight breath. "I couldn't wait any longer for him to expose himself."

I wave to two of my gunners. "Phipps has warned our enemy. Toss this traitor into the sea."

While sailors tidy my deck, I call out to Calico Mel and Celia.

"Search our guns. Search everywhere. I want to make sure Phipps has not sabotaged anything or ruined our supplies. He's been serving as our bosun since I reduced the crew."

Bahati, commanding the whipstaff, says, "Never liked him."

* * *

Trying to regain my composure, I head into the stores. Nothing seems out of place. My powder is dry. Michel taps his way into the room and closes the door.

"If you've come for your olives, Le Basque, I did have a jar brought for you."

He moves closer. "I do love them, but I'm not hungry for food."

I'm blinking in the dark. There are a lot of powder barrels around us, and he's come in wanting to talk, and I'm about to explode.

Michel puts a hand on my shoulder. "Tomás noticed Phipps following us. Then I did some checking. I unmasked him but not before he could get word to the enemy."

I grab Michel's coat. I shake him. "You should've told me I had someone on board who killed Old Jean."

"Something just didn't sit right about him, but I thought it was my jealousy. I thought he was attracted to you."

We are silent in the dark, just breathing.

Slowly he pulls me into him. His arms smother me, gathering me into an unbreakable embrace. I'm pressed against Michel's velvet coat, his linen shirt that smells of sweet soap. "You once came to me, Jacquotte, and said, 'If I have to be a wife, I should be yours.'"

"I came on board the *Marauder* to get you to love me. I chased you. Women don't often get to do that. But that was a long time—"

"I've come to you this time. I want to have a captain and a wife. They should both be you. I want to be your husband, for I have always believed I was yours."

"It's too late for us. I . . . Lizzôa."

"I'm glad Lizzôa loved you. I'm glad Lizzôa was everything you needed that I couldn't be. But I'm here to put our pieces together. I've come for you. I had de Graaf bring me to you. I want to stay."

"You have to stay. We have a mission."

"Jacquotte, I want us together after this is done. I love you deeply. I think you're magnificent."

I lean against a barrel. The solid feel of the wood under my elbow reminds me of the first time Michel and I made love. That time, those notions are thousands of nautical miles away.

His fingers find my cheek. "And if we don't survive, I need you to know I never stopped loving you."

I hear whispers of Lizzôa saying when you find love, hold on to it. Then I hear my own resolute voice. "Non, Michel. It's too late. I'm married."

"To Lizzôa? She's gone, not from your heart, but from the earth. She wouldn't want you to be alone forever."

"Non, I'm married to this ship. I am the captain of the *Canopus.* She is my mate. I'm mother and father to my crew. I have nothing left to give."

He shuffles backward. Moments later, I hear his hand clasp the door.

Then I call out, "But I can always use a friend. And I have one less crew member . . . I'd love for you to join my crew, Michel. An old salt, an old friend, is always welcome and needed."

Footfalls sound. Shadows merge, and I embrace him as I would Bahati or Mel.

He touches the chain to my crucifix. "You kept it. All these years."

"I've always carried a piece of you, Michel. Always. The past is not all bad."

There are no more disagreements between us. We emerge from the stores, just two old souls praying together and preparing for the fight of our lives.

* * *

The Windward Passage is my faithful friend. With the topgallant extended, the main and fore and topsails billowing, we've made good time. Bahati adjusts the halyard line and braces for shifts in the wind.

Calico Mel comes to me. "Captain, we've checked all the powder kegs. They are dry. But two cannons are plugged. Celia's working to see if they can be fixed."

"Good job, Calico. Go and assist her." I take a moment to smile at him. "Good to have you back, second mate. Even for one mission."

He dips his hat. "Wouldn't miss this." He turns to Michel, who's sitting on the quarterdeck. "Captain Le Basque. A group of us might need to sit with you later. We need to learn all we can about the Mughals. Captain Tew's been talking it up. I think it might be a way to make a name for myself."

Michel nods. "There are plenty of opportunities, as long as you live long enough."

"Well, I want to know. My sloop, the *Black Pearl*, might be interested in heading there."

"*Black Pearl*," I repeat. "I like that name."

Calico Mel's smile dimples his face. "Celia named it. I think it's mighty nice."

"Hey, I heard you talking about me." Celia has a list in her hands. "Bosun reporting for duty. We're down two cannons. No fixing it. The rest are operational. We have sacks and a small wagon that will fit into the pinnace to load the treasure."

"Excellent. Come up here," I say and when she does, I give her a big hug. "Glad you came for this. Can always use a seasoned sailor."

"Wouldn't miss it. Pirates are supposed to find buried treasure." She's gleeful. Celia has a little more weight in the face, and I wonder if she might give herself and Calico Mel a babe.

"Well, get rest. It's going to be a long night." I dismiss them. They head off.

It's time to be serious and deliver a hard truth. "As your captain, Michel, I order you to stay on board the *Canopus*. My ground party and I will go for the treasure. You will stay and advise my crew on what to do to avoid bombardment from Fort de Rocher. I don't want my frigate caught or sunk. You're the man to do that."

Michel doesn't respond. I wonder if that is what he'll do whenever we disagree, go silent on me. Finally he says, "You know where the treasure is, Jacquotte. If you don't think it wise for me to come, I'll follow your commands. Just don't get yourself killed. We need to complete this mission together."

"I'm bringing back enough gold to fill our hammocks. Haven't slept on a bed of gold in a while."

"Our hammocks? That's a mighty catch." His voice is deep. It sounds confident, not resigned. Face to the wind, he scoots over. "Don't need to tell an experienced captain like you how harrowing the passage can be."

"No, you don't. If it were daylight, I'd point out the variations of blue in the water in the passage. But the stars are out tonight. Michel, they are lovely. The Big Dipper and Orion—"

"Orion's Belt was right over Port Royal." He sighs.

We remain silent as I sail us through the passage. I tack the whipstaff and have Bahati adjust the sails. They look like puppets, moving the halyards, tugging braces and tying up lines.

Aren't we all puppets to something—to lusts, structures, or beliefs that limit us? My mother gave me my footing in this world, the bravery to strive for a different life. Maybe we can escape being puppets, if we find ways to live without fear and be free.

Near the bow a lantern lights. Someone's reading. Once we move beyond Cuba, I'll have the crew douse the flames. The cover of darkness will be our only protection from cannon fire.

* * *

We set anchor farther down Tortuga's shoreline. Past Cayonne, and out of the direct line of sight of Fort de Rocher, I lead the excursion crew to shore. The partially veiled Chaîne de la Selle and the highest peak, Morne La Selle, are my guides. My party paddles the pinnace softly to shore. I take a breath, fight my memories, and search the stars to find the right path. Then, as I had in San Andrés, I lead my team into the jungle.

The moonlight scatters under the thick canopies of leaves. The smells of raw mud and ferns tangle in the humid air. This was the haunt of the fille fantôme—the girl who didn't know she could do all things until she tried.

Soon we get to the split in the trail. One direction will take us to Fort de Rocher; a second, to the blond beach of Cayonne.

Something happens. I almost feel the true path calling to me. I find the deep stream that hides the caverns. With Wulf tying two ropes to trees, Mel and I take the other ends and swim into dark waters. Without fear or reservation, he follows his old captain until we emerge in the magical cavern. I find the lamp in the same place Michel put it all those years ago. I light it and show Mel a world of gold.

His eyes grow big. Piles of coins and statues shine under dripping stalactites.

Mel fastens our ropes to what looks like an old anchor. "This will hold, captain. Our crew can follow these lines to the treasure."

My plan seems to be on course. "We need to work fast and lucky."

"Aye-aye, Captain Delahaye."

We take the edge of a heavy silver platter and swim back to our awaiting crew.

Wet, but warm, we show off the prize. Men and women jump up and down, but they make no shouts. Secrecy and silence and good planning will free the treasure from where it's been hidden in for over fifty years.

Fifty-Two

1692. Tortuga

Twilight begins to brighten the world. Indigo and ebony fade into lavender as I stand at the jungle's edge, my boots moored in the blond sand while I wait for the pinnace to return for the last load. Three hours of backbreaking work yields a treasure that no one can imagine.

Calico Mel holds sacks of gold ingots. In his grin, I see plans bubbling—what he'll do with his share or what he, Celia, and the sloop *Black Pearl* will do. I'm not making plans. I'm watching the hills for resistance.

"No one has been alerted, captain. Maybe Phipps's message didn't get through."

I tap my scope on my damp sleeve. "Patience. Greedy people don't give up until they win or die."

He frowns, but I've given him truth. I know Du Casse didn't send just one spy and have Old Jean killed to give up now. I wish Sarah had set him on fire too.

"Mel, if I were going to steal gold from pirates, I'd make sure they had all of it first. These men know how well it's hidden. I count on our enemy being patient, but they will strike. We have to be better than them. And we have to be ready."

It takes another thirty minutes before the pinnace returns to the shore. Celia's commanding it.

"Why did you leave the ship?" Mel seems worried.

Her cheeks look scarlet. "The crew. They came back exhausted, so they drank from the supplies. Now they're sick. Wulf just stopped vomiting."

Calico Mel slaps his brow. "We didn't check the water. Phipps put something in it."

I take the scope. Some of my crew lie about. I see Bahati walking around. Michel too. Wulf is stretched out between gold statues. I think Margaret fans her.

Mel reaches for Celia. "Did you drink it?"

"Non. I did not. But it's bad—only ten of the crew are alert enough to sail or command a gun." She looks at me. "Captain Le Basque and Bahati are fine, but Tomás is not."

I want to scream. Tomás out of everyone is innocent. "Let's move. Get back to the *Canopus*."

We toss sacks and trunks into the pinnace and head out. In the middle of the water, I hear the most dreadful sound. *Boom*. A cannon from Fort de Rocher has fired. The noise echoes, vibrating the air. An iron ball rips through the almond blossom trees. Blanc petals scatter like feathers as the shot splashes short of the *Canopus*.

Links of chain rattle as the anchor goes up. Bahati and Michel know to get my ship free.

"Get going," I shout. "We'll catch up."

More shots rain down. Sails slowly rise. The *Canopus* moves.

Another blast. This ball nearly hits the pinnace. Calico Mel makes evasive moves. He works the rudder like Old Jean and cuts a zigzag path.

Celia and I keep low and hold on to the treasure.

The next blast hits close. The scent of sea brine mixes with gunpowder. Waves splash over our side.

Boom. Our cannons fire. Over our heads deep into the forests, we blast Tortuga. It's the best sound.

Another round of broadsides firing launches from the *Canopus*.

The sky is lighter now, showing pinks and golds, but the silhouette of the coastline shifts to emerald and flame.

I don't want Tortuga to burn, but I want the governor and Fort de Rocher to become ash.

Mel guides the pinnace closer to the stern. Bahati throws a line.

"Who's steering?"

"Captain Le Basque and His Eyes. Tomás has recovered." She tosses grappling hooks. Celia and I fasten them to the pinnace. "Climb."

Boom. A ball hits ahead of the small ship. Too close.

"Smoke," orders Michel. "Deploy the smoke."

I don't know what that is, but then I see wafts of black wind coming from the *Canopus.*

I'm screaming. Every nightmare I've had about the San Andrés fire is before my eyes.

Celia gets in front of me. "Breathe, captain. Breathe. The ship's not on fire. Look."

Baskets and demijohns are dropping into the water. Flames shoot from them, yielding the smoke. My crew has made a way to veil us.

"Captain, Celia, Mel!" Bahati says. "Come on. Start climbing."

"Forget the gold," I say. My voice is hoarse from screaming. "We have enough. Climb."

Calico Mel grabs one of the bags. He pushes Celia to climb first. Then he starts up.

I follow, but I'm watching those reed baskets. They smell of tar and straw and fear. My arms ache, but I hold on to the line. We must keep going.

Blast. Our gunners strike again. Ash billows from Fort de Rocher.

This gives me energy to climb.

The *Canopus* isn't speeding away. The weight of the pinnace and its sacks is holding us back.

I slip down the small ship. "Hold on." I take my rapier and cut Celia and Calico Mel's ropes. They bang into the stern.

I cut the end attached to the pinnace, and I slam into the hull.

I'm dizzy, but my fingers still wrap about my rapier. It's been with me too long to drop into the sea.

Calico Mel is up. He's on board, tosses the bag, and then pulls Celia over the top.

I'm hanging on, but I have nothing left in me. "Get the *Canopus* out of here."

Bahati and Calico Mel tug my rope.

"Keep holding on, captain," Bahati says.

It's a miracle. They pull me over the rail. I lie there looking at the sails. They're fully extended, bloated like glorious fantômes floating across Cayonne.

The sun pulls free from the water. It casts a warm golden hue as it soars over the horizon.

Boom. I'm still lying on the deck when the noise jolts me. My gaze locks on a shadow—it grows and hovers. It's coming too close. Before I can yell, it strikes, knocking through my crew.

Celia. Celia's hit. The grapeshot has severed an arm. A leg too.

I'm crawling to her, but Calico Mel gets there first. She's in his arms.

He weeps. I close her eyes.

I glance at Bahati. She runs and mans the cannons. Wulf's up, charging my way.

I leap to my feet and aim a cannon to fire back, but something in the water catches my eye. I swivel the barrel and point ahead and hand Wulf the ball. "Wait for my order to fire."

Then I run to Michel and Tomás and my whipstaff. "I'll take us to sea."

The *Canopus* glides, and soon the whispered image of the frigate—what I felt in the water—becomes clear. The outline of a third rate ship appears. As we get closer, I see its ebony hull, trimmed in yellow. The flag hanging from the ensign staff at the stern is the tricolor—blue, white, and red—the same glimpse of a French warship I caught with Old Jean when the Fille Fantôme was birthed in my heart. "Fire Wulf! Fire at France's frigate. Everyone fire at will."

Wulf does and leads a broadside attack on the frigate, cutting the enemy's masts—the main and the two mizzenmasts. Their sailors scream. The ones that can jump into the sea. Unlike the first time I steered this boat as helmsman of the HMS *Florence*, we, the *Canopus*, are prepared.

My crew reloads and fires again, until flames leap from the enemy's deck.

Sailing past, I slip the *Canopus* back into the Windward Passage. The heavy current, the balmy air makes us swift. Soon, we are out of reach.

No one chases us.

Michel sits on the quarterdeck. He leans against Tomás as Tomás leans on him.

Bahati takes charge of my deck.

"Michel, the sick crew?"

"They will be fine, like Tomás here."

"I'm glad I could help you, Papa Michel. I liked steering the captain's boat."

Michel rubs the boy's cheek. "You come from a line of sailors. Our captain and I will teach you more."

I agree. "Tomás, you're part of my crew too."

"How's the ship?" Michel asks. "We took a hit. Are we good?"

I shield my eyes and look at Calico Mel and Bahati wrapping Celia's body. Tears leak, then I force them to stop. "No. Not at all. We lost a sailor, but downed a French frigate. And we left a few bags of treasure on the pinnace we cut free. But we cut down a French frigate."

I wipe at my face and let them have the whipstaff. "Keep heading straight. We'll hide near Nassau. Then we'll head back into the Windward Passage to Curaçao."

In possession of myself and my sorrows, I walk to the stern to say goodbye to my crewmate and my friend. Bahati kneels and chants prayers. I whisper how proud I am of Celia to her ghost. I hold Calico Mel. Like a good maman, a good captain, I let him cry and tell me all the dreams he and Celia had for the babe now lost.

I want to say their child's in the angel arms of her mother. But I can't, can't find the words to convince him that tomorrow the sun will rise, that the extra bag of gold didn't cause this, or that this is the cost of the life we've chosen.

We're buccaneers, the best of filibusters. We live and die for adventure.

Fifty-Three

1698. Petit-Goâve, Hispaniola

The late afternoon sun bakes the docks. My slippered feet bounce on the planks as I try to adjust to the light material of the soles. I lift my face into the breeze; it smells of perspiration. Everyone around us hauls barrels, loading and unloading boats.

"I can't believe women wear these." I'm fussing with the whalebone ribs in my corset. Wulf and Margaret sold me these expensive rags—a robe with a lacy collar and yards of yellow fabric—and they've dressed me. I wear a silky corset that supports my bosom from underneath my gown. It's strange so I don shortened sloppes under everything to feel normal, to feel like me.

Michel walks at my side. When I stumble over my hem, he supports me. I curse.

He chuckles, for he's used to these complaints when we dress for society. My dearest friend looks handsome swathed in his burgundy counselor robe with black stripes. But his onyx velvet hat is something less than desirable. It has no brim and looks like a pottage bowl slapped onto his head. Nonetheless, we're the picture of wealthy French society walking along the rues of Petit-Goâve.

We are fortunate. Our escape six years ago from Tortuga was a success. The governor of Curaçao converted all the relics and ingots to silver. Van der Bosch asked no questions about the treasure's origins or the battle with Fort de Rocher. Through gossip, we did find out that Jean-Baptiste Du Casse, the governor of Tortuga, stood on that frigate we fired upon. He took a swim but lived.

My smaller crew stayed away from the Caribbean, traveled a while, but now that things are safer it's time to reunite with my brother.

Michel pats my arm. "We look respectable. The monks will let us see Josiah. I do not know why they've not answered our letters. My dear Tomás says he has written everything we asked."

The lovely boy has. He's good. "We have the money for a donation that cannot be dismissed."

"Oui. That's true. We have God's ransom."

Yes, we do. We are rich and growing wealthier without shooting a cannon. A portion of our silver is invested in the thriving Bank of England. Over the years, the monks seem to like the annual bank drafts from England. I don't know why Monsignor's letters have stopped.

"The plan is to convince Josiah to come with us. To join our crew and go to Louisiana. Right, Michel?"

"Oui. We will meet up with the de Graafs."

I breathe a little easier. In addition to Anne's three children, the couple have two more together. Unfortunately, the family was made political puppets. The English captured them in '95, but again de Graaf's connections and wealth were able to purchase freedom. They live quite well in the French colony of Louisiana.

"We'll sail the sloop. The *Black Pearl* will do nicely." I gave Calico Mel the *Canopus.* He needed the ship to build a new family. A large crew will help heal his soul. Last I heard, Mel was set to battle the Mughals with Captain Tew. Lord, help them.

"Mon amie?" Michel tightens his hold on my arm. "I'll get Josiah to listen. I'll get all the monks to listen too."

He touches my hip. "You're wearing the rapier under your skirt?"

"And sloppes." I give him a saucy smile. "I'm always prepared."

We walk a little farther. I see the other warehouses, the ones piled high with flats of tobacco and barrels of cane or cod. More likely it's sugarcane. The cash crop needs slave labor. Things have only gotten worse, here and all over the world. I take a shiny gold coin from my reticule. "Guess what I received yesterday. It's a quarter ounce of gold. The Brits call it a guinea. Hopefully this will be what is used to value goods, not men."

"Mon amie, the world changes slowly."

My heart hurts, because Michel is right. Everyone's to blame. Every government seeks to enslave someone, whether it is the Persians selling Blanc women, the Mughals punishing infidels, or for Brits, the Spanish, the Dutch, the Portuguese, the French, and the buccaneers stealing Guineas or Indigenous to work the land. We—all nations, all conditions in life—are guilty.

"Come along, Jacquotte. This is overdue. Don't be afraid. Josiah will want to go with us." He clasps my hand, fingers linking, calming my soul. He leads me to the gates that have kept me from Josiah.

I clang on the bars of L'Église de L'Assomption. I hurt my gloved hand banging against the iron. Soon a man in those familiar brown robes and pointed gray capuche appears. I'm disappointed it's not Monsignor Robilere.

The monk opens the gates. "How can I help you?"

I push inside. That's what rich women do. "We are here to see Brother Josiah Delahaye."

"Madame, sorry. There's no one here by that name."

"You're mistaken, Monsignor. I've been giving alms here to support his ministry for years, since eighty-one."

The fellow looks down on me. His spectacles slip along his nose. "You could not have, madame. There's no one here by that name."

"Get Monsignor Robilere. He knows. I've put reales in his hands. He's closed his fist on the money and praised me for my silver tithes for seventeen years."

The man's confused face turns a deeper shade of red. "Monsignor Robilere died a few months ago."

That's why the letters stopped. This can't be. I pull the correspondence from my reticule. "See these reports. Monsignor has sent them every year when I send money. Someone should know Josiah Delahaye."

The priest shakes his head. He seems genuinely confused about my letters. "These are in Monsignor Robilere's hand, but I know nothing of this. I'm sorry."

"Non. My brother has been given training. He's taken a vow of silence. He likes to clean, stack, and mop. His face is not tan like mine, but pale like yours."

"There is no one—"

I run past him to the closed doors of the limestone building. My fist stings as I bang against the knocker. "Josiah! Josiah! Come to me. Jacquotte is here."

The priest and Michel follow. "There's no one here by the name Delahaye."

"I need to see Monsignor Robilere."

"He's . . . Oui. I'll take you there."

Calming, I let him lead us through a hall of gold relics and crosses. Pewter sconces light the way. I see a gold statue in the corner like the ones we rescued and sold off from Michel's treasure.

The priest takes us to what looks like a wall, but he grabs a torch and escorts us outside. The sun is setting. We walk into a dry field. Off in the distance, beyond the new-looking stone wall are tall sugarcane stalks. The lands surrounding the monastery are habitations. The white shell bricks along the perimeter will keep the enslavers out.

"Here's the monsignor of L'Église de L'Assomption."

My heart pounds as the priest points to a grand monument, one bigger than the marble cut for Henry Morgan. Here lies François Robilere's tomb.

I kneel, not in reverie. The wind is kicked out of me. "But where's my brother? This man took my money for years, claiming to care for my brother. Then he used my shame to keep me away."

"Jacquotte, let's go." Michel reaches for me, but I avoid his hands.

"Do not be sad, madame. Your contributions have built this monastery. It's testament to François Robilere's leadership to bring in alms. If there was someone, a Josiah, ever here, know the good monsignor was kind; he'd aid the mute and put him to good work. The lord has been justified and the church increased."

"She never said Josiah was mute." Michel clasps my arm and raises me up. As he backs me away, he trips and rips off the skirt of my costume. My sloppes are exposed and my hilt is free. "Gain justice," he says.

Half wench, half warrior, I whip my blade to the monk's throat. Only a little pressure separates him from meeting his god. "I want the truth. You're not long for this world if you deny me."

In a high, squeaky voice, the priest says, "There was a mute. He was Monsignor's personal slave. He cleaned and carried things for Robilere."

"He made my brother his slave? Because he was part Guinea?"

"A slow-witted young man abandoned to the church is good for nothing but service. But he was sold off with Guineas and Indigenous coloreds in eighty-seven. We're now a Jesuit order. We can no longer have slaves."

"So Robilere gets to be here, cooling under cold marble, when he sent my brother to die in the hot fields. And you believe this right because the church has increased." I grab the torch from his hands. I want to burn away Robilere's name from his monument. His memory needs to become mute. "My skirt, the oppressions I've cast off, can become good kindling for a stew pot or this fancy cooking stone." I set it on fire, right on top of the monsignor's name.

The flames grow. I want the body of a dead man to feel the flames and incinerate to ash as his monument burns.

Heat floods my arm as everything around us ignites. I drop the torch. It rolls and spreads orange and red spikes, burning patch to patch of the dry grasses.

The priest screams for water, but flame is faster than words.

Other men in robes come outside into the growing black smoke. No one moves when I flash my rapier. Thoughts of Sarah flood my head. "Stand still, gentlemen. Let Robilere feel hell."

"Madame," the priest begs. "The dry season of Hispaniola is dangerous. L'Église de L'Assomption could erupt."

"I paid for it. I want your world to become ashes."

One monk runs at me. I sidestep him, slicing through his sleeve. He bleeds but doesn't fall dead. I'm rusty, but flames lick his robe. He dances and spreads more fire. The rear of the monastery burns.

"Captain Delahaye," Michel says. "Do we go, or do we die here?"

Rapier raised, I back away from the priests and go to him. Michel slips his arm about my gut. "Captain, I'm ready for either adventure, but Tomás is not. I think we go, for him and Bahati and the crew who still need us."

He's right. Today isn't the day to die. I grab his arm and lead him back toward the gates. Once through, we slam them closed. I find a stone, and jam it into the lock, making sure no key will ever open it. "Now the priests are the prisoners."

"Fille fantôme strikes again." Michel takes both my hands. "We leave."

I hurry through the rues but glance over my shoulder, watching the monastery redden with fire. Ebony smoke rises high. Lizzôa's mountains finally veil themselves in the floating ash.

* * *

Arm in arm, Michel and I run to the docks and leap onto the *Black Pearl*. Bahati glares at us but asks no questions. She starts untying our boat.

Michel sits beside Tomás, who sniffs at the soot in our clothes. "You and the captain been doing something bad?"

Michel shrugs. Bahati shakes her head and steers the sloop into deep water. When we are just about to leave the bay and head into the sea, I stand and gawk at Petit-Goâve and watch the fiery destruction. "For you, Josiah. From the sister you should have had—the one forever sorry."

Bahati nods and ties off lines, adjusts the sails. "Then well done."

"First mate takes us to sea."

"I'm thankful we are leaving together." Michel hugs Tomás.

The twelve-year-old boy that I've dressed in the gold tapestry of his Mughal culture wraps his arms about my rapier and hips. "Captain, you brought my other captain back safe."

"Tomás, it was the only promise I could keep."

The two let me be, and I weep in silence. The crime of enslavement I've railed against all my life has claimed my brother. Condemned not for his skin, but for his sister's neglect, I made Josiah a target. The brother who trusted me—I put into the hands of enslavers.

This is my failing. I was married to a ship, to a way of life.

The last time I saw my brother, Josiah didn't recognize my face. That must be for the best—to forget those who disappoint you.

Bahati relinquishes the whipstaff. "Captain, why don't you guide us to our new destination?"

"Louisiana is where the *Black Pearl* will head," Michel says. "Captain Delahaye has decided we are going to see the de Graafs."

I do as my first mate asks, but I will get her nieces—brilliant young women we've trained to command ships—to raise sails, trim angles once we hit the deep fast flowing waters. I want these girls to see the world and be safe to dream.

After a final look at the dark clouds of the ville, I walk to the stern and take control, steering my crew to the Windward Passage.

The sails catch the wind. I stay quiet, no longer looking back at the ville. Yet, I reflect on my life—the times I was valiant, the moments I was a fool. There's plenty of both. Though I'll never forgive myself for failing Josiah, I will make amends by sowing into the dreams of my crew—the family I have now. I promise to do right by each of them. And I, Captain Delahaye, will set the whole world on fire to save every last one.

Twilight

By the time I learned that I could be strong, I'd failed so many times, I lost count. I grew up striving to be a legacy, someone Maman would be proud of, someone who'd carry Père's Delahaye name with pride. I think those who learn of me will find me human—feminine, fierce, flawed, and lucky.

The lesson I leave—my truest legacy—is the miracle of twilight. There are two each day: one before dawn, one before dusk. Every day offers two chances to succeed, two opportunities to get things right. If you keep striving, you're bound to win—or at least find peace within yourself. Keep trying. That's what the best pirates do.

Author's Note

We love because it's the only true adventure.
—Nikki Giovanni

On holiday with my family, I joined a group of writers for a week-long tour of Kingston, Jamaica. I love visiting historical sites, particularly forts, hospitals, and gardens. I was very fortunate to tour Port Royal. Seeing its rich history through the surviving pieces of the fort, the refurbished artillery, and standing in the jail that once housed women pirates made a profound impact on me.

This experience inspired me to research piracy, leading me to discover Jacquotte Delahaye. I fell in love with her story, the pieces I found—a woman of cunning and intellect who could fight like a man and sail as well as any captain of her time. I wanted to know her: How did Jacquotte see the world? And how did the world treat her? With every new fact I uncovered, the word *adventure* echoed in my mind. I imagined Jacquotte learning to live freely—at first in the guise of a man, and later on her own terms. Glorious. Her nickname, "Back from the Dead Red," evokes the idea of resurrection—a woman returning from the death of a constrained existence, an existence in which women were denied the right to dream.

In my searches, she was closely linked to Anne Dieu-Le-Veut. Anne's life, the life of a Blanc French woman, is more documented and easier to trace. Jacquotte's and Anne's associations with well-known male pirates aided my research and became the lynchpin to reconstruct a life for Jacquotte. I used world events like the tsunami destroying Port Royal, colonization, and even the foundations of banking to enhance the storytelling.

Many characters were historical people who lived and interacted with Jacquotte. Others you meet—Dender Smith, Calico Mel, Bahati, Celia, Lizzôa, and Wulf—are archetypes of typical pirates and wayfarers of the Caribbean, matching diverse origins and circumstances to the filibusters and buccaneers found in the West Indies during this period.

While editing *Fire Sword and Sea*, one of the poets I revere died. Nikki Giovanni was a master of imagery and hope. Her poem "Resignation" inspires me, and its message—that love is the only true adventure—resonated deeply as I wrote this novel.

I like to think that Jacquotte's journey is one of love, in all its forms, unveiling itself as truth.

The Age of Piracy

What we know about the Age of Piracy needs to be challenged. The period of adventure and quests for gold and the equivalent of gold stretches around the world, connecting the wealth of Persia, Africa, South America, and the West Indies.

Television and pop culture have centered pirates as swashbuckling white heroes. While some might have done heroic deeds, they were thieves. They were outlaws. They pillaged settlements on land and native populations. Often, their tactics were brutal.

Diverse crews could have Black sailors on the top of the deck and enslaved men and women in the hull. The time of piracy's heyday in the 1600s is very different than the second golden age in the 1700s. Modern-day scholarship is advancing what we know about pirates, who they truly were, where they came from, their goals, failures, and successes.

Jacquotte Delahaye

Jacquotte Delahaye is one of the more difficult subjects I've ever researched. Facts about her life are conflicting. While I believe she was a real person, trying to build an accurate timeline of her life with even simple details such as her date of birth was extremely difficult. After months of frustration, I found it easier to look to her peers and contemporaries, particularly her relationship with Anne Dieu-Le-Veut, to build Jacquotte's timeline from her interactions with them.

My version of Jacquotte Delahaye is an amalgam of the times and themes experienced by a woman of color, a Black woman with one enslaved parent and one free parent under French colonial rule.

Lizzôa Erville

I'm a thoughtfully plotting, research-heavy writer. I've never had a character just show up and demand their story be told until Lizzôa Erville. In a time where women assumed men's identities to have freedom over their lives, men did the same. I know there will be questions about Lizzôa and how I framed this person.

While I believe there were many Lizzôa Ervilles or people who shared this identity, the language of her identity in the novel is handled in modern terms. We are never in Lizzôa's point of view. We don't know if Lizzôa aligned with the beliefs of the muxhe, who the Indigenous of southern regions like Veracruz considered a third gender. Her death was not easy to write, but it was the way her story came to me through this narrative and engenders the dangers of life on ship.

Nonetheless, Lizzôa's instructions were followed to the best of my abilities. This fits my mantra. I care about representation, about not whitewashing the past. *Fire Sword and Sea* returns us to a moment in time which was diverse and chaotic, with everyone striving for peace, income, and the right to be seen. Someone needs to research and write about the lost perspectives.

Other Key Facts Incorporated in the Story

L'Église de L'Assomption of Petit-Goâve, the monastery of Petit-Goâve, burned down mysteriously in 1698, destroying critical records.

Mel Fisher's Key West Museum made a profound impression upon me, showcasing artifacts recovered from Spanish wrecks of the 1600s and objects such as pewter basins, and showing their value in African slaves, also known as "Guinea slaves." "Guineas" were the basis of trafficking goods. African people and people of African descent were the universal currency. Pirates used money-laundering techniques to get rid of the evidence of their crimes. The slave trade played heavily into liquidating stolen loot.

Raids pictured in this novel are modeled after the true raid of San Andrés (St. Andrews), on attacks or raids on Veracruz and Indigenous colonies in present day Mexico and South America, and on Captain Henry Avery's, Sir Francis Drake's, and Captain Thomas Tew's conquests of the Mughal Empire.

The recovered treasure from the *Nuestra Señora de la Concepción*, the sister ship of the *Santa Margarita*, was used to fund the Bank of England in 1694.

Jean-Baptiste Du Casse was a governor of Tortuga. He was a former slave trader who gave half his pirated loot to King Louis XIV for favors. In 1691, he was appointed governor of Saint-Domingue. He utilized buccaneers to plunder the English colonies, including Port Royal, which had just been struck by a devastating tidal wave.

The Times When Jacquotte Delahaye Lived

An important understanding I hope readers will gain is that the 1600s were literal chaos. The concept of politics and political maneuverings, the changing nature of allyship, the power of the church, the situational nature of right and wrong, and even the way money circulated and fluctuated in value in the seventeenth century shaped the world.

Looking at lists of names—Afro-Indigenous women of Veracruz, the Caucasian Frenchwoman Anne Dieu-Le-Veut, and the thousands of African individuals documented in records—deeply informed my vantage point for this novel. Chattel slavery was the universal standard of wealth in the 1600s. While anyone from anywhere could be enslaved, the harshest and most brutal forms of enslavement were reserved for Africans.

When the world began to lust for sugar and discovered it could be grown in abundance in the West Indies, the enslavement economy grew exponentially. Enslavement shifted from Europe and Indigenous populations of South America to primarily captives from Africa.

What was also eye-opening were the fluidity of relationships. The lack of female companionship on ships and in the colonies led to men finding love and value in their fellow crewmates as well as prostitutes, etc. Men and women formed same-sex relationships or were bisexual, choosing to accept love where it was offered. The stigma that we think of arises from the Victorian age over a hundred years later. More stories of this time should be told from the diverse populations it spans.

Language Presented in the Book

While I am stickler for many things, I don't enjoy stilted language and difficult-to-read prose. The language of the 1600s was very diverse, locally based, and locally influenced. I have used jargon or older English to emphasize something important to the narrative. For readability, I used the later English of the late 1700s and early 1800s. Distinct period words are used, but sparingly and with context.

Acknowledgments

Thank you to my Heavenly Father; everything I possess or accomplish is by your Grace.

To my editor, Rachel Kahan, I love the way you push me to write the best books.

To my fabulous agent, Sarah Younger, I am grateful that you are my partner, my ride-or-die friend and sister.

I am so proud to share *Fire Sword and Sea* with both of you.

To Gerald, Marc, and Chris—Love you bros.

To Denny, Pat, and Felicia. Thank you for helping me elevate my game.

The Writers of Me and My Sisters.

The Divas.

To those who inspire my pen: Beverly, Brenda, Denny, Nancy, Sharina, Vanessa, Rhonda, Rev. Courtney, Rhonda, Angela and Pat—thank you.

And to my rocks: Frank and Ellen

Love you all, so much.

Thanks, Ma and Pa, you know why.

Bibliography

Books and Articles

Coote, S. *Drake: The Life and Legend of an Elizabethan Hero.* Thomas Dunne Books, 2005.

Cottman, M. H. *Shackles from the Deep: Tracing the Path of a Sunken Slave Ship, a Bitter Past, and a Rich Legacy.* National Geographic, 2017.

Dampier, W. *Memoirs of a Buccaneer: Dampier's New Voyage Round the World; The Journal of an English Buccaneer.* Dover Publications, 2007.

Dolin, E. J. *Black Flags, Blue Waters: The Epic History of America's Most Notorious Pirates.* Liveright Publishing Corporation, 2018.

Duncombe, L. S. *Pirate Women: The Princesses, Prostitutes, and Privateers Who Ruled the Seven Seas.* Chicago Review Press, 2017.

Ekin, D. *The Stolen Village: Baltimore and the Barbary Pirates.* O'Brien Press, 2008.

Esquemeling, Alexandre. *The Buccaneers of America.* Dover Publications, 1967.

Hill, Robert T. *Cuba and Porto Rico with the Other Islands of the West Indies: Their Topography, Climate, Flora, Products, Industries, Cities, People, Political Conditions, Etc.* The Century Co., 1899.

Johnson, S. *Enemy of All Mankind: A True Story of Piracy, Power, and History's First Global Manhunt.* Penguin Publishing Group, 2020.

Kennedy, Paul. *The Rise and Fall of the Great Powers.* Random House, 1987.

Köhler, Carl. *History of Costume.* Dover Publications, 2012.

Lane, Kris E. *Pillaging the Empire.* M.E. Sharpe, 1998.

Marley, D. *Pirates of the Americas.* ABC-CLIO, 2010.

Pennington, D. H. *Europe in the Seventeenth Century.* Longman, 1989.

Seijas, Tatiana, and Pablo Miguel Sierra Silva. "The Persistence of the Slave Market in Seventeenth-Century Central Mexico." *Slavery and Abolition* 37, no. 2 (2016): 307–33.

Severin, T. *Pirate. Privateer.* Pan Books, 2017.

Simon, R. *Pirate Queens: The Lives of Anne Bonny and Mary Read.* Pen & Sword History, 2022.

Wheat, David. *Atlantic Africa and the Spanish Caribbean, 1570–1640.* University of North Carolina Press, 2016.

Winters, Lisa Ze. *The Mulatta Concubine: Terror, Intimacy, Freedom, and Desire in the Black Transatlantic.* University of Georgia Press, 2016.

Archival and Online Sources

"The British West Indies: The British Empire in The Caribbean." Accessed n.d. https://www.britishempire.co.uk/maproom/caribbean.htm.

"Finding Sanctuary." Office of National Marine Sanctuaries. Accessed February 2020. https://sanctuaries.noaa.gov/news/feb20/finding-sanctuary-african-american-history.html.

"Slave Ship - Wreck of the Henrietta Marie." Texas State History Museum. Accessed n.d. https://www.thestoryoftexas.com/visit/exhibits/slave-ship-speaks.

South African History Online. "Khoisan." *South African History Online.* Accessed December 2024. https://www.sahistory.org.za/article/khoisan.

The Voyages and Adventures of Capt. Barth. Sharp and Others, in the South Sea. London: Printed by B.W. for R.H. and S.T. January 1, 1684. Internet Archive. https://archive.org/details/voyagesadventure00ayre.

Newspapers and Periodicals

"Berlin: On the 24th (December) His Electoral Highness Caused a Placaet (A Sanction)." *The London Gazette,* January 10, 1680.

"Four Square-Sterned Frigates Came Off from Bel-Isle." *The London Gazette,* August 22, 1678.

"Jamaica, June 15. Three English Seamen Having Made Their Escape from Petit-Goâve." *The London Gazette,* August 29, 1695.

Jones, Bart. "Raids, Not Race, Were What Mattered to Black Pirates." *LA Times,* July 2, 2000.

Philip Morgan. "Appraisers Estimate Shipwreck's Bounty at $4.7 Million." *The Tampa Tribune,* March 23, 1991.

"Port Royal in Jamaica, June 15, 1683." *The London Gazette,* September 3, 1683.

About the Author

Vanessa Riley is an acclaimed author known for captivating novels such as *Island Queen*, a *Good Morning America* Buzz Pick; and *Queen of Exiles*, an ABC's *The View* Lit Pick. She was honored as the 2024 Georgia Mystery/Detective Author of the Year for *Murder in Drury Lane* and the 2023 Georgia Literary Fiction Author of the Year for *Sister Mother Warrior.* Her craft highlights hidden narratives of power, love, and sisterhoods of Black women and women of color in historical fiction, romance, and mystery genres. Her works have received praise from publications like the *Washington Post*, *Entertainment Weekly*, NPR, *Publishers Weekly*, and *The New York Times.*

In addition to penning over twenty-five novels, Vanessa holds a doctorate in mechanical engineering from Stanford University and STEM degrees from Penn State. When she's not writing women-led sagas, she can be found baking her Trinidadian grandma's recipes or relaxing on her southern porch sipping caffeine. Stop by her website, VanessaRiley.com, and join her mailing list and musing Substack.